# The Last Chance

## Rogues of Fortune's Den
### Book 5

## ADELE CLEE

***The Last Chance***
Copyright © 2024 Adele Clee
All rights reserved.
ISBN-13: 978-1-915354-40-2

Cover by Dar Albert at Wicked Smart Designs

brandy, hissing as the amber liquid scorched her throat, determined its potency would not overwhelm her.

Aaron found her reaction strangely charming. "Now you've gathered your wits, you will tell me what the hell this is about."

She grabbed his forearm as if drowning from the weight of her burden, unnerving him as her fingers firmed over the corded muscle.

"Can I trust you? You must believe me. I had nothing to do with what happened at The Burnished Jade tonight." She shook her head in confusion as her ramblings took a worrying turn. "Perhaps my mind is playing tricks and I have imagined the whole thing. Perhaps past fears have returned to haunt me. Please say you'll come."

He held his temper. Now was not the time to gloat or remind her she'd acted against his advice and invited men into her club. He was having a hard enough time trying to imagine what wickedness had occurred.

"Did someone threaten you?"

Much to his relief, she released him and thrust the glass at Sigmund before gesturing to the door. "I'll explain once you've examined the scene."

The scene!

The comment sent a shiver shooting down his spine, but her bare feet stole his attention as she crossed the threshold. "Where are your shoes?"

"I left in a hurry."

"It's raining."

"Rain is the least of my concerns."

For a heartbeat, he considered carrying her but banished the thought instantly. "The slightest cut may lead to infection."

She pointed to his bare feet. "Then we'll die together."

Those words had a strange appeal for a man who expected to die alone.

Focusing on his current predicament, Aaron had Sigmund lock the door and accompany them to The Burnished Jade. The street was deserted except for an alley cat, a drunkard asleep in a shop doorway, and the relentless pounding of rain on the pavement.

Aaron had stood outside her club many times these last few months, contemplating why a young woman would assume control of her father's failing business. What had happened to Arthur Lovelace? Why had he upped and moved abroad, leaving a vulnerable woman in charge of his affairs? Discreet enquiries confirmed the bank had seized his Cheapside home.

Aaron knew one thing for certain.

Miss Lovelace had a secret.

One he was determined to discover.

"Follow me," the lady said, shaking off the rain before escorting them through the dim hall, painted an elegant shade of blue now she had stripped away the shabby wallpaper. "The problem lies upstairs."

Aaron mounted the stairs behind her, focusing on the new Axminster carpet and not the lure of her perfume or the gentle sway of her hips.

"Wait," he commanded, urging her to pause on the landing. He never walked into a situation without knowing the facts. "Before we proceed, you will explain your dilemma."

Her bottom lip quivered. "Where do I begin? This will be my undoing." She spoke like the world had gathered an army against her, and Wellington led the charge. "It's been a constant battle these last six months."

Aaron did not want to hear a tale to incite his pity. He did not want to hear about her personal affairs. The little he knew kept him awake at night.

"Just tell me what sent you racing across the street barefoot in the rain. What is so shocking, you'd drag *me* out of bed?"

She put one hand to her mouth and gripped the banister. "M-murder," she stuttered. "That's what had me fleeing the house. That's what leaves me fearing for my future."

"Murder?" Such things did not faze a man who'd fought thugs since the age of twelve. The horrors he'd witnessed beggared belief. "When did this murder occur? I assume you're taking me to see the body."

He doubted it was murder. More likely, a wallflower had swooned and smacked her head on the grate. Had a spinster suffered her tenth rejection and taken a lethal dose of laudanum?

"It must have happened before we closed tonight." She glanced at the stairs leading to the second floor and paled. "No one is permitted up here. It's never been a problem before, but men like to wander."

Men liked looking for places to conduct illicit affairs.

What did she expect when welcoming reprobates into her club?

"Were there any incidents prior to closing?"

She looked him in the eye. "What do you want me to say, Mr Chance? That you were right? That inviting men here was a mistake? Mr Daventry said—"

"Daventry!" Aaron straightened. He should have known the scheming devil was involved. "What the hell has he got to do with this?"

"I spoke to him at Delphine's wedding. He said under the

right circumstances, my wallflowers could achieve miracles. He suggested inviting men so the ladies could practise the art of engaging conversation."

"Engaging conversation," Aaron mocked.

"It worked extremely well until one gentleman mimicked Miss Beckett's stutter and the lady punched him on the nose. There was a terrible scuffle when he seized her arm and shook her quite violently. Miss Durrant whacked him with an iron poker. It was chaos after that."

Aaron did not laugh at her absurd story. He was so bloody angry he would wring Daventry's neck. Moreover, he suspected that wasn't the only distressing incident of the evening.

"Miss Lovelace," he began, grappling to keep his temper on a tight leash. "Trust me when I say Daventry always has a secret agenda. In future, listen to the man who deals with louts for a living."

She raised her chin, her confidence returning. "I would if your comments weren't so self-serving. You want rid of me and criticise all my suggestions."

He almost smiled at a job well done. "If I wanted rid of you, I would not be standing here barefoot, keen to help you avoid the noose. Let me speak plainly. This isn't the life for you. This isn't the right place for a ladies' club. I've made no secret of that."

She raised her hands and gave an exaggerated sigh. "Forgive me. I didn't realise change was so simple. I shall marry a wealthy merchant and retire to the country. Or perhaps I might purchase a property on The Strand like your brother Theo. Shame on me for not considering my options."

"Perhaps if you told me what you're really doing here, I might learn to be civil." He would not. Riling her temper meant she kept her distance. "Where is your father? And don't say abroad."

He caught a flicker of fear in her eyes, eyes that were usually so confident and self-assured. That said, with a dead body upstairs, she should be terrified.

"I don't know where my father is." The pain of betrayal clung to her voice. "The Burnished Jade belongs to me. I inherited the property from my maternal grandfather years ago. If you don't believe me, I have the documents as proof."

"I believe you." He was like a bloodhound and could smell a liar from a hundred yards. "I assume you've looked for your father. That you've enquired at the relevant places."

"Relevant places? You mean the morgue?"

Aaron shrugged. "Men fasten bricks to their ankles and jump into the Thames to escape their debts. Moneylenders will only listen to excuses for so long." His father was forever evading his creditors. He might have been found dead in an alley had he not forced his young son to brawl with beasts.

"People disappear all the time."

"People do not disappear," he countered. "They do not evaporate into the ether. Forgive my blunt manner, but your father is either hiding from his creditors, or he's dead."

She inhaled deeply and looked at him, hope glistening in her eyes. "There is another option. Someone may have kidnapped him. Taken him against his will."

"Kidnapped him?" Aaron gave a mocking snort. "Perhaps you drank too much ratafia tonight. What would anyone want with that reprobate?" Aaron sounded like a heartless rogue, and though he did not wish to hurt her, she had to acknowledge the truth. "Have you received a ransom note? He's been missing for months."

She hung her head. "No."

The urge to comfort her overcame him, but he shook it off like an itchy blanket. "It's of no consequence now. You have a more pressing problem."

Miss Lovelace considered him through damp eyes. "Have you ever felt like you're sinking in quicksand, and there's no one to pull you free?"

Aaron swallowed past the bitter memories. The first night his father dragged him to the fighting pits, he'd been beaten by a man twice his age and size. He'd received a slap on his bruised back and a shilling for his trouble and told he would fight again the following week. There was no respite from the torture. Some nights, he prayed he would die.

"Many times," he confessed but did not mention he found the house suffocating now his siblings had flown the coop. How the air seemed so much colder. How the chill penetrated his bones. "But I'm a man of action." Keeping busy kept his demons at bay. "Is that not why you roused me from bed in the middle of the night?"

Her gaze fell to the open neck of his shirt, and she swallowed. "I'm sorry. You have enough to deal with, but I had no one else. No one capable."

*Don't be sorry*, he wanted to say.

"You'd better show me her body. I assume you know her identity. Let's pray her death can be easily explained, and we're not hauled before the magistrate at Bow Street."

Miss Lovelace frowned. "Mr Chance, the victim is a man."

"A man?" God, he prayed he wasn't a peer.

"Yes, or a woman posing as a man. It's hard to identify him. He is lying face-down on the floor like a fallen statue, cold and in silent repose." She moved towards the stairs. "You'd better see for yourself."

He followed her and had almost forgotten Sigmund was behind him until he heard the heavy stomp of his man's feet.

"Survey the crime scene so you can be called as a witness," Aaron said, issuing instructions to Sigmund. "Then wake Godby and have him drive you to the Wild Hare. The innkeeper will send word to Lucius Daventry. Await his arrival and tell him what's occurred. Be quick. We need his advice before we summon a constable."

"Aye, sir."

Miss Lovelace showed them upstairs. She paused outside the door before gathering her wits and escorting them into the dark, musty room.

"There," she said, pointing to the body of a well-dressed man with a silver dagger lodged in his back.

Aaron inhaled a calming breath and caught the metallic scent of blood. He had Sigmund light a lamp and observe the body before sending him to fetch Daventry. Then he studied his surroundings.

The room contained nothing but a rickety bed and a worn armchair. The faded wallpaper was peeling at the corners. Dust marks revealed where missing paintings once hung, like ghostly imprints of a forgotten past.

"I sold everything of value," Miss Lovelace said, as if she couldn't wait to be rid of her father's memory. "I doubted anyone would want the bed. My father used to rent this room by the hour."

Aaron cast no aspersions and had once done something similar to fill his club's coffers. "The aristocracy expects a range of services when applying for membership. When was this room last in use?"

"My ladies listen to recitals, make pretty journals, dance and drink negus," she said, keen to rebuke any suggestion of impropriety. "What use would they have for a room like this?"

"You admitted to inviting men here so your ladies could engage in conversation." Why Daventry had made the foolish suggestion was a damned mystery. Indeed, Aaron would demand an explanation. "Do you know what happens when a man and woman are free to speak openly to each other? When they're not bound by the rules of polite society?"

"I'm sure you're dying to tell me."

"An attraction develops."

She laughed, the sound devoid of genuine joy. "We speak openly and are not bound by such strictures, yet are forever bickering."

Were he not so skilled in the art of subterfuge, she would see something other than a firm jaw and a stern glare. Had he the capacity to be anything but a dangerous devil, he would have taken her in his arms tonight and kissed away her fears.

"You didn't let me finish. Flirtatious banter and physical attraction are a lethal combination." He motioned to the lifeless body of God knows who. A body that should have been seen by the coroner an hour ago. "One of your precious wallflowers may have been attacked in this room and resorted to killing this man in self-defence."

Miss Lovelace hugged herself like she was the victim of an unwelcome assault. "Do you know the strength it takes to stab a man in the back?"

"Do you?"

"No, but I imagine one needs a firm hand."

"A woman might conjure Lucifer's strength to protect her virtue."

The dark shadows of a memory passed over her face.

"Clearly you have never had to subdue someone twice your size."

The unsolicited pang in his chest had him inwardly cursing. Any emotion he felt was not for the man he'd become but for the child who wanted an end to the pain. "Which goes to prove your point. If we were on intimate terms, you would know that's the worst thing you could ever say to me."

Not the worst thing.

She could say he had failed his family.

That he was lacking as a man.

That he was selfish. Inconsiderate.

"I assume you have the names of all those in attendance tonight." He credited her with some intelligence. When Daventry wasn't interfering, she showed good business acumen. "You do keep a record of your members?"

"Of course. I relied on my patrons to confirm the gentlemen's identities and to point out any unsavoury characters. Miss Wickford singled out more than one rake, what with her brother being an absolute scoundrel."

"Excellent," he said, keen to get to the matter of the body on the floor before it was too stiff to move. "We should have no issue identifying the victim or making a list of suspects."

Aaron crossed the room and crouched beside the corpse.

Miss Lovelace did the same, her wrapper falling open and giving him a glimpse of her pretty nightgown. "It's no ordinary dagger," she said, staring at the intricate carvings on the hilt. "Do you suppose they're real emeralds?"

"If it's as I suspect, and this is a genuine Mughal dagger, then the gems are real." A host of questions darted into his mind. But they would consider the weapon's origins once they'd identified the victim. "There's blood on the boards, but most seeped into his coat."

"How do we turn him over without removing the blade?"

Aaron considered the man's thin frame, the fine cut of his dark coat and his swathe of blonde hair. "We'll roll him onto his side. I know most gentlemen in town. One glimpse of his face is all I need to identify him. I need you to support his weight. Can you do that?"

She nodded. "I'll try."

They should not disturb the scene, but he needed to know who they were dealing with if he was to help her escape the gallows.

It did not take brute strength to grip the man by the hip and shoulder and push him onto his side. It took strength not to shout, curse and spiral into a mad panic when he gazed upon the familiar face.

"I know this man." A wave of apprehension swept through Aaron as he examined the purple discolouration on the victim's face. In front of witnesses, he had threatened to throw the fool in the Thames. He had dragged the miscreant out of his club and flung him onto the street. Warned him he would be dead if he returned.

"Who is it?"

Fear gripped his heart. "It's Lord Howard."

# Chapter Two

"Lord Howard? Are you certain?" Joanna dropped the man's body as if it carried the plague. The urge to scrub his essence from her skin had her squirming and rubbing her hands vigorously. "But he wasn't amongst the guests tonight. I have not seen him in years."

She shot to her feet, limbs shaking, barely able to stand still, barely able to suppress the need to run and put a hundred miles between her and the body of this fiend.

"You know him?" Mr Chance said sharply, observing her with a constable's scrutiny. He rose slowly, the power of his presence an unnerving force.

"I knew him once. A long time ago." A lump of shame rose to her throat. She should say nothing. To confess meant revealing a secret she had not shared with a living soul. "I assure you. He was not welcome here. I cannot imagine why he would come."

Mr Chance prowled towards her, the dark hair on his chest visible through his open shirt. In her twenty-eight years, she had never met a man who exuded such raw masculinity.

"You have a backbone of steel, Miss Lovelace." Despite the compliment, the stern look in his eyes said to expect a reprimand. "I can forgive your lapse in confidence tonight, but your odd reaction shows a severe dislike for this man. You will tell me how you're acquainted. Yours isn't the only life at stake."

Should she tell a half-truth to pacify him?

Perhaps avoidance was best.

"You'll not hang for calling a constable," she countered.

"I threatened to kill that man in front of witnesses last night." He stabbed a finger at the blackguard's lifeless body. "Now he's dead in a premises across the street. The Earl of Berridge will have my neck for this. Do you know how many men would like to see me hanged?"

"But I would testify in your defence."

"Half the men on the bench are corrupt." He laughed, a cold, hollow sound. "You'd be surprised how many witnesses they'd find to say I entered this building at the time of death. How they would say I threatened to drive a jewelled blade into his back."

"It won't come to that." The thought of Mr Chance suffering on her account left her nauseous. Bile threatened to rise to her throat. "He must have been dead for hours. The men at the gaming tables will give you an alibi."

"The men who owe me a small fortune? I don't think so." His mocking snort echoed through the room. "Of all the women I've ever met, I never expected you to be so naive."

"Naive?" The devil lying dead on the floor had stolen her innocence when she was barely eighteen. She had spent a decade learning hard lessons. "Is it wrong to believe that justice will prevail? Perhaps you should try being a little more optimistic."

"Optimistic?" He stepped closer, her heart fluttering in response. "If you'd lived my life, you would know it pays to believe the worst."

"If you'd lived my life, you'd know all I have is hope." She squared her shoulders, making it clear she was entitled to her own opinion. "Sometimes the truth is hard to bear."

"You're wrong. The truth can be liberating."

"We're allowed to disagree."

"Not when dealing with this matter." Like his stamina in the fighting pits, his steady sigh held no promise of surrender. "You dragged me into this mess. You will follow my instructions to the letter. There'll be no argument."

She stepped back. "I have a voice, Mr Chance. You'll not browbeat me into submission." Though her situation was indeed dire, she dared to test his resolve. Why wouldn't she? Every man in her life had failed her. "If you cannot accept that, I suggest you leave before Mr Daventry arrives."

He reached for her, wrapping his long fingers around her wrist. He always avoided physical contact. It seemed to pain him to touch her now. "Don't test my patience. I'm the King of Obstinacy. If I leave this room, I'll not come back."

She didn't believe him.

A man of integrity lived beneath his devilish facade.

"I'm a woman, not a child. You will consult me before making decisions on my behalf. This will be a partnership. A joint effort to clear our names. What is so difficult about that?"

He released her like her skin burned him. "Why do you persist in being awkward? Were you born to torment me? Perhaps you've failed to grasp what it means to have a murdered man in your house."

Born to torment him? Did he truly believe that? Though

the statement was absurd, he often treated her like a thorn in his side.

"I'm more than aware of what's at stake here."

With a growl of frustration, he turned abruptly and marched towards the door. She expected him to storm out, but he hesitated, his reluctance to leave evident in his rigid stance.

And so she offered a titbit to feed his curiosity. "I was eighteen when I last spoke to Lord Howard. He was The Honourable Benjamin Wilson then. A title that proved wholly unsuitable."

Mr Chance paused, one hand on the doorknob. He did not face her but turned his head a fraction. "Am I to understand you've reconsidered and mean to follow my direction?"

"I'm afraid not." She refused to surrender just yet. Then he would assume he could always get his own way. "You seemed eager to know why I despise him. And you deserve something for your trouble tonight."

"I would prefer brandy and your submission, not your feeble attempts to keep me here."

Oh, he really was the King of Obstinacy.

But he would not forsake her.

She knew that about him, at least.

Joanna inhaled deeply, letting hope infuse her heart. "Then I bid you good night, Mr Chance. I'll not mention your name to the constable when he calls. I shan't tell him I dragged you out of bed because I was so desperately afraid."

A strained silence filled the space between them.

It seemed to last a lifetime before he faced her and said, "Why do you despise him? What possible motive could you have for wanting Howard dead?"

The memory of that night seized her mind. The innocent

embrace in the garden as she cried for her missing brother. The gentle stroke of Lord Howard's hand on her hair and back, the shocking move to her buttocks. The savage kiss that swallowed her protests.

"He took something that didn't belong to him." Her voice broke. A plump tear landed on her cheek when there should be no more left to shed. "He was always weak and so terribly pathetic. He cried when he explained he couldn't marry me because of his stupid mistake." Not that she would ever consider a proposal from a selfish fiend. "As it turned out, Benjamin Wilson didn't have an honourable bone in his body."

Mr Chance stood like a monument to a god of war. His hands balled into tight fists at his sides. His rugged features set to convey a dangerous determination. His whole demeanour was a perfect picture of contained fury.

Then a muscle in his jaw twitched. The angry vein in his neck pulsed, proving he was human. A man. A splendid specimen of his sex.

"Howard ruined you?" he said, his eyes flaming.

"Ruined is a strong word. I like to believe I still have much to offer the world." She swallowed past the pain in her throat. "But yes. I am damaged goods, Mr Chance. Broken beyond repair."

The tension in the room intensified.

A string of obscenities burst from his lips. He whirled around, pressing his palms to the closed door and bowing his head. He stood for an age, chasing his ragged breaths. "Howard should be thankful he's dead. I'd have ripped him apart for what he's done to you."

His reaction proved confounding for a man who could barely tolerate her. More like that of a husband or brother.

How strange, people thought him a rogue and Lord Howard a picture of respectability.

She dashed another tear from her cheek. "Now you know why I have a motive for murder. I've spent ten years wishing he would meet a grisly end."

"You'll not mention this to another soul. Do you hear me?" He was suddenly pushing away from the door and marching towards her, cupping her elbows, touching her again. "Not to Daventry. Not to the magistrate or coroner. To no one. They'll presume you're guilty and not bother to investigate the crime."

He was still breathless. Dare she say, panicked.

It was not a good sign from a man who exuded self-control.

"Where did you meet him?" Mr Chance continued. "Who saw you together? Who might testify against you in court?"

"Lord Howard went to school with my brother. We were alone in the garden that night. I did nothing to welcome his advances. I considered him a family friend, but he acted like he was possessed by a demon."

Mr Chance's eyes turned as black as Satan's soul. "He forced you?"

She lowered her gaze and nodded, though could feel his fury.

"Then why the hell was he still walking? Someone should have put a lead ball between his brows. Did your brother not demand satisfaction?"

Good heavens.

Now came the hardest part.

But she couldn't bear to speak about Justin tonight.

"No. My brother was away from home."

It was the truth. She just didn't know where.

"Surely not for ten years." Mr Chance refused to let the matter rest. "Did you ever tell him? Is it possible he came here tonight intending to—"

"Please, no more." She placed a staying hand on his chest. The hair tickled her palm, and she felt his heartbeat pounding. "I have not seen my brother in ten years. Let that be the end of the discussion. We have a more pressing issue."

He stepped back, causing her hand to slip from his chest. After taking a few deep breaths, the storm in his eyes died. "It will be another hour or two before Daventry arrives. We should lock this room and remain downstairs."

"Does that mean you'll stay?" She clasped her hands, willing him to show compassion for a woman who always riled his temper.

"I'll stay until Daventry arrives. He helped to create the problem. He can help to find a solution."

As head of the best enquiry agency in London, Mr Daventry would know exactly what to do. Yet, to her mind, no man could match Aaron Chance's strength and capabilities.

His gaze dipped to her wrapper. "You should change out of those damp clothes before you catch a chill. Shock has kept us warm until now, but we should light a fire downstairs. Do you have brandy?"

Joanna nodded. "In the drawing room."

"I must return to Fortune's Den. I'll be ten minutes at most. I'll not meet Daventry looking like I've just crawled out of bed."

She almost smiled. She wasn't afraid of being alone. And seeing him half-dressed made him seem less like the indomitable figure who dragged drunkards from her doorway.

"I'll make myself presentable while you're gone." She

tucked a damp lock of hair behind her ear. "What must I look like?"

His eyes softened as he looked at her, his lips parting like he meant to reply, but an invisible barrier acted as a restraint. Instead, he stepped aside and gestured for her to leave the room.

She took one last look at Lord Howard's body, searching within herself for an ounce of remorse. She had none. "I'm not sorry he's dead."

Mr Chance locked the door behind them and kept the key. "I'm sorry," he said, his voice a mix of anger and regret. "I would have enjoyed torturing that louse. I would have waited in the shadows, a beast in the blackness. No one would have known it was me."

*Why?* she wanted to say.

Why did it matter?

He didn't strike her as a defender of wronged women.

"Then I'll reiterate what I said earlier. I'm glad he's dead. Your family needs you. I wouldn't want you to lose your liberty because you helped a stranger who lives across the street."

"You're hardly a stranger," he countered. "You've attended every family wedding. My brothers' wives consider you a friend."

"I'm a stranger to you." He knew nothing about her and never bothered to ask. He usually avoided conversation altogether.

"We're not strangers. We're competitors. It wouldn't do to become too familiar." Before she could contradict him, he descended the stairs and headed to her bedchamber. "I want to ensure there's no one in the house before I leave. Do you have any objection to me checking your room?"

Panic fluttered in her throat. He was always so meticulous; everything kept in its place. She had thrown off her clothes tonight, so tired, she'd fallen into bed.

"Why would I object?" she said, straightening. "As we're merely competitors, you'll glean nothing of my business secrets in there."

She didn't ask how he knew where she slept.

Her chamber overlooked the street, as did his study.

A few times, their gazes had locked as she drew the curtains.

"I didn't think you'd want a prized ape rummaging through your private things. I believe that's what you called me."

Trust him to remind her of their spat weeks ago. She might have chuckled if not for the dead man upstairs. "Were we not strangers, you'd know I hold no prejudices. I'm a great lover of the natural world."

He didn't tut or sigh but hovered outside the door as if poised on the edge of oblivion. When he turned the knob, he did so slowly.

Joanna hurried into the room behind him, gathering her petticoat and stockings off the chair. "I don't keep a maid, and it was gone midnight when I climbed into bed."

"What made you venture to the upper floor?" He was scanning the room, his dark eyes roaming over her private things, absorbing every detail despite the gloom. "Were you struggling to sleep?"

"No matter how many times I closed my eyes, I just lay there, revisiting the night's events." Despite tossing and turning for hours, she couldn't shake the terrible sense of foreboding. The feeling she'd made a dreadful mistake in listening to Mr Daventry.

"Why leave your bed and venture to that particular room?" He was kneeling now, peering under the bed, his large hand splayed on her mattress.

To admit the truth would show her in a weak light. But a woman living alone was always vulnerable. And she'd sworn never to fall foul to a man's weaknesses again.

"Having a house full of men proved unsettling. I couldn't help but fear one might be hiding in the dark somewhere." She showed him the old musket propped against the armoire, the one thing she'd taken before the bank repossessed her home in Cheapside. "I began searching the cellar and worked my way upstairs."

Mr Chance stood, brushing dust off his knees, much to her embarrassment. A faint smile touched his lips as his gaze moved to the musket. "Few people surprise me, madam. One could not accuse you of lacking courage."

"That's the third nice thing you've said to me tonight."

"I'll try not to make a habit of it. On that point, can I make something clear before we proceed any further?"

"Yes." She stiffened her spine, sensing his next words might slice to the bone.

"If I offer advice, don't take it as a personal slur. I knew you were ill-equipped to deal with a house full of excited men. That has no bearing on your character."

"It's hard to take your advice when you're always critical." She found his stubborn stance frustrating. "No woman wants to feel like a fool."

"You're no fool. But this arrangement won't work."

Despite her dire predicament, she disagreed. "With proper vetting and a man of Sigmund's skill guarding the door, it could. Lord Featherstone asked Miss Wickford to ride out with him tomorrow."

Mr Chance gazed heavenward and sighed. "Why do you care? Why play matchmaker and force alliances? You told my sister you believe one's destiny is written in the stars."

"Some people need help to find love." Miss Frampton had watched all her sisters marry but, with three failed seasons spent hiding behind potted ferns, had given up hope of meeting her match. "As a man, I wouldn't expect you to understand what it means to have a lack of prospects."

He fell quiet before offering, "Some people aren't made for marriage. And being my usual cynical self, you cannot trust the motives of the men who might frequent your club."

Joanna let a mocking chuckle slip. "There are good men in the world. Your siblings love their spouses dearly. I mean to weed out the reprobates and fulfil my ladies' dreams."

If one found love, it was worth it. Although Miss Moorland wasn't looking for marriage but to pursue a career in medicine, hence her interest in the local doctor, Mr Gentry.

"As I recall, you want a man who likes standing in the rain."

She was surprised he remembered her comment. "I said I won't settle for less than a man who waits in the rain just to spend a minute in my company. I see nothing wrong with that. Actions speak louder than words."

The fact he had come to her aid said she could trust him.

Coping with his need for control was the main obstacle.

"Is foolish behaviour not a sign of weakness?" he countered.

"Is it foolish to show a woman how much you value her company?" She had never seen his paramour enter the club but presumed he had one. Such a virile man did not spend his nights alone. "Perhaps tomorrow you might draw your mistress a bath and feed her supper."

The thought roused heat in her belly. What must it be like to have such a powerful man at one's mercy? She doubted there was a woman alive capable of bringing the formidable Aaron Chance to his knees.

His gaze rose to meet hers, pinning her to the spot with unwavering intensity. "You shouldn't make presumptions. This is the longest I've spent alone with a woman in eight years. I'm too busy for romantic entanglements."

Eight years?

Joanna frowned. The statement proved more confounding than the identity of Lord Howard's killer, who was probably another lady he had wronged. One whose father collected weapons from the Far East.

"Why?" was all she could think to say.

"Many reasons. None which have any bearing on our current predicament." He straightened, his impenetrable mask firmly in place. "I should go home and change my clothes. Do you have a spare door key? I'd rather not hammer the knocker and wake the street when I return."

Joanna moved to her nightstand and took a key from her small jewellery box. She dropped it into Mr Chance's outstretched palm, noticing the callouses and the bruise on his finger.

"You've been preparing for your upcoming event," she said, wondering why he found hitting other men so rewarding. "I'm told some contenders travel from as far afield as Manchester to demonstrate their pugilistic skills."

He closed his fingers over the iron key and slipped it into his trouser pocket. "The farther afield, the larger the wagers."

She didn't glance at the toned muscles she knew lay beneath his fine lawn shirt. She'd dared to enter his basement once. The image of him standing shirtless in the ring remained ingrained in her memory. As were the plethora of scars littering his body, the marks like the lines of a tragic tale she longed to hear.

"Are ladies permitted entrance?"

A muscle in his jaw twitched. "No. Fighting men dislike distractions. If you saw me in the ring, you'd know I'm nothing more than a savage beast." He waved his hand between them. "Don't mistake this for anything more than a need for justice. An unsolved murder is bad for business. And I'm rather fond of my neck."

"Why would I expect more than your assistance?" She admired his honesty. It was a rare quality in a man. "We're nothing more than competitors. I trust I have your word that you will help solve this problem. For both our sakes."

He nodded. "As I said, it's in our interests to bring this matter to a swift conclusion. You have my word I'll instruct Daventry's best agents to help bring the culprit to justice."

Their verbal exchanges usually left her seething.

Tonight, she felt relieved and surprisingly calm.

"I shall have the fire lit and a brandy ready when you return. Hopefully, we won't have long to wait for Mr Daventry."

"Don't open the door to anyone," he stated, not budging until she gave her solemn vow. "I'll be as quick as I can."

Joanna listened to his retreating footsteps, then hurried to the window to peer through the gap in the curtains. This wasn't the first time she had spied on him from afar.

The man was an utter enigma.

He was dominant and overbearing, rigid in his ideas and beliefs. He took stubbornness to new heights, often lacked empathy, and disliked most people.

Yet he loved his family unconditionally. It was evident in

every thoughtful action and deed, even if he never spoke the words aloud. He was truthful and loyal. Working with him would be challenging, but Joanna knew one thing with absolute certainty.

Aaron Chance would never break a vow.

# Chapter Three

Miss Lovelace was napping in the candlelit drawing room, curled in the fireside chair, when Aaron returned to The Burnished Jade and let himself in with the key. Although he had changed his clothes quickly, he had spent twenty minutes trying to suppress his burning rage.

The lady's confession plagued him like a malevolent spirit, a horrid shadow of her past he could not eradicate or erase.

*I am damaged goods, Mr Chance. Broken beyond repair.*

He wanted to haul Howard's body to the nearest heath and leave him as food for the crows. Or tie him to the Aldgate Pump with a placard saying debaucher and watch the devil slowly rot away. A maggot infested with maggots.

Aaron glanced at Miss Lovelace but did not disturb her. She had changed into a plain blue dress and fastened her golden hair into a braid draped over her shoulder. She looked peaceful, angelic, all signs of distress vanquished, if only for a moment.

He snatched the glass of brandy off the side table and

downed the contents, resisting the urge to hurl the goblet into the fire and curse his rotten luck.

He wanted to pace the floor, throttle someone, drag every lord into a dim alley and demand to know which one of them had killed Howard. If only he could summon the wastrel back from the dead. He'd wrench the murderer's name from his lips and then destroy him for what he'd done to Miss Lovelace.

"Craven bastard," he mumbled too loudly.

Miss Lovelace's eyes fluttered open, and she sat up. "Mr Chance. I didn't hear you come in. I was resting my eyes." She observed his black coat, her gaze sweeping across his shoulders before she gestured to the blue damask settee. "Would you care to sit? We may have a long wait before Mr Daventry arrives. I'm told he's often reluctant to leave his wife's bed."

The seat looked comfortable, but Aaron declined.

The room had an undeniable charm, the beautiful woman in relaxed repose making it more inviting. Soft candlelight and the fire's amber flames created a scene ripe for seduction. The lady had dabbed perfume to her pulse points, the arousing smell of roses playing havoc with his insides.

"I intend to search the rooms for traces of evidence." He would not surrender to the desires he'd suppressed for months.

"You won't find anything. I've checked all the rooms."

Her defensive tone put him at ease, so he prodded her a little more. "You were distraught and might have missed an obvious clue."

The flash of fire in her eyes said he'd hit the mark. "A man was murdered in my home. What else would I be but distraught?"

Now he had the perfect excuse to place some distance between them. "With your delicate sensibilities, I suggest you remain here and wait for Daventry. I want to search Howard's pockets. I'll not have the coroner find evidence that might incriminate me."

"What could Lord Howard possibly have in his pocket?"

Aaron shrugged. "A threatening letter demanding he pay his debts to my club. A fake love note implying he's been intimate with one of my brother's wives." Something to blame Aaron for the crime.

Miss Lovelace pursed her lips while contemplating his demand. "You should wait for Mr Daventry. He seems like a fair man and has faith in your character. Any documents might lead us to the real culprit. Someone impartial must find them."

Though loath to admit it, she was right.

Daventry could only manipulate the truth to a point.

"Perhaps you'd like to look through the list of club members," she suggested, standing to fetch a ledger from the oak bureau. "You're well informed and may know something about their families that might lead to a clue."

Being a logical man, he accepted her offer.

Dawn was fast approaching. The sooner Daventry arrived, the better, although Aaron wasn't sure whether to thank the agent or throttle him.

"I'll need the names of the men who entered your premises tonight." Seeing two men venturing upstairs drew less attention than a virgin maiden being lured through a dim corridor.

Miss Lovelace handed him the ledger and went looking for the list. She rummaged in the bureau but had a problem locating the document.

"How strange. I'm sure I placed it in the pigeonhole." She rubbed her lips with her finger while lost in thought. "I returned it to the bureau before Madame Rossellini's recital."

Clearly, the murderer had stolen the list to evade detection.

"Madame Rossellini?" He knew the name of every singer gracing London's stages. Most were the mistresses of his patrons. "Is she new to town?"

"No, she's an amateur soprano." Miss Lovelace lowered her voice as if the walls had ears. "She is Miss Stowe's maid. It's a long story which I will explain another time. I provide her with a costume and pay her fifteen shillings for an hour's performance. I cannot afford to hire a professional and must improvise if I'm to earn a living."

"I see." A rush of admiration warmed his chest.

*Hell's teeth!*

Where the blazes was Daventry?

Aaron paced the room, the ledger open in his hands, studying the names of the ladies who attended her club. The task kept him occupied for twenty minutes, though he'd read the same lines ten times or more.

Like the perfect hostess, Miss Lovelace offered him brandy and snuff and asked if he might like coffee or a light repast. She stoked the fire, watched the street through the window, and searched for the missing list.

Aaron prayed for an end to the torture.

Restlessness gnawed at him like an itch he couldn't scratch.

This intimate setting was too much to endure.

Finally the Lord answered his silent plea.

Daventry arrived, dressed immaculately in black. He did

not look tired or annoyed that they'd dragged him from his wife's bed at this godforsaken hour.

The man's confident air sparked Aaron's temper.

"What the hell were you thinking?" he said once Daventry had greeted Miss Lovelace. "You encouraged her to invite men here, knowing she would encounter problems. You must bear some responsibility for this damnable mess."

As always, Daventry remained stoic. "Miss Lovelace is a competent woman. I refuse to treat her like a child. She asked for matchmaking advice. I offered a suggestion."

"And now Lord Howard is lying dead upstairs with a dagger in his back. I threatened to kill the fool last night. Don't dare say it's a coincidence. Someone means to cause trouble." Aaron motioned to his attractive competitor. "Trouble for us both."

Miss Lovelace glared at him before offering Daventry a winsome smile. "Thank you for coming at such short notice. You must forgive my *competitor's* irate manner. He is suspicious by nature, as I'm sure you're aware."

"Do not speak for me, madam," Aaron said.

"Why? You scolded Mr Daventry on my behalf."

Daventry seemed to find their spat amusing but quickly addressed the serious matter at hand. "Take me to the crime scene. I want to see Howard's body before I summon the magistrate."

A knot twisted in Aaron's gut. The magistrate would assume Miss Lovelace was Howard's mistress, particularly as they were well-acquainted.

"You don't seem surprised he's the victim," Aaron countered. Howard was an unpopular fool, but even criminals refrained from murdering peers.

"According to my sources, Howard owes Two-Teeth

O'Toole five hundred pounds after betting on a fight on Hounslow Heath last month."

Grateful someone else had a motive for murder, the tension in Aaron's muscles eased. "That fight was rigged. O'Toole pays his men to lose previous bouts to improve the odds. It's as good as highway robbery."

"And as you know, the interest on the debt is colossal."

"Mr O'Toole was not responsible," Miss Lovelace was quick to inform them. "I would have noticed an unsavoury character on the premises. And I'm confident my gentlemen patrons possessed all their teeth."

A master criminal could enter undetected. Deciding not to embarrass her in front of Daventry, Aaron did not mention she had gone to bed, unaware of the dead body upstairs.

"What about your female members?" Aaron said. "I'll need the names of those who joined after you agreed to invite men to your Thursday soirees."

She motioned to the ledger in his hand. "They'll be listed along with the date they paid their first subscription." Turning to Daventry, she said, "I recorded the names of the gentlemen in attendance, but the list has disappeared."

"Interesting," Daventry said, then asked about the night's entertainment.

Miss Lovelace spoke of whist and cribbage in the card room and the delightful solo from the maid soprano. Tame games like charades and brain-teasing puzzles had brought much amusement.

She smiled before repeating one such riddle. "I speak without a mouth and hear without ears. I have no body, but I come alive with the wind. What am I?"

"An echo," Aaron said bluntly.

Blinking in surprise, she said, "Yes. I'm rather glad you

weren't here. The fun is in hearing all the ridiculous suggestions."

"That's where our ideas of fun differ." It reminded him they were incompatible. The more time he spent in her company, the more he needed to reinforce the point.

"My wife and I often play riddles for forfeits," Daventry said in her defence. "It can be quite a thrilling game, though I often lose on purpose, depending on what Sybil wants from me."

Miss Lovelace looked at Daventry like he'd sung a beautiful aria. "There's nothing more romantic than a man who makes sacrifices for a woman," came her veiled dig at Aaron.

"I assure you, it's no sacrifice."

Aaron ignored the hum of satisfaction in Daventry's voice. He didn't remind Miss Lovelace that he'd sacrificed sleep and his sanity to come to her aid tonight. "We have more pressing worries than riddles and games. The magistrate will wonder why we delayed summoning him."

Daventry thought for a moment. "The Thames Police Office has jurisdiction here. We can trust the superintendent, but as the victim is a peer, we'd better summon the magistrate, Mr Harriott."

Daventry left to instruct his coachman to fetch the magistrate.

That's when Miss Lovelace offered Aaron a reprieve. "Return home if you must. I can deal with Mr Daventry and speak to the magistrate. When I give my statement, I'll confirm you have not set foot on these premises before tonight."

If she believed he would walk away from a problem, she was mistaken. "I'm not leaving. I shall see this matter to its obvious conclusion."

"Which is?"

"Someone else murdered Howard." He'd wager the list of suspects stretched the length of the Thames. "I'll not rest until the hangman has the culprit's neck in a noose."

She went to touch his arm but thought better of it. "I'm sorry for involving you. I didn't know what else to do. I know we struggle to be civil, but I'm truly grateful for your help."

He struggled to breathe in her company, let alone make conversation.

"I'm thankful you did. Forewarned is forearmed. I'd prefer to be involved than have the magistrate surprise me with news of Howard's death."

Still, Aaron willed the magistrate to hurry, praying the man was competent and would bring a swift end to the nightmare.

Daventry appeared and asked them to escort him upstairs.

"Why this room?" Daventry mused, noting it was at the end of the landing. "It overlooks the street and is directly above the drawing room. What time did Madame Rossellini sing?"

Miss Lovelace addressed him. "Due to popular demand, she sang twice. At nine for an hour, then a short performance at eleven, just before the guests started leaving. They requested to hear *Costa Diva* from the opera *Norma* again. It's an extremely emotional piece. Miss Stowe and Miss Moorland played violin and flute."

"Two of your wallflowers?" Aaron asked.

"Two of my members, yes."

"Who made the request?" Daventry said.

"A handful of people. I can ask Miss Moorland who first suggested an encore." She looked at the closed door and frowned. "You believe the murderer requested the piece to mask sounds of a struggle?"

"It's possible." Daventry opened the door and stepped into the room. He appeared to absorb every detail before examining the body. "It's quite cold in here, but based on lividity and the stiffness of the smaller muscles, I suspect he's been dead at least five hours. We'll need the coroner's confirmation, of course."

Miss Lovelace's relieved sigh proved puzzling. "That means Fortune's Den was open when Lord Howard died. Mr Chance will have an alibi."

The remark knocked the wind out of Aaron's sails. She was the prime suspect in a gruesome murder, yet showed concern for his welfare. He'd always known this woman was dangerous. That she had the power to steal past his defences.

"Let's not count our blessings until the villain is in custody," Daventry said, knowing enough men would like to see Aaron hanged. "They may say Mr Chance hired someone to carry out the deed." Daventry glanced between them. "I'm confident he can find his way out of this mess. You're the one who needs protecting, madam."

"Me?" The lady gulped. "Why would anyone think I'm guilty?"

Aaron froze, fearing she might mention her history with Howard. "She has no motive. If she *had* killed that popinjay, she's clever enough to dispose of the body."

Miss Lovelace looked astounded at the compliment.

That's when Daventry chose to stir the pot. "One should never underestimate the role of gossip in criminal proceedings. Perhaps Miss Lovelace might tell us why the Marquess of Rothley proposed marriage when she took over her father's gaming house. Perhaps he saw Howard as a threat."

Aaron's heart lurched. He'd noticed Rothley watching her premises. It explained why the marquess had a sudden interest in gambling at Fortune's Den.

Miss Lovelace looked at Aaron, keen to give her account. "Gabriel went to school with my brother. He felt responsible for me when my father vanished and felt duty-bound to make me an offer. To my knowledge, no one else knew."

"You received a proposal of marriage from a marquess?" Aaron's pulse thumped hard in his throat. He could accept not having her—he would not subject them both to a life of untold misery—but he'd rather die than know she'd been forced to marry Rothley. "And you didn't accept?"

"He doesn't love me," she said, lifting her proud chin. "You know what I seek in a match. There's no point repeating my requirements."

Yes, she wanted a fool who liked waiting in the rain.

"Some members of the *ton* believe Rothley was involved in your brother's disappearance," Daventry said, adding an extra ingredient to the mix. "I would use the word *death*, but remains found in the woods were inconclusive. It's a stain on his reputation. One he has never managed to erase."

Aaron had heard the rumours, the conflicting accounts so far-fetched he doubted they were true. Rothley had killed his lover, his housemaster, his friend, his maid. Some said poison was the weapon of choice, others mentioned a garrotte.

"Gabriel had nothing to do with Justin's disappearance. They were as close as brothers." Miss Lovelace was clearly shaken by the suggestion. "Nor did anyone else in their tight-knit group."

Daventry gazed at Howard's body. "And yet, ten years to the day since your brother went missing, one member of that group is murdered in your house."

Miss Lovelace touched her throat with trembling fingers. "Is it exactly ten years? I try not to think about it too often."

It couldn't be a coincidence.

Had someone deliberately targeted her, knowing the significant date?

"Did Howard confide in you?" Daventry pressed. "Did he tell you anything about the night your brother went missing?"

Aaron's patience with Daventry had worn thin. "Can't you see she's suffered enough tonight without raking up painful memories of the past?"

"The past, the present, the future, it's all one and the same," Daventry said cryptically. "I'm only preparing you both for what lies ahead. Better we have this conversation now than before the magistrate. I advise you not to mention it when he arrives. It may buy you some time."

A tense silence ensued as Aaron tried to absorb the information. He would need to be one step ahead of the authorities if he hoped to catch the culprit.

He moved to stand over the man he would throttle if Howard wasn't already dead. "We should search his pockets before the magistrate arrives."

Daventry agreed and began rifling through Howard's coat.

They found no letters or papers, nothing but the fop's gold watch hidden inside a black velvet pouch, not tucked into his waistcoat pocket.

Daventry inspected the face before opening the back case and showing Aaron the initials engraved into the metal with an image of a stallion.

Aaron's blood ran cold. "What the blazes? Let me look at that."

He took the watch, an unwelcome memory invading his

mind. His father hadn't paid off his debts with the money Aaron earned from one particular fight. While he nursed a black eye and fractured finger, his father bought a racehorse.

"That watch once belonged to my father," he said, his tone as hard as the protective casing around his heart. "He sold it to pay his debts a month before he died. A man from Ballingers Auction House bought everything of value."

For long seconds, no one spoke.

Miss Lovelace broke the silence. "It's hard to know which one of us is being framed for murder." She paused to look at Daventry. "I know this may be considered unlawful, but perhaps Mr Chance should take the watch. If it's his father's, it will be one more piece of evidence against him."

Daventry agreed.

Aaron did not. "The devil who planned this is already one step ahead. I mean to do the opposite of what he expects. Leave the watch on the body. It shows I have nothing to hide." He did not believe in bad omens but wanted nothing belonging to his father.

Daventry slipped the watch into Howard's pocket. "Then you must waste no time investigating the crime. The pouch is from a pawnbroker's in Regent Street. I'd start there and then interview Madame Rossellini and the female members in attendance tonight. I'll do everything possible to avert suspicion elsewhere. Howard's debt to Two-Teeth O'Toole should suffice. But time is of the essence."

"I shall gather my ladies here later today," Miss Lovelace suggested. "One of them may have seen something untoward."

Daventry put paid to her plan. "This is a crime scene. I suggest you reside at Fortune's Den until we resolve the matter. Working together will be easier if you're living under one roof."

"Under one roof?" Aaron's pulse soared. And he thought finding his father's watch was shocking. "Miss Lovelace cannot live at Fortune's Den."

"Why? You have plenty of room. You're a logical man. If you're going to tackle this problem together, surely you can see it makes sense."

Have Miss Lovelace sleeping mere feet from his chamber?

Meet her in a state of undress on the landing at night?

Impossible.

"If you'd rather solve this on your own," Daventry began, "I'm sure the Marquess of Rothley will accommodate her at Studland Park. He's shrewd enough to help her find—"

"The man is a damned hedonist."

"Can you blame him?" Miss Lovelace countered. "Gabriel is haunted by my brother's mysterious disappearance. He's carried the blame for years. Have a little compassion."

"I'll save my compassion for someone more deserving."

"Someone like Miss Lovelace?" Daventry asked. "If she's forced to interview her ladies at Studland Park, you'll miss the opportunity to ask crucial questions."

"I'll not have a woman living at Fortune's Den."

"All your brothers' wives stayed there for a short time."

Yes, and their brief stay ended with a trip down the aisle.

"I lack my brothers' patience. She'll not tolerate my beastly moods." He rummaged in his bag of ungentlemanly traits to find a few others. "I fight and curse and drink to excess."

Miss Lovelace laughed. "You're not so different from

41

Rothley, then. Perhaps I'll try my luck at Studland Park. At least I'm friends with Gabriel, not merely his competitor. And I imagine he'll be keen to discover who killed Lord Howard."

*Hell's teeth!*

Every muscle in Aaron's abdomen tightened. The thought of her dining with Rothley in an intimate setting roused the devil in him. Rothley would press a lingering kiss to her knuckles and do everything possible to spend the night in her bed.

Daventry did not share his misgivings. "Excellent. Once we've given our statements and I've convinced the Home Secretary to allow you to conduct an investigation, I shall take you to Studland Park myself. I'm sure Rothley will be accommodating."

A fool could see Daventry was goading him, manipulating the situation to suit his own purpose. In truth, he had Aaron by the ballocks and was intent on squeezing until they pained him.

"Perhaps we might meet tomorrow, Mr Chance." The sparkle of hope in Miss Lovelace's eyes had the power to unnerve him. He would rather hear her scathing retorts and watch her grit her teeth angrily. "You can tell me what you learned at the pawnbroker's, and I can let you read my ladies' statements."

The thought of her spending the night at Rothley's iniquitous den brought bile to Aaron's throat. But he was no better than the marquess. Miss Lovelace needed a man she could depend on. A man capable of feeling something other than disdain. A man who'd brave a storm just to glimpse her at the window.

Yet he prayed such a man did not exist.

"Daventry is right," it pained him to say. "If we mean to

clear our names, we must put our differences aside. The upper floor at Fortune's Den is empty. You may come and go as you please."

She jerked in response. "You're inviting me to stay at Fortune's Den? It might look like we're lovers, and we conspired to put an end to Lord Howard."

"I'll speak to the Home Secretary," Daventry interjected. "I'm sure he will grant you leave to make your own enquiries. The Chance brothers have proven invaluable in helping to solve prominent cases."

"We'll be colleagues," Aaron said, "not competitors." Not friends. Not lovers. Not so desperate to sate a craving, they couldn't keep their hands to themselves. "I'm inviting you to stay for a few days. We'll have the villain in custody by then."

*Cursed saints!*

He couldn't believe the words had left his lips. But she was safer with him. He was as strong as the sturdiest dam. More than capable of keeping the powerful flood of emotions at bay. Not a single drop would spill over, not even in the face of temptation.

# Chapter Four

Mr Chance's bedchamber was on the first floor, nearest the sweeping staircase. Doubtless it was a masculine place with dark furniture and dark walls and dark velvet curtains the colour of his eyes—so black they proved disarming.

He had led Joanna past the door six hours earlier, the alluring scent of wood and subtle spice seeping from his private domain. The arousing smell had remained with her, flooding her nostrils so it felt like he was there, sharing every breath.

"You'll stay in Delphine's old room on the upper floor." He had marched ahead, carrying her valise, keen to keep ten feet between them. "It's quieter there, and the decor is more to your liking."

More to the point, it was the furthest room from his.

He didn't want her at Fortune's Den. Women were not welcome. His demeanour changed the moment he offered her sanctuary, the muscles in his shoulders bunching with tension, his mouth thinning into a grim line. He had barely spoken since they'd given their statements and waited while the coroner removed Lord Howard's body to the morgue.

So why his sudden change of heart?

Why bring her here when it was the last thing he wanted?

Mr Chance had flinched when she mentioned staying at Studland Park. He disliked the Marquess of Rothley and was right to air his concerns. Guilt was a ghost haunting the lonely corridors of Gabriel's mind. Guilt was his constant companion. He didn't want a wife but would make an exception for her.

*I owe it to your brother.*

*Taking care of you would be my retribution.*

As if she would ever choose a life without love.

Gabriel hadn't promised fidelity or given her a reason to believe their affections might grow in time. They would live separately. She would have money and a grand home miles from town but no hope of finding happiness or a husband who adored her.

Which brought her back to the confounding Mr Chance.

A man who'd denied himself female company for eight years.

Her fiercest defender and her greatest critic.

If men were puzzles, he was the most complex.

Joanna observed herself in the looking glass, imagining a suit of armour beneath her deep blue dress. Dealing with Mr Chance would be an uphill battle. She would need her wits to keep up with him. Nothing mattered but finding the killer and saving them both from a trip to the gallows.

She went in search of the intrepid gentleman.

Despite it being two o'clock in the afternoon, a calm silence enveloped the house. Mr Chance wasn't in the dining room breaking his fast. He wasn't taking his frustration out on a punching bag in the basement; the door was locked. She followed the teasing scent of his shaving soap—a classic bergamot fragrance with dominant woody accents.

Snapping her spine straight, she knocked on the study door.

Seconds passed before he called, "Enter."

Nothing quite prepared a lady for seeing Mr Chance working at his desk. Though his chair was throne-like, he filled it with ease. He sat writing in a large notebook, his shirtsleeves rolled to his elbows to reveal powerful forearms. The well-defined muscles were a testament to his physical strength. The thick veins pulsing beneath his soft skin proved an attractive contradiction. A lady could enter a room blind-folded and easily pick him as the most virile male.

Then he looked at her, a glance through hard eyes. "I trust you slept well," he said, returning to his notebook.

"Reasonably well, all things considered." Breaking down his barriers would be more challenging than she thought. How did one destroy a shield of steel? Perhaps his was forged from magical metal because there was no doubt he was a force unto his own. "Have you been up long?"

"I never sleep past noon. Visit Baptiste in the kitchen. Tell him what you want to eat, and he'll serve you in the dining room."

She'd spent less than a minute in his company, and he was already ushering her out. "Your cook is French?"

He dipped his pen into the inkwell. "Baptiste doesn't live on the premises. If you require a late supper, you must tell him in advance. If you need extra bedding, speak to his wife, Eloise." Mr Chance glanced at the mantel clock. "She's left early today. Leave a note in the kitchen if you require anything, and she will attend to it tomorrow."

"I wouldn't want to put her to any trouble." Heavens. She could cut the atmosphere with a knife. "I'm used to fending for myself."

"I pay Eloise to do a job. It's no trouble."

Although her stomach rumbled with hunger, she approached the desk and sat in the chair opposite him. "If you have spare paper and a pen, I'll write to Miss Stowe and Miss Moorland and invite them here today."

"Not today." He looked like he'd rather poke pins in his eyes than entertain her friends. "It can wait until tomorrow. I want to visit the pawnbroker's. I need to know how Howard came by my father's watch."

What happened to working together?

"I see no reason why we can't achieve both tasks. You heard what the magistrate said. We have a week to find the murderer before his constables build a case against us."

The magistrate, Mr Harriott, demanded they remain in town. They were governed by a strict curfew, forbidden to enter The Burnished Jade, and warned to remain indoors after eight o'clock at night.

Mr Chance turned the notebook to face her. "I've spent two hours searching your ledger and recording what I know about the ladies who attend your club. Did you know Howard owed Miss Fitzpatrick's brother a thousand pounds?"

"No." Joanna sat forward and studied Mr Chance's notes. Such elegant handwriting was surprising for a man with large hands and a stern disposition. "Mr Fitzpatrick only permits his sister to attend my club when he's gambling here."

"As he was last night," Mr Chance confirmed, sounding suspicious. "Might he have entered your premises under the guise of collecting his sister?"

Joanna barely knew the fellow and there was a mass

exodus at the end of the evening. "Mr Fitzpatrick usually waits in his carriage. He disapproved of me inviting men to join the merriment and permitted his sister to come because he's desperate to have her off his hands."

"Then I will add the Fitzpatricks to our list of suspects."

Guilt surfaced. While he'd been studying her ledger, she had slept late. "If I'd known you were working on the case, I would have joined you earlier."

What must he think of her?

The word *useless* sprang to mind.

"You were exhausted, and I can function with little sleep."

He could have berated her but showed compassion instead. He might have insisted he was better equipped to deal with the problem but had used the phrase *our list* to signify they were a team.

"I shall strive to make an early start tomorrow." To prove herself a worthy partner, she would rise at dawn. "I can write to Miss Stowe and Miss Moorland and have them call at six o'clock. That would give us time to visit the pawnbroker's."

His gaze moved over her hair. "Are you equipped for an outing? You packed in a hurry, and your valise seemed light. Despite pleading poverty, you always dress in the current fashions."

His veiled dig was a means of gathering information about her private affairs. While she had nothing to hide, she decided to tease him. "I'm surprised you noticed me. When did you develop an interest in ladies' apparel?"

"I have no interest in anything but running my club, and learnt to be observant at a young age." Despite the determined set of his jaw, he wasn't being truthful.

"And your family. You care deeply about them."

That's when his guard slipped. When the warmth of tender thoughts softened his gaze, she glimpsed his unwavering love for his siblings.

It tightened her throat and stole her breath.

Beneath this hard exterior lived a man who knew the value of love. It was more attractive than his muscular chest and desirable lips. It spoke to her in a way his handsome features never could.

"I'd die for them," he uttered before hiding himself again.

"Yes, I believe you would."

Eager to change the subject, he said, "Did you bring a bonnet? You'll need an elegant one if we're walking together and the backbone to hold your head high. People will make assumptions."

A chuckle escaped her. "You don't need to concern yourself with my reputation. What do you think people say about an unmarried woman who runs a ladies' club?" Some were brazen enough to call her names and cross the street.

"They'd better say nothing when you're with me."

Joanna put her hand to her chest. Such comments softened a woman's heart. "I imagine most people will be too terrified to look in our direction. But I can call at the milliner's on Bishopsgate. I was so weary last night I'm not sure what I threw into my valise."

He stood abruptly. "Write your notes, and Sigmund will deliver them. I suggest we meet your friends at five at Pickins coffeehouse. It will ruin their future prospects if they're seen entering a men's club."

Again, his concerns were not for himself.

How intriguing.

"I'll write to them now, then fetch my pelisse. I'm sure

Mrs Shaw at the milliner's will have a hat to suit me. She knows what style I like."

"Have her send the bill here."

"I can pay for my own hat, Mr Chance." Being skilled with a needle and thread, she often took work home for Mrs Shaw. The extra funds helped to keep her father's creditors at bay.

"As I demanded you wear one, I insist on footing the bill." He rolled down his shirtsleeves, an action that would have any woman reaching for a fan. "I'll visit Baptiste and have him make a basket for the journey. You need to eat. I'll not have you fainting midway through an interview."

"I prayed you'd not heard my stomach growling."

"As I said, I'm nothing if not observant." He snatched his coat from the back of the chair and thrust his muscular arms into the sleeves. "Be ready in thirty minutes. I'm just as pedantic about timekeeping." And then he strode out of the room, though his presence lingered.

Joanna relaxed back in the chair and took a calming breath.

This situation was becoming problematic. It was easy to feel like his equal when trying to prove a point. She could hold her own when tempers were frayed. But these rare glimpses of kindness were like discovering diamonds buried deep in dark rock—too astonishing to put into words. And his tailor needed a knighthood. Anyone who designed a coat that hugged a man like a second skin deserved some credit.

Worse still, Mr Chance made her feel like a helpless child, not a woman who'd taken command of her own destiny.

Something had to change.

Somehow, she had to turn the tide.

"Good heavens, have you tried your cook's pastries?" Seated in Mr Chance's elegant carriage and wearing her new pillbox hat in imperial blue, Joanna licked cream from her lips. "They're the most divine thing I've ever tasted."

Mr Chance didn't tear his gaze from the window, though there was nothing exciting happening outside. "Why do you think I pay Baptiste double what he would earn elsewhere?"

Joanna hummed with satisfaction. She knew he found it irritating. "Would you mind finishing what's left of this croissant? I want to try the sugar-coated one next. It's simply begging me to take a bite."

"Leave it in the basket." He dragged his hand down his face and refused to look at her. "Can you not eat quietly? Anyone would think you've lived in a cave for the last twenty-eight years."

"What's wrong with acknowledging the pleasurable things in life? Would you prefer I complain about our current predicament? Should I spend every hour sobbing until they hang me from the gallows?"

He looked at her then, his head shooting around as fast as a compass finding north. "Don't say that, not even in jest. I'll not rest until the real culprit is behind bars." He closed his eyes briefly and cursed under his breath. "You have cream on your chin."

"Have I? Where?" She'd hold his attention if it killed her.

"As you only have one chin, it should be obvious."

She knew exactly where it was, but human interaction

weakened his resolve. In this game of wills, the friendly card unsettled him more than the angry one.

"Has it gone?"

With a fleeting glance, he said, "No."

She tried not to laugh as she wiped the wrong side of her chin. "Can I reach it with my tongue?"

"Saints preserve us. If you can't keep cream off your chin, what hope is there of you catching a murderer?" He pulled a black silk handkerchief from his pocket and thrust it at her. "Here. Keep it."

Strange that his last comment should cause her heart to pound. Owning something belonging to Aaron Chance was a remarkable feat indeed, more so because he gave nothing of himself.

The silk was soft in her hand, the smell of his shaving soap divine. She wiped her chin with her finger as he glared out the window, then slipped his handkerchief into her pelisse pocket.

"It's probably best I eat no more," she said.

"If it means saving me from hearing the constant licking of your lips, I agree. I'll tell Baptiste you want ham and eggs tomorrow."

Joanna chuckled to herself.

What was his problem?

Did he spend his life in perpetual bitterness? He was present in body and mind but not heart and soul. What made him happy? What filled him with joy? He never laughed. He never smiled. Though she thought she'd seen the corner of his mouth twitch when she'd called him a prized ape.

It was not a topic for conversation now.

Not when he had retreated to his lair.

Despite being unable to find her father and brother, she

would try her utmost to find Mr Chance. He was hiding somewhere beneath that magnificent body and gruff temper.

"Lord Howard had a new mistress," she said, drawing him out with a snippet of gossip. "By all accounts, she is new to town. I heard mention of it last night when Mr Jenkins accused Madame Rossellini of being the elusive paramour."

Mr Chance turned in the seat, ensuring their knees didn't touch. "That explains the argument that erupted shortly before Howard accused my croupier of cheating. When I spoke to Sigmund this morning, he remembered men goading Howard, saying he lacked the skills to keep an exotic woman entertained."

Why any woman would waste a minute of their time on such a feeble fool was a complete mystery. "It shouldn't be difficult to find her. You could ask your patrons, or I could call on Gabriel. He will surely—"

"I'll not involve Rothley," Mr Chance said sharply before modifying his tone. "The fewer people who know of our predicament, the better. We were told to conduct a discreet investigation."

"The word *discreet* does not exist within the *ton*." People were suspicious by nature, none more so than those who idled their days away. "The gossips will soon discover Lord Howard was found dead in my house. I'll be surprised if Daventry can keep it a secret for a day, let alone a week."

Mr Chance relaxed against the squab and dragged his hand through his thick, black hair. "I have an idea, though I expect you'll disagree."

"What? That we conduct separate investigations to speed up the process?" He'd probably spent the last twenty minutes thinking of ways to get rid of her.

"No." He shifted in the seat. "That we plan your escape."

"My escape?" Her blood ran cold.

"If the evidence is stacked against you and they mention taking you in for questioning, I can have you out of the country within hours. We must be one step ahead of the authorities."

Joanna couldn't quite catch her breath. "Leave my home and my friends?" She had put her heart and soul into making The Burnished Jade successful. "I'm innocent. Surely it won't come to that."

"Let's hope not," he said, sounding sincere. "But I'm a pessimist, remember. I plan for every scenario. Money is no object. I'll fund everything. You could live in France until the true villain is caught and locked in Newgate."

He would give her the money to flee?

"But I couldn't repay you."

"It would be a gift, not a loan."

"You'd give money to a stranger?"

"My sister would never forgive me if I let you perish."

Joanna clasped her chest, fear creeping into her heart for the first time today. "What about you? You're just as likely to be accused of the crime."

"I'll not leave London," he said, his tone resolute. "I made an oath sixteen years ago. I would rather die than break that vow."

Joanna stared at him, this handsome picture of perfection who boasted about his many flaws. Sticking to his principles wasn't one of them. When the Lord gave men integrity, Mr Chance had the lion's share.

"An oath to whom?"

"Myself."

She swallowed deeply. "You'll not save yourself, but you'll save me?"

He shrugged like it didn't matter. "There is nothing I hate more than injustice. You're innocent. I'll not let you die because of that"—he stopped abruptly and gritted his teeth— "fool."

"There's no need to curb your language on my account."

"What I think of that fop is not fit for your ears." He cracked his knuckles to show what he'd do if Lord Howard wasn't dead. "Well? Will you permit me to put a plan in place?"

She snorted. "I'm surprised you've asked. You usually do what you want, regardless of other people's opinions."

He fixed her to the seat with his impenetrable gaze. "I can issue demands if you prefer." His voice held the dangerous undertone that excited her more than unnerved her.

"Yes. If the time comes, you must force me to comply. Kidnap me if necessary." She would not leave The Burnished Jade willingly. And though loath to admit it, she trusted him to make the right decision. He acted with his head, not his heart. "It's the only time you will ever play the domineering patriarch with me, Mr Chance."

He nodded. And the deal was done.

The carriage stopped outside Mr Josiah Grimshaw's Pawnbroker and Curiosities shop on Regent Street. An odd assortment of items filled the bow windows: dusty hats and brass-topped walking sticks, tarnished silverware, old pocket watches and signet rings.

Mr Chance alighted. He lingered on the pavement as if he'd never assisted a woman from a carriage before and appeared confused about what to do.

Joanna lifted her skirts, ducked her head and reached for him.

He went to grip the tips of her fingers, but she slid her

palm over his and clasped his hand. That's when the world shifted. When the only thing on her mind was the delicious wave of warmth flooding her body.

He looked shaken. Like he did the night she entered his basement in her dressing gown and found him wearing nothing but his trousers.

She was attracted to him.

She'd never felt this with any other man.

Most of the time, their rows masked the odd flicker of feelings. Which was just as well, because only a fool would have romantic fantasies about a man who could barely tolerate her.

She released him, frustration bubbling because life was always unfair. "Perhaps *I* should speak to Mr Grimshaw. You're far too intimidating." And oddly charming, she thought, especially when plotting to rescue a damsel in distress.

He made no protest and gestured for her to enter the shop. He even held the door open, so had no issue playing the gentleman when it suited him.

A stout fellow stood behind the counter, holding an eyeglass to his left eye while examining the jewels in a necklace. "I'll be with you in a moment. You're welcome to look around while you're waiting."

"We're not here to make a purchase," she said, approaching the counter, "but to ask questions relating to a police matter."

Mr Grimshaw's hand shook as he returned the necklace to the roll of red velvet on the counter. He looked at Joanna, then at Mr Chance. "I ain't never heard of a lady working at Bow Street. But I know of crooks who pretend they need to confiscate stolen goods and then pocket the booty."

"Then perhaps you should pay attention to current affairs. Ladies work in covert operations because criminals don't suspect them." Joanna turned to her colleague and held out her palm. "Might I have the evidence, Mr Chance?"

He made that face again, the same grimace he'd given the magistrate when told to take the watch and prove Lord Howard had purchased it and not stolen it from Fortune's Den.

Mr Chance handed her the watch and addressed the pawnbroker. "Unless you want us to inspect the paperwork for all your recent purchases, I suggest you answer the lady's questions, Grimshaw."

Mr Grimshaw moved the necklace to a drawer under the counter. "What do you want to know? I sell ten watches a week. Sold as seen. I can't be held responsible if they're faulty."

Joanna placed the full hunter on the velvet roll. "This was found on a murdered man's body. We need to know when the victim bought the watch and the name of the person who sold it to you."

Mr Grimshaw ran his hand down his stained mustard waistcoat. "I'll need a name if I'm to find him in the receipt book. Might I take a closer look at the timepiece?"

Joanna smiled. "Of course."

The pawnbroker weighed it in his palm, studied the gold chain, opened the front case and examined the face. Nothing sparked his interest until he noted the image of a stallion engraved inside the back case.

"I remember this all right. It's the oddest sale I ever made." His grin died as panic set in. "Here, I suspected it was stolen, but she didn't want any money. All I had to do was convince the gent to buy the watch when they came in a few hours later."

Joanna failed to contain her excitement. "When was this?"

Mr Grimshaw shrugged. "Last Thursday or Friday."

"A week ago?" Mr Chance stepped up to the counter. "I want the name of the woman who gave you the watch. Reputable pawnbrokers take an address. I presume you have it to hand."

"I didn't take the details because I didn't pay her."

Mr Chance's temper flared like a struck match. "Describe her."

"Pretty. Foreign looking. Hair as black as coal. Spoke with an accent. I'd put her in her twenties." Mr Grimshaw turned to the cluttered shelf behind him and removed his receipt book. "I sold it to the gent and took his name. He was a toff. Mass of wavy blonde hair. Thin as a penny's edge."

The description fitted Lord Howard perfectly. Except Mr Grimshaw had forgotten to say a mean devil lived beneath his angelic facade.

"Here it is." Mr Grimshaw pressed his dirty finger to the entry in his book. "Mr Simpson. Staying at the Clarendon Hotel. I sold it for the bargain price of twenty pounds. He wanted a half-hunter, but she insisted he have that one."

She must have insisted Lord Howard give a false name and address, too.

"Did you not question the provenance?" Mr Chance said.

"I don't care where it came from, only that I can turn a profit." The broker returned the book to the shelf. "If it's any help, I'd say he's paying for her keep." He nodded at Mr Chance. "I'm sure you take my meaning."

"Have you ever seen the woman before?" Joanna asked.

"No, but her sort often sells trinkets to pay the rent." Mr Grimshaw jerked as he remembered something else. "The gent bought the watch to please her, though I got the impression he didn't want to wear it. Like he knew it was some sort of game."

That might explain why Lord Howard kept it in the velvet pouch. Perhaps he planned to see his mistress later that night, and she would expect to see him wearing the watch.

"We'll wait while you write a statement detailing exactly what you told us," Mr Chance said in the masterful tone that left most men quivering. "Or you can close the shop and accompany us to the nearest police office."

Wanting rid of them, Mr Grimshaw obliged while Mr Chance loomed over his shoulder, insisting he record every detail.

They left the shop with their first piece of evidence and the watch Mr Chance carried like it was possessed by his father's evil spirit.

"We'll call at Daventry's office in Hart Street before our meeting at the coffeehouse." He opened the carriage door for her. "Now we have Grimshaw's statement, let him be the custodian of this damnable timepiece."

"It's just a watch," she made the mistake of saying.

"It's not the watch," he snapped, retreating into his fortress and slamming the portcullis shut. "It's what it represents. A selfish blackguard who hurt his own children to line his pockets. You should know better than to make light of something others find painful."

She climbed into the carriage without his assistance, though she felt the power of his burning gaze on her back.

"How am I to understand if you don't tell me what you're thinking?" she said once they had settled into their seats.

"You don't need to understand. I'm not in the habit of sharing my private thoughts with anyone." He looked out the window as the carriage lurched forward and picked up speed. Something made him modify his tone and make a concession. "I warned you. I'm not easy company, particularly when it comes to personal matters. Remember that, and we may still be on speaking terms next week."

That's when she knew laying siege to his fortress would only force him to increase his defences. She needed to disguise herself as one of his men and sneak past the guard-house undetected.

She'd need to prove she was his ally, not his enemy.

# Chapter Five

As with most Friday afternoons, Pickins coffeehouse was a bustling hive of activity. Aaron ordered coffee for himself and Pekoe tea for Miss Lovelace. Then he lingered at the counter for brief seconds to bolster his defences.

It wasn't the prospect of locating the mysterious woman who once owned his father's watch that unsettled him. Nor his body's fierce reaction upon hearing Miss Lovelace devour a *crème pâtissière*. Or the sudden spark of attraction the moment she gripped his hand.

It was the thought of her leaving London. Perhaps for good.

No more stolen glances.

No bickering that fed a need he didn't quite understand.

No wishing he were a different man.

It would be for the best. They were destined to part ways, and he'd rather her visit France than the gallows. Besides, the more time they spent together, the harder he had to fight to keep his fortress walls intact.

He didn't need a friend. He didn't want a lover. Life was

complicated enough. Soon, he would be an uncle, and the relentless desire to protect the child would consume him night and day.

"I hear the seed cake here is exceptional," Miss Lovelace said when Aaron returned to his seat in a booth they'd been lucky enough to secure.

"Cake will spoil your dinner." Aaron withdrew his watch and checked the time. "I'll not let Baptiste's hard work go to waste."

Miss Lovelace didn't snap at him like he'd hoped. "Don't you think it strange Lord Howard used an alias but kept the watch in a pouch embellished with the pawnbroker's name?"

"Mr Simpson might be the name he uses when staying at hotels with his mistress." Aaron distracted himself by looking for the waiter bringing their refreshments. He did not wish to discuss lovers' antics with Miss Lovelace. "Howard was a dolt and probably had no idea he was being used as a pawn."

"A pawn? Then you believe someone targeted Lord Howard to frame you for murder? Why not kill him elsewhere and leave the body in your club's yard? Why involve me?"

Aaron relaxed a little. Logical questions needed logical answers. They did not chip away at the ice encasing his heart.

"Because they feared I would dispose of the body and their efforts would be in vain. A witness will say they saw me entering your club." They might suggest Miss Lovelace was Aaron's mistress and accomplice, but he couldn't think about that now. "You'd be surprised what men will do to please a woman."

She tilted her head, little lines appearing between her brows. "You seem calm for a man who may face a murder charge."

"None of us leave this world alive." The blasé comment did not reflect the riot of panic inside. Who would protect his family when he was gone? The question kept him awake most nights, staring at the ceiling until dawn. "Anyone who's fought me in the ring knows I'm a formidable opponent."

She pulled gently at her lips, which she always did when worried or nervous. "I have a suggestion, though you will probably raze the roof in protest."

"I'm not leaving London."

"Not even for a short time?"

"No. What if the villain comes for Aramis in my absence?" If their estranged uncle, the Earl of Berridge, was involved in this debacle, he wouldn't rest until all the Chance brothers died. "My uncle has no heir. He'll see me hanged before I'm named the next Earl of Berridge."

Miss Lovelace gasped. "You're the heir to an earldom?"

"Not anymore." He explained that his reprobate father had traded his birthright for an exorbitant sum of money, a move sanctioned by the monarch thirty-five years ago. "My father's family cut all ties and forced him to change his surname from Delmont to Chance."

It took her a few seconds to absorb the information.

"Aaron Delmont," she mused, repeating the name three times to test the sound. "I prefer Aaron Chance. It sounds more masterful and reflects your two greatest hobbies—fighting and gambling."

"I don't gamble." He needed to change the subject. Hearing his Christian name on her lips did strange things to his insides. "Building an empire took more than blood, sweat and tears. It took my heart and soul." She would never understand what he'd sacrificed. His life was not his own.

"All the more reason to reclaim your birthright. The Crown will not render the title extinct if there's an heir."

"An earl cannot own a gaming hell."

"You could sell Fortune's Den." She paused to thank the waiter who brought their beverages. "Or your brothers could run the business without you."

Without him?

The notion was unthinkable.

Explaining what the club meant to him would involve revealing aspects of his painful past. He didn't want to venture into that dark abyss. He didn't want to face the demons living there.

"I'll never leave Fortune's Den."

"Not even—"

"Never. Let that be the end of the matter."

A tense silence enveloped them. Miss Lovelace poured her tea while Aaron stared at his coffee, a drink as black as his heart. A minute passed, though it felt like an hour. His pulse had barely settled when his inquisitive *colleague* asked the question no one else had ever dared.

"Who are you angry with?"

Those five words slipped through a chink in his armour. The urge to stand and storm out, to put a vast ocean between them, battled with the lost child who had been denied a voice.

"The world," he said darkly.

It wasn't the whole truth. He was angry with himself.

"Anger is an easy emotion to feel," she said, absently stirring her tea. "It gives you a sense of control when everything around you is chaotic. Acceptance takes strength. Forgiveness is reserved for the special few who are no longer afraid to feel vulnerable. Sadly, I am not one of them."

Aaron shifted in his seat. He would rather tolerate her

hands on his naked body than suffer this intimate probe into his psyche. Forgiveness was for fools. He would never accept the past or make excuses for his father's cruelty.

Indeed, he breathed a sigh of relief when the coffeehouse door burst open and two women entered. They craned their necks and scanned the room before waving at Miss Lovelace and hurrying to join them. Then they saw him and came to a crashing halt at the table.

Aaron stood while the temptress opposite introduced a nervous Miss Stowe and Miss Moorland. He called the waiter and ordered more tea, though both ladies remained rooted to the spot.

"Do sit down. Mr Chance doesn't bite." Miss Lovelace moved to sit beside Aaron, invading his space, her thigh too close to his, while her friends occupied the opposite bench. "I imagine you're wondering why I called you here."

Miss Stowe's bright blue eyes conveyed a desire to know everything. "Does it have something to do with the attack on Miss Beckett? When the assailant left, he—"

"Mr Parker," Miss Moorland added, looking studious in spectacles. "That's the name of the man who left The Burnished Jade with a broken nose and bruised knuckles after being hit with the poker."

"Mr Thomas Parker? Sir Geoffrey's brother?" Aaron asked.

Miss Moorland, who had kept her gaze fixed on Miss Lovelace, gulped when she glanced at him. "Yes. He left promising to sue and called us a menagerie of oddities."

"He said he would ensure the club never opened again," Miss Stowe added.

Miss Lovelace put the threats to bed. "It's nonsense. I

doubt he would want all and sundry knowing two young women chased him out."

Aaron agreed though he would question Parker. "Do either of you know Lord Howard? Did you see him at The Burnished Jade last night?"

Miss Moorland removed her spectacles and placed them on the table. "I know him. I saw him lurking in the street but don't recall seeing him on the premises."

"I saw him peering through the drawing room window," Miss Stowe added, her cheeks reddening when she looked at Aaron. "What is this about?"

"Howard is dead," Aaron said, though he wasn't prepared to reveal more than they could read in the broadsheets.

Miss Lovelace threw caution to the wind, leant across the table and whispered, "Someone killed him at The Burnished Jade and is trying to frame one of us for his murder." She gestured to Aaron, touching him briefly on the arm. "We have a week to find the culprit before we're hauled into the police office for questioning."

Both ladies gaped.

"Why would anyone wish to frame either of you?" came Miss Stowe's naive reply.

"I ruin men for a living," Mr Chance said.

"I'm sure you don't drag them in at gunpoint."

"Those facing a stint in the Marshalsea always look for someone else to blame." Gamblers ignored their own failings. Addicts fooled no one but themselves.

Miss Moorland reached to clasp Miss Lovelace's hand. "Do you suspect this has something to do with your poor brother? I'm sure you said Lord Howard belonged to the same group of friends at Cambridge."

"It's been ten years since Justin disappeared. There's no

proof the body found was his or that his friends were involved." Miss Lovelace nudged Aaron's leg beneath the table, a covert signal to remain silent. "What other motive could I have for killing the man?"

It was clear she had not told her friends about Howard's brutal attack in her garden all those years ago. Yet she trusted Aaron with the information. Trust was fundamental to all thriving relationships, so he quickly told himself she had no choice.

The waiter returned with the ladies' tea. Miss Stowe poured a tiny amount into her cup and left the tea to steep while she asked an important question.

"What can we do to help?"

Miss Lovelace wasted no time in giving them a few tasks. "Can you find out who encouraged Madame Rossellini to give an encore? I'm also curious to know if any ladies were seen sneaking upstairs. Perhaps you might make discreet enquiries. And I need a list of all the men who entered my premises last night. Someone stole the record I made."

"The murderer, no doubt," Miss Stowe said.

Miss Moorland was more interested in the murder scene. "May I ask how Lord Howard died? Was it terribly gruesome?"

Aaron thought to test the wallflower's metal as she did not seem that shy. "He was stabbed in the back with a Mughal dagger. Might you know anyone who collects Indian weaponry? A person whose ancestors may have been granted the honour of being presented with one from an emperor?"

Miss Moorland tried to look him in the eye and seemed almost angry with herself when her gaze wandered. "No, sir."

"Your manner says you're lying."

Miss Lovelace jumped to the lady's defence. "Miss Moorland is being entirely honest. Despite our many lessons in the art of talking to gentlemen, she finds eye contact the most difficult."

"Talking is an art form now?" he mocked.

"You find it difficult on occasion. When I interrupted your fight in the basement a few months ago, it took an age before you could string two words together."

She had descended the stairs in a dressing gown that hugged every curve, her golden hair hanging in lustrous waves around her shoulders. He'd been dumbstruck. He'd battled to breathe, let alone form a coherent word.

"I was about to punch a man. I believe I told you to get out."

"Your sister dragged me there because you were about to assault Mr Flynn. She said I was her last hope. The one person who might make you see sense."

Aaron gritted his teeth. "Flynn ruined her."

"They were in love, not that you'd know what it means."

"Do you?" he countered, not wanting to hear the answer.

"Of course not. But I imagine one loses all grasp of reality."

Miss Moorland sighed. "The poets say love is sublime. Though when it comes to marriage, I would happily settle for a kind man who accepts my interest in the macabre. Perhaps a handsome doctor like Mr Gentry."

Gentry! The man was married to his work. And a woman with Miss Moorland's timid disposition would not convince him to push his responsibilities aside and indulge in carnal pleasures.

Finding romantic chatter mind-numbing, Aaron snatched an opportunity to avoid this drivel. "On the subject of the macabre, let's return to the more sensible subject of murder."

Miss Moorland took offence, any fears of speaking her mind vanishing like a puff of smoke. "You believe worrying about one's prospects is foolish? Do you know what it's like to have no control over your life? To have your wishes discarded like peelings thrown on a compost heap?"

An unwelcome memory invaded Aaron's thoughts.

*You're coming with me, boy.*

*I'll hear no more of your whimpering.*

"Trust me," he said, striving to keep the menacing edge from his tone. "I know the feeling better than you ever will."

A tense silence ensued, broken by the lively chatter in the other booths, someone coughing up a piece of cake and Miss Stowe stirring her tea.

"It seems we have more in common with Mr Chance than one might expect," Miss Lovelace said, playing peacemaker. "As a man who knows the true meaning of desperation, perhaps we might enlist his help with our cause."

Aaron sensed he'd stepped into a trap. "Your cause?"

"Helping my ladies in the fight to find suitable husbands."

"What the devil has it got to do with me?"

Excitement shone in Miss Stowe's eyes. "There is no man more intimidating. We might practise the art of conversation with Mr Chance."

"Like hell you will."

"You see." Miss Stowe was pointing at him now. "He's totally disagreeable and a perfect candidate for our studies."

"What an excellent idea." Miss Lovelace beamed at her protégés. "What would you consider to be Mr Chance's best physical feature? I'm sure he's keen to know. Don't be afraid to voice your opinion."

Aaron stood abruptly and tossed back the remains of his coffee. "I'm not a performing monkey. I'll pay the bill and wait outside. May I remind you we have a week to solve the crime?"

The infuriating Miss Lovelace grabbed his arm and stared at him with doe eyes. "Please, Mr Chance. What if someone had offered you a helping hand? You can reply as you see fit. The sharper the better."

"Your ladies won't withstand my criticism." They lacked her strength and undeniable resilience. "We have enough to deal with without this circus show."

"I think his shoulders are his best feature," Miss Moreland said, popping on her spectacles to study him in greater detail. "You're—"

"Dare say another word, madam, and you'll not like my reply."

Miss Lovelace encouraged her student. "Don't be intimidated. Mr Chance is exceptionally good at making a woman feel foolish." She looked at him, a pleading he found hard to ignore. "Allow her to finish, and we will turn our attention back to solving the murder."

Were he not the prime suspect, he would curse them all to Hades. "You have one chance to explain why, Miss Moorland. Then I never want to hear your empty compliments again."

Miss Moorland waited for him to sit before she rose to the challenge. "You're practically bursting out of that coat."

Aaron scoffed. "If you want to leave a man intrigued, you might try being a little more subtle."

"Allow me to show you." Miss Lovelace turned in the seat, her vibrant eyes observing the breadth of his shoulders. "You must give me the name of your tailor, Mr Chance. I've never seen a man fill a coat quite so well."

Their eyes met, and he felt the ache in his loins that made

him want to clear the coffeehouse, knock the cups on the floor, and take Miss Lovelace over the table. "Your comment screams of insincerity."

She smiled. "How odd. I meant every word."

Her honest response only heightened her appeal.

"Your banter is hardly original." Unlike the lady herself. He had never met anyone quite like her. "I'm not as shallow as most men. I don't care what you think of my physique."

"You have exceptional eyes," Miss Stowe chimed. "They say black is the colour of rebellion."

Miss Lovelace grinned. "Well done, Miss Stowe. Mr Chance does indeed carry an air of defiance. Yet you must dig deeper if you want a man to know you have noticed him."

Aaron's heart skipped a beat when Miss Lovelace gazed into his eyes again. He should have put an end to this nonsense yet he was too damn desperate for her praise.

She moistened her lips. "People make the mistake of thinking your eyes are black. Those people have never seen you speak about your family or witnessed a kind gesture. Then your eyes gleam like a starry night—so bright and full of promise. One must be quick to catch the spectacle before storm clouds shield them again."

Aaron swallowed past the tightening of his throat.

Why did she see something no one else did?

"How perceptive," he said with necessary arrogance.

"I have an advantage," she confessed. "I've seen the best and the worst of you, Mr Chance. Most people are denied the privilege."

He didn't correct her. She had not seen him pummel his opponents, seen blood and sweat dripping down his face, or heard his feral growl when he put a man twice his size on his arse.

71

She had not seen him on his knees when his brother was shot, praying at Theo's bedside, tears filling his eyes and rolling down his stubbled cheeks. She had not heard him whisper words of love and loyalty. Had never seen him without his guard raised.

But he needed to batten down the hatches and prepare for every eventuality if he was to keep her out in the future.

"Enough of this nonsense," he said, fixing her friends with his stern gaze, reminding them he was a sinner, not a saint. Turning his head a fraction, he gave Miss Lovelace a similar warning. "Do not presume to know me. You'll be making a foolish mistake."

"How could I presume to know you?" she whispered. "You don't even know yourself." Before he could reply, she faced her friends. "I'm staying with Mr Chance at Fortune's Den, though you're not to mention a word of what we've discussed to anyone. Send a note if you discover anything of interest, and we can arrange to meet here."

Looking a tad nervous, both ladies nodded.

Aaron wasn't ready to leave until he had answers to his remaining questions. "Tell me about your maid soprano, Miss Stowe. I assume she is Italian. I have yet to meet a maid with the time to learn a second language."

"Lucia came from Naples when she was ten. Her parents took ill and died during the crossing. An English lady aboard the ship took her in. Lucia speaks fluent Italian and sings like an angel."

"Who lives in your house?" he pressed.

Miss Stowe swallowed, the pained look of a sad tale evident in her eyes. "Me and my ailing father. He is bedridden and hasn't left the house for almost a year."

Aaron softened his hard tone. "I'm told a guest at The

Burnished Jade thought she might be Lord Howard's new paramour. Might Lucia have met the lord? Is she permitted to leave the house at night? Are you aware of her movements during the day?"

Miss Stowe failed to suppress a chuckle. "Lucia is not Lord Howard's paramour. I can assure you of that. We spend most of our evenings together. She barely finishes her daily tasks in time for supper."

Still, Aaron would pay a man to watch the house. "What is your opinion of Miss Fitzpatrick's brother?"

Miss Moorland was the first to answer. "His liver is pickled. The man spends more time sotted than sober. He plays the caring guardian well, but it's a facade."

"He is unkind to her when they're at home," Miss Lovelace added as if to remind him of his own cold manner. "Cruel is too harsh a word."

Miss Stowe glanced around the coffeehouse before revealing a snippet of information. "She believes he's paid someone to ruin her so he could send her to live with the nuns of St Agnes in Hertfordshire."

"Might Lord Howard have accosted Miss Fitzpatrick, forcing her to defend herself?" Aaron asked, though felt sure the answer was no.

A man had the strength to drive a blade into someone's back. A lady would need to be terrified, panicked, to commit such an act. That said, he'd be wise to remember there were wicked women in the world. Time spent living on the street had taught him that.

The ladies looked at each other and shrugged.

Aaron would find Fitzpatrick tonight and drag the truth from the devil's lips if he were not bound by a curfew. He'd question his patrons but couldn't open the club until the case was solved.

He stood. "Send word to Miss Lovelace when you have the information she requires. I would also appreciate your discretion." Needing time alone, he glanced at Miss Lovelace. "Stay here and talk to your friends. I'll pay the bill and walk home. My coachman will wait outside for you. You're to leave with no one but him."

She didn't argue. "I'll be an hour at most. I'll not risk breaking curfew. I'm sure you have business matters that require your attention, so won't disturb you unless I have new information to impart."

He had a family matter to attend to first. Having cancelled this morning's meeting, his brothers would demand to know why he'd closed the club. But it could wait until tomorrow. Answering their endless questions was the last thing he needed tonight.

After hearing Miss Lovelace's thoughtful appraisal, knowing she had noticed him more than she should, he would put all his energy into avoiding her. There'd be no candlelit dinner for two. No reading together by the fireside. No chance meeting on the stairs.

There would be him.

Just him.

Alone in his study, banishing a dream he would never fulfil.

# Chapter Six

The early morning knock on Joanna's bedchamber door made her start. She hurried to tidy the bed and place her nightdress under her pillow, then patted her hair, calmed her nerves and called for Mr Chance to enter.

It wasn't Mr Chance but Eloise, a beautiful French woman with pale olive skin and black hair tied in a braid. "Pardon, madame. Mr Chance, he asks that you join his family downstairs in the dining room. Their daily meeting begins at nine. Mr Chance said you must have breakfast in your room before joining them."

Joanna had eaten supper in her room last night while trying to remember the names of the men who had visited The Burnished Jade. Mr Chance did his utmost to avoid her, hiding in his study, a sanctuary barred to intruders.

"Thank you, Eloise. What time is it now?" Joanna was sure she'd heard a church bell chime eight and the half hour.

Eloise gave an apologetic shrug. "It is almost nine, madame. The family are seated in the dining room, but Mr

Chance said to join them once you have finished your morning meal."

"I see." Did Mr Chance have personal matters to discuss? Did he not want her to interact with his family? "Why invite me and then insist I arrive late? The man grows more confounding by the day."

Eloise pursed her lips, but a chuckle escaped. "I am sorry. I did not mean to laugh, but I think Mr Chance is afraid they will mention your … erm … *sobriquet.*"

"S*obriquet*?"

"*Oui*, your pet name. Your moniker."

Joanna straightened. "My moniker?" She dreaded to think what it might be. "Are you telling me they mock me behind my back?" And yet they were all so warm and welcoming, except for their eldest brother, who had made his disapproval of her known.

"*Non*, it is not like that." Panic flashed in Eloise's dark eyes, and she clasped her hands together in prayer. "Your moniker, it is adorable. All the brothers have nicknames. Mr Chance is the King of Clubs."

Yes, Joanna knew the men teased each other about being kings and thought the names were all quite apt. The King of Clubs was a symbol of wisdom and authority. A born leader. A powerful ruler of his domain. The epitome of Aaron Chance.

"Then who am I?"

Eloise hesitated. "I—I cannot say."

"You have my word I will not repeat it."

The housekeeper remained defiant. "Mr Chance would—"

"Please, Eloise. It might help me understand my place

here. Mr Chance is kind and considerate one minute and avoids me the next. Please, tell me what the family calls me. I'll worry it's something terrible."

One could see an inner war in Eloise's expression. "You … you are Miss Scrumptious." Eloise put her hand to her mouth like she had committed a cardinal sin. "Madame, you must not repeat it to another soul. Mr Chance will throw me out."

"Miss Scrumptious?" Shocked and a little flattered, Joanna repeated it silently a few times. "Why would the family call me that?"

Eloise waved her hands as she stepped back and said '*non*' ten times or more. "Baptiste will sew my lips together if he knows I told you. Ignorance, it is bliss. Nothing good can come from knowing the answer. Mr Chance, he will never change. He will always be a stubborn mule."

Joanna could barely stand still. Her curiosity was like a flame feeding off these sparks of intrigue. "Do they think I'm sweet?" It was the only explanation that made sense.

"*Non.*"

"Well, what then?"

"*Il te regarde comme s'il mourait de faim.*"

"In English, Eloise. Please tell me. I'm not sure how long I can endure his odd silences."

Eloise made the sign of the cross. "They say he looks at you like he is starving. That is why they call you Miss Scrumptious."

"Starving?" Joanna couldn't catch her breath. She had seen indifference and annoyance in Mr Chance's dark eyes. The occasional flash of kindness. Never anything more.

"They say he wants you."

"Mr Chance? Are we speaking about the same gentleman?"

"He denies it and curses them all to the devil, but it is there in his eyes if you know where to look." Eloise reached for Joanna's hand. "He will send you away if he knows I have told you. He will do everything possible to make you despise him. Please, do not speak of this to anyone."

"I give you my word this will be our secret," she said, her legs shaking from this bolt from the blue. "You must trust me. I would never break a vow."

His behaviour last night made sense now. He was hiding, hiding the fact he was attracted to her. It explained his odd reaction in the carriage, and why he refused to let her accept Gabriel's help, a man who had already proposed marriage.

Joanna took a moment to consider her own feelings. The news did not have her reaching for her valise, desperate to flee. She didn't hug herself, scared to walk the corridors of Fortune's Den. Mr Chance would do the honourable thing and keep his distance. And yet she longed to probe his mind and learn more about him.

There was no better time than the present.

"I'll not be late for the meeting and will eat in the dining room," she said, keen to observe Mr Chance now she was armed with this enlightening information. "I'll have tea and one of Baptiste's delicious pastries."

"Mr Chance ordered eggs and ham and toast for you."

"Give it to Sigmund. He has the appetite of a heathen army. He will ensure nothing goes to waste this morning."

Joanna reassured Eloise for a final time, then tidied her hair and hurried downstairs to join the family meeting in the dining room.

If Mr Chance was surprised to see her, he gave no indication. He sat at the head of the table, wearing a black waistcoat moulded to his torso, observing her over the rim of his coffee cup.

Though her heart pounded, Joanna smiled when the Chance brothers and their wives turned towards her. "Good morning. Sorry I'm late."

Everyone grinned and welcomed her, except for Mr Chance. Like a skilled actor on the King's stage, he held the usual steely look in his eyes.

"Have you eaten?" he said, the remark a veiled reprimand. "We have a busy day ahead of us. I want to visit Parker and the Fitzpatricks. There'll be no time to stop en route. I'll not have crumbs in the carriage."

He didn't care about crumbs, though seemed to be averse to the sound of her licking her lips.

Everyone looked at her, anticipating her reply.

"May I sit here?" Joanna gestured to the chair opposite Mr Chance, the seat traditionally reserved for the mistress of the house, eager to witness every nuance, any hint his thoughts and actions were misaligned. She sat before he demanded she occupy the space beside his brother, Christian.

Eloise arrived with tea and two petite pastries. "I have the breakfast you ordered, madame." The poor woman's hand shook as she lifted the teapot off the silver tray, though she did not look Mr Chance's way.

"Thank you, Eloise."

Eloise took an order for more beverages.

"Are there more pastries?" Aramis asked, his eyes alight with mischief. "Bring what you have. I think we would all agree they look scrumptious."

Christian chuckled. "So scrumptious, Aaron must be

eager to try one. I know sweet things are a real test of his restraint."

Aaron Chance firmed his jaw. "Miss Lovelace, perhaps now you understand why I asked you to eat before the meeting. My brothers will spend the next hour devouring the contents of the pantry."

"Oh. I thought it was because you hate me licking my lips and humming with pleasure. Baptiste's pastries really are the best I've ever tasted."

He held an indifferent expression. "If you want to eat like an animal, I suggest you dine with Mrs Wilcox, the zoological expert of Mayfair. She keeps a menagerie of feral beasts in her garden."

Joanna met his gaze. "As you often consider yourself a beast, I'm in good company. Perhaps you should begin the meeting. I promise to eat like a nun bound by a vow of silence."

She realised Mr Chance hadn't informed his brothers of Lord Howard's murder. Judging by their playful manner, they must presume she had other reasons for staying the night.

"Well?" Aramis said, prompting his brother to confess. "Why cancel the meeting yesterday? Why close the club last night?" He glanced at Joanna. "If it's because you needed personal time, you don't need to explain to—"

"When have I ever needed personal time?" Mr Chance countered, rousing a vision of him working alone in his office until dawn. "When have I ever put my own needs before opening the club?"

"Why did you not explain the problem when I called last night?"

Aramis had arrived a little after eleven, his concern turning to frustration when Mr Chance informed him they would discuss it at the family meeting tomorrow. Joanna had listened from the landing and heard them argue as Mr Chance ushered his brother out. He'd had Sigmund follow discreetly behind to confirm Aramis made it home safely.

"Because he wants you to listen and heed his advice," Joanna said, surprising everyone by speaking for their brother. "He wants to ensure you do not embroil yourselves in our problem."

Mr Chance's dark eyes rose to meet hers, a lingering look that caused an odd ache in her chest, a look she could not define.

"Miss Lovelace asked for my help because she found a dead man on her premises," Mr Chance said calmly. "I summoned Daventry because I publicly threatened to kill the victim. As you all know, Lord Howard owed me a great deal of money. Someone drove a Mughal dagger into his back."

There was a collective gasp.

They all looked at Joanna as if she were to blame.

"I assure you, I am innocent," she said.

"I have a motive for murder," Mr Chance said, before describing his altercation with Lord Howard. "I found our father's gold hunter in Howard's pocket. A watch sold sixteen years ago." He gave a brief account of what happened at the pawnbroker's shop. "We have a week to solve the crime before we're taken in for questioning. We have Daventry to thank for that, or we would be eating bread and gruel in Newgate this morning."

"I'll kill Berridge for this," Aramis growled, thumping the table.

"Which is exactly what I'm instructing you not to do." Mr Chance spoke in the masterful tone of someone who expected to be obeyed. "What I want you to do is be vigilant. If Berridge hopes to ruin me, he'll be hoping to ruin us all."

"Should Eleanor cancel her clients?" Theodore said, reaching for his wife's hand. "Should she close the shop while the murderer is at large?"

Christian was equally concerned for his wife. "Isabella is giving a lecture at the library today. There's no telling who will be in the audience."

"Then take Sigmund. He will observe the crowd and help keep Isabella safe." Mr Chance raised a hand of reassurance when his siblings voiced other concerns. "Go about your business, but take precautions. Keep a loaded weapon. Remain at home when possible. I've written to Mrs Maloney. She'll be in Oxford with Delphine and Flynn until next week, but they, too, must be on their guard."

Mr Chance lived to protect his family.

And yet he could not be in five homes at once.

His sangfroid was something to be admired. His complete self-possession did not reflect the panic that must be rioting in his veins.

"I think it wise to restrict your movements," she said, wanting to support him because she knew what it felt like to live in constant fear. "Until we know who and what we're dealing with."

Mr Chance gave a curt nod of approval. "There is nothing I wouldn't do for this family," he said, worrying her slightly because he would give his life to save theirs. "I'll not rest until we can all breathe easily again."

A heaviness fell over the room, the family's happiness replaced with a dread of the unknown.

"Would it be better if everyone came to live here?" Joanna suggested, despite a pang of reluctance. Mr Chance would have every excuse to avoid her then. "Would it be easier if we all lived under one roof?"

Mr Chance surprised her by saying, "No. It's more difficult to attack five targets than one. Until we gather more evidence, it's better for all of us if we live separately."

"It was just a thought."

"A considerate one," he said, keeping his mask in place. His gaze moved to his brothers. "I need to question Two-Teeth O'Toole. There'll be a price for information. He'll want me to fight for him out on the heath. I fight for no one but this family."

Aramis misunderstood his brother's meaning. "I shall fight."

"No. You'll find me something to use as leverage."

Aramis nodded.

"We'll not meet tomorrow." Mr Chance paused when Eloise returned with the pastries and fresh pots of tea and coffee.

Joanna took the opportunity to eat one of her own delicious treats. It took effort to use a napkin and not lick sugar off her lips. Her eyes kept fluttering closed as she savoured every bite.

Mr Chance watched her.

She smiled and mouthed, "They're so good."

His gaze dropped to his coffee, though she was convinced she saw the beginnings of a smile grace his lips. Why the action should cause a flush of heat in her core was anyone's guess. Why she had a sudden desire to make him happy proved confounding, too.

"We need to vary our usual routine," Mr Chance continued. "We'll meet at Daventry's office on Monday at noon. Any notes we exchange via the penny boy must contain the sacred rule and the symbols of our monikers in order of our birth. That way, we cannot be drawn into a trap."

"The sacred rule?" Joanna said, amazed at his thoroughness.

"There must be no secrets between us, no lies," Christian said, gazing upon his brothers with abiding love and loyalty. "It's a rule we've lived by since our stepmother threw us out on the streets."

Joanna's home had been ripped from her, too. Unlike the Chance brothers, her grandfather had ensured she always had somewhere comfortable to live.

"Honesty is always the best policy," she said but did not look at Aaron Chance. "Secrets rarely remain hidden forever."

The last statement did not reflect her own personal journey. Her brother's fate would always remain a mystery. A mystery that would haunt Gabriel beyond the grave. The same might be said for her father, but she suspected he would reappear once his creditors had grown tired of looking for him.

"Perhaps you would like to stay with us, Miss Lovelace," Aramis' wife Naomi said. "An unmarried lady should have female company."

As Naomi had kidnapped Aramis at gunpoint and married him the same night, she was hardly one to worry about society's strictures. Indeed, Joanna wondered if the comment was made to test Mr Chance's resolve.

"As Mr Chance explained, we're bound by a curfew," Joanna said. Something else bound them together, too, an unnameable something she felt deep in her bones. "I'm not sure I'm permitted to reside elsewhere."

The constable had called at eight o'clock last night to

ensure they had not absconded. She had seen Mr Chance for all of five minutes before they parted ways in the hall, bidding each other good night.

"It's more practical for her to remain here," came Mr Chance's logical reply. "Focus on looking after each other. I shall protect Miss Lovelace should any problems arise."

He was alluding to the escape plan. The plan to bundle her into a carriage during the early hours and set her on the first ship bound for France. Might he have an ulterior motive for playing the errant knight? In his battle to keep her at arm's length, would he seek to send her miles across the sea?

"No one can protect her better than you can," Theodore said with glowing pride. "One might think you've spent your whole life preparing for this moment."

"I've spent my life fighting to survive," he corrected before returning to the arrangements to meet in Mr Daventry's office on Monday.

They finished their beverages, and his brothers left Fortune's Den fifteen minutes apart. Each man assured Mr Chance they had survived worse and would survive this setback, too.

Naomi drew Joanna aside to deliver a cryptic message. "Most men have a gambler's instinct. They keep their cards close to their chest and master the cool expression that confuses their opponents. The trick is to call their bluff and force them to play their hand." She looked Mr Chance's way. "I'm confident the prize is worth the wager." With that, she hugged Joanna and left.

Then it was just her and Mr Chance again, just the two of them standing awkwardly in the hall. She searched his face, looking for the telltale sign Eloise mentioned, anything that might suggest a hunger to have her.

Nothing.

She would have convinced herself Eloise was mistaken had his brothers not mentioned the word *scrumptious* twice during the meeting.

"I'm ready to leave if you are," she said.

His brow furrowed. "Leave?"

"To question Mr Parker and the Fitzpatricks."

"Yes, let me fetch my coat."

"The coat you fill so well?" she teased.

The flash of amusement in his eyes was gone before he took the next breath. "Intelligence and physical strength are equally important when fighting for one's place in this world."

"How fortunate you have both in abundance."

He held her gaze for a little longer than necessary, long enough to rouse butterflies in her stomach, for warmth to fill her chest, the gentle glow lighting her from within.

"Fetch your pelisse and the hat I bought you."

She grinned. "I told Mrs Shaw to send me the bill."

"I paid while you were trying it on, and for another in midnight blue. It should be ready to collect on Monday."

She swallowed past the rising lump in her throat. No one had ever treated her so kindly. But it was more than that. It mattered because *he* had bought them, and she had an awakening desire to have him lavish her with gifts.

"For a cold-hearted devil, you can be quite charming."

"It was a logical decision based on necessity."

Mr Chance had a Norseman's skill for defending his position.

She gave a playful shrug. "You thought of me, even for a few seconds. That sets you apart from any other man of my acquaintance. Though take heed, a gentleman makes such purchases for his wife or lover. Now there is evidence to suggest we are more than colleagues, Mr Chance."

He arched a brow. "I shall record the purchases as work apparel." Every hand he played trumped hers. "It was a business decision, not a personal one."

She laughed at his absurd response. "You really are quite funny." Why would someone so strong and capable have to maintain a facade? "When did you develop such a dry sense of humour?"

In a fit of giggles, she laughed again. To an observer, these were not the actions of a suspected murderer.

Mr Chance watched her, his mouth drawn into a thin line, his jaw rigid, yet his compelling eyes turned traitor. From behind his mask of annoyance, his pupils dilated, betraying a fascination he failed to hide.

Wishing to unnerve him a little more, Joanna clutched her abdomen and touched his upper arm. Her fingers rested on his bulging bicep. "Don't be cross. If I don't laugh, I shall probably cry."

"There's nothing to fear. I won't let anyone hurt you."

Now she did feel like crying. Crying because he said the nicest things without realising. Crying because the wall he'd built around himself was strong enough to keep an army of marauders out.

She made a mental note to begin work on a siege tower.

"I'm confident this will all be resolved within the week," she said. Though her fingers itched to learn every hard contour, she released his arm. "Time is of the essence. We should go. I'll fetch my pelisse."

"I'll wait in the carriage."

She was climbing the stairs when he called out to her.

"I've asked Baptiste to prepare an extra course tonight. We'll be gone most of the day and won't have time to eat."

Would she be eating in her room again? Would they spend the evening in separate parts of the house? Would the loneliness feel even more profound?

"Can we not take a basket?"

He glanced at her mouth. "I can tolerate most things, madam. Your soft sighs of pleasure are not one of them."

# Chapter Seven

Thomas Parker owned a townhouse on Dean Street near Soho Square. He supplemented his income by gambling and placing ludicrous wagers. "When would Captain Monroe trim his wild moustache?" was one such bet. "Who would be the first debutante to fall foul of the season's most notable rake?" was another. He was a tedious bore, an average card player and suspected cheat.

Although Parker was in bed when they arrived, Aaron refused to let the arrogant butler turn them away. With his temper prowling like a caged animal, the first person to test his patience would pay.

"Summon Parker now," Aaron yelled, barging into the hall and beckoning Miss Lovelace to follow. "We'll wait in the drawing room. Don't force me to mount the stairs and drag the devil from his bed."

The drawing room was in a shambles. They stepped over dirty plates and discarded newspapers. Thick dust coated every surface. Stale smoke and the sharp odour of neglect filled the air.

Miss Lovelace peeled creased clothes off the sofa, holding one dirty stocking aloft. "I think the maid's duties involve more than emptying chamber pots and cleaning the grates."

Aaron glanced around the room in disgust. "Men who abuse their positions should be hanged. Owning a gaming hell is considered scandalous, yet they say this is a gentleman's entitlement."

"The hypocrisy is astounding," she agreed.

"You can wait in the carriage if you prefer."

A grateful smile touched her lips, the sort that might disarm him. "I have a strong constitution and will give you my full support. I owe you my life, Mr Chance. Heaven knows where I would be had you not come to my aid."

The air between them sparked to life, the charged energy heightening his senses. He could smell her perfume and hear the cadence of her breathing. The many ways she might show her gratitude filled his tortured mind.

"I fear you've been used as a pawn in a game to dethrone me." He needed to feel the fire of vengeance in his blood, not these unwanted stirrings of desire. "I'll not rest until this dreaded business is behind you. On my oath, you will reopen your club and return to the life you love."

She stared at him. "Will we go back to bickering?"

"We like bickering."

"Do we? I'm not sure I can berate you now that I consider you a friend. It's an unlikely friendship, I admit, but I have a newfound respect for you, Mr Chance."

Could they be friends?

Could she be his trusted confidante? A person who understood the boundaries and knew a sexual relationship was taboo. A friend who expected nothing but his abiding loyalty?

"We are friends," he agreed. "Friends are allowed to bicker."

She smiled like she'd found gold at the end of a rainbow.

In that moment, he wished he could love her. That he could make her his priority over those he had sworn to protect. Wished he wasn't so cynical, so brutal, so emotionally detached.

Parker burst into the room—snapping Aaron out of his reverie—dressed in a flamboyant green banyan. He had never been more glad of an interruption.

"What the blazes do you—" Parker stopped upon recognising Aaron. Unable to get the next words out, he gaped like a marionette without a puppeteer.

"You know why I'm here." Aaron considered the man's crooked nose and the purple shadows beneath his eyes. "You abused one of Miss Lovelace's guests at her club on Thursday night. You left threatening to sue and have the place closed down."

Parker raised his hand in surrender, revealing the bruise from being struck with a poker. "I drank too much brandy and acted the lark." He jabbed a finger at Miss Lovelace. "I was the one abused. Abused by two of her ladies. They attacked me and chased me out."

Miss Lovelace stepped forward. "You shook Miss Beckett quite violently. And you were not in your cups but quite sober, sir."

"Be quiet, woman. That house of ill-repute you call a club—"

Aaron was on him in a heartbeat. He grabbed the fellow by the throat and pinned him to the wall. "Speak to her in that derogatory tone again and you'll suffer more than a broken nose. You'll show her some respect."

He released the fool, waiting while Parker caught his breath.

"You left in a temper," Aaron continued.

Parker rubbed his neck. "A lady hit me with a poker."

"A witness said you returned later that evening," Aaron lied. It was easy to convince a reprobate he'd committed a cardinal sin. "You were seen creeping upstairs to seek revenge. A woman claims you attacked her during the soprano's encore."

Parker pleaded innocence. "She's lying. I left The Burnished Jade and went to my club. A place barred to crazed females."

"Brooks's." Aaron made it his business to know everything about the men who gambled at Fortune's Den. "How strange no one can vouch for you there."

"I played cards with Walmsley."

"Walmsley was at Fortune's Den until midnight. He lost his racehorse to Sir Albert Compton." Aaron cracked his knuckles. "You've lied to me twice. Don't make it a third time. I'm not a tolerant man."

Parker looked panicked. "I swear I never went back. Why would I? There's not a gently bred lady amongst them. None of them have a hope of finding a husband. Heathens. The lot of them."

"I didn't realise you were in the market for a wife," Aaron snapped. "Perhaps I should warn the good families of the *ton* that you live in a hovel and your maid warms your bed."

Parker shrugged. "I doubt they'll care."

"Your future in-laws might. Sullying the hired help is hardly a Christian pastime." Aaron drew his watch from his pocket and checked the time. "I'm a busy man. You have a minute to tell me where you were or face the consequences."

Aaron waited.

Parker lowered his head and whispered, "I went to meet a woman. It's a delicate matter. I cannot give you her name."

"You will, or I'll purchase every debt you owe and beat you when you cannot make the payments."

The lily-livered fool paled. "I only know her as Venus." Parker glanced at Miss Lovelace. "I'll not speak of it in front of her. This is for a man's ears only."

Miss Lovelace was not deaf. She raised her chin and confronted the gentleman. "Nothing you could say would have me reaching for a vinaigrette. My ladies have brothers. Many are scoundrels. I'm well aware of the disreputable things your kind do."

Aaron smiled to himself.

Miss Lovelace had courage abound.

In some other life, they would make a formidable couple.

"Who is this woman?" Aaron demanded to know. "Where did you meet her, and why is she using a moniker? Unless you want me to hound you night and day, prove you left The Burnished Jade and did not return."

Parker rubbed his forehead as if it might help him remember. "Truth be told, I don't know who she is. I met her at Mrs Flavell's masquerade."

"A demimonde gathering?" Aaron said.

"Yes. She came as Venus." Parker's eyes glowed at the arousing memory. "She approached me in the garden, said she knew I liked to make silly wagers, kissed me and said if I won the bet, I could—" He stopped speaking, his cheeks reddening as he grimaced.

Miss Lovelace chose to finish the tale. "She invited you to share her bed if you were successful. I imagine it was a pointless wager. To seek you out, she must have wanted you to win."

The comment stroked the man's pride. "She seemed desperate to have me, spent forty minutes playing the coquette and then disappeared when I went for refreshments."

Suspicion formed like a knot in Aaron's chest. Before Parker could describe the woman or explain what she wanted him to do, he knew it was connected to Lord Howard's murder.

"Let me guess," he said, hoping he was wrong and that someone wasn't plotting his downfall. "Venus was young, pretty and spoke with an accent."

Parker straightened. "Yes. I thought Italian or French, but she refused to tell me and said it was part of our guessing game."

"But you did what she asked?" Miss Lovelace said.

The answer was obvious. Few men had Aaron's fortitude to fight lustful cravings. Miss Lovelace was more tempting than Venus and Aphrodite combined.

"Some women know how to pique a man's interest," Aaron said, determined not to look at Miss Lovelace. "I imagine Parker would have panted like a dog and piddled up a tree to spend a night with his Venus."

Parker's temper surfaced. "She wasn't Venus but a manipulative hag. I did what she asked and waited at The Cock Inn until two in the morning. If I need an alibi, the landlord will confirm I sat in the taproom, waiting for a woman who failed to keep our bargain. He's the one who clicked my nose back into place."

One did not need Daventry's acumen to know what bargain they'd struck. "Venus asked you to cause trouble at Miss Lovelace's club."

"I was to make a scene and rouse the ladies' tempers." Parker touched his bruised nose and winced. "How was I to know Miss Beckett had an excellent right hook?"

There was no question Venus was the woman who'd accompanied Lord Howard to the pawnbroker's. But why have Parker make trouble so early in the evening? During the commotion, had the murderer stolen the list of attendees? Amid the chaos, had someone entered the building and hidden upstairs?

"Monsieur Xavier taught my ladies to throw a punch." Miss Lovelace made a perfect fist, correct thumb placement, straight wrist, knuckles aligned. "We've had three classes on the art of defending ourselves. You'd do well to remember that in future."

The creak of the upstairs boards drew Parker's gaze.

"Look, I've told you everything I know." The gentleman stepped aside and tried to usher them out. "The doctor advised rest. If you have anything more to say, call tomorrow."

With Aaron's suspicions roused, he decided to search the upper floor. "If there is someone else upstairs, speak now."

Parker shook his head. "No one but Nancy. Check if you must."

"I will go." Miss Lovelace was already at the door. "I doubt Nancy would want a strange man finding her naked in bed."

Aaron reluctantly waited as Miss Lovelace mounted the stairs. The need to protect her grew fiercer by the day. But the lady valued her independence and would not take kindly to him treating her like a child.

He held his breath until she reappeared in the hall. "Well?"

"The maid ducked under the sheets when I entered. There's no one else upstairs. I checked every room, beneath the beds and in both armoires."

"I don't know which harpy made an accusation against me," Parker said, referring to the lie that he'd attacked a woman during the soprano's encore, "but when you check my alibi, you'll know I've told you the truth."

"I pray you're right." Aaron nudged Parker's shoulder as he stepped past the sluggard. "Your life depends on it."

Aaron escorted Miss Lovelace to his carriage, bracing himself as he gripped her hand and assisted her ascent.

During the journey to visit the Fitzpatricks, he aired his frustration. "I can't invent the same lie to trick Fitzpatrick. I can't tell him Howard is dead and accuse him of murder, either. He'll deny being in the club, and his terrified sister will be his alibi."

Howard's only relative lived in Northumberland. It would take days before his obituary appeared in *The Times*. Hence they had a week's grace to find the murderer. But keeping Howard's death a secret caused other issues.

Miss Lovelace agreed. "Perhaps we should focus our efforts on finding Venus. She may not have killed Lord Howard, but she is the mastermind behind the plot to incriminate us."

How did one find a nameless woman in London?

Aaron groaned when the answer came to him. "It would mean venturing into the world of the demimonde." Howard was known to attend the odd event. Did he meet Venus at a party, too?

"We could question Mrs Flavell. She must know the identity of those who attend her wild parties."

"Very well, but I'll go alone." Mrs Flavell was always on the hunt for fresh blood. Who better than the beautiful daughter of a wastrel? "The demimonde is not the place for you."

Miss Lovelace sharpened her gaze. "Allow me to judge what is suitable. I warned you, sir, you will only play the domineering patriarch with me once."

*Damnation!*

"Have you ever been to a party at Mrs Flavell's lavish abode?"

"Of course not. Have you?"

"Many years ago. A man leaves his conscience on the doorstep and rarely departs with his soul intact."

Miss Lovelace sat forward, her brow furrowed. "What did you do there? You're not the sort to indulge in fanciful pleasures."

Aaron snorted. Did he detect a hint of jealousy?

"A young man needs to know where he belongs. It was reassuring to know I did not belong there." His conscience had followed him through the candlelit corridors, past an orgy of people wearing animal masks, past the naked dancers urging him to smoke in the opium den. "Make no mistake, I have the same urges as other men." Urges that were hard to control in her presence. "I choose to abstain because I cannot keep my vow to my family if my mind is engaged elsewhere."

"Your vow to protect them always?"

He held her gaze, his throat tightening, his heart heavy with regret. "No one can ever be more important to me than them." Keen to put paid to any notion they might be more than friends, he added, "That is why I will never marry."

"That's quite a sacrifice." She swallowed deeply, a shadow of sadness settling over her. "Are you not lonely? Do you not long to be a father or fall in love?"

He gave a mocking snigger but didn't admit that he locked himself in his study to feel close to her. By watching her house, he felt as if he were protecting her, as though she were part of his family, too.

"What sort of role model would I be?"

Her eyes grew watery. "A remarkable one."

Those words hung between them.

He didn't ask her to elaborate. She was supposed to despise him, think him cold and arrogant. He couldn't bear to hear her praise.

"I'm fighting next week. I shall save you a front-row seat." She would see the animal—the ruthless beast who could tear a man to shreds. "Then I'm confident you will have a different impression."

"Perhaps."

He thumped the carriage roof and asked Godby to pull over, then faced the woman who haunted his dreams. "We'll find a way to question Miss Fitzpatrick alone. I'll speak to Daventry tomorrow about visiting Mrs Flavell. Today, I want to meet Miss Stowe's maid and see if she resembles Venus."

Miss Lovelace gasped in horror. "Lucia isn't Venus. She remained in Miss Stowe's hired carriage between performances, hiding from the amorous vultures who thought her mistress material."

"She may have seen something important."

The maid confessed to seeing nothing important. Despite her mobcap and drab dress, the young woman had an exotic appeal anyone would find enchanting.

"Who asked for the encore?" Aaron said as they stood in Miss Stowe's drawing room, the worn upholstery hinting at the family's dwindling fortunes.

Lucia shrugged, admitting in a mild, Italian accent, "I do not know. I waited in the carriage until Miss Stowe asked me to sing again."

"The request came from someone in the crowd," Miss Stowe replied. "Then people began calling for Madame Rossellini, and the initial voice was lost amid the chorus."

"Did anyone enter the club while you waited in the carriage?" Aaron knew it was a pointless question. A maid could not identify the lords of the *ton*.

Lucia looked at Miss Stowe. "I took a nap. My working days are long, singing is tiring, and I am usually asleep by ten o'clock."

Miss Lovelace found it necessary to prove she was not exploiting the servant. "Lucia is saving to return home to Naples. She has a cousin there but wants to earn enough money to support herself until she finds work. She hopes to sail in the spring."

"I offered to pay for her passage," Miss Stowe said, "but Lucia insists on earning every penny."

"How commendable." Aaron might have a use for her after all. Someone who could enter a house and gossip with the staff might prove invaluable. "I'll pay you five sovereigns if you accompany Miss Stowe on a visit to Miss Fitzpatrick. I'll double the fee if you discover anything about her brother hiring someone to ruin her."

Miss Lovelace had some reservations. "What if Miss Fitzpatrick recognises Lucia? On what pretext would they visit?"

"Maids are practically invisible," he said, inclining his head, for he meant no offence. "And Miss Stowe is intelligent enough to think of something."

Leaving Miss Stowe glowing from his praise, and with Fortune's Den being a few minutes' drive, they returned home to take refreshments and plan their next visit.

"We're running out of options." Aaron withdrew his key and opened the front door. "There's nothing left to do but search Howard's abode."

He could not question Two-Teeth O'Toole or Mrs Flavell without something to trade. He could not accuse men of murder when few people knew Howard was dead. There would be calls for their arrest once the truth came to light. Gossip would spread through the *ton* like wildfire.

But fate had other plans.

The smell of an unusual cologne assaulted Aaron in the hallway. The aroma roused a vision of spice markets in Marrakesh. It was the scent of a man who enjoyed many vices.

"Rothley is here," he growled.

"Gabriel?" Miss Lovelace said.

Aaron hated that she used Rothley's given name.

Sigmund hurried into the hall, quick to explain. "I wasn't expecting you back for an hour or more." He gestured to Aaron's study. "I told the marquess to call tomorrow, but he insisted on waiting. Eloise is fetching coffee and a newspaper."

Aaron did not ask the purpose of Rothley's visit but glanced at Miss Lovelace. "He wants to know why The Burnished Jade is closed. He'll insist you return with him to Studland Park."

"Then he's had a wasted journey."

The thought ignited a fire in Aaron's blood. He barged into his study and found Rothley relaxing in the leather fireside chair. "No one enters my house without an appointment."

Rothley stood, his gaze moving past Aaron to the beautiful woman in the doorway. "Get your things, Joanna. We're leaving." He had something of a wolf about him: dark, penetrating eyes, prominent cheekbones, and a stare that could make weak men tremble.

Aaron clenched his jaw. "As an independent woman, she can make her own decisions. I would never force her to do anything against her will."

Rothley prowled closer, his voice low and gravelly when he warned, "If you've laid a hand on her, you'll meet me at dawn."

"Only a libertine would make that assumption. Miss Lovelace is here as my guest."

Rothley bared his teeth and thumped the desk. "She's here because you killed a man in her house and need her to take the blame."

*What the devil?*

"That's not true." Miss Lovelace came to stand beside Aaron.

Aaron used anger to disguise his panic. He refused to let Rothley take her. "You'd better tell me what you know and who the *bloody hell* told you."

Rothley reached into his coat pocket, retrieved a letter and slapped it on the desk. "Someone who knew I would rescue Joanna from this iniquitous den and keep her from the scaffold."

Snatching the letter, Aaron read it quickly, shocked the sender had identified Howard as the victim. "How do I know you didn't write this?" He handed it to Miss Lovelace. "How do I know you didn't kill Howard to force Miss Lovelace to marry you?"

"Despite what the *ton* believes, I'm not a murderer. The letter was delivered to my home this morning. I visited Howard, but he has not been seen for days. Then I hear The Burnished Jade has been closed since Thursday."

"I called here when I found the body," Miss Lovelace said. "With the magistrate's support, Mr Chance is doing everything he can to help me find the culprit."

"Of course he is," came Rothley's cynical reply. "Has it occurred to you that he has a motive for murder? That this is all part of a carefully constructed plan?"

"*I* have a motive for murder," she confessed.

"What motive could you have for killing a family friend?"

"You don't need to explain," Aaron said.

Miss Lovelace remained defiant. "No. It's time Gabriel heard the truth." She gathered herself. "Lord Howard ruined me ten years ago. The night he returned to London to say they had called off the search for Justin." She looked at Aaron, her gratitude evident. "Mr Chance is the only person who knows. I told him after I found Lord Howard dead."

Rothley paled. "Ruined you how? What the blazes did he do?"

Tears filled her eyes. "He took my virtue. Ignored my protests. I'm sure you're able to picture the scene."

The need to hold her in a tight embrace had Aaron flexing his fingers. This woman always made him feel so helpless.

Rothley turned away, his muttered curses conveying a desire to murder Howard himself. The thought of failing to protect his friend's sister would hound him to the grave.

It was why he swung around and said, "Fetch your things, Joanna. I'm the only person who can save you. I'll have a special license by the morning, and we'll marry tomorrow night."

Like hell they would.

Fury twisted inside Aaron. He'd always known he would lose her, but not like this. Few women refused a man of Rothley's notoriety. Fewer refused to marry a marquess.

"She doesn't want to marry you," he said darkly.

"She has no choice," Rothley barked. "I couldn't save Justin, but I will give Joanna the life she deserves."

*Stop using her damned name!*

"You're too late," Miss Lovelace said, clutching at the last vestiges of hope. "Should we fail to find the culprit, I've agreed to marry Mr Chance. In my opinion, there's no finer gentleman."

He was no gentleman. And though she had invented the marriage tale to buy herself time, he could never make her his.

Rothley's mirthless laugh echoed through the room. "You'd marry a gaming hell owner over a marquess? Don't be absurd."

"Mr Chance's blood is as blue as yours. He values my opinion and doesn't treat me like a hapless female."

"We've been friends for twelve years," Rothley countered. "You've barely known him twelve minutes."

103

"As you know me so well, Gabriel, name my most attractive quality."

"What?" The marquess found the question confusing. "You have many. Why does it matter? What bearing does it have on our current situation?"

"It matters to me. Name one."

Rothley shrugged. "You're a beautiful woman, Joanna. Is that what you want to hear? I imagine you turn heads wherever you go."

"But not yours."

"Of course not. We're friends."

"What about my character?"

Rothley gave a nonchalant reply. "You're good-natured."

Aaron snorted, grateful for Rothley's apathy. "Neither of those things set her apart from other women."

Miss Lovelace turned to him. "What does set me apart, Mr Chance? I'm keen to hear your observations."

*Hellfire!*

Though he had reservations about voicing his opinion and was not a man of great sentiment, it was essential to show Rothley in a negative light.

"Your eyes remind me of a summer sky. It's the only place I've ever looked and felt past sorrows drift away." It was not a lie. "Your abiding loyalty strikes such a deep chord in me. It's like we're woven from the same cloth."

Her slow smile had a teasing quality. "I might accuse you of being insincere, but I believe you meant every word." She turned to Rothley. "I shall remain at Fortune's Den until the murderer is caught. If you're a true friend, you will support my decision. If you want to help us in our endeavour, find evidence to show someone else killed Lord Howard."

Knowing Rothley would never betray her, Aaron

extended an olive branch. "Well? Do you care to hear what we've uncovered, or will I have the pleasure of throwing you out?"

Rothley narrowed his gaze but said nothing.

Aaron prompted him. "The sooner this matter is resolved, the safer Miss Lovelace will be. We need someone to search Howard's house."

"To look for what exactly?" Rothley replied.

"We need to know what social events he attended recently and who visited him at home. I estimate we have a day or two until the world learns he's dead. Then the *ton* will be baying for our blood."

Rothley looked at the letter in Miss Lovelace's hand. "Someone informed me of the crime. Similar notes may be in circulation."

While all of London might know their secret, Miss Lovelace's suspicions mirrored his own. "The villain wants the blame to rest on Mr Chance's broad shoulders. You were sent here to drive a wedge between us."

"All the more reason you should leave now and marry me," Rothley pressed. "The great Aaron Chance can defend himself."

Aaron could not argue with Rothley's logic. Though it pained him, he could not be selfish. "Rothley is right. You'll be safe if you marry him. He can protect you in ways I cannot."

Miss Lovelace shook her head. "But they'll invent lies about you. Find fake evidence. Throw you to the wolves."

"I have suffered worse and survived."

"No!" she cried. "You were there in my hour of need. I'll not forsake you now." With a defiant glare, she faced Rothley. "I'm staying here. You can help us, or you can leave."

"Your brother would drag you out and force you to comply."

Aaron clenched his jaw. "Touch her, and you'll deal with me."

"Justin is no longer with us." Miss Lovelace strode to the study door and motioned to the hall. "Decide where your allegiances lie."

Rothley cursed under his breath. He scowled at Aaron before gritting his teeth and surrendering. "Fine. But you will tell me everything."

# Chapter Eight

"Good night, Gabriel." Joanna escorted the marquess through the Den's opulent red hall. She opened the front door, gripping it firmly when the blustery November wind threatened to slam it shut. "Thank you for your support and for abiding by my wishes."

"I had little choice in the matter," he grumbled.

Gabriel had listened to the evidence gathered thus far and agreed to help them find the culprit. He had left Fortune's Den three hours ago, returning with Lord Howard's diary, his recent letters and a pile of social invitations tied together with a tatty red bow.

They had examined the elegant cards from people who valued Lord Howard's company and wanted to pack their ballrooms with titled gentlemen. People who knew nothing of the monster hiding behind his affable facade.

"Why the devil didn't you confide in me?" Gabriel's voice held the agony of a man always scrambling in the dark. "I would have made Howard pay for what he did to you. He always was the odd man in our group, always boasting and seeking ways to feed his vanity."

"His social calendar suggests he hid a licentious appetite."

While flicking through the lord's diary, they found he had visited Mrs Flavell's abode on many occasions. His last sojourn into the demimonde was as recent as two weeks ago.

"Men often display one personality while secretly harbouring another." Gabriel nodded at Mr Chance's study door. "You owe him nothing. Think of yourself, Joanna. Leave this place while you can still salvage something of your reputation."

She placed her hand on his arm. Gabriel was a handsome man, though she felt nothing but the warmth of friendship. "What reputation? My brother died mysteriously. My father—"

"We don't know Justin is dead."

They had the same tiring conversation whenever they met. Gabriel could not accept what was obvious to most. "My father is a wastrel who left me alone to face his creditors. My brother's friend stole my virtue. In supporting myself and other women, I have earned people's disdain."

"There's only one way to silence the gossips. Become the next Marchioness of Rothley." Gabriel must have seen her eyes roll in frustration. "The offer is there should you come to your senses. As I have no desire to sire an heir, I would ask nothing of you."

His response carried the chill of the November air.

She would wait for a man who wanted everything. A man who yearned for her love and loyalty. A man who would die for one kiss.

"You know why I must refuse. One day, you might meet someone special and regret your benevolent gesture."

Someone who might help him exorcise her brother's ghost before it drove him mad.

A cynical snort was his only reply.

"Good night, Gabriel. I will tell you what Mr Daventry says once we meet with him tomorrow."

"Send word to me in Hanover Square." Gabriel drew his greatcoat across his chest and pulled his beaver hat down over his brow. Prepared to brave the cold, he stepped out onto the street. "I shall remain in town until this sorry business is over and you've regained your sanity." Then he disappeared into the night like the spectre haunting his dreams.

Joanna locked the door and drew the bolts, inhaling deeply before slipping into the study and closing the door gently behind her.

The fire had dwindled to amber embers, the smoke from the snuffed lamp a fading white trail in the dimness. The soft flicker of the solitary candle sent shadows dancing across Mr Chance's handsome features, but he didn't look at her as he placed Lord Howard's letters in his desk and moved to extinguish the last light.

"Is it not a little early for you to retire?" She glanced at the fire, wishing the distance between them would burn away just as easily. Was he desperate to avoid spending time alone in her company? "You often sit at your desk until the early hours." She didn't say she spied on him sometimes.

He seemed surprised she had noticed his daily habits. "We have a busy day tomorrow, and there's less paperwork now the gaming tables are empty."

"Will you manage while the club is closed?"

He'd agreed to fund her trip to France, but she didn't want to make assumptions.

Mr Chance snorted. "The club generates a third of my

yearly income. I plan to reduce that to a quarter when I rent the apartments I'm having built north of Regent's Circus."

"You mean to strengthen your empire," she said, impressed.

"I mean to ensure my family's long-term future."

*And what about your future?* she wanted to say while battling a host of strange sensations: a longing in her heart and a newfound ache in her loins, a swell of pride for him rising like a warm tide in her chest.

"You've given them everything they could want. Money keeps a man safe and dry from the elements. Love and friendship nourish the soul."

"I strive for a balance in all things," he said.

"That's not entirely true. You neglect yourself."

"I have everything I need and want."

Would he ever admit to wanting her?

Or had Eloise misheard, her confession just a silly mistake?

"And yet your tone lacks conviction."

He blew out the last candle, plunging them into darkness. Despite the abrupt end to their conversation, the palpable energy flowing between them did not need eyes or a voice.

The atmosphere shifted, unspoken desire humming in the air like a hypnotic melody. Did he feel the sudden crackle of electricity dancing over his skin? Did he struggle to think of anything but their bodies pressed together, swaying in time to the music? Had she imagined the soft brush of his fingers against hers as he moved past her to open the door?

"We shouldn't linger." He stood in the hall now, a stoic figure, a martyr to his cause. "It's cold tonight. I suspect you'll want to hurry upstairs and bury yourself beneath a mound of blankets."

"I might light a lamp and read for a while."

"I suggest you sleep." He waited for her to climb the stairs and followed behind. "We'll need our wits when Daventry tries to draw us deeper into his devious trap."

"His devious trap?"

"They say Daventry is the most cunning matchmaker in London." He caught up with her but kept his gaze trained ahead. "Be warned. He may try to take advantage of our current living situation."

She cast him a sidelong glance. "I'm sure he knows you vowed never to put a woman before your family. It's not like he has the power to make people fall in love."

"It won't stop him interfering in our affairs."

"I shall tell him I plan to marry Gabriel." She knew Mr Chance disliked her speaking about the marquess. "He is quite open about his desire to make me his wife."

"It's hardly a case of desire," he said bluntly. "Rothley made it sound like a business proposition. A marriage in name only. Besides, you told him you would marry me."

"Yes, I do apologise." Thankfully, he had not contradicted her in front of Gabriel. "It's all I could think to say. You know I would only ever marry for love."

They reached the dimly lit landing, the soft glow of a single wall sconce casting shadows on the dark wood wainscoting. She touched his upper arm and bid him good night.

Heavens, he was built like a gladiator of Rome.

Mr Chance inclined his head. "Good night."

"Did you order my breakfast for tomorrow?"

His half-smile stole her breath. "And inconvenience my staff? You enjoy causing mischief, and it's easier to let you."

"I'm a woman. I was born to turn your life upside down."

He did not peruse her female attributes as some men

would and agree she was a fine example of her sex. "Finally, a point on which we both agree."

On that amusing note, they parted ways.

She walked a few steps and stopped. Mr Chance had lowered his guard tonight: the brief touch of their hands in the dark, the subtle smile that said he enjoyed their conversation. He would never be as vulnerable as he was in that moment.

"Mr Chance," she called, turning to face him.

"Yes?" He stepped away from his bedchamber door, dragging a hand through his raven-black hair. There was an undeniable magnetism about him, a raw masculinity she found irresistible.

"Would you answer a question before you retire?" She moved towards him when he made no reply, something other than excitement coiling low in her belly. "It's a simple one. I merely wish to understand your logic."

He waved for her to continue, though did not move an inch.

"I proved I am loyal to our cause tonight. I have been nothing but honest with you, and I know you will be honest with me."

"I never skirt around the truth."

She couldn't ask the question burning her tongue.

She couldn't betray Eloise's trust.

"Delphine's room is the coldest in the house. A logical man would care more about my physical comfort than my desire to sleep in a pretty place." Slowly, she closed the gap between them until she stood outside his bedchamber, too. "It would only make sense to put me far from the gaming tables if the club was still open."

He arched a brow. "I hear your observations, but not this simple question you're dying to ask."

Joanna raised her chin by way of a challenge. "What logical reason could you have for giving me the coldest room when the weather is bitter?"

The amused glint in his eyes said her argument impressed him. "Perhaps I want you to leave."

"Then you would tell me so in your usual blunt manner. You could have forced me to go with Gabriel tonight."

"Stop using his given name like you're more than friends." His sharp tone matched the flash of irritation.

"If we were more than friends, I would be at his home, not yours," she countered, letting him see she was equally vexed. "You're avoiding my question. I deserve an honest answer when I have trusted you with my greatest secret." Joanna had him cornered and refused to let him escape. "Are you afraid to tell me? Do you want me to suffer? Is it a way of punishing me for adding to your burdens?"

She saw panic in his eyes before his temper surfaced like a titan bursting from the sea. "You're the last person I would punish. Nothing scares me but breaking my vow. If a man shows weakness, his demons will devour him."

Beneath his anger, she could sense a civil war.

"What has your vow got to do with me staying in the coldest room in the house? Answer my question, and I shall leave you in peace."

He exhaled deeply, but his lips remained pursed.

"Fine," she said, about to turn on her heel. "Never question my friendship with Gabriel again. He doesn't keep secrets. He knows I would rather hear the truth than have him spare my feelings."

She moved to walk away, but Mr Chance clasped her wrist and drew her back to face him. "A man finds it harder to conjure amorous thoughts of a woman when she is sleeping in his sister's chamber. That's why you're in Delphine's room."

Euphoria flooded her veins, but she kept an intrigued expression. "And you don't want to have amorous thoughts about me? Is that it?"

"Our relationship must remain purely platonic."

*Yet I'm deeply attracted to you*, she said silently.

He was still holding her wrist, perhaps unaware his thumb moved in light circles. His eyes were softer now, the faint amber flecks making them appear nowhere near as dark and dangerous.

"Yet you touched me in the darkness." She had not imagined the feather-like stroke of his fingers over hers or the hitch in his breath. "The air is electric when we're alone like that. I know you feel it, too."

"I would need to be in the grave not to feel it." He sounded annoyed and solemn in equal measure. "It's not the first time I've experienced the unwelcome intrusion. Were we not embroiled in a murder investigation, I would insist you return home."

If Eloise had not disclosed his secret, she might have felt the sting of rejection. Indeed, she was keen to see how he would react if he thought his remarks had hurt her.

"I understand. You don't need anyone, and certainly not a woman like me. A failing club owner who brings nothing but problems to your door."

"It's not you," he snapped, pulling her a little closer, the smell of his cologne so good she could spend forever breathing him in. "I'm not made like other men. I cannot be gentle. A beast lives inside me. You've felt the mild whip of its tongue but never seen the sheer brutality of its actions."

She could contradict him and reveal his many fine qualities but decided to take a different approach.

"Have you thought we might not suit?" They would suit. She knew it like she knew her own name. "A quick experiment would put all your troubles to bed. If one tells themselves they cannot have walnut cake, it becomes the most appetising one on display. The painting that's not for sale becomes the greatest masterpiece."

"What are you saying?"

"You know what I'm saying, but you're afraid to test the waters."

They were alone, the soft candlelight creating a sensual ambience. If she couldn't get him to kiss her now, she never would.

"You have my permission to kiss me." Desire unfurled in her belly as the words left her lips. "What harm can it do? It will probably be a relief to get it over with, and then the masterpiece will seem like any other bland painting on the wall."

He did not argue with her reasoning.

"And I would like to move to a warmer room." She placed her hand on his chest and kept an impassive expression. She had never been this close to him before. He was breathtaking. "A quick peck should suffice. Should I close my eyes? This will be the first time I have ever been kissed. I pray it's mildly pleasant."

She felt like Eve tempting Adam to eat the apple. But the world would be a better place once Mr Chance lowered his defences.

"I'm not someone a lady chooses for her first kiss."

"Because you're rough and uncouth?"

"Because I'd devour you."

Why did that sound so appealing?

"Then I'm glad I'm not a lady."

"You won't like it when I lose control."

"When have you ever lost control?" She could imagine his inner devil tugging on his restraints, willing them to snap.

"I suspect I might with you," he uttered, the longing in his voice undeniable. He wanted to kiss her but refused to surrender.

The confession sent her pulse soaring. It felt like her happiness pivoted on this single moment. This one crucial decision could shift the balance either way. Dare she take a risk?

She moved her fingers slightly before gripping his waist-coat lapel. "Forgive me. I have always been too curious for my own good and lack your restraint."

Before he replied, she came up on her toes and pressed her mouth to his. His lips were warm and soft and utterly immovable. That didn't stop her from brushing hers slowly over his, relishing the feel of him, savouring the faint taste of cinnamon and brandy from their late-night dessert. It didn't stop the butterflies in her stomach or the giddy excitement urging her to continue.

But he released her wrist, forcing her to break contact.

"I should have known you'd play a winning hand."

"A lady must sneak past your defences. What a shame my first kiss was less than average. Perhaps it proves we don't suit."

"That wasn't a kiss. A kiss requires two willing participants."

"Agreed." She released him, her formidable foe. "Good night, Mr Chance. Let's pray I'm not frozen to death in the morning."

He shocked her by saying, "Good night? Do you think I'd let you leave believing I'm less than average? You must experience the reason for my reticence. If only this once. Though you will make certain promises before we continue."

She swallowed hard. He was going to kiss her.

"Yes?"

"You won't mention it to anyone. We won't have this discussion again. Do you understand? You'll pretend it never happened."

"You have my word." A desperation to feel close to him would have her agreeing to anything.

"And you must tell me to stop if I'm too much for you."

Too much for her?

What did he intend to do?

She nodded. "I will."

That's when he looked at her, really looked at her. His dark eyes roamed over her figure, a wicked smile curling his lips as he gazed at her breasts. "I may touch you inappropriately. I'm counting on you to be the voice of reason."

Maybe she should tell him she'd left her common sense at The Burnished Jade, but he robbed her of rational thought when he reached into her hair and slowly pulled out the pins.

He spent moments running his fingers through her golden locks, admiring the softness before draping her loose hair over one shoulder.

"No woman has ever tempted me the way you do." With his guard gone, he looked tortured. Conflicted. "I'm almost afraid to kiss you."

He pressed his finger to her lips so she couldn't reply. Moving slowly, he traced the outline as if her mouth were a marvel of science.

"I pray the beast behaves," he whispered, capturing her chin.

And then he closed his eyes and kissed her lips, and she thought she might die from the pleasure.

He was kissing her, the woman who lived under his skin, the woman he'd worshipped from afar for so long. He didn't know how he had fallen into her trap or under her spell, but the moment their mouths met, he didn't give a damn.

Perhaps he did know.

He would be no one's disappointment. He would leave her in no doubt of his ability to arouse her or of the dangers she faced. And yet he was hard in his trousers, solid from one chaste kiss.

*Don't lose control,* he whispered to himself.

*Breathe, damn you.*

But lust licked his body, scorching him like the hottest flame. His heart pounded. His lungs ached for air. And yet the dominant feeling as he coaxed her to kiss him open-mouthed was one of pure joy. To kiss her once was a gift. A present he did not deserve. One he should unveil slowly, not tear at the wrapping and devour the contents.

*Slow down.*

Beneath the heat of her mouth, his problems became unimportant. The past faded away, leaving nothing but the sensation of her lips against his and a peace he had never known.

Peace and pleasure.

Two things he denied himself.

Two things that made a man weak.

*It's just this once*, he uttered silently, knowing he had to make every second count. He could not let his emotions overwhelm him. There was no room for sentiment when easing a physical ache.

But he'd missed the flaw in his plan.

It didn't matter that he kept his feelings for her chained to a dungeon wall, that there was no room for manoeuvre, that he'd spent months forging the strongest iron shackles and the sturdiest cell door.

Miss Lovelace had the key.

The temptress slipped her tentative tongue into his mouth, her passionate hum trembling against his lips, releasing the locks and setting the beast free.

A guttural growl escaped him.

She wanted this as much as he did. The thought hardened his cock, the throbbing ache unbearable as it strained against the placket of his trousers.

He wrapped his arms around her waist, his tongue mating rampantly with hers, desire tearing through his veins. She smelled of roses, sweet like summer air. An intoxicating scent that aroused him to near madness.

He felt her hands glide up his chest, exploring the firm contours of his muscles. Then she flung her arms around his neck, pulling him closer, the heat of her body pressed against his as they stumbled back against the wall like desperate lovers.

Aaron lost control.

The King of Clubs was relegated to a lowly knave.

Every sensual movement of her tongue fed his craving. He plunged deeper into her wet mouth, the primal urge to hike up skirts and drive home causing a heavy ache in his loins. Erotic visions bombarded his mind. His mouth hot on her womanhood, his fingers plunging in and out of her wet sex. Her panting while calling his name.

*Take me, Aaron.*

Cursed saints!

He tore his mouth from hers. "Tell me to stop," he cried, unable to subdue the hunger, aware of the discordant actions of his body and his rational mind. "For heaven's sake, demand it."

Even as the words left him, he was hiking up her skirts, his fingers grazing the soft skin of her thigh. If he edged higher, he could slip his fingers through her folds, make her come hard.

She looked at him through dreamy eyes as her mouth parted on a pant. "Don't stop. Not yet. You still need to show me the reason for your reticence."

"Isn't it obvious?" Both hands were up her skirts now. He gripped her bare buttocks, pressing the hard ridge of his erection against her abdomen, his arousal deepening. "I'm a heartbeat away from having you. I'll not stop until I've wrung the last whimper from your lips." He would make her come again and again just to feel the splendour of her hugging his cock. "You should leave. It's not safe for you here."

She swallowed hard. "You swore to protect me."

"I'm the one you should fear. I'll pay for you to stay at Mivart's hotel, pay for a companion and a handful of guards. If you stay here, it will end in disaster. You've been hurt before. I don't want to be the one who hurts you again."

"You can't hurt me if I'm a willing participant."

"You might want me now, but you'll regret it later. You deserve better."

It took all the strength he possessed to release her and step back. Sweet mercy. He wished he were a weaker man, that he wasn't consumed with the need to protect her. Who would have thought he'd be saving her from himself?

"Wait." She stepped away from the wall.

But he couldn't wait. If he hoped to dampen his ardour, he needed mental clarity. Indeed, there was only one way to knock sense into his addled brain.

"There's somewhere else I need to be."

"You can't leave. What about the curfew?"

He dragged his hand through his hair and tried to temper his lust. "I'm going to the basement. I have to fight next week. I can't afford to lose." He didn't stop to hear her reply but descended the stairs as if the house were ablaze.

There was but one way to satisfy the beast. He would punch the boxing bag until anger swallowed every conceivable emotion. Then he would retire to his study and sit alone, his heart bleeding in the darkness.

# Chapter Nine

*Office of the Order*
*Hart Street, Covent Garden*

Aaron escorted Miss Lovelace into Lucius Daventry's premises promptly at ten, though the housekeeper asked them to wait in the hall because the gentleman was otherwise engaged.

"The master will be with you shortly," Mrs Gunning said before hurrying away because she had biscuits in the oven and timing was everything.

"Daventry is always punctual. He never runs late." Aaron glanced at Miss Lovelace, the woman he'd not stopped thinking about since he left her on the landing last night. The memory of their kiss lingered in his mind, the yearning to kiss her again so intense it was almost painful. "Perhaps he's forgotten our lives hang in the balance."

She smiled at him like he was a mere acquaintance, not the man who'd left her panting with pleasure. "I'm surprised the housekeeper didn't ask us to wait in the drawing room."

"She seemed more bothered about burning her biscuits."

"They do smell delicious."

"Indeed."

Silence descended.

He had made her promise not to discuss their amorous interlude, yet he was beyond desperate to know her thoughts. Had the urge to kiss him again kept her awake last night? Did she know they were so well suited it was like they'd been made for each other? Had she touched herself and thought of him? Because he'd taken himself in hand twice this morning—*Joanna*, the only word on his lips.

A feminine giggle echoed from the study, along with Daventry's playful request for the lady's silence.

Aaron would wager a king's ransom that Sybil Daventry was the recipient of her husband's attentions. The man made sure everyone knew how deeply he loved his wife.

A bang preceded the faint feminine groan.

Miss Lovelace chuckled. "Perhaps he knocked something off the desk, and the lady is frustrated."

"*Frustrated* is not a word I would use to describe Daventry's wife."

The Lord must have granted the man extra hours each day. How did he manage to be an exceptional enquiry agent and a devoted husband?

The study door flew open and the vivacious Sybil Daventry appeared, her vibrant red hair a little tousled, her lips red and swollen.

"Mr Chance. Miss Lovelace. Good morning." The lady's cheeks were flushed, and she wore a smile as broad as a summer horizon. "Sorry to have delayed your meeting, but I had important business with my husband." She touched her abdomen affectionately, the child she carried a testament to the couple's abiding love.

Daventry came to stand in the doorway, but he stared at his wife, not them, as if his hunger for her had never been sated.

Aaron knew the feeling all too well.

"I'll be home for supper tonight." Daventry spoke like the words were a code for something salacious. "Tell the boys I'll take them riding in the morning before breakfast."

For no explicable reason, Aaron's throat tightened. Thoughts of an alternative future bombarded his mind: Miss Lovelace pushing his coat off his shoulders, kissing him frantically, a wild and wicked welcome home.

Daventry greeted them and ushered them into his study, insisting they take a seat while he escorted his wife to their carriage.

Aaron drew out the chair for Miss Lovelace, his fingers brushing her arm as she sat. He should be grateful for small mercies. When she returned to The Burnished Jade, he'd be back to stealing glimpses of her through the study window.

"Do you regret asking me to kiss you last night?" He took the seat beside her and stretched his legs, crossing them at the ankles to look relaxed, not so pent up with need he could barely breathe. "You've been quiet since breakfast."

Miss Lovelace smiled. "I thought we were going to pretend it didn't happen. You made me promise never to mention it again."

"I'm just curious. We barely spoke afterwards and—"

"Because you left to take your frustration out on the boxing bag in your basement."

"I'm not sure you appreciate the effort it took to walk away." They had been a few feet from his chamber, a short distance from his bed. The desire to have her burned so hot in his veins, he feared he might combust.

She nodded like she understood perfectly. "You mean the war between your mind, body and conscience. I have no such issue."

Stillness settled over them again. The mantel clock ticked as incessantly as the question echoing in his mind.

"Do you regret it?" he repeated, needing an answer.

Miss Lovelace looked at him, her eyes bright with the memory. "Not for a second. It was the most thrilling moment of my life."

He found himself smiling. "You're an exceptional kisser."

"And you're a surprisingly passionate man."

Though he wanted to look into her eyes and lose himself in those cool blue pools, he averted his gaze. "Now you know why I gave you Delphine's room, though I suspect it's not as cold as you portrayed."

"I'm sure it's chilly in the dead of winter."

"When the temperature plummets to minus five?"

"Indeed."

Silence ensued.

"You were wrong about the painting." He promised himself this was the last time he would refer to their kiss. "You're nothing like the others on display. Like a true masterpiece, you command a room of your own, leaving everything else waning in your shadow."

The remark had her clasping her chest, but not from the compliment. "Please," she said, her voice raw with emotion, "you mustn't say such things. Not when we're trying to forget it happened. Can we abide by our promise and not discuss it again? It's in the past now. Let us focus on trying to find the devil who killed Lord Howard."

It was a sensible request. He ought to say a silent prayer of thanks, but the urge to kiss her was like a relentless addiction, an irresistible tug deep in his gut.

Daventry returned. "Forgive the delay. I wished to put my wife's mind at ease. My agents were assisting in an operation to catch river pirates last night. I went to check their progress and became embroiled in the fight. I only left the Limehouse Basin an hour ago."

While Aaron wished to throttle Daventry on occasion, there wasn't a man outside his family he respected more.

"It's why I could never marry," Aaron said, keen to put paid to Daventry's matchmaking plans. "I couldn't let my wife lie awake at night fearing I was dead."

"Yet you and your brothers live with that constant fear every day. A man must balance his business ambitions with his personal desires. To deny oneself either is to live a life unfulfilled."

Before last night, Aaron would have disagreed. But now he had a hole in his chest that only Joanna Lovelace could fill.

"Might we discuss the reason we're here?" she said, keen to avoid the topic of marriage and personal desires. "Time is of the essence. We have a few days remaining until we're hauled to the Thames Police Office for questioning."

Daventry gestured for her to continue. "Let me hear what you've discovered, and then I shall inform you of the new developments."

Aaron straightened. There were new developments?

Might their worries be over in hours, not days?

Might Miss Lovelace return home tonight?

The rush of relief was short-lived. There'd be no more

late-night experiments on the landing. No clever traps to tie him in knots. No forbidden kisses.

Miss Lovelace told Daventry about their visit to the pawnbroker's and their interviews with her friends and Thomas Parker.

"It's fair to assume Venus is the woman who persuaded Lord Howard to buy the watch," she said, "and that they met at one of Mrs Flavell's gatherings."

Daventry agreed. "It's obvious she had Parker make a scene at your club so the murderer could enter unnoticed. Or did Parker invent the story because he killed Howard in a fit of jealous rage?"

"Both are possible," Aaron said, though it didn't explain the missing list. "I checked Parker's alibi. The landlord at The Cock Inn remembers a toff with a broken nose but was vague on the timing. As for Venus, based on the pawnbroker's description, she bears an uncanny likeness to Miss Stowe's maid soprano."

Miss Lovelace was quick to defend the maid. "Lucia is not Venus. She's far too innocent to entice men with her womanly wiles."

*Unlike you*, Aaron wanted to say.

*You had me wrapped around your finger last night.*

Daventry made a note in his book. "Does she have an alibi for the time of the murder?"

"I sent Sigmund to question Miss Stowe's coachman." Aaron trusted his man to uncover the truth. "He states the maid remained in the carriage until summoned for an encore."

"A woman capable of pitting two men against each other could easily seduce the coachman into lying," Daventry said.

Miss Lovelace's mocking chuckle said the notion was ludicrous. "Oh, please. Lucia is not Venus."

"Why is she so desperate to return to Naples?" Aaron countered. Could they trust any information the maid provided? "With her talent and beauty, she could secure a wealthy patron in London."

"You, of all people, should understand the importance of family. She has no one here and misses her homeland. And a patron will expect her to perform more than a stirring aria."

Daventry drummed his fingers on the desk while in thought. "Why target Howard? Has he wronged someone? Did someone kill him to ensure one of you hang for murder? And if so, which one?"

Aaron glanced at Miss Lovelace, the thought of losing her causing his chest to constrict. "It's obvious someone wishes to punish me." There was an endless list of debt-ridden lords who had the means to arrange an elaborate charade.

"Then why not kill Howard and dump him on your doorstep? Why use a Mughal dagger? I have an expert in weaponry coming to assess the dagger this afternoon. He may offer valuable insight."

"The Earl of Berridge is involved." Aaron felt the truth of it coursing in his blood. "He's telling everyone we framed his son for fraud, that Theo was the mastermind behind the forged bank plates."

Daventry reached into his desk drawer, removed a letter and gave it to Aaron. "The treasury received this three days ago. The nameless sender accuses your brother Theo of stealing forged bank notes and killing Berridge's only heir. You're lucky I was there that night to witness the murder and arrest the culprit. Thankfully, I have the Home Secretary's trust."

Hot, murderous fury ignited in Aaron's veins. The primal instinct to fight had him shooting out of the chair. No one threatened his family and lived to tell the tale.

"Then there is only one course of action left." His heart pumped so fast his hands shook. "I'm grateful for everything you've done, and I ask that you work to clear Miss Lovelace's name. Rothley is still willing to marry her." He felt sick to his stomach at the thought. In his heart, she belonged to him but they were destined to walk different paths. "He will protect her now."

"No!" Miss Lovelace jumped to her feet, grasping his arm, her touch the sweetest form of torture. "What do you mean to do?"

"What I should have done years ago."

Daventry stood, bracing his hands on the desk, determined to make a point. "You cannot kill the Earl of Berridge. It will solve nothing and set your family back decades. They'll no longer be the sons of a scoundrel but the brothers of a cold-blooded killer."

"At least they'll be alive," Aaron argued.

"Their children will wear the stain of your misdeed." Daventry tutted. "I credited you with more sense than to let your heart rule your head."

"I'll not let you do this." Miss Lovelace placed her hand on his back, the action going some way to settling his boiling blood. "You're a good man. We'll find a way out of this mess. I know it doesn't mean much, but I will do whatever it takes to help you."

Her support meant more than he could say. He'd lost count of the nights he'd sat alone in his study, looking for ways to solve his family's problems. Needing someone to confide in who wasn't his kin.

"Pull yourself together," Daventry said firmly. "I can only keep the authorities at bay for so long. Things will get worse before they get better. There's something else you should know. I suggest you sit and let me help you find a sensible solution."

"If Berridge is involved, I *will* make him pay." He would make it look like a tragic accident, have rats nibble the carcass and disguise the evidence. "But I'll keep my temper —for the time being."

They all took a deep breath and sat down.

"There's more at stake here than your family's future." Daventry offered Miss Lovelace a sympathetic smile. "For a woman, a loveless marriage is akin to slow torture."

"I will never marry Rothley," she said. "I don't love him."

"Rothley is a powerful man, but he will never see you as anything more than a sister. I'm sure Mr Chance was only thinking of your long-term welfare. One day, you will fall in love with someone who deserves you. The fact you'd settle for nothing less is admirable."

The thought of her kissing someone the way she'd kissed him caused a roiling in Aaron's gut. "I don't want you to suffer more than you have already."

She lifted her chin. "Allow me to judge what I'm willing to do. Don't speak on my behalf like my feelings don't matter."

Though his instinct was to argue, he inclined his head.

"Back to our pressing problem." Daventry took a moment to study his notebook. "Too many questions need answering. How did Venus know about your father's watch and where did she get it? Was the soprano moonlighting as a wealthy man's mistress?"

"She was not," Miss Lovelace said in a sabre-sharp tone.

Daventry ignored the interruption. "If Venus attends Mrs Flavell's parties, did a member of the demimonde want to implicate you in a crime? Stabbing a man in the back is a symbol of betrayal. I'll make discreet enquiries at Howard's club. See if anyone made threats against the fellow."

"We need to know if Mr Fitzpatrick paid someone to ruin his sister," Miss Lovelace said. "That someone may have been Lord Howard. And I shall question Mr Parker's maid. Perhaps if I reveal his affection for Venus, she might betray his trust."

Daventry nodded. "An excellent idea."

Aaron's heart sank to his stomach. There were too many lines of enquiry and time was running out. "Hopefully, the weaponry expert will know where the dagger came from."

Daventry relaxed back in the chair and considered Miss Lovelace over steepled fingers. "There's a mental exercise I would encourage you to try, one to prompt the memory. Mr Chance will assist you."

"What would you have me do?"

"Sit in a dark room and imagine you're at The Burnished Jade on the night of the murder. Retrace your steps. Search your mind's eye and tell Mr Chance everything you see, particularly when the maid is singing. He will make notes. Do it the moment you wake and just before bed when your eyelids are heavy."

*What the blazes?*

There wasn't a chance in hell Aaron would enter her chamber.

"I guarantee you will see results," Daventry continued. "A minor fact your conscious mind has overlooked."

Miss Lovelace gave a curious smile. "I will try."

Daventry looked at Aaron and spoke in a cautionary tone.

"As to the other point I must mention." He paused, pressing his lips into a thin line. "An accusation of theft has been made against your brother's wife, Isabella. Made by someone on the British Museum's Board of Trustees. Unaware there is a conflict of interest, the Board hired my agent to investigate the theft of an Egyptian artefact."

Aaron might have flown out of the chair and sent the damn thing tumbling, but Miss Lovelace clutched his arm.

"What can we do to stall the investigation?" she said on Aaron's behalf. "These timely attacks on Mr Chance's family are a ploy to hinder our enquiries."

Daventry nodded. "Agreed. I've put Evan Sloane on the case but asked him to investigate the Board, not the theft." He looked at Aaron. "You must warn your family to be on their guard."

"I have." Guilt slithered in Aaron's chest when he considered this new dilemma. "But I can't tell them about these personal allegations. They will take matters into their own hands. I suspect that's what the fiend wants."

"Which is why you will refrain from going after Berridge."

With burning reluctance, Aaron nodded.

Daventry closed his notebook and returned his pen to the inkstand. "I'll visit Mrs Flavell today. The lady is in my debt. I'll arrange for four invitations to her soiree tomorrow evening. I'm told the regular event is called Temptation Tuesday. I think we all know what to expect."

Aaron inwardly groaned. "Four invitations?"

A slow smile curled Daventry's lips. "You'll both go. You can break curfew. I'll arrange it with the magistrate. Sybil and I will accompany you. A woman with child cannot attend social gatherings. My wife will relish the prospect of wearing a costume and enticing me to visit dark corners of the garden."

Not giving a fig for Daventry's romantic pastimes, Aaron said, "Should we men not go alone? The demimonde is not the place for an unmarried woman, certainly not one with Miss Lovelace's allure."

Every licentious devil would seek an audience, a means to seduce her with fake words and false promises. Society's polite rules did not apply. There was no such thing as personal space.

The heat of the lady's gaze warmed his face. "You consider me attractive, Mr Chance?"

She was teasing him. Surely the way he devoured her mouth said he found her irresistible.

"I'm stubborn, madam, not blind."

Daventry considered them both. "Finding Venus will give us the answers to many questions. Let's make that our priority. You'll need a costume for tomorrow, Miss Lovelace. Might I suggest something verging on indecent?"

The lady shifted in her seat. "Indecent?"

"Bare your shoulders. The lower the neckline, the better."

*Bloody hell!*

A string of silent curses bombarded Aaron's mind. "I doubt she will find something at such short notice."

Daventry eyed her figure merely as a matter of course. "I'll have Sybil send you a suitable gown. Make any necessary adjustments." He paused as if conflicted. The reason quickly became apparent. "Until my carriage calls for you tomorrow night, you're not to leave the house. Your safety is paramount. We're being played like puppets, dancing while a devil pulls the strings."

Aaron sat forward. "We don't have time to waste. I'll not

sit like a craven fool, afraid of his own shadow." He would slip out in the dead of night, steal into suspects' houses and terrify them into confessing.

Miss Lovelace sided with Daventry. "The villain is one step ahead. He's been planning this for months. It's like he has written the script and is directing us from behind the scenes. We must do the opposite of what he expects. My friends are on the case and will make contact if they discover anything important."

Aaron felt like a lion in an ever-shrinking cage. He wanted to roar and bare his teeth, not hide like a helpless cub in the dark. He was the King of Clubs, the ruler of his domain.

But every beast had a weakness.

Miss Lovelace turned to him, her eyes seeking his before making her heartfelt plea. "Please, Mr Chance. I sense danger ahead and beg that you err on the side of caution. Just this once. For me."

The power of the last two words rendered him speechless. They stripped him bare, exposing what lay beneath his stony facade.

He would do anything for her.

Anything that did not involve his kin.

That was the root of his problem. A problem he had tried to fix with his beastly moods and gruff temper. But his mind and body betrayed him at every given turn. And so, he nodded and surrendered to her persuasive power, just as he had last night.

# Chapter Ten

Joanna stared at herself in the looking glass, smoothing her hands over the blue silk gown and grinning like she had found hidden treasure. The bodice hugged her like a second skin, accentuating her slender waist before spilling into a voluminous skirt. She had never looked so frivolous, so feminine, so carefree.

Confidence stirred within her.

She barely recognised the sensual woman smiling back.

The last ten years had taken its toll, a decade marred by loss. Loss of family and fortune. Loss of her dignity and virginity. It's why she fought to make The Burnished Jade a success, why she couldn't afford to worry about her reputation. Such things mattered to the privileged. It did not matter to her.

She twirled before the tall mirror, a chuckle escaping.

What would Mr Chance think?

She never dressed to rouse a man's interest. She had never cared to see desire burning in a man's eyes, yet her stomach performed somersaults as she anticipated his reaction. Anger always flared first, but would his passions betray him?

There was more to admire than her womanly silhouette. The sleeves fell gracefully off her shoulders. The sweeping décolletage exposed the upper swell of her breasts. One firm tug and they would spill out. She trailed her fingers over her bare flesh where she longed to feel Mr Chance's hot mouth.

"Madame," Eloise began a little breathlessly, "you look so beautiful. It will not matter that Mr Chance had an extra helping of dessert. He will still stare at you like he is starving."

Joanna's heart skittered.

Two nights ago, she had caught more than a glimpse of the hungry man. Mr Chance had devoured her mouth with a passion that belied his cool mien.

"Thank you for staying late and styling my hair." Joanna touched the black velvet ribbon around her neck, the choker that added a touch of mystery. "And for trusting me enough to reveal Mr Chance's secret. It's helping me see his true nature, who he really is inside."

A kind, tortured man, though no less dangerous.

"Mr Chance has been different today. Forgetful. Troubled. Baptiste, he thinks it is odd." Eloise looked at her with glowing admiration. "But I know you are feeding a feeling inside him. He will want you tonight more than ever."

"What if attending the party is too much for him?" Would he retreat to his lonely lair if forced to lower his guard?

She had to tread carefully.

He had to instigate their next kiss.

If there was to be one.

"There is no need to worry. Enjoy yourself." Eloise drew Joanna to the stool and encouraged her to sit. "A bold white feather in the hair adds a certain playfulness." She slid the feather into Joanna's hair, then pressed a false mole to her cheek. "The patch will draw his attention to your mouth. A woman must use such ploys to attract a stubborn man, *non*?"

It was all too much. Joanna might have objected—Mr Chance disliked artifice, and she wanted to explore their feelings, not win his favour—but if they were to mingle with the demimonde, the more vivacious she looked, the better.

Joanna stood and hugged Eloise. Living alone made one appreciate every kindness. "Wish me luck."

"You do not need luck." Eloise clasped Joanna's hands. "You are everything he wants and more."

Aware she was running a little late, Joanna snatched her mask and cloak and hurried to meet Mr Chance in the hall.

He was pacing, tugging at his collar and the ends of his coat sleeves, each step a muttered complaint. He hated parties. He hated the demimonde. He refused to wear a mask. He was liable to punch someone tonight, and it might be Mr Daventry.

Then he glanced at the stairs and came to a crashing halt.

He faced her, swallowing so hard she feared he was choking. Intense dark eyes moved from her hair to her lips to her bare shoulders.

"We're not going."

She descended the last few stairs. "Of course we're going."

"Then you must wear something else." He scrubbed his face with his hand and groaned. "They'll eat you alive."

"Mrs Daventry only sent one gown." She ran her fingers over the lace neckline, tears threatening to fall. The last thing she needed was an argument. "I had to make a few adjustments. The lady is a little larger in the bust."

"Every man there will seek ways to get you alone."

He was afraid. The truth was there in every tense muscle.

"I've taken care of myself all my adult life. I'm capable of putting a drunken sot in his place." She decided to mention her ruination before he did. "I'll not make the mistake I did ten years ago."

"You'll be out of your depth."

"I'm always out of my depth. It's how I learned to survive." She inhaled deeply, keeping her disappointment at bay. "I have never felt so confident, so feminine. Don't spoil it for me."

He pushed his hand through his hair and sighed. "God help me. I have never seen anything more beautiful in my life. You take my breath away."

Her heart swelled. "You need to work on your delivery. Compliment a lady first, then let her see your insecurities. Allow me to demonstrate."

She stepped back, raking her gaze over his torso—remembering the muscled physique beneath his fine clothes. In his all-black ensemble, he looked like Lucifer come to survey his minions. As sinful as hell.

"You're a dangerously handsome man, Mr Chance. When I look at you, my body is not my own. It answers your silent call. Every woman will want you tonight, but they'll have to fight me first."

He smiled, and her heart missed a beat.

"You don't need to change clothes," she said, smiling too. "I'm confident I can deflect their unwanted attentions." She stepped closer and patted his chest. "Trust me. If you decide to kiss anyone tonight, it will be me."

He held her gaze. "We agreed not to mention kissing. We said we'd pretend our mouths had never met."

"Yes, but your shoulders are so tense, you look like you need to lose yourself for a few hours. Remember, tonight we're entering a world that exists outside of society. We can do as we please, and it doesn't count."

The hard lines of his mouth softened, but he said nothing.

"Let me be transparent," she said because she had her own list of demands. "I will never give up The Burnished Jade. I'll never be beholden to a man again. We both have responsibilities to other people. I can't think about my future until I see my ladies settled."

"That could take forever," he mocked.

"Yes. Like you, my life is not my own. But we're allowed to relax and enjoy ourselves a little." She pushed a lock of hair off his brow and he didn't catch her wrist to stop her. "We're friends who might kiss occasionally. Where is the harm in that?"

He looked at her like she was a mathematical puzzle. "You make everything sound so simple."

"And you complicate everything. Perhaps we might meet somewhere in the middle." She paused, waiting for him to make a demand or refuse to play games, but he didn't. "You'll need to wear a mask."

"And have those pathetic fools think I'm one of them?"

"We don't want Venus to recognise you. And if you do decide to kiss me again, is it not better to pretend we're strangers?"

"I doubt I'll have time. I'll be batting vermin away like an overworked rat catcher." He strode to his study, returning with a black domino and stuffing it into his coat pocket.

"I can take care of myself." She hoped the lessons in pugilism would help if cornered by a rakehell. Failing that, Mrs Daventry had ensured she was armed. "On Mrs Daventry's request, I have a blade strapped to my thigh. A pretty silver *verijero*. Though I fear it's asking for trouble. She said to tell you before we leave for Belgravia."

Mr Chance's eyes rolled in their sockets. "Has the woman lost her mind? You're suspected of murdering a man with a dagger. If you're caught with a knife, it shows intent." He beckoned her with a sharp, impatient flick of his fingers. "Give it to me. I'll not have you putting yourself at risk."

Agreeing it was an odd request on Mrs Daventry's part, Joanna turned away but struggled to hold her skirts and unbuckle the belt. Eloise was still tidying the room on the third floor and wouldn't hear her calls.

"You'll have to help me, Mr Chance." She faced him, her gown raised to her knees. "You'll have to hold my dress or remove the dagger."

He looked like she'd asked him to scale the dome of St Paul's blindfolded. He glanced at her silk stockings and groaned. "Where the hell is Eloise?"

"Upstairs." The sound of a carriage rattling to a halt on the street had Joanna checking the viewing window. "Hurry. Mr Daventry is outside."

"*Hellfire!* Hold your skirts. A little higher. I'll not fiddle with the buckle but just remove the blade." He did so swiftly, barely touching her as he drew the weapon. "Mrs Daventry has a lot to answer for," he grumbled, depositing the knife in the console table and slamming the drawer shut.

Minutes later, they found themselves squashed beside each other on Mr Daventry's leather carriage seat, her skirts spilling over Mr Chance's thighs as the vehicle charged through the dark London streets.

Mrs Daventry looked stunning in an emerald green gown, her red curls piled high, a few tendrils teasing her bare neck.

Mr Daventry mirrored Mr Chance and wore all black. It was hard to tell who looked more dangerous.

"I gave the magistrate my word you'd be home no later than one," Daventry said, reminding them he was their chaperone. "A constable may call, so we must abide by the rules. We can discuss recent updates later."

"And if Venus doesn't show?" Mr Chance said.

"We lock the door, hold everyone hostage and question the guests individually. I warned Mrs Flavell I might make an arrest. I said we'd be discreet unless forced to act otherwise."

"You told Mrs Flavell we're looking for Venus?" Joanna doubted the woman could be trusted.

"No. She knows we're looking for someone but doesn't know who. I said we would mingle. Give the impression we've come seeking entertainment."

Mr Chance stiffened beside her. "It will look odd if we're not cavorting with the guests."

"I shall cavort with my wife. We'll wear masks. As long as it looks like we're seducing someone, people will pay us no mind."

"What about us?" Heat crept up Joanna's neck at the memory of Mr Chance pushing her against the wall, his rampant hands sliding under her skirts. "How are we to make it look convincing?"

She knew how.

He needed to kiss her, and she needed to pant and moan and grasp his collar like she had the other night. He needed to stand between her thighs, the hard ridge of his arousal pressed against her belly.

"The power of one touch can be mesmerising." Mr Daventry turned to his wife, tilted her chin with one finger and gazed at her lips. "If you speak in low hushed tones, people assume you're saying lewd things." He released his wife and faced them. "There's no need to do anything more. Perhaps you should use the journey to practise."

"We're not children," Mr Chance snapped.

Mrs Daventry chuckled. "In that gown, it's quite clear Miss Lovelace is every bit a woman."

They spent the rest of the journey to Belgravia in silence. Mr Chance stared out the window, his annoyance palpable in the confined space. Yet every time the carriage bounced through a rut in the road, his arm became a protective barrier to prevent her from slipping off the polished seat.

The carriage stopped outside an imposing four-storey townhouse in Grosvenor Place opposite the majestic Green Park.

Joanna stared at the impressive facade. "Mrs Flavell entertains the demimonde here?"

It was a house fit for a king. The vast portico and towering stone columns exuded an air of opulence and grandeur. It wasn't just a home—it was a statement, where every carved detail whispered of wealth and timeless sophistication.

"Mr Flavell made his fortune in the steel industry," Mr Daventry said with a hint of admiration. "He was a forward-thinking man. Don't be fooled by the widow's friendly demeanour. She's astute and uses these parties to find new investors."

Mr Chance gave a distrustful sneer. "I wouldn't be surprised if she arranged Howard's death. Perhaps she's purchased a gaming hell and means to dispose of the competition. I'd wager Mrs Flavell knows Venus' identity because she hired her."

Mr Daventry shrugged. "At this point, anything is possible."

They alighted, and Joanna donned her mask while Mr Daventry instructed his coachman to park directly opposite and note anything suspicious.

Music and laughter spilled onto the street, mingling with the lively hum of conversation echoing from within the grand mansion.

"You'll not leave my side." Mr Chance placed a possessive hand gently on her back, the merest touch sending tingles dancing down her spine. "Not even for a second."

She didn't argue. Why would she?

No one had ever cared about her to this degree.

Mr Daventry led the way, mounting the steps and tugging the bell.

Mrs Daventry smoothed her hands over her swollen stomach, hidden by a cascade of green silk. "She senses my excitement. Lucius would like a daughter. He says the world needs mischievous redheads to challenge the status quo. Do you see yourself marrying and having children, Joanna? Oh, you don't mind me using your given name?"

"Not at all—to using my given name. I don't know what the future holds for me. I'm merely trying to get through each day and keep myself out of Newgate."

The lady offered a sympathetic smile. "It won't come to that. Lucius will do everything in his power to ensure you walk free."

The loss of Mr Chance's hand on her back brought a cold rush to her skin, the only warmth in her life snatched away. She turned to find him wearing his black silk mask. If he looked sinful before, he looked downright wicked now.

Her pulse soared, a surge of heat flooding her cheeks. His

ADELE CLEE

eyes were darker, like hidden caves promising untold treasures. And his lips seemed softer somehow, an intimate focal point she found captivating.

Arousal slid through her body.

She wanted him. Would she want him more when presented with the erotic displays of Temptation Tuesday?

Mrs Flavell's strapping butler took their invitations and outdoor apparel and welcomed them into the vast hall, its marble floors gleaming beneath glittering chandeliers. A group of men lingered at the bottom of the sweeping staircase. A woman dressed as a milkmaid hurried past, tugging the rope belt of a man in a monk's gown.

All heads turned Joanna's way.

She felt their eyes crawling over her like insects on her skin.

"Prepare to be shocked," Mr Chance whispered when she took his arm. "Whatever you do, do not go anywhere alone."

They passed the open door to the opulent dining room. Guests in animal masks occupied all twelve seats around the table. Their hands were tied behind their backs, leaving them to gobble food with their mouths from the body of a naked woman strapped to the walnut surface. They grunted like beasts. None of them were Venus.

Joanna clung to Mr Chance and inhaled to calm her nerves.

A strange smell lingered in the air—a sweet scent mixed with the earthy aroma of tobacco and incense. It irritated her nostrils and teased her senses.

"Hold your breath when we pass the next room," he urged.

*Take me home*, she wanted to say, but mingling with the

debauched brought out the protector in him. And he didn't object when she hugged his firm bicep.

Joanna tried to breathe as smoke wafted from the salon on their right. People relaxed on red damask sofas, puffing on pipes, entranced by the white wisps coiling into the air. Some kissed like depraved citizens of Sodom and Gomorrah. Some swayed in time to the orchestra's music, their rampant hands exploring each other's bodies.

The string quartet in the drawing room played Beethoven to a crowd of eager revellers. Alas, the musicians failed to hold the throng's interest. Men turned their heads, mischief glinting in their eyes, their mouths moist where their tongues skimmed the seams. Women lowered their masks to stare at Mr Chance.

It was like walking through the African savannah, past starving lions lounging openly in the grassland, waiting for one to roar and pounce.

Joanna squeezed Mr Chance's arm. "Unless you want to be a dish on the supper menu, I suggest you refrain from going anywhere alone, too."

"The sooner we leave here, the better."

Excited whispers breezed through the air.

A woman with ebony curls and large breasts stepped forward to block their path, longing to be the first to secure dinner. "Good evening, sir. With such a confident strut, this can't be your first party." Her feline gaze journeyed over Mr Chance's physique, but she didn't remove her mask. "Perhaps we might find a quiet alcove and you can tell me how badly you want to come tonight."

Mr Daventry had warned them to mingle lest they rouse suspicion.

So, it came as no surprise when Mr Chance gave a curious hum. "I'm otherwise engaged. Perhaps we might talk later."

The brazen devil glanced at Joanna. "Is three a crowd?"

"Indeed. When it comes to her, I'm exceptionally greedy."

"Show me how greedy she makes you," the woman insisted, beckoning her friends to come and watch. "Newcomers must put on a show."

Mr Chance didn't curse her to Hades and demand she move. He smiled like he lived for pleasure, not wallowed in pain. "You'll get a glimpse of what she does to me, no more. I'm protective of the things I own."

Joanna's heart nearly thumped out of her chest when he faced her and captured her chin with firm fingers. He was going to kiss her in front of the crowd.

"Shall we show them why I'm your one and only master?" His low, husky voice melted her insides. "You know I like you to beg for my mouth."

It was his way of asking for permission.

A way of telling her to play the damn game.

Good Lord! The Daventrys were nowhere to be seen and were probably outside hunting for Venus. She had to prove herself. She'd told him she was used to feeling out of her depth. That she could cope with what life threw her way.

"Why should I give it to you?" Mr Chance prompted.

Joanna moistened her lips. "I've been such a good girl, sir."

"Yes, you have," he purred while people looked on. "So good. Tell me again. Whose good girl are you?"

"I'm your good girl, sir."

"And you think you deserve a reward?"

Joanna nodded. This was merely a ploy to show they belonged here, but her sex pulsed so quickly she was panting now.

"Say it! Speak up. Tell me what you want."

"I want your mouth, sir." It was not a lie. She might die if he didn't kiss her soon. She wanted everything he had to give. "And your tongue and your hands on my body. Please, sir. I'll do anything you ask."

A man in the crowd chuckled. "I do like hearing her beg."

The faint twitch of Mr Chance's cheek muscle said the thread holding his temper was about to snap. He gave no further warning. His mouth came crashing down on hers like that of a scandalous libertine.

He didn't try to coax a response or tease her with the faint touch of his tongue. It wasn't a kiss but a passionate explosion. Like the greedy man he professed to be, he drove his tongue deep into her mouth, the long, powerful strokes sending shocks of pleasure to her core.

Her nipples hardened, another ache to add to the many. She didn't care that people were watching, that she was moaning into his mouth. She was riding so high on the waves of pleasure, she hoped she never came down.

But he broke contact to an applause from their audience, the cries for an encore drowning out Beethoven's symphony.

Mr Chance didn't acknowledge them.

She was the focus of his intense gaze as his chest rose and fell rapidly as he chased his next breath. Those obsidian pools carried the mystery of the unknown, yet twice, he had invited her to explore their hidden depths.

The ebony-haired coquette gestured to the gold sofas, offering them champagne and inviting them to join her party.

"Perhaps later," Mr Chance said, his voice strained as he

147

reached for Joanna's hand and grasped it firmly. "For the moment, we require a little privacy."

The woman glanced at his trousers, laughed and stepped aside. "Yes, being a greedy man, I suspect you need something warm and moist to eat."

Mr Chance inclined his head and led Joanna away.

"Do you need air?" she said as he pulled her through the open terrace doors.

"No. I need something else entirely." He saw the Daventrys mounting the terrace steps and might have marched straight past them had Mr Daventry not stopped to ask an obvious question.

"Any sign of Venus? I take it she's not in the drawing room."

"No."

"She's not in the orangery or the Chinese pagoda." Mr Daventry noticed their clasped hands. "We'll wander upstairs and conduct a thorough search. If we're caught in a bedchamber, we won't find ourselves fumbling awkwardly."

"Avoid lingering in the drawing room." Mr Chance spoke like he was late for an appointment. "We'll check the garden again in case she's hiding and meet back on the terrace in half an hour."

He didn't wait for a reply and descended the stone steps, pulling Joanna through the garden towards the tall boxwood maze. "Say now if I've misjudged the situation and you have no desire to continue what we started." Before she could reply, he said, "Do you want to kiss me again? Would you like me to touch you the way I longed to do the other night?"

Her body flamed, hot like the braziers spread around the garden to chase away the late autumn chill. "You know I do.

And after that heart-stopping kiss, you've earned the right to call me Joanna."

He drew her to a halt outside the entrance to the maze. "You played the part well. Too damn well. I've a cockstand like you wouldn't believe. But that's not why I've brought you here."

"Oh?"

"You're strung as tight as a bow. While Daventry hunts for Venus, I need to ease your tension."

"Ease my tension?"

"I need to make you come, Joanna. I'll go out of my mind if I don't. Tell me it's what you want too."

She swallowed hard. "You want to touch me in the garden?"

He jerked suddenly and cursed. "Damn. Not the garden then."

"Why not the garden?" It was quiet, secluded, and she was desperate to explore this irresistible attraction. She had never felt so desired in her entire life.

"You know why."

He was referring to Lord Howard's *mistake*.

"If we're to kiss, I would rather it was in the garden." Mr Chance was not Lord Howard. And this was an affair, a delicious dalliance involving mutual feelings and the utmost respect. "You can help to erase the bad memories."

His arm snaked around her back. "You said we can be anyone we want tonight. That we might indulge ourselves and not worry about it tomorrow."

She wrapped her arms around his neck. "We're just two people seeking comfort, nothing more."

"From a life neither of us planned," he agreed.

"Nothing beyond this moment is guaranteed." She released him, held his large hand and drew him into the dark maze. "Let's disappear. Let's pretend we're living a different life. One with no responsibilities, where the rules do not apply."

# Chapter Eleven

Aaron followed Joanna into the darkness, convincing himself that whatever happened here would have no bearing on the case or their friendship. He rarely lied to anyone, least of all to himself, but if he didn't sate this need to touch her, he'd be a candidate for Bedlam.

"Hurry," she whispered, excitement lacing through her voice as she drew him further into the gloom. "How far should we go?"

Her hand was soft and warm in his, the charge of attraction an electric pulse beating between their palms. Her eagerness kept his cock hard, a solid strain against his trousers. She enjoyed this game as much as he did. When were they ever this carefree? When had they ever indulged their desires or acted on a whim?

Never.

"Just a little further," he said. The maze was small but he would hear the gravel crunch if someone entered. "Walk to the end of the avenue and turn left."

The dense evergreen walls loomed on either side, their

shadows swallowing any light from the house. The thrill of anticipation hung in the air, along with the sweet, earthy scent of boxwood. It was the perfect place for a secret liaison, a place where nothing mattered but the woman he adored.

"Shall we stop here?" She came to a halt, facing him, her hands moving to his chest like she was desperate to touch him, too. "We're still wearing our masks. Should we pretend we're strangers? Would you like me to play the good girl, sir?"

Aaron pressed her against the hedge, cradling her throat gently, tracing her lips with his thumb. "I like the strong woman, not the good girl. I like it when you make demands on me. I like the fire burning in your eyes and the sting of your sharp tongue."

She sighed softly. "It sounds like you want us to be ourselves."

"Us as we might have been had life treated us fairly."

She caressed his chest. "Sneaking into hidden places to steal forbidden kisses? Where nothing else matters but pleasing each other?"

She painted an idyllic picture. A glimpse of heaven on earth.

"Yes." A life where she would be his priority.

"It sounds divine."

He could not afford to dwell on the thought. He had to meet with his brothers tomorrow and inform them of the threats. They were grown men who deserved to know the truth. Their safety would be his focus then.

"Did you mean what you said, Joanna? Do you want me to devour your mouth? Do you want to feel my tongue sliding over yours, my hands on your body? Or was it all an act to please the crowd?"

"I want all of those things," she uttered, her breath a mist of white in the cool night air. "The crowd merely allowed me to say what I've wanted to say all day."

His gaze moved to her bare shoulders. "Are you cold?"

"A little, but I have a plan to keep warm."

She responded by wrapping her arms around his neck and kissing him in the darkness. Her lips were soft and pliant and *his*. She would always be his. Touching her would always feel like he had found his way home.

He deepened the kiss, drinking from her like he was dying of thirst. The desire to touch her intimately, to be the first man to make her climax—the only damn man—throbbed in his fingers, his lust a potent beat in his blood.

He tore his mouth from hers with a gasp. "I'm going to take liberties but don't want to frighten you."

She pressed a chaste kiss to his lips. "You could never frighten me."

"You're one of the few people in London who can say that."

"No one knows you like I do."

"You only know one part of me." He dreaded to think what she would do when she saw the savage in him, pounding men with his fists, reclaiming debts, knowing the innocent would suffer. "I've done things you would find abhorrent. I'm ruthless in business. I take no prisoners."

"You're a loving family man."

"I'd tear anyone apart who tried to hurt them."

"And yet I find your strength arousing, not terrifying."

"Why?" he demanded.

"I cannot define what exists between us. All I know is it's mutual and so powerful I'm not thinking about finding Venus, only anticipating the moment your lips take mine."

That moment came less than a second later.

Their mouths collided in a kiss to rock the heavens. The sudden urgency to ease a physical ache had them grasping each other, their roving hands mimicking the frantic movements of their lips.

He was drowning in the smell and taste of her. He was lost as he drank her in, her essence filling his body like she belonged there. Yet it wasn't enough.

"Tell me you want more," he growled, moving to rain kisses down her slender neck and bare shoulder. He meant to brand her, leave his mark on every inch of her porcelain skin.

She tilted her head. "When it comes to you, I'm insatiable."

"Do you touch yourself, Joanna?"

She hesitated.

"Tell me," he whispered. "You can tell me anything."

"Sometimes."

"Have you touched yourself and thought of me?" He tugged at the shoulders of her gown, grateful for the style of corset because it took no effort to free her breasts.

Good God! She was magnificent.

A temptress touched by slivers of moonlight.

She sucked in a breath as the chill air hardened her rosy nipples.

"Have you?" he repeated, kissing her neck and palming her plump breast, grazing his thumb back and forth over the pretty pink peak.

"Yes," she said with a throaty moan, her head falling back. "You're all I think about lately. I can't get you out of my mind."

"When did you last touch yourself?" He moved to

worship the hard bud, flicking it with his tongue, sucking it into his mouth. "When, Joanna?"

She pushed her hands into his hair, urging him to lavish her other breast. "Last night … and …"

"And?"

"Tonight, when I bathed."

"I came to the thought of you so many times today that I've chaffed my damn skin." He reached under her skirts, the rustling of silk preceding his guttural groan as he slipped his fingers over her sex and found her wet.

*Merciful Lord.*

He could be inside her in seconds, pushing into her wetness, driving deep. But she would be his then. The most important person in his life. This … this beautiful moment was a test of his resolve. Never had he been so close to abandoning his family and forgetting every vow he'd ever made.

He looked at her, searing the glorious sight into his memory. "Do you want me to ease the ache, Joanna?" His fingers massaged the centre of her sex. "Will we share such an intimacy and pretend it never happened?"

"Yes," she panted, her lashes fluttering against her cheeks as she closed her eyes against the waves of pleasure. "It doesn't have to mean anything."

"It's nothing more than two people enjoying the evening."

It was the greatest lie he had ever told.

It meant everything. There would not be a day in his life when he wouldn't imagine himself right here, loving her the only way he could.

"You're certain?"

"Yes. Don't stop touching me."

Nothing prepared him for the moment she came. The minx grabbed his coat, writhed against his hand, and insisted on pressing her open lips to his though didn't kiss him. Her taut nipples brushed his waistcoat as she moaned against his mouth.

When she came apart, he felt every shudder.

As the ripples subsided, she held on to him like he was a pillar of support, not someone who might one day break her heart.

"You were right," she said, pressing her forehead to his as her lungs fought for air. "You're the most dangerous man I have ever met."

"It's not me," he said, dragging her sleeves up and covering her breasts. "It's your passionate nature that makes this a dangerous pairing."

*It's the way I feel about you that makes this unique.*

Now it was over.

And it would be unwise to share such intimacies again.

"If only things were different." She cupped his cheek like this was goodbye. "I wish you were free and life was less complicated."

"After all my family has been through, I could never wish for that."

"No, you've all survived a great injustice."

Not having her was the greatest injustice of his life.

Perhaps when the Earl of Berridge was dead, things would be different. Yet he couldn't shake the fear of impending doom. A storm was coming. He could sense it gaining momentum, gathering force and growing stronger each day.

"We should return to the house and assist Daventry." It was still early by the demimonde's standards, and the thought of being cajoled into sharing more intimate moments with her would test Aaron's sanity.

"It would be impolite not to greet our hostess." She patted her elegant coiffure and brushed the creases from her gown. "When we see Mr Daventry, we'll need to explain where we've been."

"If he asks, we've been looking for Venus."

"Yes." She seemed forlorn, like she'd heard a sad tale, not come apart beneath the stars, her beauty bared to the heavens.

"Is something wrong?"

"No. Nothing." Her half smile said she was lying.

In truth, he felt deflated, too. He'd lived his greatest fantasy but had woken from the dream. They should be racing home to make love until dawn, not allowing a strained distance to open up between them.

"Neither of us is good at pretending each kiss doesn't matter," he said.

Woeful blue eyes searched his face as if he were off to war and she might not see him again. Did she feel like she had lost the man she'd kissed mere moments ago? Could she sense him slipping away with each passing second?

"I'm a wallflower, remember," she said, her forced laugh a bid to lighten the mood. "I know life doesn't always work out as one planned."

"You're not a wallflower."

"Why? Because I'm old enough to be a spinster?"

He had to touch her, though his fingers lingered at her elbow a little too long. "No. Because you steal my attention every time you enter a room."

Her eyes glistened beneath the moonlight's embrace, her deep sigh almost mournful. She hugged her abdomen like it pained her. "Can we spend the rest of the evening just being colleagues? My emotions are somewhat fragile. Too fragile to cope with another kiss or compliment."

"Hurting you is the last thing I want." Aaron ignored the crushing pain in his chest. Whatever happened, they could not indulge their desires again. "It was easier for both of us when we kept our distance."

"I wouldn't change anything that's happened between us. Every perfect moment will live with me always." She averted her gaze, shutting him out. "But I cannot kiss you again, Mr Chance. Not even when we pretend to be other people. Please do your utmost to respect my wishes."

He stepped back and bowed, his throat so tight it was hard to speak. "I'll do anything you ask. You're the only woman I have ever wanted. The only woman I respect. We must be strong for each other."

She nodded. "We'll play at being enquiry agents and throw ourselves into our work. In the throes of passion, we've forgotten our lives are at stake."

He wanted to tell her she was beautiful inside and out. To admit he felt something other than lust. That his heart wasn't dead because it hurt like the devil now. He had lost many things—his mother, his home, pieces of himself stolen with every childhood beating. Joanna was the greatest loss of his life.

"I still need a friend, Joanna."

She dabbed her eyes. "We're the best of friends, Mr Chance. Nothing will ever change that." She slipped her arm through his and hugged him so tightly he could cry. "Now, come. Let us hunt for the elusive Venus. I can't help but feel she lured us here tonight."

They left the maze and began searching the garden.

Wherever they went, they met couples locked in passionate clinches, their aroused cries a testament to their freedom. The tangle of four bodies writhing on the orangery floor turned Aaron's stomach. He would treasure Joanna always, not share her with other men.

"Didn't Mr Parker say Venus approached him in the garden?"

Aaron glanced around the autumn landscape. The only people outside were those engaged in amorous activities. "Yes, though I wonder what Parker was doing out here alone."

"Perhaps she slipped him a note and lured him outside."

Aaron considered the point, which took longer than usual because Joanna dominated his thoughts. "Or Venus wasn't invited to the party and she sneaked in via the mews. This is the only house on the row with access from the garden."

He paused, registering a presence behind them.

"Experiencing the pleasures of the outdoors, Mr Chance?" came a woman's sultry voice. "I hear you have been causing quite a stir."

*Damnation! How the blazes had she recognised him?*

He turned to find Mrs Flavell, their flamboyant hostess. The forty-year-old wore a red silk *robe à la française* with an oriental pattern. Her powdered white wig was large enough to hide a small aviary.

"I could make a fortune auctioning you to the highest bidder," the widow continued. Her wicked grin spoke of mischief, though she'd forgone a mask. "Most ladies in London would give an organ to spend the night with the formidable Aaron Chance."

Mrs Flavell's gaze shifted to Joanna. "You must share your secret, my darling. How the devil did you lure him into the maze?"

Joanna smiled. "One must appeal to the man behind the scandalous reputation. It's not an easy task. More akin to laying siege to a Norseman's fortress with a blind beggar and a lame donkey."

Mrs Flavell laughed like her sides hurt. "Oh, how utterly amusing you are, my dear. Perhaps you might return without your chaperone. With your wit and beauty, the world could be yours." She glanced at the house. "They're already squabbling over you. You could take your pick tonight."

Aaron's anger snapped as easily as thawing ice on a raging river. "The first man to touch her loses his hand. You'll tell them she's mine."

"My friend is somewhat protective," Joanna said.

"Your friend?" Mrs Flavell narrowed her gaze. "I've seen men fornicate like beasts to appease their physical cravings. I rarely see one kiss a woman like she owns a piece of his soul."

Aaron shifted uncomfortably. "What do you want?"

"Changing the subject so quickly. I think that proves my point." The lady produced a letter she had tucked inside her bodice. "This came for you ten minutes ago. I would have brought it outside, but I didn't want to spoil your little adventure into the verdure."

Aaron snatched the letter, noted his name scrawled in elegant script, then broke the seal and read the missive.

> *I shall bring your house down brick*
> *by brick until you're the only one*
> *standing in the rubble.*

*Hellfire!*

Alarm shot through him, his heart hammering in his chest as every muscle tensed. Either his nemesis followed him to

Belgravia, or Mrs Flavell's mouth was as loose as her silk drawers.

"Did Daventry say I would be here tonight?"

"No. Mr Daventry refused to disclose your identity, even when I mentioned asking you to play master with a small group of ladies upstairs." Mrs Flavell feigned concern. "I trust all is well."

Aaron firmed his jaw. "Don't toy with me. I own most of your patrons' vowels. One threat and I could empty your house. Who delivered the note?"

Mrs Flavell seemed to find it all so amusing. "A penny boy. I doubt you'll catch him. The sprightly little thing took off down the street, a gangle of arms and legs."

Aaron thought to wipe the smirk off her face. "Someone is out to hurt my family. I don't need to tell you what I'll do when I find the culprit. Our enquiries led us here. Don't force my hand. Believe me, you'd rather be my ally than my enemy."

The widow shrugged. "I don't know what to tell you."

Joanna spoke, her sweet voice bringing an element of calm. "We need the names of the women Thomas Parker enjoyed at your parties."

"I made an oath to protect my patrons' anonymity. Besides, the list would fill more pages than Walter Scott's *Waverley*. I'm not exaggerating when I say Mr Parker leaves no stone unturned. His brother, Sir Geoffrey, asked that I withdraw his membership."

Perhaps Sir Geoffrey hoped his brother would find a willing bride.

And the mention of membership roused an interesting point.

"Are all guests members?" Aaron said.

"Of course. I'll not allow any riffraff in. Frivolity can be expensive. The fee is five hundred pounds per annum. Paid in advance."

"Then Lord Howard and Mr Parker are members."

Mrs Flavell gave a covert nod. "I would have to check my ledger. If you and your *friend* join the private party later, I'll grant you access to the records."

Aaron would rather carve the words *Berridge's Flunkey* on his forehead than watch other men seduce Joanna.

"Both men entertained the same woman," he began, hoping the widow might answer one last question before he refused her offer. "She's foreign, pretty, with ebony hair and came dressed as Venus. Is she a member?"

Mrs Flavell's mouth curled into a coy grin. "Please my ladies tonight, and I'll tell you what you want to know."

Women like Mrs Flavell always wanted payment for their favour.

"If you watched me kiss my *friend*, you know why I must refuse. I'll never kiss another woman as long as I live." He arched a challenging brow. "There. You've heard the private thoughts of a man who always keeps them hidden. Surely that's worth a simple answer to a simple question."

But Mrs Flavell did not let it rest there. "Have you given her assurances for the future?"

Aaron glanced at Joanna. "No. Present problems force me to focus on the vow I made to my family. Someone threatens to destroy what I've built. I cannot fail those who need me most."

"Sometimes a man must be selfish," she said, sneering.

"My father had that attitude, and I despised him."

Mrs Flavell's gaze turned reflective. "Life often presents painful choices. We rarely know we've chosen incorrectly until it's too late." She sighed like the conversation bored her. "The woman you mentioned is an interloper. She crept in with a party of people, and I presumed she was their guest. She left with Lord Howard. He paid for her membership the following week. While Howard smoked in the den, she went outside and spent an hour with Parker. The name she gave is false. No one has ever heard of her."

Despite the wealth of information, they were still clueless.

"Have you seen her since?"

"Yes, tonight, while you were in the maze but she disappeared. How the devil she got into the house is anyone's guess. She didn't enter through the front door, and the gate to the mews is locked. I believe Mr Daventry is conducting a thorough search of the house."

Aaron turned and scanned the shady depths of the garden. "Do we have your permission to inspect the mews and coach house?"

The woman gave a nonchalant wave. "Be my guest. All I ask is that you never return here again. You've worked my guests up into a lustful frenzy. I'll have a devil of a job pleasing them all tonight."

"I mean to avoid this place like the plague."

"Good." Mrs Flavell flounced away but came to an abrupt halt and paced back so quickly her wig wobbled. "Tell Daventry he's wrong about the Mughal dagger. My husband didn't purchase it at the auctioneers but won it in a bet twenty years ago. It went missing recently. The night Howard and Parker argued over Venus."

Aaron's heart skipped a beat. The evidence gave Parker a motive for murder and proved Parker or Venus might have stolen the weapon. He was about to demand Mrs Flavell give a statement, but her gaze moved past them, her eyes bulging from their sockets.

"Be gad! That woman has got the devil's cheek." She pointed to the raven-haired beauty strolling at the bottom of the garden, her mask firmly in place, her white gown billowing in the breeze like a ghostly shroud.

Joanna gasped. "It's Venus."

Venus hadn't noticed them as she hugged the darkness and disappeared behind the trunk of an oak tree. Was she meeting someone? Had she arranged an assignation? If Parker appeared, surely Daventry could arrest him.

Mrs Flavell was ready to march to the bottom of the garden, but Aaron urged her to wait. "We need to speak to Venus, not frighten her away."

"It looks like she's in a trance," Joanna said when Venus reappeared and ambled aimlessly towards the maze. "Like she's lost her way."

Or flying high after a visit to the opium den, Aaron thought.

They moved towards the maze, trying to keep to the shadows. Venus gazed up at the house but peered right through them. Even when they came to a halt before her, she merely inclined her head and tried to move past them.

Mrs Flavell grabbed Venus' wrist, startling the young woman. "What sort of game are you playing, gal? Who are you? Take off that mask. I'll not stand for your flagrant disrespect for the rules."

Venus panicked and said in a soft Italian accent, "Forgive me. I meant no disrespect, but I know nothing of your rules. I am new here."

"New?" Mrs Flavell cried. "And I live under a toadstool."

As always, Joanna brought calm to a tense situation.

"There's nothing to fear. We simply ask that you remove your mask and explain why you're wandering around the garden."

Aaron studied the timid woman. He'd expected an impudent creature, overtly sexual in manner. A woman who could persuade a man to choose the watch he didn't want and force another to play the cruel tormentor.

"Remove your mask, Lucia," he said, raising his to reveal his face.

"M-Mr Chance?" With shaky hands, the maid did as she was told. Her doe eyes stared with childlike innocence. "What are you doing here?"

"We're looking for a pretty young foreign woman dressed as Venus," Joanna snapped, tearing her mask off, too. "Someone who bears an uncanny resemblance to you. And to think I vouched for you. Does Miss Stowe know of your secret identity?"

Tears filled Lucia's eyes. "Please, you mustn't tell her."

Despite Aaron's earlier misgivings, instinct said Lucia wasn't Venus. "Tell us why you're here, or we must place you under arrest."

"While you're at it, charge her with theft and trespassing," Mrs Flavell blurted. "I want my husband's dagger back, gal. No one steals from me."

Lucia looked to be drowning in a sea of confusion.

"Why are you here?" Joanna pressed.

"I—I was paid to come and walk in the garden."

"Paid?" Mrs Flavell said. "By whom?"

Lucia's tiny shoulders rose and fell. "I do not know. A letter came. The sender offered to pay me a hundred pounds if I wore this costume and made sure I was seen in the garden. The person arranged for a hackney cab to collect me from the bottom of the street. The driver paid me and brought me here." She gestured to the mews beyond the garden gate.

Aaron wasn't sure why, but the far-fetched story rang true.

"Is he coming back for you?" Aaron said, hoping to throttle the truth from the jarvey.

"No. I must make my own way home. I can leave at the stroke of midnight. I only pray Miss Stowe does not notice I am missing."

Mrs Flavell's eyes shone with suspicion. "Liar! I locked the gate and took the key. How did you get in?"

Lucia opened her clasped hand to reveal an iron key. "The driver gave it to me when he brought me to the mews."

"This is all very convenient." Mrs Flavell grabbed Lucia's arm. "I want to question you myself. I want to know what else you've stolen from me."

"But I have never been here before tonight."

Daventry suddenly appeared and made his own demands. "As she's a suspect in a criminal case, she's coming with me." He faced Mrs Flavell. "Don't argue, or I might be forced to mention your illegal shipment of raw opium to the Home Secretary."

Mrs Flavell paled, the fight leaving her in an instant. "Then get her out of here. If she is Venus, I want my husband's dagger and anything else she stole."

Aaron turned to Daventry. "Mr Flavell won the dagger in a bet."

"From whom?"

Mrs Flavell shocked everyone when she pointed at Aaron. "From his rotten father. That dagger belonged to Ignatius Chance."

# Chapter Twelve

It was fifteen minutes past curfew when Joanna entered the hall of Fortune's Den with Mr Chance. Amid the stillness, they both sighed, glad the constable wasn't waiting to cart them away in his prison wagon. Relieved the night was at an end, and there might be some respite from the confounding feelings plaguing them both.

There would be no respite for her.

Not when he filled every space in her heart and mind.

She wanted to slip into his warm embrace, kiss him, indulge in wicked fantasies, but she had to be strong. She was falling in love with him. A slow tumble that began weeks ago and gained momentum the moment their lips met.

But one could not make a life with half a man.

While Gabriel wanted nothing, Mr Chance's demons left him wavering between worlds, drifting between darkness and daylight, between freedom and fear. A wanderer on a quest to escape his emotions.

It hurt to think about it. She had gripped his arm and promised friendship, but how did one douse the flames of desire? Like the sacred fire on Mount Olympus, would her need for him always burn this fiercely? Would she die with his name on her lips?

"I shall write to my family in the morning and insist they reside here," he said, jostling her from her reverie. "I was wrong to think we'd be safer apart. As we learned tonight, my nemesis has Lucifer's cunning."

He referred to the threatening letter and the villain's plan to use Lucia to throw them off the scent—the scheme to blame a maid, not a master criminal. The devil was always one step ahead. But Aaron Chance had another reason for not wanting to be alone with her.

"Can I ask you something?"

He looked at her in the gloom. "You can ask me anything."

*Do you believe we can be friends and nothing more?*

*Is it possible to kiss like we did and forget it ever happened?*

"When did you realise nothing would ever be more important than your family?" A wave of emotion tightened her throat. A selfish part of her hoped she haunted his waking hours and stalked his dreams. "Help me understand what the vow means to you."

He stared at her like she'd asked him to descend into the bowels of hell. "I try to avoid revisiting dark memories, but I will for you." He stepped closer, the power of attraction sparking between them. Standing in the gloom, he inhaled as if bolstering his defences. "I was barely thirteen when I realised I would die to protect my brothers."

"So young?" What was he like then? Had he always possessed a commanding presence? Had he been a fearful boy forced to become a man?

"It wasn't by choice." He averted his gaze, not wanting her to see how much the memory pained him.

"You enjoy philosophy and medieval history. I imagine you were quite studious then." When did his thirst for knowledge become a thirst for blood?

A sigh of regret escaped him. "Tales of the Crusades are unimportant when you're trying to survive. Nothing matters but living to see the sunrise."

Fractured memories of her own past entered her mind. A frightened girl of eighteen searching taverns and brothels looking for her absent father. The hunt for lost pennies to buy food and coal. Lying awake in the dark, wondering when he would come home.

"I understand," she said. His scars were thin white lines weaving a path across his chest. Like an iceberg, the real depth of his pain remained hidden beneath the surface. "You were fighting in the pits then."

"More dodging and defending than fighting, but I was quick on my feet and learned to punch back. I imagined every opponent was my father. Hatred can give a boy the power of the gods."

Her heart wept for him. He must have been terrified.

"And your brothers didn't suffer in the same way?"

"He came for Aramis once." Mr Chance gritted his teeth and cursed his father to Hades. "He needed a weak, inexperienced boy because it pleased the punters, and he had already taken his fee."

"Was there no end to your father's cruelty?"

"Ignatius Chance lived to please himself."

"So you strive to be the father your brothers never had."

He nodded. "We all deserved better."

"Did he take Aramis that night?" Joanna imagined a boy

waking amid a violent thunderstorm, a flash of lightning illuminating a slobbering beast lingering in the doorway.

"No. I pleaded with him and agreed to take a beating. I suffered three cracked ribs, a split lip and a fractured wrist. He made me fight a fortnight later."

His eyes held a haunted look.

That's when she knew the nightmares still plagued him.

"Did he try to take your brother again?"

"No," he said proudly. "I did what he wanted as long as he left my brothers alone. Then he died, disowned by his family and drowning in debt. Our stepmother stole what little was left before dragging us from our beds and dumping us in the rookeries."

Joanna barely remembered her mother but knew she was kind and had the patience of a saint. "Your stepmother sounds as wicked as your father."

"She choked on a chicken bone years later. I regret not being there to witness her clawing her throat in an effort to breathe." His eyes were cold like flint as he spoke about the woman he despised. "I was grateful for the education. It hardened me in ways you cannot imagine."

Yet he was a different man when he kissed her.

He was passionate and tender.

Keen to offer light relief, and because she wouldn't sleep without asking the question rebounding in her mind, she said, "Did you mean what you said to Mrs Flavell tonight? That you won't kiss another woman as long as you live?"

"I meant every word."

"I see." The tragedy of it was too hard to contemplate. She should be thinking about Lucia and her persuasive confession. They had taken the maid home and searched her room, but the girl kept repeating the same story. "Thank you for being honest with me."

"Friends don't lie to each other."

She wished they could be more than friends, but he was right. There was a side of him she didn't know. She wanted all of him, not the part he was willing to share.

"Well, it's late," she said, knowing she should leave before they fell into each other's arms and kissed like they were two halves of a whole. "I suspect this is the last time we'll be alone together."

"If my family agree to come home tomorrow, we'll not get a minute's peace." A wistful smile touched his lips. "Yet, there's beauty in the chaos."

Joanna agreed. The hours spent listening to her friends' problems and amusing tales left her feeling blessed, not burdened.

Nerves had her shifting her feet, but she had to speak truthfully. "In case we're denied an opportunity to speak privately again, I want to apologise for calling you a prized ape some weeks ago. In truth, I think you're a remarkable man, Mr Chance."

His eyes brightened. "Mr Chance? Do friends not use given names?"

She smiled or else she might cry. "Maintaining a certain formality between us is best. You've spent months striving to keep your distance, and for good reason. The world fails to exist when we kiss."

He glanced at her mouth, the air between them alive with unfulfilled longing. She felt the deep tug in her gut, the profound pull of attraction, the ache only he could sate.

"Good night," she said before she acted on impulse.

She left him alone in the hall, her stomach churning, her legs shaking, and mounted the stairs quickly.

He called out to her. "Joanna."

She turned, gripping the banister. "Yes."

"Thank you."

"For what?"

"For helping to keep the darkness at bay. These moments with you make me forget I'm the dangerous devil men fear."

Tears filled her eyes. Not because she wanted to kiss him but because she could hear the boy still trying to dodge life's punches.

"I lost sight of myself this last week, too." She should have raced to her room but took a step towards him, drawn by a force she could not explain. "My grandfather bought the house across the street forty years ago. I don't remember him, but he changed my life when he left it to me."

Mr Chance moved to grip the newel post.

"I can't help but feel I was destined to live opposite you," she said, confused why she could not push him from her mind when there would be no happy ending for them. "Perhaps whatever exists between us was meant to cause chaos. That this is all part of a bigger plan." A spiritual education.

There was an unmistakable look in his eyes, a silent plea for something more intimate than words. "Do you know what prevents me from mounting the stairs and inviting you to my bedchamber?"

"Yes, your vow."

"No, the fact I would rather die than hurt you. I would rather suffer your indifference than your disappointment. I would rather be a man you admire, not one you grow to hate."

Their eyes remained locked, their breathing no doubt

mimicking the erratic train of their thoughts. Should she take a step forward or make a hasty retreat? Could she begin a love affair with him and keep her heart intact?

Fate made the decision for her.

The clopping of horses' hooves and the rattle of carriage wheels on the cobblestones outside drew their attention to the front door. The vehicle stopped. A man called to the driver, the muffled voice impossible to identify.

A chill of fear swept through her.

Had there been a new development in the case? Had the magistrate come to make an arrest? Or was Mr Daventry the bearer of bad news?

The caller knocked on the door—the thud like a death knell—then he turned the handle, grumbling when two dogs began barking in the street.

Mr Chance tutted and marched to the door. "If that's a wastrel come to ask when the club reopens, there'll be hell to pay." He looked through the viewing window, gave a shocked gasp and opened the door.

Three people hurried into the hall, escaping the cold weather.

"Oh, what a dreadful night," Mr Chance's sister, Delphine, exclaimed. "We left Oxford at three o'clock, but there was a terrible accident near Waddesden. The road was blocked for hours. Then a vagrant tried to steal our luggage, and Dorian gave chase. We thought we'd never get home."

Joanna watched from the gloomy depths of the stairs.

"We planned to arrive before the club opened," the lady's husband, Dorian Flynn, said. He removed his hat and combed his fingers through his dark hair. "Hoping to cover sixty miles in five hours was wishful thinking on my part."

"Did you not receive my letter?" Mr Chance snapped.

Mrs Maloney—a kind, loving woman who had given the family lodgings as children and was like a second mother—wasn't concerned about the accident or the delay. "It's as I thought. The problem is more serious than you mentioned in your letter." She tugged off her glove and cupped Mr Chance's cheek. "Are your brothers well?"

"Presently. You were told to remain in Oxford." He did not sound pleased. "No one knew you were there. Now, you've merely added to my burden."

"We were worried," Delphine said in their defence. "Where else would we be than here, offering our support?"

From amid the shadows, Joanna cleared her throat and descended the stairs. "Good evening. Mr Chance is just relieved you arrived home safely. You must be tired and cold after your long journey. I'll light a fire in the drawing room and make tea."

"Miss Lovelace." Delphine's gasp became a slow smile as she scanned Joanna's daring dress. "What a pleasant surprise to find you here late at night. And what a beautiful gown, and such a fetching shade of blue. You look breathtaking."

"I borrowed it from Mrs Daventry for the soiree we attended tonight."

Mrs Maloney's eyes widened. "Aaron went out?"

"To a demimonde gathering," Mr Chance said impatiently. "We're working with Daventry on a case. It was business, not pleasure." He cast a covert glance Joanna's way, the warmth in his eyes so opposed to his cold, abrupt tone.

"We've both been framed for murder," Joanna informed them.

"Murder?" all three said in unison.

"It's a long story." Mr Chance motioned to the drawing room. "I'll explain everything, but I insist you reside here until the matter is resolved." He drew the villain's letter from his pocket and gave it to Mr Flynn. "Threats have been made to our family. You'll do exactly as I say. Is that understood?"

Mr Flynn read the missive.

The men shared a look of genuine concern.

"Do you know who sent this?" Mr Flynn handed the note to his wife. "What other threats have been made?"

"Berridge is involved, though I have no proof. The magistrate has granted us a temporary reprieve while we hunt for clues."

"I knew that ingrate would come for my boys one day," Mrs Maloney said in a venomous voice. "Perhaps I should just shoot him and be done with it. It's not like I have long to live."

Mr Chance wrapped his arm around Mrs Maloney's slumped shoulders. "I'll not see you rotting in gaol. Every day you're in our lives is a blessing."

The elderly woman melted into him. "That's the nicest thing you've ever said to me." She tapped his chest directly over his heart. "Perhaps the iron casing is cracking."

"Or perhaps I'm preparing you for bad news. I told Aramis to close your bookshop. Although Naomi agreed to take care of things in your absence, she wasn't safe there."

Mrs Maloney shrugged. "They're just books. Protecting the people we love is more important. I suppose I'm to remain here, too."

"Yes. Don't force me to tie you to a chair."

Delphine hugged her husband's arm. "I have fond memories of you sneaking into my room. Now you can stay the night."

Mr Chance cleared his throat. "Miss Lovelace is staying

in your room. The crime was committed at The Burnished Jade. She had nowhere else to go."

That wasn't entirely true.

She could have stayed with Gabriel.

"You put her on the third floor when the house is empty?" Delphine sounded more amused than shocked. "It makes sense, I suppose, what with debt-ridden wastrels wandering about the place."

"I closed the club almost a week ago."

"Oh."

"I can move rooms in the morning," Joanna said, not wanting to cause problems. If she rose early enough, she could help Eloise with the bedsheets.

Delphine was quick to accept the offer. "I don't want to be a nuisance, though it would be nice to stay in my old room. The chamber next to Aaron's is vacant. The bed is huge, and it's much more spacious. I'm sure Aaron will give you the key to the adjoining door."

"We will discuss it in the morning," came Mr Chance's sharp reply. "Miss Lovelace is a guest here. She can have whichever room suits her needs best."

"I could always stay with Miss Stowe," Joanna suggested. It would allow her to keep a watchful eye on Lucia.

"Perhaps you should explain what's occurred before any decisions are made," Mr Flynn said, his impatience evident. "I'm skilled at finding people. I may be able to help bring the matter to a swift conclusion."

Mr Chance gestured to the drawing room. "Pour the drinks while I change. I suspect we all need a stiff brandy."

"I shall leave you to talk privately and bid you good night." Joanna remained on the stairs. "It's been a long day."

And Delphine was looking at her most peculiarly. "Mr Chance has the full measure of the situation."

His family wished her good night and moved to the drawing room while Mr Chance insisted on accompanying her upstairs.

"All I can smell is the smoke from burnt opium on my clothes. The stench reminds me of everything I hate about the demimonde." His hand rested on the small of her back, heat infusing every cell in her body. "If you're comfortable upstairs, Delphine can occupy the room next to mine. You don't need to reside with Miss Stowe."

"Are you sure you want them next door? Their hunger for each other is evident even in the most mundane conversations."

Hunger clawed the air now—a thick and tangible desire to continue what they had started in the maze—swamping them with every step, every breath, every shaky exhale.

"Delphine wants to spend time with her husband in her old room," Joanna continued, knowing what would happen if she was alone in a bedchamber with Mr Chance. "I think they wish to revisit a treasured memory. You mustn't persuade her to sleep elsewhere. I'll consider my options in the morning."

They reached the landing, expecting to part, but it was like their feet were fixed to the floor. Their eyes remained locked on each other.

"Before you go, perhaps you should inspect the room next to mine." His husky voice spoke of an entirely different inspection. "Delphine will insist it's the best option. You may think differently."

"You mean I might refuse to sleep next door to a beast," she said with a coy grin. "It might be best if I stay with Miss

Stowe. I suspect Delphine is a pupil at Mr Daventry's school for matchmakers."

He didn't smile or laugh, though his breathing quickened. "Don't leave," he suddenly uttered, the words almost a plea. "I want you to stay. At least look at the room."

He offered his hand and she took it, lacing her fingers with his.

*Foolish girl!* her father would have said.

But Joanna followed him along the hall, lured by the prospect of sharing an intimate moment, longing to feel the warmth of his lips.

Mr Chance brought her to a halt outside his bedchamber. "Delphine's matchmaking efforts are wasted. I've known you're the only woman I need for some time." His gaze dipped to her mouth. "Perhaps you might permit me to demonstrate."

Fascinated by him, she nodded.

He captured her chin and kissed her slowly, his tongue stroking hers in the same hypnotic way his fingers had explored her sex. "Don't leave." The words sounded pained this time. "I want you here, not with Miss Stowe. Say you'll stay."

It was pointless arguing. Her body sang to his tune. The tightening coil in her belly had command of her senses. "I'll stay for a day or two, but we play a dangerous game."

He drew her into his chamber and kicked the door shut.

It was dark, but he didn't light the lamp.

"Tell me I'm not the only one losing my mind," he hissed, pressing her against the wall, crushing her to his hard body. "Tell me all you think about is the feel of your mouth on mine."

"I've thought of little else."

"How can we ease the cravings?"

She shrugged. "We could stop talking and kiss."

He claimed her mouth in fierce possession, the kiss almost savage in its desperation. Each thrust of his tongue had the muscles in her core clenching while greedy moans rumbled in his throat.

She felt drunk on the taste of him, intoxicated by his earthy masculine scent. There wasn't a place he didn't touch her, a palm skimming her breast then the curve of her hip, fingers squeezing one fleshy buttock, his skilled hands igniting a fire in her blood.

*Don't ever stop touching me, Aaron.*

"Say you need more. I need to hear those pretty moans when you come again, Joanna," he said, answering her silent plea. "I can't get enough of you. Every part of me aches to feel close to you. Say you'll stay until we solve the case."

"We'll never solve the case if I sleep next door." Yet she was already anticipating the night they would make love, their naked bodies entwined until dawn. "We'll be lovers, consumed by our passions."

"Maybe we should accept the inevitable. We could move between rooms without anyone knowing. I could lounge on your bed and watch you bathe."

What had brought about this sudden change in him? Did he believe things would be different now his family were home? Was it her threat to stay with Miss Stowe? Or the fear their time together might soon end?

"We don't have long," he panted, shrugging out of his coat and throwing it to the floor as if the garment offended him. "I need to join my family in the drawing room, but I'll feel your hands on my body first."

Lust was akin to madness.

179

Her heart thumped a frantic rhythm.

She practically tore the clothes off his back, dragging his shirt over his head like the material burned him.

"Touch me, Joanna."

His skin burned beneath her palms, though every muscle was hard like granite. She caressed him, her fingers roaming over the scars cutting through the dark hair, her heart breaking while he closed his eyes and groaned with pleasure.

*Who did this to you?*

*Who hurt you when you needed love?*

Though silent, the words still choked her.

But she could love him now.

She touched every inch of him, pushing her hands into his hair and tugging hard while raining kisses over his jaw and throat. Her fingers followed the tantalising trail of dark hair disappearing below the waistband of his trousers.

"Don't," he said when she slipped the first button. "They're the only thing stopping me from having you. If you free me, I'm done for."

Joanna bit back a smile.

She had Aaron Chance at her mercy.

Who'd have thought it was possible?

"When I take you into my body, Aaron, we'll need hours, not minutes, to slake our desire." She liked being brazen. Liked the power of taking control of her destiny. "And I will have you inside me. If not now, then soon, very soon."

"Don't tease me when I'm this aroused."

She ran her hand over the placket of his trousers, stroking his solid length. His manhood was long and thick and hard against her fingers.

"Joanna," he breathed, his head falling back despite the warning.

"Perhaps I might make *you* come, Aaron." She didn't know how but would improvise. He seemed to like it when her thumb grazed the head of his shaft. "We'll sneak outside when everyone is in bed, and I'll touch you beneath the moonlight."

"Save that thought." He scooped her into his strong arms and carried her to his bed. "You'll move into the room next door tonight while I'm downstairs discussing our dilemma. It's not up for negotiation."

"What if I hate the decor?" She laughed when he threw her onto the bed. "Should I not inspect the room first?"

"It doesn't matter. You won't be sleeping there." His hand slid under her skirts and over her stocking to the leather sheath still buckled to her thigh. "You'll come to my room wearing nothing but this tomorrow night."

"I thought you disapprove of me carrying a blade."

"A dangerous man needs a dangerous woman. It took all my strength to remove the blade and not ravish you on the stairs." Cool air breezed over her thighs as he shoved her skirts to her waist and parted her legs. "Will you permit me to take liberties now, Joanna? I'll not remove my trousers. Not tonight. You have my word."

"We're lovers, Aaron." There was no denying it. They were destined to be lovers from the moment they kissed. How long this love affair lasted was a question she refused to consider. "My body is yours. I give it to you freely."

"Are you sure that's wise?" The glint of mischief in his eyes heightened her arousal. "I shall tongue your sex the way I did your mouth."

As long as she lived, she would never forget the first glide of Aaron's tongue over her bud. The warm waves of heat. The brush of stubble over the sensitive skin. The tingles down her spine. Every muscle tensing, anticipating release.

But that's not what made her climax so powerful.

It was him.

The smell of him. The humming sound he made against her sex. The intensity of his gaze when their eyes met. The feel of his fingers pushing deep inside her. The beauty of knowing how badly he wanted her.

"Aaron." His given name burst from her lips as she shuddered against him, clamping around his fingers while he whispered words of encouragement.

"Hug me and don't let go. God, you're so beautiful when you come. I'm so desperate to be inside you it's driving me insane."

Somewhere in her hazy mind, she heard a loud thud on the front door. Seconds passed before voices echoed in the hall and Mr Flynn raced upstairs to hammer on Mr Chance's bedchamber door.

"Aaron? You need to come downstairs."

He cursed against her bare thigh. "What is it? I'll be down in a minute."

"Daventry is here."

"Pour him a drink. Entertain him while I change."

But Mr Flynn uttered the damning words that would change Joanna's life irrevocably. "Daventry said it's urgent. Something about the magistrate issuing a warrant. They're going to arrest Miss Lovelace for murder."

# Chapter Thirteen

Aaron was too stunned to move.

Fear crept into his heart like a malevolent spirit out to destroy every shred of hope. It choked the breath from his lungs. It taunted him and left him feeling as helpless as the night his stepmother barged into his bedchamber with hired thugs and threw him and his brothers out.

"Aaron." His name was a terrified whisper from Joanna's lips. She scrambled to sit up, grabbing his arms, clinging to him as if afraid to let go.

"Should I fetch Miss Lovelace?" Flynn called from beyond the door, his grave tone adding to Aaron's torment. "I can send Delphine."

"No. Pour Daventry a drink. I'll fetch her." Aaron waited to hear Flynn's retreating footsteps before helping Joanna to her feet. "Take a breath. We've prepared for this. I'll not let them take you."

She fell into his arms, holding him tightly, her fingers sinking into his flesh as she anchored herself to him. "What if we're too late? What if I must leave with Mr Daventry now?"

The scenario played out in Aaron's mind. "I'll restrain him and tie him up and we'll make a hasty escape." It would be a fight that would alter his destiny.

She looked at him through teary eyes. "But you would be arrested upon your return. I can't let you do that. I can't let you sacrifice everything you've worked hard for, everything you've achieved."

*I'll leave with you*, he wanted to say.

But the bonds of brotherhood were an anchor, as strong as the iron chain that held it secure. Abandoning his family was not an option.

*You could marry Rothley*, he thought to suggest, but the words burnt like acid on his tongue.

Aaron brushed a lock of hair from her face and cupped her cheeks. "You'll not hang for a crime you didn't commit. I have a boat waiting and a crew willing to sail at a moment's notice. Sigmund has agreed to accompany you and remain with you indefinitely."

Tears slipped down her cheeks. "I don't want to leave."

"You must. You have no choice. I shall keep your club open in your absence." And there would be a war. No more tiptoeing in the shadows. He would sweep through the *ton* like a tempest of destruction, forcing his foes to their knees. "I shall do everything in my power to bring you home again. Ignore what I say to Daventry tonight. He cannot know of our plan."

Her hands moved over his back as if memorising every muscle. "How has it come to this? Why are we being punished when we've suffered more than most?"

He wished he knew the answer.

"One day, it may all become clear." He exhaled deeply. "I

need to find a shirt while you straighten your skirts. Then we'll ask Daventry about the warrant."

They dealt with the tasks silently amid a heavy cloud of despair.

Aaron led Joanna to the drawing room where Daventry was pacing, not lounging in the chair, casually sipping brandy.

"I thought we had another day until the magistrate called us in for questioning." Anger infused Aaron's tone, though it wasn't Daventry's fault they were in this predicament.

Daventry came straight to the point and confirmed their worst fears. "The Thames Police received an anonymous letter informing them of Miss Lovelace's unpleasant history with Lord Howard."

Aaron's pulse soared. Who was this anonymous devil causing havoc with their lives? "They cannot arrest her on hearsay."

"It proves she had a motive for murder."

"It proves nothing."

"The letter was quite detailed," Daventry said, trying to be delicate. He turned to Joanna. "Your acquaintance with the maid, Lucia, has been called into question. A witness places Lucia at the pawnbroker's shop with Lord Howard. It's been suggested you were in cahoots to snare him in a trap. Lucia lured him to your house because he believed she was the opera singer Madame Rossellini. Lucia stole the murder weapon while at Mrs Flavell's party and together you conspired to kill him."

A chill swept over Aaron. They were dealing with a master manipulator. "It's supposition. None of it is true."

"It's enough for a jury to convict her of murder." Daventry looked uneasy. Was he out of his depth for the first time in his professional career? "Finding your father's watch in Howard's pocket doesn't help matters. It's thought she might have been trying to frame you."

"That's preposterous," Joanna cried, dashing tears from her cheeks while Aaron's family looked on. "Everything is being twisted to suit the villain's purpose. I would never hurt Mr Chance."

An unwelcome thought entered Aaron's mind. One certain to offend the woman he might lose for good. "Could Rothley be involved? He's obsessed with the death of his friend. Marrying Miss Lovelace would ease his guilt, but he knows he must force her hand."

"Even Rothley couldn't save her from this."

Joanna's nostrils flared. "It's not Gabriel."

"Then he won't mind answering a few questions when I visit him tomorrow." Aaron turned his attention to Daventry. "Are you here to arrest her?"

"No. I persuaded the magistrate to give you the time you requested. You have until eight o'clock tomorrow night. Then you'll both be taken in for questioning. There's a constable stationed across the street outside The Burnished Jade. I've been ordered to remove your carriage from the mews to ensure she cannot abscond. Your coachman will follow me to the Thames Police Office."

Aaron kept calm. Joanna's life depended upon it. "I'll come with you. We need to call at The Saracen's Head. Godby has a room there."

Daventry narrowed his gaze. "I expect you have a plan. Don't breathe a word of it to me. I'll not lie under oath."

"You'll escort me to the inn while I rouse Godby. That's all. And you will accompany me when I question the suspects tomorrow. Miss Lovelace will remain here with Delphine.

You'll tell the constable you've placed her under house arrest. He can access the premises at any time to vouch for her whereabouts."

With a curious frown, Daventry nodded. "Agreed."

"Does anyone have the time?" Aaron said.

Flynn checked his watch. "Almost half-past two."

"I'll meet you at Parker's residence at noon," he informed Daventry. "Bring Lucia with you. Godby knows Miss Stowe's address." Aaron reviewed the plan in his mind. "My family will arrive in the morning. Until the murderer is in custody, I insist they reside here."

"Your family pose no threat. As long as Miss Lovelace follows orders, I see no issue." Daventry glanced at Aaron's open-necked shirt. "I'll wait while you fetch a coat."

"I don't need a coat. Time is of the essence."

The plan went smoothly.

Daventry escorted Aaron to The Saracen's Head across the street and waited in the yard while he fetched Godby. For the second consecutive night, his coachman occupied a room with Sigmund and a woman named Miss Bryant.

Sigmund pushed out of the rickety wooden chair he used for a bed. "Happen your worst fears have come true, then."

Aaron nodded, banishing the rising dread that threatened to overwhelm him. "Be ready to leave in half an hour. Do you have the money, letters and jewels?"

"I have everything I need." Sigmund patted his greatcoat pocket as proof and gestured to Joanna's portmanteau near the door. "I forced the back window and packed what I could off the list. I hope the lady appreciates you risking your neck to save her."

"I've evaded death more times than I can count. Let's pray I'm as lucky this time." Aaron studied the woman whose brother owed him more money than most men earned in a lifetime. "Do this without rousing suspicion, and I'll give you the vowels. Remember, if questioned, say you warm my bed on occasion. Tell them you undressed in my chamber and discovered someone had stolen your clothes when you woke."

Miss Bryant gave an unladylike snort. "I assure you, I'll not admit to helping a suspected felon escape. That would make me a criminal."

Aaron left with Godby and met Daventry in the yard beside the horseless carriage, the empty shell a symbol of a journey come to an end.

Daventry kept the conversation to a minimum. "I've spoken to the constable as requested." He told Godby to ready Aaron's carriage and follow him to the Thames Police Office. "I'll drive you home again."

Aaron returned to Fortune's Den, stopping to talk to the constable stationed outside The Burnished Jade. He explained his plans for tomorrow and that Miss Lovelace would not be leaving the house.

"My mistress will join me for an hour." He described Miss Bryant as a luscious brunette with a mouth made for sin. "As I'm not under arrest, I see no problem with a brief visit. Do you?"

The constable grinned. "I'm to watch the premises and make sure Miss Lovelace doesn't leave. Mr Daventry didn't warn against nocturnal visits."

"Good." Aaron patted the man's back. "Someone with Miss Lovelace's golden hair and striking looks would be impossible to miss."

"That's what my sergeant said."

Once back at Fortune's Den, Aaron found his family

comforting Joanna in the drawing room. The sight made his heart lurch. She didn't deserve to suffer. But his enemy had played a winning hand in this game of wits.

Who despised him so much he'd hurt an innocent woman?

The answer Aaron had been avoiding assaulted his mind.

Was his father alive?

Had Ignatius Chance returned from the grave to give him a beating?

No. Aaron had stood beside the body in the open casket and condemned his father to eternal damnation. Still, doubts surfaced. Was the scene staged? He'd not checked to make sure the body was cold. Mere hours later, Aaron had been evicted from the house.

"We don't have much time," he said, banishing bitter memories from the past. "You need to change out of those clothes, Joanna. Delphine will help you."

"What's this all about?" Mrs Maloney said, worried.

"You heard what Daventry said, but I'll explain it in greater detail later. You can help by sending notes to my brothers, instructing them to pack a valise and be here by ten o'clock." He explained what to include in the letters.

"It sounds like we're at war," Delphine said.

"We are, though I'm still trying to identify the enemy."

Flynn offered some insight. "In cases like these, timing is key. Why now? What threat do you pose? It strikes me the answer lies with the Earl of Berridge."

They had avoided questioning the earl, but there was no reason to hide anymore. "I'm convinced Berridge is involved and will visit him later today."

Unbeknownst to his kin, Aaron had climbed the steps to their uncle's house once before. They'd been on the streets for days, and he'd gone cap in hand to ask for help. He'd been left standing in the cold, shivering to his bones. Berridge appeared, threw a bucket of vegetable peelings over him, called Aaron the scum of the earth and slammed the door shut.

He thought of that moment every time he raised his fists to fight.

A sudden knock on the front door brought the decoy.

Miss Bryant had hidden her blonde hair beneath a chestnut-brown wig. Her breasts were practically spilling out of her fashionable red dress, and her rouged cheeks made her look every bit a courtesan.

She stroked Aaron's arm affectionately, and he tried not to flinch. "The constable is watching. I suggest you kiss me if you want to make this look authentic."

Every muscle in his body stiffened, but he smiled for the constable's benefit and kissed Miss Bryant on the mouth. For good measure, he patted her bottom as he shut the door.

"You know what to do," he said, annoyed he'd broken his vow not to kiss another woman. Surely it didn't count. "You've been through this with Sigmund ten times. I'll return your brother's vowels to you tomorrow. I can give him a beating, too, if you think it will knock sense into his addled brain."

The young woman sighed. "Sadly, there's no hope for him. I'm having him kidnapped and put on a boat to India. First, I need to be sure his creditors won't come banging on my door demanding payment."

The news brought light relief. It was reassuring to know other people faced similar burdens. "I hope you've told no one else of your plan."

"Of course not. I'm telling you so you know you can trust me."

As time was precious, he ushered the woman upstairs.

Half an hour later, Aaron was waiting in the hall.

Joanna descended the stairs, the brown wig hiding her golden locks, her heaving breasts almost spilling out of the red dress that was a tad too big around the waist.

It hurt to look at her.

It hurt to think of what might happen tomorrow.

Tears streaked her cheeks, but she dashed them away. "Will I ever see you again?" She reached for his hands and squeezed them tightly. "Will this nightmare ever end?"

He didn't care that Delphine lingered in the background. He kissed Joanna tenderly on the lips. "I'll do everything in my power to put this right. But I need you to be brave. Surviving must be your priority."

She sniffed back tears and nodded. "Will you reassure my ladies? Tell them I've not abandoned them. If my father returns, you must prevent him from taking ownership of The Burnished Jade."

If her father returned, Aaron would toss him in the Thames.

"I will deal with everything in your absence." Knots twisted in his stomach. Emotions gathered in his chest like storm clouds, ready to burst. "But you must go now. I'll follow later to ensure you've reached your destination but will keep my distance."

Her eyes widened. "You can't ride all the way to Dover. You'll not be back in time to meet Mr Daventry at noon."

He drew her closer, kissed her cheek and whispered, "You're not going to Dover. Do as Sigmund says. You'll be safe with him. He's waiting for you in the yard of The Saracen's Head. Hush. Say nothing." If questioned, he did not want Delphine to lie. "I'm going to kiss you at the door. Let the constable think we've spent a rampant half an hour together. Tell me when you're ready."

She brought his hand to her lips and pressed a lingering kiss to his palm. "Saving yourself must be your priority now. Don't let the devil beat you. Don't die, Aaron. The world needs strong men like you."

Strong? He felt as weak as a kitten.

"And you must be a good girl," he teased, "not a mischievous imp."

"I'll try." She inhaled deeply a few times. "Open the door."

He obliged, raising a hand to the constable before taking Joanna in his arms. He took her mouth, anchoring her to him like she was his life force, like his heart would stop beating without her, like his lungs would be depleted of air.

He tasted her salty tears. Felt the agonising torment in every deep plunge of her tongue. Inhaled the sweet scent of roses on her skin. Heard every desperate sigh. Knew she wouldn't stop kissing him, and he must be the one to break contact.

"Follow Sigmund's instructions," he said.

She cupped his bristled cheek. "I pray I'll see you again."

"You must believe it's possible. Now go before the constable grows suspicious. And giggle like you've just had the ride of your life."

He would never forget her parting smile.

One of pleasure tinged with immense sorrow.

"Same time tomorrow, minx," he called.

She laughed and waved. "You might last longer next time."

Aaron stood in the doorway, watching until she entered The Saracen's Head, the crushing ache in his chest a sensation he had never known. He didn't breathe again until Sigmund drove the hackney cab out of the yard, and the vehicle disappeared into the blackness.

He closed the door, resting his forehead on the wood.

Seconds passed as memories of their last days together repeated like a well-loved play—a kaleidoscope of unforgettable moments.

"It's obvious you're in love with her," Delphine said, closing the gap between them and placing a comforting hand on his shoulder. "We always teased you about it, but I've never witnessed a greater display of love in my life."

Aaron pushed away from the door and faced Delphine, the pain in his throat making it hard to speak. "Loving someone isn't always about happy endings. I can live without her as long as she's safe."

She brushed his hair from his brow. "Your ability to do the right thing distinguishes you from other men. It would have been easy to keep her here and risk fighting your foes."

In this moment of weakness, he revealed his greatest fear. "Many men want to hurt me. What better way than through those I love? I had to let her go. I must let her go if she returns."

"Is that why you've not told her you love her?"

"She needs a man who'll battle a storm for her." Not someone who had complicated his life with a constant fear of failure.

"Is that not you?"

He sighed. "She makes me forget everyone else exists. You know why that's dangerous. I can't protect you all and be everything she needs."

A coy smile touched Delphine's lips. She didn't make the foolish mistake of advising him to forget his family. "There is a way to strengthen your defences though you won't like it one bit."

He narrowed his gaze, knowing the road she referred to was one he refused to tread. "I'll not appeal to the King to be named heir to an earldom. I'd rather cut out my tongue and serve it for supper."

Delphine shrugged. "Aramis could run the club. You could sit in the House of Lords and terrify them into making sensible decisions. As a peer, you would be practically untouchable."

"I'm a gaming hell owner, not a lofty lord."

"Your grandfather was the Earl of Berridge, as was his father before him. You're the true heir, not an imposter. Ignatius Chance sold *his* birthright, not yours. You could right the wrongs of the past."

Everything she said made sense, but even if the King agreed, it would mean bearing a title he despised to the depth of his bones, adopting the family name he hated with a vengeance.

"It's too much to contemplate when my heart is heavy." He straightened. All that mattered was proving Joanna's innocence. "There is much to do tomorrow. I need to rest for a few hours, though I doubt I'll sleep."

Delphine laughed. "We both know sleep isn't on your agenda. I heard you say you're following Miss Lovelace to ensure she arrives at the destination."

Aaron smiled. "As far as you know, I'm asleep upstairs with my door locked." Not clambering over the high wall in the yard and claiming his tethered horse from St James' churchyard. "Once I know Joanna has made the first leg of the journey, I'll return home to demand our brothers move into their old rooms."

"Is Miss Lovelace staying at an inn?"

Aaron tapped his finger to his lips. "The less you know, the better."

"You might have said goodbye there and had an hour's privacy. You might have shown her how deep your passions run without saying it in words. Given her a memory to treasure." She tapped his arm playfully before walking away and calling, "Just a thought."

It was a thought he couldn't shake from his mind as he dressed. A thought he considered as he scaled the wall and broke curfew. A thought that plagued him every mile on the ride to Gravesend.

Joanna wasn't staying in the popular Pier Hotel but in the quieter Pope's Head tavern. Sigmund was in the taproom when Aaron arrived, supping ale at a table by the window, watching the schooners and barges navigate the Thames. Dawn was upon them, the sunrise slowly illuminating the river in a soft, misty glow.

Aaron threw off his heavy riding coat and pulled up a chair. "How is she?"

"As anyone would be when they feel they've lost everything."

"Did you find McMillan?"

Sigmund nodded and downed a mouthful of ale. "He took the cab and horse as payment for passage. We're leaving for Southend at nine and boarding a ship to Ostend at high tide tonight. I'll know more when McMillan returns."

"When you reach Ostend, send a blank letter to Godby's sister." Then Aaron would know they had arrived at their destination. "Find a remote hotel while you look for permanent lodgings. I'll come for you once I've buried the Earl of Berridge."

Sigmund shifted in the seat. "There's something different about this one—a bad feeling gnawing away in my gut. You need me at home, not miles across the North Sea."

Aaron could feel Sigmund's frustration but needed him to concentrate on the task. "If I'm to fight to the death, I need you here. I can't be a ruthless bastard when she consumes my thoughts."

Sigmund gripped his tankard in his meaty paws like it was the villain's scrawny neck. "I hate feeling helpless. You know that."

Aaron reached across the table and gripped Sigmund's arm. "You've been a loyal friend all these years. Protect her like you would me. That's all I ask of you."

Sigmund sighed and then offered every reassurance. "Will you visit her before you return to London?"

No! It would add to the torment.

"I'm not sure that's wise."

He had an hour to spare before taking to the road. Saying goodbye would be harder this time, and he was already dying inside.

"There's nothing wise about any of this, but happen you know that already." Sigmund glanced at the ceiling. "Remember, some memories have to last a lifetime. A few good ones might keep the nightmares away. Nothing destroys a man like the pain of regret."

Aaron forced a grin. "When did you become the voice of reason?"

"When you cracked a smile for the first time in ten years."

# Chapter Fourteen

Joanna lay on the bed in the quaint room, trying to stem the flow of tears. Her white handkerchief was a damp, crumpled mess. Her heart hurt, and her eyes stung from rubbing them dry. She sniffed while still wondering how she had veered onto this treacherous path when she had planned each step with such care and precision.

Take control of her inheritance.

Earn money to pay for new furniture and repairs.

Open a club for ladies in need, a sanctuary for those without friends or family. Somewhere she might have found solace from scoundrels and the endless nights spent alone.

She'd been focused on her future. Determined to succeed.

Then she met Aaron Chance, and her world spun out of control.

Some might say he had been right to avoid her, sensible to let her believe she roused his disdain. But when they kissed … heaven help her … nothing felt so glorious. That's why the river of tears would not stop flowing.

With hard work, she could replace her material possessions.

She could not replace him. The man who tortured himself for his father's mistakes. The caring man who believed he was a monster.

Now, she would never get an opportunity to love him, to show him how beautiful he was inside. That's what hurt the most.

It was a tragedy worthy of Shakespeare.

An elegy for a life lost.

A heartbreaking tale of injustice.

A light knock on the door drew Joanna from her reverie. Dawn was upon them. Soon, she would be miles across the sea while her heart was still in London.

"Just a moment." She dried her eyes and gathered herself. Sigmund would insist she ate before setting out on their journey, though the thought of food turned her stomach.

She opened the door, though her brain struggled to make sense of the handsome vision standing in the corridor. She stared at Aaron in his fitted black coat, her heart thumping hard in her chest, excitement racing through her veins.

"Miss Lovelace."

His deep voice stirred the hairs on her nape.

"Mr Chance."

"I came to ensure you arrived safely. I must leave in an hour and had to see you one last time." His gaze trailed over her body like he was mentally undressing her, but then their eyes locked, and she saw her own sorrow reflected there. "How I spend the hour is up to you."

As she struggled to keep the tenuous hold on her composure, she reached for him, slipping her hand into his and pulling him across the threshold. "This is an unexpected gift."

"I haven't the strength to stay away."

"You're stronger than any man I know."

"You're my Achilles' heel, Joanna. My one weakness." He glanced at their joined hands and sighed. "I confess, I've never wanted anything quite so much."

He was not alone in his torment. Her waking moments were filled with thoughts of him, too. "Then we should not waste a single minute. Every part of me aches for you, Aaron. I know how I want to spend the next hour. I want to spend it naked in bed with you."

Heavens, she sounded wanton, like the women at Mrs Flavell's parties, but she could feel his pain, pain as raw as her own. What if tragedy struck, making this the only fulfilling moment of their lives?

Aaron hissed a breath. "Lock the door."

She saw to the task, then flew into his arms. "I don't want to talk about our problems. I don't want this to be a sad moment. We'll make no promises. I'll not hold you to another vow. Let our actions be our words."

He cupped her nape, his thumb stroking her cheek gently. "I need to see you smile. I need to watch you glow with pleasure. I need you to pretend all is well."

"I don't need to pretend." She was already pushing his coat off his shoulders, her hands gliding over the firm muscles, relishing the power beneath her fingertips. "All is well. You're here. I have never been happier."

He drew her close, devouring her mouth as if they'd waited years, not hours, to taste each other again.

"Let me make love to you, Aaron," she said against his lips, determined he would leave here knowing he was adored. "I haven't the first clue what to do, but you must give me free rein over your body. Let me touch you as I please."

*We both have wounds that need to heal.*

The hitch in his breath was an odd mix of want and nerves. "I'll need you in every way possible. I need to squeeze a lifetime of lovemaking into an hour. I'll be tender and rough and will make no excuses for it."

Desire unfurled in her belly, a tantalising heat coiling low.

"Then why are we still talking?" She smiled while clambering to undo the buttons on his waistcoat, her hands quick to roam under his fine lawn shirt and feel the sumptuous heat of his skin. "If I'm too much for you, you must tell me to stop," she teased.

"I uttered the same words the first time we kissed. Now it's clear our passions are perfectly entwined." He captured her chin, his fevered breath stroking her lips. "When I'm alone at night, I shall let this memory move languidly through my mind, but I'm on fire. I need to be inside you. I need to take you slowly, and thrust hard and deep. I need you against the door, on your back, on your knees, sitting astride me."

A shiver of delight chased down her spine. "Then get me out of these clothes. I don't want the beast to behave. I want all of you. Hold nothing back."

Their next kiss cried of desperation, a rampant mating of mouths, of shared moans and breathless pants. A ravenous hunger she knew would never be sated.

How did one convey a lifetime of need without words?

Aaron knew how.

He dragged his lips over her jaw and neck like he couldn't bear to break contact, like they were joined together forever and nothing could tear them apart. Despite attempting to undo the side buttons on her dress, his eager hand wandered, palming her breast, pushing into her hair and tilting her head back. He kissed the column of her throat, reached under her skirts to grip her bare buttocks, squeezing hard to leave his mark.

*You're mine.*

Those possessive words echoed through every action.

It was like an erotic dream where time stood still.

But they didn't have such luxury.

She took control, her fingers moving to the placket of his trousers, resisting the temptation to stroke the thick shaft bulging against the material. She wanted to touch his erection, feel his bare skin, hold the power of his pulsing arousal in her palm. She wanted the great Aaron Chance at her mercy.

He inhaled sharply when she freed his manhood. "If you touch me, I'm done for. Do you know how many times I've imagined this moment?"

"Too many," she breathed, daring to take hold of him. His skin was soft, a veil of satin over steel. Despite his immense strength, he surrendered to the pleasure gained from every inexpert stroke. "You were done for when you entered the room," she said, his musky scent a silent call to her sex. "You were done for when you agreed to let me stay at Fortune's Den."

"I was finished long before that."

"When?" she demanded to know, loving how he groaned when she firmed her grip. Touching him was so addictive she couldn't stop. "Tell me, Aaron."

"The first night I saw you brushing your hair at your bedchamber window. The first time you put me in my place. The first time you touched me accidentally. When your hand brushed my arm and it was like a jolt from the heavens."

*Stubborn man*, she uttered silently.

What if Eloise had never confessed?

"You've wanted me for that long?" she whispered, noting the tiny bead of moisture weeping from the engorged head of his shaft. She imagined it was the only tear Aaron Chance had ever shed. "And you said nothing?"

He responded now, his mouth forming a perfect O as his head fell back, exposing the sculpted line of his jaw. There was a tiny scar she had not noticed before, from a previous wound that had never fully healed, but he was no less magnificent.

"Joanna," he growled, stilling her hand. "If I come now, I'll need time to recover, time we can ill afford." He looked at her, his eyes deep, inky pools of longing. "Before we continue, I need to know you want this just as badly, that you're not afraid."

"Afraid?" As soon as the word left her lips, a haunting vision of Lord Howard assailed her. The memory of his sickly scent turned her stomach, even now.

The betrayal hurt more than anything. She had replayed the scene in her mind a thousand times, those precious seconds where he'd hugged her tightly, and she had been utterly clueless of the horror about to unfold.

Had she missed the signs?

Had she said something he had misconstrued?

Had grief made him lose his mind?

Was it a calculated attack or an impulsive mistake?

For a long time afterwards she felt numb, weak, half a person paralysed by her thoughts, but soon realised Lord Howard was a feeble excuse for a man. A pathetic creature who would one day get his comeuppance.

Now he had. What a shame she had not witnessed him draw his last breath, to watch the light in his eyes dim, to apologise for the crime and explain she could do nothing to help.

"I don't want to hurt you," Aaron said, drawing her back to the loving man who was leagues above Lord Howard. "We don't have to be lovers to make this moment memorable."

*We do because I'm in love with you*, she longed to say, but had vowed to let her actions be her words, agreed they would not be bound by oaths and promises.

"I need you, Aaron. I need a beautiful memory I will never forget." She would not let Lord Howard steal every shred of happiness, too. "Be the light in the darkness. I shall be the same for you. Nothing exists beyond our need for each other." She cupped his cheek to reassure him. "I know you will be mindful. That you have my interests at heart."

When they kissed again, it was deep and tender. Butterflies fluttered in her stomach. Her heart raced wildly, though she had never been so relaxed.

When he undressed her, slowly peeling off one item of clothing at a time, one would think he had days, not minutes, to complete the task. He stood still, rubbing his jaw as his greedy gaze devoured every inch of her naked body. He swallowed more times than she could count.

"I don't deserve you," he said, like the weight of his past deeds hung over him, a penance he had to pay. "I thought I knew my place in the world, yet you force me to challenge it at every turn."

*That's what love is*, she thought. It made people reconsider their hopes and dreams and prioritise what was important.

"This is a surprise to me, too," she admitted, drawn to the raw carnality in his eyes, puzzled by her lack of urgency to cover her modesty.

"You're so beautiful, I'm afraid to touch you."

"Then I will touch you."

She reached for his shirt, grasping the fine lawn and dragging the garment over his head. God, he was beautiful. She didn't gape in awe of his rugged physique or weep at the sight of his many scars. Her hands were on him, pushing through the dark hair on his chest, smoothing a path across his broad shoulders.

The feel of his hot skin dragged a sweet moan from her lips.

"Aaron," was all she could say, not the measure of her feelings, not a list of fine qualities that made him the most impressive man she had ever met. "Time is precious. Remove your trousers and sit in the chair."

They both had hurdles to climb.

She needed to be in control at the beginning, to choose the moment he claimed her. Despite his earlier confession to have her in every conceivable way, to fit a lifetime of love-making into an hour, he was scared to hurt her.

Aaron released her to tug off his riding boots and slowly push his trousers down over his lean hips, each movement deliberate, as if relishing the intimacy of undressing while she watched.

Her gaze wandered over him, starting at the wide expanse of his chest, then gliding down to the taut muscles of his abdomen. She felt her pulse quicken as her eyes trailed lower, drawn to the solid length of his manhood, the burn of desire flaming with every passing second.

He tried to lure her to the bed, but she put her finger on his lips and guided him towards the seat. He was too big for the wooden chair, his shoulders broader than the back rail, his powerful thighs overhanging the base when he spread them wide. She glanced again at his engorged manhood. He was too big for her in every regard.

A hungry anticipation lurked in his gaze as he took himself in hand. "You're the only woman who's ever seen me like this," he groaned, his eyes flickering like passion's flames licked his skin. "So relaxed and carefree."

"You're the only man who's ever looked upon me." She touched herself, palming her breasts, a light twist of her nipples, the slow glide of her fingers through the damp folds of her sex. "The only man I want and need."

*The only man I'll ever love.*

"God, you make me forget a world exists outside this room." Eyes as black as jet raked over her body, a visual caress that tugged at her insides. "You can trust me, Joanna. I'll be careful. You don't need to worry about a child."

A pang of disappointment hit her squarely in the chest. If only she could leave England with a part of him growing inside her, a child to tie them together forever. But she could never be that selfish.

With tentative steps, she closed the gap between them. They were wasting precious time. "Tell me what to do. Tell me how to please you."

"Straddle my thighs. Let me touch you."

He closed his legs to make room on the chair.

She did as he asked, gasping when he clutched her hips and held her firmly on his lap. "Don't let me fall, Aaron."

"I doubt I'll ever let go." He held her while blowing gently on her nipples as they grew to solid peaks. "I see you like that, love," he whispered darkly, sucking one hard bud into his mouth, the rapid flick of his tongue sending a bolt of heat shooting to her core.

Lust was a gnawing tension in her stomach, a fever in her

blood. Every touch of his mouth on her sensitive skin made it impossible to sit still. The hard ridge of his erection rubbed against her sex, desire a deep quiver in her belly.

"I need you, Aaron. I need you now."

"Look at me, Joanna." His hot mouth covered hers, their tongues meeting with a feverish hunger. "I need to watch you as I take you."

Holding her steady with a strong hand splayed against her back, he gripped his manhood, rubbing the head over her sex, his mouth parting, his smouldering gaze never leaving her for a second.

"I can see how badly you want this," he groaned like he wanted it so badly it pained him. "I need you riding my cock, Joanna. Tell me when."

"Now. Don't wait."

He entered her, the first inch stretching her wide, pushing against the slight resistance. Another inch deeper, and his eyes rolled in their sockets, his breath coming in shallow pants.

"God, Joanna."

She welcomed the intrusion, unprepared for the unrelenting pull on her heartstrings, the sweet ache of love banishing the slight sting as Aaron filled her full.

He gazed up at her, allowing her to glimpse the man beyond the veil, his dark eyes softening, shimmering like deep pools at dusk. She saw the intense warmth of adoration, a burning passion that spoke the words his lips could not.

*We belong to each other now*, her heart whispered.

"Does it pain you?" he said.

"How could it? It feels like we were made to fit together."

"In all my wildest dreams, I never believed this was possible." He gripped her hips and rocked her slowly, the movement making him swell inside her as excitement built in her, too. "You need to ride me and find a rhythm. Take what you want, love. Be greedy."

"Show me how."

With strong arms, he lifted her, driving deeper into her as he lowered her down. "Like this. You control the pace. Don't be nervous. You don't need to be nervous with me."

She came up on her knees and sank slowly down, whimpering as she sheathed him, taking every solid inch. The friction of him sliding in and out of her, his guttural groans of appreciation, and the slick sound of the act heightened her arousal.

There was something primal in his eyes as he watched her. His hands moved over her body, caressing the soft swell of her breasts, his thumb sliding through her folds to strum her aching sex.

"Don't stop, Aaron. I've never known such bliss."

"You'll come for me like this," he panted. "You'll come around my cock, Joanna. Lord knows I've thought of little else the last six months."

The tension inside her built, like the sea's ebb and flow, she was being pulled closer to the shore. Her release broke through her like the crashing of a wave, a sudden surge of pleasure that had her body clenching around the man she loved, hugging his manhood hard as she whimpered and called his name.

"Hell, yes!" Aaron stared at her, passion burning in his eyes like embers in a night without stars. "Things may become frantic. Do you need to rest? We don't have to continue."

Her nipples were aching peaks, her bud engorged, her heart still pounding. She didn't want this moment to end, and neither did her lustful body. "Don't stop. We need to fit a life-time of lovemaking into an hour."

Before she'd caught her breath, he held her tight to his solid body and stood. "Wrap your legs around me. If I'm too rough, you must tell me. Look at me, Joanna. Tell me how it feels."

"It feels so good."

She was against the wall, Aaron driving into her again and again. The power in every movement, the frenzied desperation, belied the man who'd feigned indifference.

"Tell me what you're thinking," she said, loving that he had lost control, taking pleasure in the fact he couldn't get enough of her.

"This won't be the end of us," he growled, moving her to the bed and laying her on her back. He slowed the pace, holding her hands above her head, their fingers entwined, rolling his hips as he filled her, the sensation sublime.

Such passion could not be tempered.

She'd wait years for him, a lifetime if necessary.

"Let our thoughts control our destiny," she said, her mind a haze of desire. "We will see each other again, Aaron. We have to believe it's possible."

"You're mine, do you hear me?" he said when she climaxed again. "You'll wait for me. I'll work night and day to clear your name. I'll not rest until you're home and in my bed."

He sank in and out of her hard and fast, then withdrew suddenly, spilling his seed over her abdomen, his guttural groan like the casting off of chains.

The hard angles of his face softened, the gleam of plea-sure in his eyes like a serene sunset in a break between storm clouds. As he fought to catch his breath, his gaze was everywhere at once, on her lips, her breasts, her hair, lingering on the swollen folds of her womanhood.

"Let me fetch water and a towel." Aaron moved to the washstand, but not before she witnessed a shadow of sadness mar his handsome features.

She let him wash her, even though he took his time and the air turned cold.

They lay on the bed together, her brushing his hair with her fingers, him tracing patterns on her shoulder.

"You didn't have me on my knees," she said in jest, though her heart felt like it was breaking. "There's no time for an encore. You'll need to leave soon."

He stared at her, stroking the backs of his fingers across her cheek. "I need to look at you when we make love. I can't do that if you're on your knees. Watching you is an addiction. It will kill me to look through the study window and know you're not there."

Tears gathered behind her eyes. The euphoria had subsided, leaving nothing but grief in its wake. "I'll never forget you. I'll never forget what we had. No matter how long I'm away, there'll be no one but you, Aaron."

A heaviness clung to the air as if it, too, mourned in silence.

They lay there until the dreaded time arrived for him to dress and depart. She helped to straighten his cravat and insisted on fastening his waistcoat, desperate to touch him a little longer.

"Remember, you're to send word when you reach Ostend." The deep timbre of his voice carried a pain he couldn't hide.

She nodded as tears rolled down her cheeks. "Be careful.

I can live in exile if I know you're safe. Don't take unnecessary risks."

He wiped away her tears and pressed a lingering goodbye kiss on her forehead, though he never uttered the word. "Close the door. Don't watch me walk away. I can't look back."

"I'll see you again. I know I will."

He cupped her cheek as he stood in the doorway. "You have no idea how much you mean to me. You'll live in my heart and mind always."

Then he left, closing the chamber door behind him.

# Chapter Fifteen

*Fortune's Den*
*Aldgate Street, London*

Aaron strode into the dining room, brushing road dust off his clothes and breathing deeply to calm his racing pulse. He was late. An hour late. On the bright side, his family were lucky he wasn't on a boat to Southend. Lucky he had come home at all.

Nine heads turned towards him.

Nine gasps echoed through the room.

Nine people stood, voicing their fears all at once.

"Where the hell have you been?" Christian cried.

*Making love to the woman who owns my heart,* he said silently. *Riding home, wondering how I'll cope without her.*

"We've been out of our minds with worry," Theo complained. "Did you not think to consult us? Why didn't you take one of us with you?"

*And spoil a treasured moment?* Aaron wanted to say.

Aramis thumped the table with his clenched fist. "We thought you'd been arrested. Taken against your will. I was about to march to Hart Street and drag Daventry to every police office in London."

*Oh, I've been taken, but not against my will.*

The memory of Joanna sitting astride him, taking him deep—her golden hair falling wildly about her shoulders like a waterfall of sunlight—brought a smile to his face. One destined to be short-lived.

"Are you ill?" Christian said, glancing at his wife Isabella as if his eldest brother were mad. "I fail to see what's amusing when Berridge is baying for our blood."

"Let him catch his breath." Delphine cast Aaron a knowing grin. "He's not slept a wink. Can you not see he's exerted himself? Pour him coffee and butter a triangle of toast. I fear he's expended all his energy."

Aaron winked at her.

He never winked at anyone.

Mrs Maloney chuckled. "Who are you, and what have you done with my eldest boy? You're pedantic when it comes to timekeeping, yet you don't seem the least bit fazed."

Aaron shrugged. "Some things can't be helped. But I'm here now and haven't much time. I trust Delphine updated you all on recent events."

Aramis was the first to respond. "Yes, though she refuses to explain why Miss Lovelace locked herself in the room next to yours and won't come out."

"Miss Lovelace isn't here." He glanced at the mantel clock. She would arrive in Southend soon, the distance between them widening by the hour. "It wasn't safe for her to remain in England." His stomach twisted at the memory of her crying as they said goodbye. "We must keep the secret until tonight. Then she'll be on the last leg of her journey, out of harm's way."

Christian paled. "But they'll hang you for aiding her escape."

"Not if we stick to the same story." Aaron sipped his coffee. "I have nine hours to prove she's innocent. It's a tall task, but I will drain my personal account and draw blood if necessary."

Amid the tense silence, Aramis said, "What do you want us to do? I speak for all of us when I say we are at your disposal."

They would not like the answer.

"You're to remain here and promise you won't leave." Aaron raised a calming hand at the first grumbles of protest. "I cannot work quickly if I'm worried about your safety."

"What about your safety?" Mrs Maloney said.

"I'm invincible, remember." Stomach rumbling, Aaron reached for a slice of toast. "I've made huge sacrifices for this family. I'm asking you all to do one small thing for me."

No one argued.

How could they?

"There is work you can do in my absence." Aaron reeled off the list that would keep his brothers occupied. "Compare the handwriting on the letter Rothley received to the one delivered to Mrs Flavell, and the one sent to the treasury. They're in my desk drawer. And study the list of men's names Miss Stowe sent. Mark any with a gripe against me."

"Anything else?" Aramis said.

"Search the ledgers from The Burnished Jade. Look for names you don't recognise. A woman who joined the club recently but has no connection to anyone in society. And

213

write to Ballingers Auction House. We need to know who bought our father's watch all those years ago. It's a distinctive timepiece. A clerk may remember the sale."

"I'll send Sigmund."

"He's not here. Send Baptiste. We need the answer today."

Flynn spoke up. He thought like an enquiry agent and offered valuable insight. "We must consider how Venus is connected to the Earl of Berridge. Did Berridge meet her at one of Mrs Flavell's lavish parties? Might Mrs Flavell be the earl's mistress?"

Aaron was forced to reveal another secret he had kept to himself. "I've had men watching Berridge since the thugs shot Theo. I'd know if he had a mistress. He spends his nights alone at home. It begs the question: how did he meet Venus if he rarely leaves the house?"

"Logic would suggest the earl is innocent," Flynn said.

"Then we're missing a vital clue." Aaron scoured his memories for the lost piece of the puzzle but kept returning to the same question. Why now? "Berridge has threatened us for years but has never dared to act."

"His son and heir is dead," Theo said. "What has he to lose? Though, why the elaborate plot? Why have you chasing your tail?"

Hatred for the Berridge family surfaced. "Killing me isn't enough. He wants to make me suffer. He wants to hurt me by threatening the people I love."

Delphine jumped at the opportunity to force a confession. "Then why involve Miss Lovelace if she's nothing more than your competitor?"

Like a soothing melody, Joanna's words drifted through his mind.

*We're the best of friends, Mr Chance. Nothing will ever change that.*

*I'll never forget you. I'll never forget what we had.*

His grief was a crushing sadness that sucked the life out of every breath.

He coughed to loosen his throat. "Because I'm in love with her. Someone knows she means everything to me." Saying the words aloud felt good. For once, his heart and mind were aligned.

A stunned silence ensued.

Then Aramis clapped his hands and laughed. "Praise the Lord. I feared we would have to tolerate a lifetime of brooding."

"Self-flagellation can be tiring for those forced to watch," Christian added. "I would rather not see you add to your scars."

Mrs Maloney sobbed into her handkerchief. "Your love could move mountains. You'll find a way through this. I know you will."

He didn't say he might leave England if he failed to prove Joanna was innocent. He didn't say it was becoming increasingly difficult to live without her.

The mantel clock chimed the half hour.

A reminder every minute was precious.

"Flynn, I need to borrow your vehicle." Aaron stood, snatching one of Baptiste's pastries from the plate Aramis hogged. He would eat it slowly, savour every bite and think of Joanna. "I'll be back by eight o'clock." He faced Aramis. "At seven, help Miss Bryant escape over the back wall. I cannot risk her being arrested. She will need her brother's vowels. You know where to find them."

Aramis frowned. "Miss Bryant?"

"Delphine will explain." Aaron turned to the family he would die for and firmed his tone. "No one leaves here. To disobey my orders is to say the beatings I took meant nothing."

Everyone nodded, though apprehension lined their brows.

"Be safe," Delphine called. "We love you. More than you know."

Muttered words of agreement echoed around the table.

Money had been the means to end their suffering.

Their suffering had brought a gift greater than wealth.

Despite his eagerness to leave, Aaron paused at the door. "My love for you all knows no bounds." He looked at them, compelled to utter words he'd never spoken. "I'm glad our father died. Being head of this family has been the greatest honour of my life."

*Home of Thomas Parker*
*Dean Street, Soho Square*

Aaron found Daventry sitting in Parker's worn leather chair when he barged past the irate butler and stormed into the grimy drawing room.

"You're late." Daventry scanned Aaron's creased clothes and grinned. "You look dusty and dishevelled. Like you've journeyed fifty miles on a farmer's cart and have barely slept a wink."

Ignoring the comment, Aaron glanced at Lucia, perched on the cluttered sofa like a prim debutante, hands clasped in her lap, knees shaking. "I trust Miss Stowe had no objection to you borrowing her maid," he said.

"Miss Stowe wanted to come, but I refused. There's too much at stake to risk her interference." Daventry motioned to the maid. "Lucia insists she's innocent, even when I shouted at her in Italian."

Aaron silently cursed. He knew when a punter was bluffing at cards, but the maid was skilled at adopting different identities. It took courage to wear a costume and sing opera, yet she acted like a timid mouse now.

"Where the hell is Parker?"

"In bed. He has ten minutes to dress before I drag him downstairs." Daventry drummed his fingers on the arm of the chair. "How is Miss Lovelace faring?"

The question caught Aaron off guard. He flinched as an inescapable anguish flooded his chest. "Distraught. As any innocent woman would be when accused of murder."

"Murder?" Lucia inhaled sharply. "But Miss Lovelace is innocent. Where is she? Miss Stowe will want to see her. She will want to help."

"You can help by telling the truth," Aaron snapped. "How long have you worked for Miss Stowe?"

Lucia's bottom lip trembled. "Six months."

"Six months? Where did you work previously?"

The colour drained from Lucia's face. "At Lord Hutton's house in Manchester Square. Miss Stowe found me crying in the market and took me home. I have worked for her ever since."

Daventry looked at Aaron and arched a brow. "I suspect Hutton couldn't keep his hands to himself."

"No, his lordship was kind," Lucia protested. "His friends were wicked. One lady beat me for spilling a drink. She came to my room at night and hit—" A sudden sob escaped her. She put her head in her hands and wept.

Parker chose that untimely moment to amble into the room, scratching his stubbled chin, stinking of brandy and still half-sotted.

"What is it this time?" Parker tightened the belt on his silk robe and pointed at the tearful Lucia. "Is this the woman who claimed I assaulted her at The Burnished Jade? I assure you she is lying."

"This is Venus," Daventry said, insisting the maid raise her head.

"Venus?" Parker stepped back. "Are you sure? She looks a little young."

Aaron lost his temper. "You should know. You kissed the woman. Are you saying this isn't her?"

Parker shrugged. "It was dark, and she wore a mask. You know how it is at Mrs Flavell's parties. One's mind becomes fuzzy. I need to hear her speak in that sultry foreign voice." He beckoned the girl to stand. "Show me those delightful hands, darling. I'll never forget the feel of those."

Lucia stood on shaky legs and obeyed Parker's order. When asked to speak, she said, "I have never met you before, sir. People confuse me with Venus, yet I have never been known by that name."

Parker scratched his head. "I suppose asking her to kiss me would be inappropriate. A man never forgets the taste of a mysterious woman's lips."

Aaron's heart lurched.

Would it always be this way? When people mentioned love and kissing, would he always think of Joanna and wish he were somewhere else?

"You'll not lay a finger on her." Aaron grabbed Parker by his fancy robe. "Look at her. Is she Venus or not? Don't test my patience. Not today."

"It c-could be her," Parker stammered. "Venus was spectacular. This girl lacks that special something that makes her attractive to men. She looks too pure, too timid."

The reprobate made Aaron's skin crawl.

Why had Venus targeted this degenerate? Probably because he was gullible enough to do her bidding. Was insulting a lady who stuttered his only prank?

"You were so desperate to bed her you'd have done anything," Aaron cried.

Daventry spoke up. "So desperate she persuaded you to demonstrate your loyalty by accepting a dare. We know what you did," he bluffed. "And why she chose a man who makes silly wagers."

Parker's agitation escalated. "For heaven's sake, you can't tell Mrs Flavell. She'll revoke my membership. I'll be barred for life. It was a prank. I was going to return the dagger. Venus was supposed to give it back when I met her at The Cock Inn."

The permanent knot in Aaron's chest eased slightly, though the confession only proved Venus had handled the murder weapon. He prayed the meek maid wasn't Venus. It reinforced the theory Joanna and Lucia were in cahoots.

Daventry stood. "You will put that in writing."

Parker threw his hands in the air. "I can't. Mrs Flavell will flay me alive. Look, I've told you everything I—"

"I will have your testimony now," Daventry boomed. "Or

I will haul you to the Thames Police Office and charge you with theft and conspiracy to commit murder. The Mughal dagger was used to kill a man. You could hang for the part you played."

Parker heaved and retched. The threat of the noose caused him to deposit his breakfast and a bellyful of brandy on the floor behind the chair.

Lucia covered her mouth with her hand.

Aaron dragged the fool to the study and stood over him while he committed his confession to paper.

"You're a disgrace," Aaron said through gritted teeth as he was leaving. "You may not have abused a guest at The Burnished Jade, but you've abused your staff and your brother's generosity. I shall make sure Sir Geoffrey knows of your antics."

He left Parker on his knees, begging for mercy.

"I'll meet you at the pawnbroker's in Regent Street," Aaron said, handing Daventry the statement. He craved time alone. Daventry would bombard him with questions. Aaron couldn't speak about Joanna and keep the mindset needed to catch a killer.

The pawnbroker was just as clueless. He rubbed his hands over his paunch and stared at Lucia. "She may have been a bit taller. I mean, she looks similar. I want to say it's her, but I can't be sure. I mainly spoke to the gent." He studied Lucia and shook his head. "No, she had a special kind of confidence, if you take my meaning. There was nothing feeble about her."

Daventry thanked the man and left his card on the counter.

"How hard is it to identify one woman?" Aaron grumbled as they left the pawnbroker's and lingered on Regent Street.

He turned to Lucia. "You'd better be telling the truth. An innocent woman's life is at stake."

The maid started crying.

Aaron felt like an ogre, the beast he professed to be, but made no apology. Tears dried. The maid would recover. The noose awaited Joanna.

What happened next proved an odd twist of fate.

The pawnbroker appeared at the shop door and beckoned them closer. "I've remembered something. It's a silly thing but might be important."

Blinded by a desire for the truth, Aaron turned his back on Lucia.

"The woman had a mole," the pawnbroker began as a group of political zealots came darting past, carrying placards and complaining about a corrupt Whig government. "I remember because my wife had one the same on her left wrist."

The clacking of rattles brought ten constables charging along Regent Street in pursuit of the zealots. Panic ensued. Bystanders took to their heels and ran in the opposite direction. Somehow, Lucia got swept up in the chaos and disappeared amidst the crowd.

Aaron ran the length of the street, pushing people aside and grabbing strangers, but couldn't find the devious vixen.

Daventry searched shops, darting from the barbers to the perfumers, but Lucia knew to blend into the background.

Both breathless, they returned to stand outside the pawnbroker's.

"It's fair to assume Lucia is Venus." Aaron braced his hands on his knees while he caught his breath. "For people to believe she is Madame Rossellini, she must be versatile and skilled in deception."

"Either way, Lucia absconding hinders the investigation." Daventry craned his neck and scanned the crowd. "She had the dagger and was present at the murder scene. It suggests Miss Lovelace conspired to kill the man who took her virtue."

Aaron's heart sank like a brick in a well. "Tell me this isn't happening. I don't know how to help her. There's no time to fix this."

Daventry gripped Aaron's shoulder. "We'll take a statement from Miss Stowe. She will write something in support of Miss Lovelace. I'll speak to the Home Secretary. Ensure they postpone the trial for a week or two."

"It's too late." Aaron wore his failure like a heavy cloak, the damn thing swamping him. "I can't prove Joanna is innocent before the magistrate calls tonight."

Silence ensued.

"Don't blame yourself," Daventry said, his tone gentle, reassuring. "I would send Sybil away, too, if I thought her life was in jeopardy. If the authorities can't find her, it gives us time to catch the culprit. I can manipulate the truth a little if necessary."

"What the hell am I missing?"

"Nothing. The villain is cunning enough to cover his tracks. We know Lucia is Venus, but we don't know why she framed Miss Lovelace for murder or who else is involved. That must be our focus."

"Berridge is involved." The name brought bile to Aaron's throat. How could he adopt the title and keep his self-respect?

"Then we must find proof. We'll visit Fitzpatrick first. If he paid someone to ruin his sister, that man may have been Lord Howard. It gives Miss Fitzpatrick a possible motive for murder. It won't explain how she obtained the murder weapon, but the magistrate will have a second suspect."

"Very well," Aaron said, glad someone could think logically. "Casting doubt on Joanna's guilt may appease the magistrate and convince him to give us more time."

"I'll ride with you." Daventry removed a small book and pencil from his pocket, scribbled a few notes and handed the slip of paper to his coachman. "I've instructed my agents to look for Lucia," he said as the carriage pulled away. "They'll make it a priority. I've told Sloane we need to know who complained about your sister-in-law stealing from the museum."

A niggling in Aaron's gut had him suggesting a change of plan. "We should visit the earl first." Berridge was guilty. No one else would dare goad the devil. No one else wished to hurt Aaron and erase a whole family from existence. "What if Lucia warns Berridge and he flees to his country estate?"

Giving it some thought, Daventry reluctantly agreed. "You'll be professional. Berridge is in his sixties and incapable of taking one of your punches. We need solid evidence before accusing a peer and forcing him to name his accomplice."

Aaron couldn't afford to make a mistake. "Something tells me I'll find answers there. I'll keep my rage on a tight leash."

They were about to leave when an imposing black carriage, pulled by a team of muscled black Friesians, came to a crashing halt on the street. The crest on the door was unmistakable—a gold dragon flying above crossed swords.

Rothley alighted, vaulting from the vehicle like he'd escaped from the underworld. Staring from beneath hooded lids, he strode towards Aaron, his greatcoat billowing. "Where the hell is she? I visited Fortune's Den, but your brothers refused me entrance. Something is amiss because Aramis threatened to flatten my nose."

Aaron had no choice but to add to Rothley's torment. "I'm afraid I can't tell you. Joanna's life depends upon me keeping the secret."

A dark cloud passed over Rothley's features. "If she comes to any harm because of you, I'll kill you myself. The law be damned."

Aaron clenched his fists at his sides. Threats always brought out the devil in him. "Come to Fortune's Den tonight at eight o'clock, and I'll tell you everything. I'm trying to help her, but time is short." While he longed to put Rothley on his arse, he knew it would upset Joanna.

Rothley considered him through narrowed eyes. "This better not be a ploy to appease me. You'd better be there tonight, or there'll be hell to pay."

Blood rushed to Aaron's fists, but he kept control of his temper. "I'll be there. In the meantime, there's something you can do to help."

"Name it."

"Find Fitzpatrick. I need to know if he paid Howard to ruin his sister. I need to know what Howard was doing at The Burnished Jade. I need a motive for murder that doesn't involve me or Joanna."

Rothley nodded. "I have your assurance she is alive?"

"She's alive." Or else he would be drowning in despair.

"She's not missing?" Rothley said, more a plea than a question.

"No. I know exactly where to find her."

The marquess released a weary sigh. "I'll get what you need."

Rothley made to leave, but Aaron called after him.

"What is it, Chance?"

"A word of warning," Aaron said darkly. "No man threatens to kill me and lives to tell the tale. Lucky for you, I'll make an exception, just this once."

Rothley said nothing.

Aaron watched Rothley's carriage charge away before turning to Daventry and voicing his fears. "Rothley is in love with Joanna. His actions border on obsession." Aaron should know. There was a reason the rug near his study window was threadbare.

"Rothley is in love with Kate Bourne and has been since he was nineteen. He feels duty-bound to protect Miss Lovelace. That's the cause of his frustration."

Aaron had never heard of Kate Bourne, nor was he interested in the reason for Rothley's gruff temperament.

Nothing mattered now.

Nothing but saving Joanna.

*Upper Brook Street*
*Mayfair, London*

"Lord Berridge is indisposed," the butler said, raising his chin as if expecting an argument. "A strict mourning period is being observed. If the matter requires immediate attention, I suggest you contact his secretary."

Aaron kept the rim of his hat pulled low and said nothing.

"We must speak to his lordship today." Daventry removed a letter from his coat pocket and gave it to the lean fellow guarding the door. "We're investigating a crime on behalf of the Home Secretary."

It was a small lie that left the butler shaky on his feet. "I'll speak to the housekeeper, Mrs Lowry. We've been instructed to turn all visitors away. Call again later, and you'll receive a reply."

"We'll wait," Aaron insisted. He imagined storming into the house and informing the servants they would answer to him when the earl was dead.

The butler nodded politely when he should have been firm.

"We've no valid reason to be here," Daventry whispered as they lingered on the steps. "I can't barge into his home demanding answers, not when there's no evidence to tie him to the case. I need to justify my actions."

Sadly, Daventry was right.

"Then wait in the carriage and have Flynn's coachman move around the corner. I'll deal with Berridge alone."

"You'll do something rash."

"I need to see Berridge, that's all." He needed to stare into the earl's soulless eyes to find the truth. "I'll know if he's guilty. He'll gloat if he thinks he's hurt me."

The butler appeared, returning the Home Secretary's letter. "His lordship is upstairs, resting. It's a difficult time. Contact his secretary."

And with that, he closed the door.

"A difficult time?" Aaron mocked. "Berridge doesn't know the meaning of hardship." He glanced at Daventry. "Wait for me in the carriage. I'll be a few minutes."

"Don't stoop to his level. Think with your head, not your heart."

"Have faith. I can't help Joanna from a gaol cell."

Muttering his reluctance, Daventry left.

Aaron waited beneath the portico until the carriage was out of sight, then hammered the brass knocker loud enough to wake the dead.

The flustered butler yanked open the door. "If you don't move, I will call a constable."

"I'll move."

Aaron barged into the hall, almost colliding with the bespectacled housekeeper, a sturdy woman in her fifties whose weary face looked vaguely familiar.

"His lordship is asleep in bed," she cried, raising her hands like she might perform a miracle, urging him back like Moses had the Red Sea. Her faith may have prevailed were she not fighting for the devil. "You need to leave, sir."

"You're a terrible liar," he said when Mrs Lowry, a name wholly unfamiliar, made the mistake of glancing at the drawing room door.

Two scrawny footmen, their black armbands stark against the green livery, arrived to throw Aaron out.

"Lay a hand on me, and you'll have assaulted the earl's heir and nephew. You know who I am." He had no intention of pleading to the King but enjoyed seeing the flare of panic in the footmen's eyes when they realised they were threatening Aaron Chance. "Touch me, and I have a reason to retaliate."

Aaron left the servants quivering. He stormed into the drawing room and found the grey-haired earl sitting in a chair, a plaid blanket draped over his lap, his gaze absent as he stared at the floor.

Aaron stood before him, cold fury filling his heart. The memory of the earl's hatred, the vile comments made to a boy, fuelled his temper. "You evil bastard. Villainy is in your blood. You lacked the strength to kill my father but think hurting women and children makes you a man."

Berridge looked up slowly, a sinister smile forming. "Have you come begging again, boy? Do you think expensive clothes and a clean face change anything? You'll always be a filthy delinquent. You'll always be your father's lackey. His brave little whipping boy."

The last remark cut deep, but Aaron remained stoic. "When you're dead, I shall take what is mine. I'll live in this house and dine at your table. While you rot in the ground, weeds will swamp your grave. Your memory will pale in my shadow."

"You killed my son," he said in a raspy voice.

That's when Aaron knew the earl was guilty.

That Berridge was the orchestrator of his downfall.

He would never get answers.

There would never be a truce.

One of them would die soon.

"Your son was selling forged bank plates and was killed by his accomplice. The culprit confessed to the murder and their criminal misdeeds. I had no part to play." Aaron stepped closer, gripping the arms of the chair and looming over the fool. "But I will bury you. The time for reckoning is nigh."

Aaron left before he did something stupid. But the visit had not been a waste of time. He knew Berridge must be using his servants to deliver messages. That the housekeeper slotted into the puzzle—a missing piece from the past. That if he wanted to save Joanna and his family, he had to kill the Earl of Berridge.

# Chapter Sixteen

*Southend-on-Sea*
*Essex*

Joanna stood, a lonely figure on the sandy beach, hugging herself against the biting November chill. The cold wind rolled off the sea like whispers of forgotten ghosts, whipping her hair and wrapping around her like a shroud of sorrow.

She looked at the expanse of blue sky, at the sun as low as her spirits, but nothing brought the same glow of contentment as being held in Aaron's arms. She missed him.

Had he arrived safely in London or fallen foul of the villain's trap and was dead on the roadside somewhere?

She hated not knowing.

Endless wondering was the bane of her existence.

Was her brother Justin dead? She had to believe he had perished, or she would not sleep at night. Was her father missing or merely hiding from his creditors? She was past caring.

One thought surpassed them all.

Would she ever see Aaron again?

She closed her eyes and tried to imagine the deep timbre of his voice, the warmth of his touch, the arousing scent of his skin. Yet the memories faded by the hour.

"McMillan wants us ready to sail at seven o'clock tonight," Sigmund said, coming to stand beside her on the sand. "Best eat early. It will be a rough crossing. I pray you've got sea legs. Mr Chance will murder me if you fall overboard."

She looked at Sigmund and forced a smile. He didn't want to visit Ostend any more than she did. "Mr Chance is lucky to have someone he trusts so implicitly. Have you known each other long?"

Sigmund stared at the sea. "Eleven years or thereabouts."

"So, just before he bought Fortune's Den."

"Aye, we beat each other black and blue the first night we met."

"You fought with him in the pits?" she said, eager to learn everything about the man who owned her heart. "Rumour is the men there are ruthless."

"Not the pits. It was an important fight at a fancy estate south of Bromley." Perhaps sensing she enjoyed talking about Aaron, Sigmund elaborated. "There were ten bouts. We were the last in the ring. Aaron was my opponent, but he was quicker than me and desperate to win the purse."

"Desperation and anger make a lethal combination."

Sigmund snorted. "He was angry, all right, snapped like a rabid terrier. He'd bite off your finger if you came too close."

Sadness filled Joanna's heart. She wished she had been there to comfort Aaron then, to tend to his bruises and bathe his wounds. To love him.

"Did he win?" She couldn't bear to think of him lying bruised and bloodied, feeling like he had failed his family.

"Aye, with a punch I didn't see coming."

She smiled. "He is rather skilled in the art of surprise." He had stolen into her heart and set up camp, making it his home now.

Sigmund didn't smile. A dark shadow passed over his rugged features. "The crowd were wicked that night. Nabobs wanting bloodsport. Men more brutal than any I've met on the streets. As it was the last fight, they jeered for Aaron to finish me off good and proper, like pompous Roman emperors giving a gladiator the thumbs down."

Joanna gasped. "They wanted Mr Chance to kill you?"

"To wedge his foot on my neck and crush my windpipe. I remember looking at him as they cried *kill*. One eye was the size of a ripe plum. Blood dripped from a cut on his lip, yet I saw a sad boy, not a fearless warrior."

Her heart raced like she was there. "What did he do?"

Sigmund smiled then. "He offered his hand and helped me to my feet. He marched over to the lord in charge and told him he would thrash anyone who tried to stop us leaving. Told him to shove his purse up his arse. Aaron Chance saved my life that day. It's a debt I can never repay."

Pride swelled in her chest. She considered saying fighting was a way to fill the coffers and that Aaron didn't want to hurt anyone, but that wasn't true.

"Why does he still fight if he doesn't need the money?"

Sigmund bent to pick up a shell off the sand. "You could not stop Aaron fighting any more than you could change the tides. It gives him the strength he lacked as a boy. The more people who think he's dangerous, the safer his family will be."

"Yet we're on a beach waiting to sail to Ostend. He's battling to keep everyone safe when the walls are closing in on him."

"I've every faith he'll win this fight, too." Sigmund reached for her hand and placed the shell in her palm. "You might wonder how something so fragile could survive the high seas. Like Aaron, it's strong enough to take a battering. Tougher than normal folk can comprehend."

"But Aaron has another side to his character." A loving side. A vulnerable side. A side so beautiful she could barely describe it in words.

Sigmund nodded. "Happen I've seen a gentler man of late. What's a shell if not proof things evolve?"

Joanna met his gaze. "It's comforting to know he's had you beside him all these years. You're a good friend, Sigmund."

"I'm his right hand when he needs one. I don't take charity—never have—and insist on earning my keep. I'd follow him to the ends of the earth if he asked."

"Or live with his colleague in Ostend," she said.

"We both know you're more than his colleague. He risked his neck to ride here this morning, though he knows I'd make sure everything went as planned."

Her body melted at the memory of how they had spent that precious hour. How he looked at her like she was an angel. How he lost himself in her body, filling her, pleasure alight in eyes that were often troubled.

"How can we help him? There must be something we can do." She had never felt so useless. "A way to lighten his burden."

"We can help him by staying safe and doing what we're told." Sigmund gathered his greatcoat across his broad chest.

"Best come inside now. The tide will be in soon. And he'll have my guts for garters if you catch a chill."

The thought of sitting for hours in The Ship's taproom filled her with dread. The endless weeks, months or years in Ostend would be unbearable, too.

Desperate to do something, she told Sigmund about Mr Daventry's idea to prompt her memory. "He said it's remarkable what one might recall when in a trance-like state. You must revisit the scene and find what isn't obvious."

"It's nonsense if you ask me," he said, trudging across the sand towards the esplanade. "The sort of gibberish spouted by crones at the fair."

"But what if I remember something important?" She raised her skirts and lumbered behind him. "One minor detail might be the key to unlocking the puzzle. Please, Sigmund. It's worth a try. You said you'd do anything for Aaron. I would rather exhaust every line of enquiry than desert him."

Sigmund glanced over his shoulder and sighed. "You know how to pick your words. Now I see why the most notorious man in London is falling over himself to please you. What do you want me to do?"

She smiled to herself. "Just guide me while I search through the memory of that night. Ask questions and note my responses. It's unlikely anything new will spring to mind, but I have to try."

Sigmund grumbled to himself. "Let's get it over with. We'll use the taproom at The Ship Inn. Best we stay close in case McMillan changes the plans. We might have to rent rooms if there's a storm brewing."

"We can sit on that bench." She pointed to the lonely wooden seat on the esplanade overlooking the beach. "I should be able to relax there."

Before Sigmund could protest, she hurried ahead, mounted the stone steps and took a seat. The sea stretched to the horizon, endless miles she had to cross, each one taking her farther away from everything she loved.

"Well?" Sigmund said, sitting down beside her. "I suppose you should close your eyes and breathe deeply."

"Yes, I suppose I should." Joanna clasped her hands in her lap, the tiny shell cradled between her palms, a reminder she was resilient, too, and would do anything for the man she loved. "I shall imagine myself back in the drawing room of The Burnished Jade. It may take a minute or two."

"Take your time. We've seven hours to spare."

Joanna closed her eyes and willed herself to think, but all she saw was a spectacular vision of Aaron, naked and rising above her on the bed. Mr Daventry mentioned looking through closed eyes at a forty-five-degree angle. That it left one relaxed and in a meditative state.

He was not wrong.

A warm tingling chased up her arms the second she raised her gaze. Strength seeped from her muscles as each one relaxed. She let her mind drift to the night of the murder, ignoring the wind and the whooshing sound of the sea.

Thirty people had crammed into her drawing room. More lingered in the hall, the library and the refreshment room. A few ladies hugged the wall. Miss Pardue found a seat in the corner and remained there all night.

The hum of laughter and lively chatter filled her head.

Familiar faces appeared in her mind's eye. Miss Moorland conversing with a gentleman, though her gaze sought every distraction. Miss Beckett proudly showing off her bruised knuckles as people laughed about Mr Parker's broken nose.

The smiles on her ladies' faces were as broad and bright as moonbeams.

"Where did it all go wrong?" she whispered.

She tried to relax and focus on searching for clues—an odd look or conversation, something ordinary yet out of place.

"I saw a group of men smoking in the street," Sigmund said, his soft voice belying his hulking physique. "Mr Chance sent me outside to look. He'd have moved them on if he thought they were trouble."

"I'm surprised he didn't have his nose pressed to the window," she said, smiling while keeping her eyes shut and holding on to the memories.

That's when she recalled looking out the drawing room window and chuckling because Miss Stowe's hired carriage blocked Aaron's view. Miss Stowe had alighted outside the tobacconist, yet Lucia asked the driver to park nearer the club.

"Madame Rossellini suffers with nerves. She hid in the carriage for fear of casting up her accounts. She asked the driver to park directly outside my premises in case she felt ill again."

Was the move a way of preventing Aaron from identifying the murderer? Was Lucia agitated, or did she have another reason to return to the carriage?

*Lucia can't be involved.*

The words entered her head yet left her examining the maid's behaviour that night. Innocent actions could easily be cunning steps in a strategic plan.

"Miss Stowe beckoned me to the hall." It was fifteen minutes before Lucia's recital. "Madame Rossellini wasn't sure she could perform and had requested five minutes alone upstairs to gather her composure."

What if Lucia was Venus?

What if she stole the dagger from Mrs Flavell and hid it in the bedchamber? Lucia wasn't the murderer because she was singing an aria to disguise the sounds of a scuffle. She was an accomplice. But who was she working for, and why would she help someone commit a heinous crime?

Had Lord Howard hurt the maid?

No. This was about hurting Aaron Chance.

This was a different sort of revenge.

"The villain has to be Lord Berridge," she uttered.

"Aye, but Berridge would get someone else to do his dirty work."

Perhaps someone Lucia spoke to that night.

The list was endless. Men surrounded her after her first performance, eager to be the first to bed the young singer, none keen to hear an encore. The women were in awe of her talent, though few dared to approach her. Only Miss Stowe and Miss Moorland knew Madame Rossellini was a maid.

Joanna watched as images moved into her field of vision. Someone spoke to Lucia in the hallway. A woman touched her arm and congratulated Lucia on her performance. They smiled at each other, but then Lucia glanced at the stairs.

"Madame Rossellini spoke to a woman. It looked like a friendly exchange, though I got the impression she found the attention overwhelming. Perhaps she wasn't overwhelmed but afraid. Perhaps she passed the woman a covert message."

"A message about what?" Sigmund said, curiously.

"To say she had hidden the dagger upstairs."

Joanna opened her eyes, her vision a little blurred while adjusting to the light, and relayed her thoughts to Sigmund. It was supposition, her mind making something out of nothing, creating a version that might not reflect reality.

Sigmund shifted on the bench. "Who was the woman?"

"She purchased a subscription two months ago. I believe she's in her late thirties, maybe older." She looked at Sigmund, needing to explain. "We accept ladies of all ages. They're often a stable influence on the younger ones."

Then another thought struck her.

One that made her stomach roil.

"If hurting Mr Chance is the motive, could the woman be a disgruntled mistress?" Someone he had cared about once but was reluctant to mention. "If I remember rightly, her name is Miss Goswell."

Sigmund surprised her by laughing. "A mistress? Happen you haven't been paying attention. Aaron was no saint in his youth, but since owning the Den, he's avoided female company."

"He said he's been alone for eight years."

It was hard to believe.

"He's been alone all his life. He's never had more than the odd dalliance. Other things have always taken priority." Sigmund cast her a knowing grin. "He's never loved a woman, if that's what you're asking. He put up a hard fight to stop loving you. It's the only battle he's ever lost."

Was Sigmund right? Did Aaron love her?

This morning, she'd caught the glow of affection in his eyes, felt it in every touch, in the whispered words alluding to the possibility.

*You have no idea how much you mean to me.*

*You'll live in my heart and mind always.*

Unshed tears stung the backs of Joanna's eyes. Aaron fought everyone's battles, and here she was, running away.

Who loved him enough to defend him? Who loved him enough to risk their life?

She did.

"I don't want to leave," she said, the ache in her heart unbearable. "This is wrong, Sigmund. I've never run from my troubles. I'm not foolish enough to believe justice will prevail, but I've never been a coward."

"It's not about being a coward. It's about giving Aaron time to find answers." Sigmund's tone darkened. "If anything happens to you, it will be a war to end all wars. He'll earn his seat at the devil's table."

Joanna suspected he was trying to frighten her into submission. But how could she live in ignorance when the man she loved suffered?

Lord Howard had assaulted *her*. He may have been responsible for her brother's death. And he had died on her premises. Threatening a patron was Aaron's only crime. Surely he'd warned other gamblers over the years, men who were still breathing. The only physical evidence against him amounted to an old watch and a Mughal dagger he couldn't have stolen.

"What if me leaving is part of the villain's plan?" she said, unable to shake the persistent dread. "What if angering Aaron plays into the devil's hands?"

Sigmund felt the same unease because he failed to settle her fears. "Happen Aaron knows that. Maybe he's hoping to lure the blackguard out."

Joanna stood, looking at the delicate shell before slipping it into her pelisse pocket. "I have risked my life for the Chance family. I tackled the lunatic who was about to shoot Delphine. I helped to confront the men stalking Theodore and injured one in the yard of The Saracen's Head."

"And Aaron loves you all the more for it."

"What is there to love? When he needs me most, I'm brooding on a bench at the beach, staring at the sea and scouring my mind for clues."

Sigmund hauled himself up. "Aaron needs his wits and can't think unless he knows you're safe. He made me promise to follow his orders."

Joanna firmed her tone. "You won't break that promise. Keeping me safe will be your priority. I will be the one who's failed to do what I'm told."

Sigmund scratched his head, confused. "You make it sound like you're not boarding the ship. That you've no intention of sailing to Ostend."

"I'm not." She steeled herself, waiting to defend her position.

"Thank the Lord." Sigmund chuckled. "I thought we were doomed to eat Flemish stew and dance the Polka."

Joanna laughed, then frowned. "You mean you won't try to stop me?"

"No. I've been waiting for you to come to your senses. Only a fool breaks an oath to Aaron Chance. He'll never trust me again if he thinks it was my idea."

She released a long exhale. "Then I insist you take me back to London. We need to reach town before the magistrate calls at eight."

"You'll need to twist my arm, quite hard, I suspect."

It would be impossible to hurt him physically.

She would have to play the shrew.

"If you don't agree, I'll run away and accept a ride from the first unsavoury gent with space in his carriage." Joanna raised her skirts. "You had better pray you're quick enough to catch me." She took to her heels, purely so neither of them had to lie to Aaron.

Sigmund was surprisingly fast for a burly man. Despite heaving for his next breath, he caught up with her in the yard of The Ship Inn.

"Forgive me," she said, slapping his face lightly and stamping on his foot. "Nothing you could say or do will make me change my mind."

A hoarse laugh escaped him. "We'll have a job finding transport home. Don't make me bind your wrists and hurl you over my shoulder."

"You brute," she teased. "Mr Chance won't be happy if you manhandle me."

"He'll kill me if he knows I've restrained you. Though I don't suppose it matters. I'm a dead man anyway."

# Chapter Seventeen

Tension clung to the air in the drawing room like a storm on the verge of breaking. Aaron's family sat rigid, their emotions hidden, no one daring to mention the grave situation.

The incessant ticking of the mantel clock heightened Aaron's unease. Soon, the magistrate would know Joanna had absconded. She would be a fugitive—a felon on the run, a wanted criminal—until he found Lord Howard's killer.

What if they caught her before then?

What if the truth eluded him forever?

A sharp knock echoed through the house. Their eyes met in silent dread, each of them straightening like they were on trial, each drawing shallow breaths.

The magistrate was early. Damn him. There were real criminals to apprehend. Why harass an innocent woman?

In Sigmund's absence, Aramis went to greet the caller. He returned, clutching an unsealed note. "It was a penny boy. Miss Bryant escaped without detection. I asked her to inform me once she arrived home safely."

Aaron gave a curt nod. "That's one less worry, I suppose."

Silence ensued.

Aramis settled into his seat, gently took his wife's hand and kissed it with quiet affection.

The loving gesture tightened the knot in Aaron's gut. Living without a woman's company was no hardship. Living without the woman he loved would be unbearable.

For the second time in his life, he considered letting his family fend for themselves. They were children when he first crept out of the house, leaving them sleeping. He walked thirty yards before guilt gripped him with hawk-like talons, the piercing pain in his heart forcing him to abandon the moment of madness and return to their room above Mrs Maloney's bookshop.

The situation was more complex now.

If only he could be in two places at once.

Another loud knock on the front door cut through the silence.

Aaron stood slowly, dread coiling in his gut. "Wait here. I'll deal with the magistrate. He will demand answers and a full explanation. Expect me home by dawn unless Berridge has another trick up his sleeve."

Delphine stood, her face etched with grief for a tragedy yet to occur. "I'll wait with you in the hall. You'll need someone to pretend to fetch Miss Lovelace."

*Joanna!*

Aaron prayed she was safe. She would be aboard the ship now, alive and free, not shackled in leg irons and shuffling towards the scaffold.

"Make it look convincing, like you believe she is resting upstairs. I don't want the magistrate thinking you had prior knowledge of my hare-brained plan."

It wasn't the magistrate banging on the door but Rothley.

Aaron had forgotten he'd told the marquess to call.

"You'll not evade my questions a second time." Rothley pushed past Aaron, whipping off his beaver hat like he meant to use it as a weapon. "You will tell me where I can find Joanna. What the hell is going on here?"

Aaron faced Rothley, unsure whether to trust him completely. "She's on a ship bound for France," he lied. "The magistrate will arrive shortly with a warrant for her arrest." He ignored the look of horror on Rothley's face. "I needed time to dispose of the threat. I'll not have her tried and hanged because Berridge paid a corrupt judge to hasten the process."

Sensing Rothley's mounting fury, Delphine said, "The evidence is enough for a jury to convict her of Lord Howard's murder. Mr Daventry said no one can save Miss Lovelace from the noose, my lord. Not even you."

"Did no one think to tell me?" Rothley bellowed.

"We've been busy trying to uncover the truth." Aaron explained the claims made against Joanna and what he had learned thus far. "Lucia is Venus. She had Parker steal the murder weapon, which she took with her to The Burnished Jade that night. Even a mediocre barrister could convince a jury the maid was working for Joanna."

Rothley drew his hand slowly down his face and groaned. "God, this is a damnable mess. You know what will happen if they find her."

"They won't."

"This is your fault," Rothley spat.

"It's not, but I accept Berridge used her to hurt me."

"I'll gut Berridge like a fish for this."

"As will I, but we cannot help Joanna from a cell in Newgate." Aaron's hands had been tied since the start of the investigation. Killing Lord Howard was a cunning move, almost too clever for a weasel like Berridge. "We need to know how Berridge persuaded Lucia to be his accomplice. Howard must have told her what he did to Joanna."

"And Lucia told Lord Berridge," Delphine said, looking at Rothley. "My lord, the letters sent to you and the police office were written by the same person, though Christian believes a woman wrote them."

"Can the maid even write?" Rothley scoffed. "I suppose we could ask her if your brother hadn't let her escape."

Quick to defuse the tension, Delphine gestured to the drawing room. "I would appreciate your help on a matter. A few ladies mentioned in Miss Lovelace's ledger are unfamiliar. You may help to identify them."

Rothley might have agreed had the front door not burst open.

Baptiste hurried into the hallway, shivering from the cold. With a trembling hand, the Frenchman offered Aaron a foxed receipt. "It is a copy of the sale docket from the auction house," Baptiste said, his teeth chattering. "To prevent the sale of stolen goods, the clerk keeps records of all items bought by the nobility."

Aaron studied the docket and grinned. "Excellent work." He patted Baptiste on the back. "Pour a large brandy and warm yourself by the fire."

Baptiste didn't linger in the chilly hall.

Aaron showed Rothley the receipt. "Berridge bought my father's watch all those years ago. No doubt he wanted a trophy. Now, he must account for its whereabouts."

"It's a small move in the right direction," Rothley said, slightly appeased. "According to my sources, Fitzpatrick offered Howard a thousand pounds to ruin his sister. Howard was supposed to lure the girl upstairs and have someone catch them in the act." A muscle twitched in Rothley's cheek. "It's obvious that's why Howard was at The Burnished Jade that night."

"And it gives someone else a motive," Aaron said, refusing to count his blessings just yet. "Though I doubt Miss Fitzpatrick is the killer, either."

"Then we must find more evidence."

"I have a man watching Berridge's house." Aaron had given the fellow new instructions upon leaving the earl's home today. "I've told him to watch the servants, the house-keeper, in particular."

Aaron had seen her somewhere before.

He fell silent while trying to recall where.

The housekeeper had been much younger, her hair dark, not grey, her face thinner, gaunt even. And she had not worn spectacles. He was certain it was the same woman—a dreaded ghost from his past.

Rothley made to speak, but Aaron raised a stalling hand.

Who was she?

The answer danced in his mind, a fraction out of reach.

A loud rap on the front door jolted Aaron from his musings. The sound came just before the hall clock chimed the dreaded hour.

Aaron swallowed past the lump in his throat. "If they arrest me, I need you to free me from gaol," he told Rothley. "You'll work with my brothers to—"

"And with me," Delphine added. "We will all work to uncover the truth, Aaron. You have our word. We will do it for Miss Lovelace, too."

"Yes," Rothley agreed, ignoring the second knock on the

door. "I'll not spend my life plagued by more unanswered questions."

Aaron gathered himself and opened the door.

Daventry looked nervous as he ushered the magistrate, Mr Harriott, into the hall of Fortune's Den. They were surprised to see the Marquess of Rothley, who barked orders, demanding someone better prove two innocent people were being framed for murder.

Mr Harriott, a short tubby man with hair as thin as his patience, gripped the warrant. "We need Miss Lovelace to come to the Thames Police Office to answer some questions," he said eloquently. "You should come, too, Mr Chance. It will save time, and we need your statement."

"I gave you a statement on the night of the murder."

"New evidence has come to light."

Aaron sent Delphine to fetch Miss Lovelace.

While they waited, Rothley mentioned Miss Fitzpatrick's motive. Thankfully, he did not say Lucia was Venus. "Chance has proof Berridge purchased his father's watch from the auctioneers. How blind can you be? Berridge has been making threats for years. He wants retribution for his son's death. He's making a laughingstock of you all."

Nervous about challenging a marquess, Harriott said, "I have no option but to follow procedure. All suspects must answer the claims made against them. The evidence is compelling."

"You do have a choice," Daventry said, deciding to risk his reputation. "You could delay questioning them for a few days. They're obviously making progress. And I disagree with your opinion of the evidence. You've based the hypothesis on anonymous letters with no clue as to the sender's identity."

Harriott argued the point. "The fact remains, Miss Lovelace knew the man who was murdered on her premises. I need to question her about her motive."

"Question her or arrest her?" Aaron countered.

Harriott shifted nervously. "Arrest her on suspicion of murder. She will have legal representation. There's time to determine whether the letters are legitimate."

Aaron lost his temper. "Why is she even a suspect? Twenty reliable witnesses corroborate her story and place her in the drawing room when the murder took place. Speak to the coroner. Howard was stabbed with some force."

"The coroner agrees a woman may have delivered the lethal blow."

"May have?" Aaron scoffed. Whether fighting with fists or logic, it was important to win the point. "Question all ladies present that night. You must admit, the letter arrived at a convenient time."

"Well, yes," the magistrate said, wavering.

"Release her into my custody." Rothley spoke with an aristocrat's aplomb. "I will act as surety while we gather more evidence to support their claims. Based on Mr Chance's history with Lord Berridge, you must accept this all seems rather suspicious. No man wants to look a fool in front of his superiors, Harriott."

A sudden sense of inadequacy weighed heavily on Aaron's shoulders. A weakness he had not felt since he was a boy. He could kill with his bare hands and had money to do as he pleased. Yet, in the eyes of the law and society, he remained insignificant. A mere mister held no sway. He couldn't use his title as a weapon to bend people to his will.

Rothley was more powerful.

The fact left Aaron facing a startling truth.

Men did what he said because he owned their debts, and they were terrified. Without the club, he lacked the means of controlling the lofty lords. And what if he lost a limb and couldn't fight?

Delphine returned. "I knocked twice, but she's not answering."

"Try again," Aaron said, stalling. "She might be sleeping. Try the other bedchambers. She complained the upper floor was cold."

The entire house was cold. It was November, for heaven's sake. But Joanna had used it as an excuse to draw him out of the dark and force him to express his feelings.

Delphine nodded and hurried upstairs.

To buy time, Aaron told the magistrate what he knew about the murder weapon. "It was stolen from Mrs Flavell's home in Grosvenor Place. She will confirm Miss Lovelace attended her first function this week to gather evidence and couldn't have stolen the dagger."

The magistrate came to the wrong conclusion. "An attractive woman living alone will doubtless have a lover. He may have stolen the weapon."

"Miss Lovelace is not that sort of woman," Aaron snapped.

"What sort of woman?" came a feminine voice behind him.

Daventry's eyes widened. "Miss Lovelace. Good evening."

*Miss Lovelace?*

Aaron's heart stopped beating. He turned slowly, fear forming a lump in his throat. Their eyes met, and the sudden ache in his chest was overwhelming. "Miss Lovelace. There you are."

*What the hell are you doing here?* he wanted to yell.

Rothley looked furious.

While Aaron was a maelstrom of conflicting emotions.

She smiled like she didn't have a worry in the world. "I was out in the yard, taking some air, and didn't realise it was eight o'clock." She brushed dust off her blue pelisse and patted her hair. "It's a little windy out tonight."

Feeling the pressure of their relentless questions, the magistrate gestured to the door. "As you're dressed for an outing, it's best we leave now."

"She's not going anywhere." Aaron noticed Sigmund lingering behind Joanna and hit him with a stare hot enough to sear his soul. "I request a few days grace. Rothley will act as surety. Miss Lovelace is not a flight risk. If she were guilty, she would have escaped over the yard wall."

"I will assist with the investigation," Daventry assured the magistrate. "I'll ensure your office shares the credit if we catch the killer."

The magistrate considered their proposal.

Joanna stepped forward. Her clothes smelled of musty seats and road dust, not sweet like roses. Still, Aaron's muscles firmed with the need to carry her upstairs and make love to her until dawn. Which is precisely what he would do once they'd got rid of the magistrate.

"With Sigmund's help, I remembered a few pertinent points about the night at The Jade," she said, admitting to seeing Miss Goswell creeping upstairs. "She's a spinster who joined the club recently, though no one knew her. Despite her pleasing countenance, none of the men recognised her, either."

"I know most people in society," Rothley said when

Joanna gave a brief description. "I don't know anyone named Miss Goswell."

Daventry turned to the magistrate. "Perhaps your men could interview Howard's staff and see if they know her. Maybe ask at his club. With Miss Lovelace's help, I'll question her guests." He paused. "Shall we agree to meet in my office at noon on Saturday and compare notes?"

A heavy silence followed.

Daventry sweetened the deal. "I will ensure we have the Home Secretary's full support, though you must lift the imposed curfew."

With a persuasive nudge from Rothley, the magistrate conceded. "You have until noon on Saturday. If no further evidence comes to light, I will speak to Miss Lovelace at the Thames office."

Everyone agreed.

Aaron showed the magistrate out.

Anger simmered. He had never relied on other men to solve his problems. He had never stood mute and left his fate in other men's hands. As God was his witness, it wouldn't happen again.

He faced Daventry and Rothley. "Call in the morning at ten. We'll decide what to do from there. My brothers will assist us."

The men nodded and lingered, as if expecting the offer of brandy.

"I would invite you to stay," Aaron said, glancing at Joanna, "But my attention is needed elsewhere."

That's when Delphine reappeared, grinning at Miss Lovelace before returning to the drawing room. Daventry and Rothley left. The slam of the front door was Aaron's cue to berate Sigmund.

"You vowed to protect her," he said, glaring.

"He *has* protected me," Joanna countered.

Sigmund raised his hands in mock surrender. "I didn't think you'd want me restraining her or giving her a hefty dose of laudanum. But she ran like the clappers, then attacked me in the yard."

"She attacked you?" Aaron gazed at his slender lover and then at his burly friend. "Is this a joke to rile my temper?"

Joanna straightened her spine. "I hit him in the face and stamped on his foot. There was a brief tussle."

"And that crippled the best pugilist I know?"

"She threatened to climb into a rakehell's carriage," came the next excuse in Sigmund's ludicrous defence.

"Do rakehells frequent Southend in November?" Aaron suppressed a grin as he imagined poor Sigmund trying to tame a vixen. "Did you suffer more distress at Miss Lovelace's hands? Is there anything else to confess?"

Sigmund averted his gaze. "I had to grab her bottom as I pushed her over the wall. Happen I caught sight of her ripped stockings, too."

"You didn't think to knock on the door and summon me?"

"Oh, for heaven's sake." Joanna barged in front of Sigmund and braced her hands on her hips. "Sigmund is not to blame. Shout at me if it makes you feel better. I insisted on returning home because I love you." She prodded him in the chest. "I'm so in love with you, I would rather face the noose than let you fight this battle alone."

The hum of conversation in the drawing room died.

Aaron tried to breathe because it felt like his heart might burst through his chest. He'd been afraid to say what he'd uttered silently for so long. Yet here was the woman he adored, voicing her feelings proudly.

"We'll continue this conversation elsewhere," he said, pointing to the staircase.

Their eyes met, and she read his thoughts.

She raised her skirts and marched upstairs.

"Go pour yourself a brandy," he said, patting Sigmund's chest before mounting the stairs behind Joanna, and following her into his bedchamber.

"Of all the foolish things," he said, slamming the door.

"Is it foolish to love someone?"

Aaron tore off his coat and threw it on the chair. "Are you trying to kill me? Do you want me to die of apoplexy?"

She began unbuttoning her pelisse. "I don't want you to die at all. That's why I came home. To be with you."

He closed his eyes as a wave of love for her washed over him. "Against my strict orders?" he said, desire for her cooling his temper.

"You don't own me."

"I will as soon as we're out of these clothes."

The hitch in her breath said she wanted him just as badly. "Then perhaps we might hasten the process."

He watched her fiddle with the buttons on her dress. "Just rip the damn things. That dress is fit for the bonfire." His waistcoat and shirt hit the floor. "I'll buy you a wardrobe of new clothes."

Longing burned in her eyes as she gazed at his bare chest. "Have you been sparring in the basement?"

"Sparring? I've been running around town like a hapless fool, trying to prove you're innocent." With a quick yank, his shoes were off and they landed somewhere near the bed. "Lucia is Venus." He would explain everything later. "She's disappeared, though I couldn't tell the magistrate because he already thinks you're in cahoots with her."

"What? But Lucia is too meek to play the coquette."

Slipping the last button on his trousers, he pushed the garment past his hips. His manhood hung between his legs, thick and heavy, but the sight of Joanna rolling down her stockings stiffened his cock in seconds.

"The best actresses know how to fool people."

"I think Lucia stole the dagger and hid it upstairs in my club. I think she moved the carriage to block your view of the entrance." She paused, petticoat half-raised, and admired his engorged flesh. "You have a body made for sin. After an hour of passionate lovemaking this morning, what made you think I could ever stay away?"

"It would have killed me, too," he said, closing the gap between them and helping her undress. "But I'm used to making sacrifices. Why would I risk your life for selfish reasons? That's not love."

She stared as he drew her chemise over her head.

"What is love for you, Aaron?" she said, smoothing her hands over his chest. "Is it that the heat of my skin sets you on fire? Is it the gnawing ache when you see me, the one that never goes away?"

"It's that and more." He bent his head, grazing his mouth over hers, moving along her jaw to the sweet spot below her ear. "It's everything about you," he whispered. "I'm in love with you. I feel like I've always been in love with you."

Something about those words stoked the flames of their desire. He was suddenly kissing her neck, inhaling the scent of her skin, gripping her hips.

"There's nothing more romantic than a man who makes sacrifices for a woman," she breathed, tilting her head to give him unrestricted access. "But I'd rather you were selfish. I'd rather you take me to bed and show me why I'm right to risk my life, why there's nowhere I belong but in your arms."

With a growl of hunger, he carried her to bed.

"How many ways will you have me tonight?" she teased.

He wanted her in every way possible, wanted to use his tongue and his cock to brand her. Wanted to devour every inch of her porcelain skin. To breathe her in so she consumed him.

"Only one way," he said, rising above her and nudging her legs open. "I want to look at you and feel your skin pressed to mine. Tonight isn't about gratification. It's about the incredible bond neither of us ever expected to feel."

She gazed up at him as he settled between her thighs. "I love you."

Hell, he felt like the richest of men. "I love you. More than I can express in words." He claimed her mouth in a searing kiss that had her wrapping her thighs around him and grinding against his erection.

"I want you inside me, Aaron." A haze of desire darkened her blue eyes. "Don't wait. We have hours to indulge in other pleasures."

"I need to go on a short journey first."

"A journey? Where?"

"To paradise," he teased, moving down between her legs, impatient to sate his hunger. "I intend to devour every inch of you." He hooked his arms under her legs and pulled her closer.

The scent of her arousal was more potent than the smoke in a demimonde opium den. He hissed sharply before slipping his tongue through her pretty pink folds.

"Aaron!" She arched her back, rolling her hips in time to every deep suck and circle of her bud. "Don't stop."

He buried his face in her sex, indulging in an erotic, open-mouthed kiss. She came apart when he entered her with his tongue, her body shuddering as she came hard.

Aaron rose above her, taking his cock in hand. "Say you want me, love."

"I want you so badly, I can barely breathe."

He pushed into her body, her wet heat hugging him as he stretched her wide and buried himself to the hilt. He looked down at her, this beautiful woman who had changed his life, an all-consuming blaze of affection stealing his breath.

Then he moved, sliding in and out of her, a slow, hypnotic kind of lovemaking. Hot. Intense. Each thrust measured to bring ultimate stimulation.

Joanna ran her hands over his tense biceps, over the taut muscles in his back, every caress drawing his ballocks tighter, sending his pulse soaring.

He liked the way she panted as she took him deep.

He liked her muttered moans of appreciation.

This was love.

A bond too strong to break.

She climaxed again, her muscles milking his cock. The primal urge to pound hard had him quickening the pace, sinking into her so fast the bed creaked beneath them. He wanted to spend inside her, pour everything of himself into her.

"God, you have no idea how much I love you," he cried.

He didn't care who heard them as he raced towards release. He didn't care that his guttural groan rang through the room as he came violently over her abdomen.

Nothing mattered but knowing Joanna loved him.

# Chapter Eighteen

Joanna couldn't sleep. She lay in Aaron's warm arms, absently stroking his chest and listening to the patter of rain on the windowpane. She had spent the last hour counting her blessings, not sheep. While her life had crumbled around her like a neglected ruin, she had fallen in love.

Deeply in love.

Her heart skipped a beat when she looked at him. A lock of ebony hair hung rakishly over his brow. Long, dark lashes rested against his cheeks. The soft, steady murmur of his breath spoke of a man in peaceful repose, not one plagued by demons.

Love was like medicine. A means to mend a damaged heart.

It was a lot like opium, too.

The need for more, a sweet form of addiction.

She cast her gaze around the room, feeling content.

Everything about Aaron's bedchamber—a masculine space befitting the owner of a notorious gaming hell—reminded her of him. The rich mahogany panels spoke of brooding elegance. Thick velvet curtains hid the world beyond, hinting at the private man no one knew.

*You only know one part of me,* he had said.

It was a warning. A warning to guard her heart and keep her distance. But it was too late. She wanted him in every way a woman wanted a man—as a friend and lover, her husband and father of her children. A lifelong companion.

The real question was: could she be his lover indefinitely? Could she accept not being his wife and never having a family?

Because one fact remained.

If they married, he would protect her with his life.

No one would be more important.

"A penny for your thoughts," he said, his voice husky from sleep. "I can almost hear the cogs whirring."

She ran her hand over the hard ridges of his abdomen. "It's nothing. I was contemplating the road ahead, though one would think I'd be used to dealing with uncertainties."

He trailed his fingers over her upper arm in featherlike strokes. "Once we've dealt with the threat, I'll hire an investigator to find your father," he said, mistaking the cause of her anxiety. "I'll pay Daventry to help determine what happened to your brother."

Did he think Gabriel had left a stone unturned?

The marquess had spent ten years searching for the truth.

"Justin is dead. His body is interred at St Michael's churchyard."

"Then why the confusion? Rothley is adamant he's alive."

She didn't want to dredge up the ghosts of the past. If Justin was alive, he didn't want to be found. "We were unable to identify his body. The coroner based the decision on his hair and clothes, height and build. There was evidence to suggest he had met someone. He was found at a secret hideout deep in the woods."

Aaron was quiet for a moment. He pressed a tender kiss to her hair and said, "I'm sorry. I can imagine how painful losing a sibling must be."

She tried not to think about it.

She tried not to think about a lot of things.

An unmarried woman could not afford to grieve or dwell on what might have been. Nor could she place her life on hold to focus on suspicions.

"When we're no longer suspects in a murder enquiry, I would like to have a funeral and lay a proper headstone." Perhaps it would bring her closure and help Gabriel to focus on the future, too. "Justin was committed to the ground, but my father couldn't bear to say goodbye."

"I'll make the arrangements." Aaron pulled her closer to his hard body, the heat of his skin chasing the chill of sadness away. "I'll do whatever brings you the peace you deserve."

She rolled on top of him, eager for love in any form. "Perhaps you might bring me peace now, Aaron. I need a distraction from these maudlin thoughts."

With mischief in his eyes, he gave a sinful grin. "Is this distraction enough?" He gripped her buttocks, his fingers sinking into her soft flesh while gliding her back and forth over his growing erection. "Straddle me."

He didn't need to ask twice.

He was inside her in a heartbeat.

Buried so deep, she arched her back and sighed sweetly.

Trust Sigmund to choose that moment to rap lightly on the door.

Aaron stilled. "What the hell is it?"

Sigmund cleared his throat and called from the corridor,

"There's a young lady here to see Miss Lovelace. She's waiting in the study, said it's important. Said her name is Miss Stowe."

"Can she not return in the morning?"

"Happen she wouldn't have come if it could wait."

Joanna leant forward and kissed Aaron's lips. "I asked for a distraction, and the Lord answered my prayer."

"We both know you had something else in mind."

"We'll finish this later." She smiled, but a sudden pang in her chest said nothing in her life was guaranteed. Happiness might be stolen from her at a moment's notice. "I'll be right down, Sigmund."

Aaron sat up, wrapping his arms around her waist and flipping her onto her back. He was still inside her, as if sensing another goodbye was imminent.

"Don't go. Don't leave this room. Not tonight."

She cupped his cheek. "Why? What are you afraid of?"

"Nothing," he hissed. "Everything."

The admission was a milestone in their relationship. The fears one buried as a child were never far from the surface. They informed every decision one made.

"We can control some things," she said, stroking his back, "but we cannot control fate." Knowing she could not reason with him, she revealed her own method of coping. "Have you ever wondered why we all walk different paths? Why some people suffer more than others?"

"Every damn day," he growled.

"What if we all chose a lesson to learn? What if everything in our life happens to ensure we receive an education?"

"I must have chosen more than one," he said bitterly.

"Not necessarily. Your whole life has been marred by fear. Fear of being physically hurt. Fear of failure. A fear of being poor and unable to protect your family. You're afraid of what will happen to them if you put your own needs first." She wrapped her legs tightly around him, holding him inside her even though his manhood had grown flaccid. "You will always live with secret fears until you master the emotion."

Aaron wasn't angry with the world.

He was afraid of all the ways it might hurt him.

He stared at her, his annoyance tinged with a glimmer of fascination. "Perhaps fear is a demon, one too strong for a mortal man to slay."

"We might debate the theory later." She released him and urged him to help her up so they might dress quickly. "Miss Stowe has come about Lucia. Either to assist us or accuse us of tormenting her helpless maid. She might have information we need or may have helped Lucia board a ship to Naples."

Aaron stood, his body glorious, his expression grave. "Let's pray it's not the latter. Getting the truth from that woman is our only hope of freedom."

They found Miss Stowe pacing the floor in the candlelit study, wringing her hands and sniffing back tears. When she saw Joanna, she flew across the room.

"Can you ever forgive me?" Miss Stowe gripped Joanna's hands like her life depended on it. "Lucia has fooled us both. Tricked us into believing her sad little tale."

"She told a convincing story," Joanna reassured Miss Stowe.

"It's all a lie. Her mother isn't dead but living in Lambeth.

I doubt she's even Italian." Miss Stowe's hands shook as she caught her breath and rummaged in her reticule. She tugged crumpled notes from the velvet bag and thrust them at Joanna. "I found these in her room. After Mr Daventry came to tell me what happened, I ripped the place apart."

Joanna glanced at Aaron, guilt rising in her chest. Initially, he had been suspicious of the maid, but she had convinced him otherwise.

*Lucia is not Venus*, she had protested.

In truth, no one knew who Lucia was.

Aaron stepped forward and asked to read the letters. He did not say, "You fool, Joanna," or berate her for trusting a maid. He did not use those he loved to prove a point or bolster his self-worth.

"Lucia is perhaps the most convincing liar I have ever met," he said, taking a plaid blanket from the leather chair and draping it around Joanna's shoulders. "I trust you're warm enough, Miss Stowe."

The lady gathered herself. "Yes, thank you, Mr Chance."

"Let's sit and try to understand what we're dealing with." Aaron gestured to the chairs facing his desk. He didn't perch on his throne but pulled up a seat and settled beside them. "Where did you find the notes?"

"Hidden inside her spare boots."

How odd. They had searched Lucia's room the night they found her wandering around Mrs Flavell's garden.

"We scoured the room and found nothing," Aaron said calmly before unravelling one note and reading the missive. He handed it to Joanna. "I need you to think, Miss Stowe. Has Lucia ever had another servant visit her? An older woman? Someone she confessed to knowing from a previous position?"

While Miss Stowe thought, Joanna read the penned words. It was a simple message, an invitation for Lucia to dine with the woman on Sunday. It was signed *your loving mother*, but that's not what shocked Joanna most.

"The person who wrote this note also wrote to Gabriel." Joanna pointed to the letters' curling tails. "The writing bears the same exaggerated flicks and sweeps that give it a distinctive flare."

Aaron agreed as he read the other notes. "It's a woman's writing, someone educated, not a servant or a mother whose child might work in service."

"Lucia often met a woman at the market," Miss Stowe said. "A servant she worked with at Lord Hutton's house."

Aaron sighed. "I doubt she worked there. I called today. Lord Hutton doesn't remember her, and neither does the housekeeper."

"Oh." Miss Stowe hung her head.

"How convenient of the sender to mention her new address in Lambeth," Aaron mocked, slipping that note into his trouser pocket. "It's a trap to lure me there. Every move I've made has played into this devil's hands."

"Who is she?" Joanna said, her voice breaking because this person had one goal in mind. To destroy the Chance family.

He shrugged. "The wife of a man who lost his fortune at the tables. Someone who blames me for her husband's addiction and is in cahoots with the Earl of Berridge. Someone clever enough to have me chasing my tail."

Fear crept into Joanna's heart, filling every chamber like a frigid morning mist. "We should hire an enquiry agent to check the address. Have a man watch the premises."

"There's no time." Aaron stood abruptly upon hearing the

upstairs board creak. He glanced at the ceiling and lowered his voice. "I mean to play the game and visit Lambeth tonight. I don't want my brothers to know I've left the house."

"But it's almost midnight."

"I expect Lucia and this mystery woman will be waiting."

A sudden knock on the door brought Aramis, who cut a commanding figure despite him wearing nothing but trousers and a loose white shirt. "I heard a commotion." He stared at Miss Stowe and frowned. "I trust all is well."

Aaron nodded. "Miss Stowe found a few notes in Lucia's room. The maid corresponded with someone who knew she wasn't an orphan of Italian descent. Daventry will be interested in the handwriting."

"It bears similarities to the other letters sent," Joanna said.

Aaron gave Aramis the note he held. "It's from Lucia's mother, though she told Miss Stowe her parents died on the ship from Naples. It proves she lied and is working with Howard's killer."

Miss Stowe sniffed. "How could I have been so blind?"

Joanna tried to ease her guilt. "Kindness is not a weakness. Lucia is the only one who should be ashamed."

Aramis studied the elegant script. "Yes, I would say it's identical to the other letters in your desk. Though until we find the maid, we can't prove anything."

Aaron stifled a yawn. "It's late. We can discuss it at the family meeting in the morning. We need a plan of action. We need answers before the magistrate loses patience."

"A plan that involves your brothers helping you," Aramis stated.

"We've been over this a hundred times."

"I demand we discuss it again."

"Tomorrow."

"We're men now," Aramis complained, perhaps glad of an audience because it meant Aaron had to control his temper. "How long do you intend to keep treating us like children?"

Aaron jerked like he had been hit with an arrow. Despite everything he had sacrificed for his family, he wore the pain of failure in his strained expression. "I wasn't aware my concern for your safety grieved you."

"You're twisting my words," Aramis said through a strained sigh. "I would like to fight for this family, too, but you rule with an iron fist. Let me help you."

Aaron nodded. "We'll discuss it tomorrow. It's been a long day, and I must ensure Miss Stowe arrives home safely. Send Sigmund in on your way out."

It was Aramis' cue to leave.

He did so, calling his brother a stubborn ass.

Sigmund came to the study, but Aaron ushered him out onto Aldgate Street so they might speak privately. He returned to inform Miss Stowe there was a hackney waiting to take her home.

"If Lucia returns, you must call a constable." Joanna hugged Miss Stowe, offering a warm smile when every cell in her body feared what Aaron planned to do. "I'll visit you tomorrow and inform you of our progress."

Miss Stowe left with Sigmund.

"It's bitterly cold tonight," Aaron said, pulling the blanket tighter across Joanna's chest. "Wait for me in bed until I return."

Joanna ripped the blanket off her shoulders and threw it onto the chair. "I'm coming with you to Lambeth. I'll wake the whole house if you refuse."

He exhaled calmly, which proved more unnerving than

his blunt retorts. "I'm walking into a trap and need to go alone." He tucked her hair behind her ear and kissed her so deeply it was like he had slipped beneath her skin.

"You can't bribe me with a kiss."

"I can't fight if I'm worried about you. Stay here. Please, Joanna."

She laid her palms on his chest. "I'm in love with you, Aaron. I'll not sit here, mindless with worry. Besides, if it is a trap, they won't be expecting me."

He remained silent.

"Trust all will be well." She alluded to their earlier conversation about being ruled by fear. "Believe we're living the life we're meant to, regardless of what happens tonight."

His smile was tepid at best. "That's easy to say, but nothing scares me more than venturing into unknown territory."

"I can think of something. If I'm left here to worry, I might nibble off my fingers. Then I'll never be able to touch you again."

His broad grin spoke of surrender. "You're right. That would be terrifying."

The address in Lambeth led them to a modest terraced house a stone's throw from Searle's Boat Yard and Astley's Amphitheatre. Light shone from the single downstairs window of 2 Stangate Street while darkness shrouded the row.

The night carried the threat of winter, a biting wind

rolling off the Thames, bringing with it the pungent stench of the river. The rank smell of decay was like an omen, a stark reminder that nothing lasted forever.

Seated inside the hired hackney coach, Aaron reached for Joanna's ungloved hands and rubbed them warm. "You should have stayed at home. You'll catch your death tonight. The cold cuts through the air like a sabre."

"We're in this together," she said, letting him feel the flick of her temper. "I'm not leaving you alone to deal with Lucia. Besides, I know you. You're happy to brawl with men but would not hurt a woman."

She was right.

It's why he agreed she could accompany him to Lambeth.

Aaron removed his coat and draped it around Joanna's shoulders. "You'll wear this. I'll not take no for an answer. Keep the blanket for your legs."

She'd spent the journey on his lap, the blanket wrapped around them both. They had not kissed but held each other tightly, keeping the chill at bay.

"I should have fetched your coat and gloves," he complained.

"Had we not crept out of Fortune's Den when we did, we'd be part of an entourage. Every member of your family would have followed us." She thrust her arms into the sleeves of his coat, letting him fasten the buttons. "I'm used to the cold. My father went missing the week before Christmas once and didn't come home until New Year. There wasn't a spare shilling in the house."

Aaron cursed the man to Hades. He prayed Arthur Lovelace never returned, or he would have to teach the wastrel a hard lesson.

"There's a flask of brandy in my coat pocket. A swift nip

will warm your bones. It's my emergency supply. I took it from the desk drawer before we left."

Joanna wrinkled her nose. "What sort of emergency would prevent you from walking six feet to the drinks table?"

"You have a habit of gazing out the window while wearing your nightdress." A vision of loveliness flashed through his mind. Her hair a cascade of golden waves around her shoulders. Her skin smooth and pale as fine porcelain. "The sight of you leaves me rigid in my seat. I need a dram to settle my pulse."

She narrowed her gaze like she didn't believe him. "Teasing me won't solve our problems. I get the sense you're stalling." She placed her hand on his leg, stroking his thigh. "I don't want our love affair to end. I don't want to lose you, Aaron, but we need answers before it's too late."

A desire for the truth burned inside him like wildfire.

It was as simple as arresting Lucia and her mother and using them to seal his uncle's fate. But he was avoiding a confrontation.

Everything would change once they'd solved the case. From a front-row seat, Joanna would watch him fight and realise he was a brute, not the man she loved. She would return to her club, unwilling to trade her independence for a dying dream.

The pain would cripple him.

Perhaps even finish him for good.

"Very well," he said, wishing they were both on the boat to Belgium, not lingering in Lambeth on a dreary night. "But keep your blind down. No peering outside. Hired thugs may be watching the vehicle. If I'm forced to alight, I don't want them to know you're here." A chill of foreboding crawled over his shoulders. "I'll not lose you tonight."

"This won't be the end of us," she said with such conviction he almost believed it. "How can it be? I need to learn how to trust a man implicitly. You need to stop expecting the worst."

"How can I when there's so much at stake?"

Aaron called to the jarvey he'd paid to comply, instructing him to rouse the occupants and bring them to the carriage. "Ask for Lucia," he said, lowering the window when the driver climbed down from his box. "Say I'm alone in the vehicle but refuse to enter the house."

"Right you are, sir."

Aaron would not risk walking into a trap.

Nor would he leave Joanna alone in a hired hackney.

The jarvey trudged up to the front door and knocked.

Aaron knew someone would answer. They were expecting him. This was a carefully laid plan which made him question his own stupidity. A woman could fire a pistol. Two could throw a dead man into the Thames. A brick tied to the ankle might keep him submerged for days.

A woman did answer the door, but it wasn't Lucia.

Aaron peered through the darkness, but it was impossible to identify her. Perhaps they had the wrong house. What if the plan was to have him leave Fortune's Den? To ensure he was the last brother standing?

His heart thundered, the rapid beat pounding in his throat. "I warned Sigmund to keep the doors locked and watch the street in my absence." He held his head in his hands. "What if coming here is a mistake?"

Joanna tapped his arm. "It's not a mistake. The women are leaving the house and following the jarvey. I see Lucia. The other person must be her mother."

Aaron looked up as the jarvey opened the door, and the

two women climbed into the vehicle. They fell into the seat opposite, looking like terrified victims, not murderous villains.

"Keep your hands on your laps where I can see them." Aaron glared at Mrs Lowry, his uncle's bespectacled housekeeper. "How the hell do I know you? We've met before. Years ago."

"I beg you not to shout, sir," Lucia said in her faint Italian accent. "It is not our fault. We had no choice but to follow orders."

"Stop this charade," Joanna countered. "You're not Italian and didn't come here on a boat from Naples. The earl forced you and your mother to kill a man in cold blood. You could have come to Mr Chance for help instead of plotting his demise."

Lucia started sobbing so hard she couldn't speak.

"She's just a young girl," Mrs Lowry said, reaching for Lucia's hand. "Only recently turned sixteen. She wanted no part in this but had no choice."

Timid Lucia looked sixteen.

Dressed as Venus in a mask, she looked twenty-three.

"A mother is supposed to protect her child," Joanna said.

"I'm not her mother, miss. I only wish I were."

Confusion kept Aaron's temper at bay. "Then how do you know Lucia? How do you know me? What is this about?"

Mrs Lowry removed her misty spectacles and wiped them with a handkerchief. "I was employed at your father's house in Hill Street. Started as a scullery maid and worked my way up to ladies' maid. Sadly, the years abroad have taken their toll."

Abroad?

Aaron stared at her, a bitter taste in his mouth because the past was like poison. "Did you work at Hill Street when my mother was alive?"

A vague memory of his mother slid into his mind, a smiling face, a glimmer of sunlight catching her ebony hair. He had never dared ask his father to describe her in greater detail, partly because Ignatius Chance remarried within months. Aaron remembered Christian and Theo's mother because he was nine when she died just as mysteriously.

"Yes, sir. There was no one kinder. No one more loving."

Aaron covered his mouth with his hand. He wished he could remember his mother's face. Wished his childhood wasn't tainted by his father's evil misdeeds.

Tears gathered behind his eyes, but he leant on years of honed arrogance to beat them back. "I recall you were dismissed the week before we were thrown out onto the streets." His father's third wife, the witch known as Natasha, had fired most the staff, including her own maid.

"That's what Mrs Chance wanted everyone to think."

*Mrs Chance!* he grumbled silently. It grated that they would forever bear the same surname, like the woman haunted him from beyond the grave.

"I didn't fill my valise with clothes," Mrs Lowry continued. "It was crammed with jewels, silver, and anything valuable I could carry. I had to do it, or the mistress said she'd see me hanged for stealing."

Plagued by thoughts of Natasha's wickedness, Aaron fell silent.

"What is this all about?" Joanna said. "Why are you working for Lord Berridge? Why risk your lives to assist in his devious scheme?"

Mrs Lowry looked at Aaron and paled. "I'm forced to

work for Lord Berridge and play the messenger. It's part of a bigger plan."

"What plan?" Aaron snapped.

Lucia dashed tears from her eyes. "You are the last person I wanted to hurt. I wanted to tell you everything, but she threatened to kill Miss Lovelace."

"We should have run away the moment the ship docked in Southampton," Mrs Lowry said, wrapping her arm around Lucia and hugging her tightly. "I've helped raise Lucia since she was born. We returned to England on a boat from Naples nine months ago."

"I have something for you." With a shaky hand, Lucia retrieved a note from her coat pocket and gave it to Aaron. "It will be a dreadful shock."

Aaron tore open the note and read the missive.

> *By the time I'm finished, you'll wish you'd*
> *kept your brothers in the rookeries.*
> *I heard you cried like babes that first night.*

Aaron shivered as if cold fingers from the past were tracing down his spine. "Who wrote this?"

"The letter is from my mother, N-Natasha Chance." Lucia looked terrified at the mention of her own mother's name. "The person you hate most is not dead."

Natasha was alive?

Time stopped for a heartbeat.

"Is this your idea of a sick joke?" he barked.

"No, it's true, sir. I swear it." Mrs Lowry clasped her hands in prayer. "May God strike me dead."

"But I read the coroner's report and interviewed the constables." Bile stung the back of Aaron's throat. What the

271

hell had he missed? "Witnesses watched her die. I had a man ride to Petersfield to check the parish records."

"Mother paid people to lie. She said she would never be safe if you thought she was alive. We left for Naples with her Italian lover when I was three. Roberto died last year, leaving Mother four hundred pounds in his will."

"Natasha was furious," Mrs Lowry added. "Despite her wicked plot, Roberto's son inherited everything."

"What does she want with me?"

"You swore to seek vengeance." Lucia hung her head before finding the courage to reach for Aaron's hand and plead, "You must stop her. She is possessed by the devil and will not rest until your family is dead. She had documents prepared, naming me heir to your fortune, to your share of the gaming hell and the properties you own. Killing you is just the beginning."

Aaron tried to remain calm, but his thoughts were rioting. "Why, in Lucifer's name, would I leave my fortune to Natasha's daughter? Any court in the land would see it as blatant fraud."

That's when Lucia delivered an unexpected blow, an unforeseen twist in the tale. "Because Ignatius Chance was my father. I am your sister, sir. Lucia Chance."

# Chapter Nineteen

Aaron froze.

It was a clever plan. Everyone knew how much he loved his kin. Everyone knew he would not leave a sibling out in the cold. But for Natasha to achieve her goal and avoid his brothers' wrath, she must kill an entire family.

It was an impossible task.

Unless she set the club ablaze while they slept upstairs.

He turned to Joanna, fear rising through him like a tidal wave. "We need to leave. I warned Sigmund to expect an attack, but he can't watch every room. Natasha could raze Fortune's Den to the ground."

A blackguard might scale the wall in the yard, force the door and torch the downstairs rooms. There would be mass panic, jumping from the upper windows, his family's only means of escape.

"You can't go," Mrs Lowry said, a tremble in her voice. "Natasha has a boat waiting, moored down past the yard. Once you're aboard, the skipper will take you to the meeting place. Natasha wants you to leave your share of Fortune's

Den to Lucia. She'll manage Lucia's affairs until she's of age, though she promises not to hurt your family."

That was a lie.

Natasha would shoot him and dispose of his brothers.

Aaron gave a mirthless chuckle. "Natasha is a fool if she thinks I would subject my brothers to a lifetime of misery. Why the hell would I trust her?"

"We can't stop her. She has men watching the house." Mrs Lowry's voice quivered like the tenuous hold on her nerve might snap. "We've followed the plan because Lucia was afraid Natasha would kill you. Just like she killed the gent at The Burnished Jade."

Joanna gasped. "Natasha killed Lord Howard? Why?"

"His father hurt her years ago, and she said his son must repent." Mrs Lowry cast a pitying glance at Lucia. "Lucia was told to cause trouble between Lord Howard and Mr Parker and get one of them to steal the dagger. We thought Natasha wanted to make life difficult for Lord Howard."

Lucia shivered like she could feel the men's clammy hands on her skin. "Mother said she wanted the dagger because it belonged to Ignatius Chance. I did what I was told. I didn't know she would take it to The Burnished Jade and kill a man. I didn't know you'd be a suspect."

"What did you think she would do?" he snapped, angry that Natasha would use her daughter to do her dirty deeds. "Keep it as a souvenir? She made you an accessory to murder."

Probably so she could control Lucia.

Water welled in Lucia's eyes as she looked at him. "I didn't know Mother was watching Fortune's Den. She's been looking for a way to destroy your family and steal your fortune."

And she had come close to succeeding.

"Why use The Burnished Jade and involve Miss Lovelace?"

Lucia turned to Joanna. "She knew you were friends with Mr Chance and discovered what Lord Howard did to you. That's when she decided to use you to hurt him."

Joanna inhaled deeply. "Lord Howard must have confessed to his crime. You told your mother. What sort of mother would leave you alone with him, knowing he's a monster?"

"I am just a pawn in her game," Lucia said through a sob. "But if it is any consolation, Lord Howard was sorry for what he did. He confessed to me the night I cried when he tried to touch me."

"Howard lied." Aaron relayed what he'd heard about Miss Fitzpatrick's planned ruination. "He came to The Burnished Jade to hurt another innocent woman."

Lucia looked confused. "No. He came to The Burnished Jade looking for Mr Parker. Mother sent him an anonymous note. He thought Mr Parker was planning to hurt me. Whatever else you've heard is untrue. Mother stole the list of attendees so it would look like he came of his own volition."

"It's my fault," Mrs Lowry said, sniffing back tears. "I should have done something years ago. But once Natasha sinks her claws into you, there's no hope of escape."

Aaron paused to think.

There was only one way to stop Natasha hurting his family.

A way fraught with danger.

"Why should I trust you?" he asked Lucia. "You were born to wicked parents, two of the most evil people I've had the misfortune to meet."

"It's not a life I chose." Lucia delved into her coat pocket and retrieved a miniature in an ornate gilt frame. "I have always longed to be part of your family, and hoped you might regard me as kin."

Mrs Lowry spoke up. "She's a kind, caring girl, sir, who's been forced to do terrible things against her will."

Aaron gave a nod of recognition. "Our parents treated us like puppets in their cruel games. When you've known nothing but wickedness, you'll bear the scars for a lifetime."

"I know affection, devotion and friendship," Lucia argued. "Mrs Lowry loves me like kin."

How could he argue? Mrs Maloney loved him, too.

"I told Lucia about your mother, Diana, sir."

Hearing his mother's name pierced like a blade through the heart. Nothing prepared him for the moment the girl handed him the miniature of a beautiful raven-haired woman and said, "This belongs to you, Mr Chance."

Mrs Lowry was quick to explain. "I took it from your father's desk when I left Hill Street but kept it hidden. I showed it to Lucia when she was old enough. I wanted to explain not all mothers are wicked."

Aaron hung his head and stared at his mother's image. A lifetime of regret squeezed the breath from his lungs. He felt his mother's anguish, the grief for a life cut short. He imagined her in heaven, watching every beating, trying to guide him towards a better path.

"Did my father kill her?" He had to know if the gossip was true. "Tell me. Surely Natasha knew. My father found his match in her."

Mrs Lowry shook her head. "Your father loved your mother. Part of him died when he found her dead at the bottom of the stairs. I heard his brother was involved, but there was no proof."

"Berridge?" Aaron sat forward.

The earl was a dead man walking.

"A servant disappeared the night your mother died. A maid. I heard she gave your mother a hefty dose of laudanum and a gentle shove in the back, but it was just gossip, sir."

All stories contained fragments of the truth.

"The Earl of Berridge didn't want our father to have more sons," Lucia said. "He was afraid you would cause trouble in the future. Ignatius remarried quickly to show the earl he could not be beaten."

Aaron could believe that was true. Knowing he had four vengeful nephews, Berridge must have been quaking in his boots. It explained why he left them to die in the rookeries.

Joanna hugged his arm and said softly, "Don't torment yourself over things you cannot control. I know how these thoughts make a person weak. Nothing matters but protecting those you love and ending this nightmare."

Knowing she was right, Aaron fell silent while he considered the options. There was one. He had to confront Natasha.

"Once I'm in the boat, what are your instructions?" he asked Mrs Lowry.

"The skipper will transport you to the destination while we wait here. You're to drink a vial of laudanum before I walk you to the boat."

So, Natasha needed him subdued.

"Where will he take me?"

It would be somewhere quiet, maybe out of town.

"Natasha didn't tell us. She said a woman would destroy you where strong men failed." Mrs Lowry glanced nervously out of the window. "We can't linger here without rousing suspicion. Happen we've been here long enough."

"Then let's not waste time. I'll play Natasha's game." Aaron handed Joanna his mother's miniature and had every faith she would do as he asked. "Give this to Aramis. Explain what happened tonight and tell him he must take charge." He removed the sovereign ring from his finger. "Give him my ring. He's to protect our family, not concern himself with me. He must focus on the future."

Joanna shook her head. "You can't go. She means to kill you."

"If I'm to end this, I have no choice." He cupped her cheek and let his love for her flood his heart. "These times spent with you have been the happiest of my life. I'd withstand a daily beating to feel the pleasure of one kiss."

"Don't go. There must be another way."

"There isn't. I must learn to master my fears. I'm afraid of losing everything I love, but I'm not afraid to face Natasha."

Her face grew taut as if she balanced on a razor's edge. "We can't keep saying goodbye like this."

"This will be the last time." It had to be.

Mrs Lowry handed him a small vial. "Natasha told me it's laudanum."

"It could be arsenic," Joanna said, horrified.

Indeed, he could not risk making assumptions.

Natasha was a cunning cat.

"I can't drink that."

Lucia retrieved a tiny brown bottle from her pocket. "I agree, Mr Chance. This is laudanum." She removed the stopper and took a small swig. "There. That proves I've told the truth. Drink some. Mother needs you drowsy so she can

278

restrain you. She will want you awake to sign the documents and won't try to kill you until you do."

"It will give Miss Lovelace time to alert your family," Mrs Lowry added. "They might know where Natasha plans to take you."

Aaron stared at the medicine bottle—then at the two women—wondering if this was an elaborate story to fool him or the absolute truth.

*Trust all will be well.*

Joanna's earlier comment drifted into his mind.

*All is well*, he said silently, surprised three simple words had the power to calm his restless spirit. Not knowing the strength of the opium tincture, Aaron sipped an average dose equivalent to ten drops. The solution tasted bitter and needed time to travel through his bloodstream.

"What now?" he said. The road ahead was an uncertain path.

Mrs Lowry moved to alight. "I'll walk Lucia back to the house, then escort you to where the boat is moored. The skipper will take things from there. What happens afterwards, I cannot say. The only saving grace is Natasha needs Lucia alive."

Mrs Lowry climbed down from the coach, but Lucia paused in the doorway. "I always dreamed of making you proud. That I would be a famed opera singer and you would attend my performances. I'm sorry if I have been a disappointment."

Aaron knew that guilt was a leaden anchor dragging you down.

He touched his sister's arm. Something told him everything she'd said was true. "I hear you have the voice of an angel. Let's pray I live to see you sing an aria for the King."

Lucia smiled. "I imagine your mother would have said something just as kind. You have inherited her good heart." And with that naive comment, she alighted.

It hurt to look at Joanna.

Distress lived in every line on her brow.

"Aaron, I wish we were back in Aldgate, and you were dragging drunken louts from my door. I wouldn't care if you were rude. I would smile and thank you for being a gentleman."

"I was rude so I might save myself from feeling the pain I do now," he confessed. "You're strong enough to overcome whatever happens tonight. Your club will be a huge success. Women are breaking free from their shackles and seeking their own identity. When it comes to matchmaking, trust Daventry's advice. There's no man wiser."

"I would sacrifice it all to spend my life loving you."

He cupped her cheek. "You'd be afraid of the man you saw fighting in the pits. He's vicious when there's nothing to keep his temper in check. If I don't return, at least I'll know your last thoughts of me were favourable."

She clutched her abdomen. "I feel sick with worry."

"All will be well." He sounded too relaxed, which was probably a consequence of the opium taking effect. "Kiss me. But not like this is goodbye."

She kissed him like she wanted to tear off his clothes and straddle him on the coach seat. Their lips collided with fierce intensity, their breath mingling as he gripped her waist, pulling her closer. She touched him, her hands moving so rapidly it made him dizzy. Again, it must be the opium.

"I love you," he uttered, his head growing heavy.

"I love you," she said as Mrs Lowry returned to escort him to the boat. Panicked, Joanna turned on the woman.

"Make sure he reaches the boat and doesn't end up in the river. If you've lied tonight and he dies, I'll not rest until I find you. You'll wish to God you'd killed me."

The tremor in Joanna's hands mirrored the pounding of her heart. The pain in her throat was like fingers crushing her windpipe. She could hardly see from crying but gripped the seat as the coach lurched forward and picked up speed.

She wanted to die.

She wanted to curl into a ball and sleep through the immeasurable pain. But there was a chance she could save Aaron, a chance he would survive. Somehow, she had to find the strength to help him.

As the coach rattled over Westminster Bridge, she pressed her face to the window, scouring the inky blackness for Natasha's boat. The odd lit lanterns hanging aboard the barges on the Thames cast shadows across the water, but the man she loved was lost amid the gloom.

The coach jolted suddenly, the jarvey cursing as he brought the vehicle to a crashing halt. Prepared to fight one of Natasha's thugs, Joanna was surprised when Lucia opened the door and clambered inside.

The poor girl's cheeks were flushed, and she was panting so hard she struggled to speak. "Have the jarvey drive on," she said, her expression strained as she clutched her chest. "Hurry."

Joanna called to the jarvey, instructing him to drive like

the devil was at his heels. Then she faced Lucia. "Has something happened? Is it Mr Chance?"

*Please don't say he's dead.*

"No, but you need me to speak to the magistrate. I can tell him you're both innocent, and I must be as brave as my brother." Lucia's eyelids flickered. "The opium, it is making my muscles relax but I may be of some help."

Joanna clung to the overhead strap as the vehicle raced through the dim streets. Lucia fell into a haze, drifting somewhere between sleep and blissful ignorance. A carefree place where her problems slipped away like mist in a morning sun.

Half an hour later, they arrived in Aldgate Street. Joanna flung open the carriage door, desperation forcing her to leap from the vehicle while it was still rolling. She fell to her knees on the pavement before scrambling up and hammering on the Den's door.

Sigmund answered. A heavy frown marred his brow as he looked to the open carriage and saw Lucia asleep in the seat. "Where's Aaron? What happened?"

"Let me rouse Aramis, and I'll explain. Carry Lucia into the drawing room, and tell the jarvey to wait. Be careful. There may be men outside ready to attack." Who knew what Natasha had planned?

Joanna charged into the house, crying, "Aramis!" five times from the hallway.

Aramis appeared on the stairs, dressed in black like his brothers behind him. He looked at Joanna, then at the open door, his face turning ghostly pale.

"Where is he? Where the hell is Aaron? We were about to leave to visit Miss Stowe. I knew something was amiss when he ushered me out of the study earlier."

A sob ripped through her, her body jerking as grief took

control of her limbs. "Natasha is alive. She plans to kill Aaron tonight."

"She's a-alive?" Aramis stuttered.

Other family members appeared in the hall, dressed and ready for battle. They were unharmed. There was no fire. Natasha knew how to use Aaron's fears against him.

"Lucia is Natasha's daughter," Joanna said as Sigmund carried the drowsy girl into the house. "She's your sister. Ignatius was her father."

Aramis jerked in shock. "Good God."

Joanna fumbled through her pocket, handed Aramis his mother's miniature and his brother's signet ring, and conveyed Aaron's message. "Aaron said protecting your family must take priority."

"He is our family," Delphine said.

"You need to think where Natasha might take him. A place one can reach by boat. A place that means something to Aaron. Somewhere one might kill a man and dispose of a body."

Aramis stared at his mother's likeness, his Adam's apple bobbing in his throat. Then he shook himself, aware he needed to concentrate on finding his brother. "Aaron rarely goes anywhere. He's dedicated the last ten years of his life to this club."

"What about somewhere he liked as a boy?" she said, a vision of a sad child filling her mind, a boy without sanctuary.

All the brothers shook their heads.

Delphine stepped forward. "Aaron worked lugging barrels by day and fought in the pits at night. He never took time to rest. He never considered himself, only how we would escape poverty."

Impatience left Joanna's temper frayed. "Think! All of you! His life depends upon us finding the answer. Natasha won't rest until she has destroyed him." She rubbed tears from her eyes. "Please. We need to bring him home."

*I need him to come home!*

Mr Flynn offered a sensible suggestion. "I'd be more inclined to think of a place he despises. A place where he might feel powerless. Where Natasha can use his thoughts against him and he might be easier to defeat."

Joanna had an idea. "Where is your mother buried?"

"St Audley's, Mayfair," Aramis said solemnly.

A sudden knock on the open door had them all jumping to attention. A young man, tall and bony, gripped the doorframe to keep himself from crumpling with exhaustion. "I need to speak to Mr Chance. Aaron Chance. He said to call day or night."

Aramis stepped forward. "Why?"

The man gauged the size of Aramis' chest and answered the question. "He's had me watching a house in Upper Brook Street. Wanted to know if I saw any shifty business or if the cove had visitors. Said he'd pay double if I watched through the night."

"You'll find money in the drawer, Miss Lovelace." Aramis pointed to the console table. "Pay the fellow, and let's hear what he has to say."

Joanna took three sovereigns from the purse in the drawer. She dropped the coins into the man's grubby hand. "What had you racing to Aldgate?"

"I'll need a bit more for the ride home." He gave a tooth-less grin. "I used every shilling I had to hire a hackney to follow the cove."

Joanna obliged him. "You followed Lord Berridge?"

The lackey nodded. "The old toff headed across town, past Tower Hill and Shadwell Church, towards the Limehouse Basin. That's where I ran out of coins and the jarvey turfed me out."

"Where the blazes is Berridge going?" Aramis mused aloud.

"There ain't much out there. There's the West India Docks on the Isle of Dogs and the marshes."

"The earl could be leaving town," Delphine said.

"I don't reckon so," Aaron's watchman replied. "He went in a hired coach, not a nabob's carriage. A right old rickety thing. I'll wager the driver takes him to the marshes and robs him blind."

Joanna turned to Aramis. "Might Natasha take Aaron to any of those places? She said something about a woman destroying him where strong men failed. Might she be talking about a past event, a fight his father forced him to attend?"

Sigmund spoke up. "Aaron told me about a bare-knuckle brawl north of the Ferry House on the Isle of Dogs. He was only fourteen but had beaten four brutes that night. His last opponent was a woman with fists like mallets. No matter how much she provoked him, Aaron couldn't hit her."

"I know the place," the lackey said. "They call it the Dog Pit. No-Neck Harry won there a few months ago."

"How long will it take to get there?" A bud of hope blossomed in Joanna's chest. She looked at the crowd of people huddled in the hall. People who loved Aaron. "There's no room for us all. We've got a hackney coach and Mr Flynn's carriage."

"The fewer occupants, the quicker we'll be," Aramis said.

"We'll need weapons." Joanna imagined them closing in

on Natasha, surrounding her, giving her no option but to surrender. "We don't know how many men Natasha hired."

"I—I know of four," Lucia said weakly, shuffling into the hall. "You must let me come, too. I may be able to reason with her."

"You're hardly fit to travel."

"But without me, my mother's plan won't work."

"What plan?" Aramis demanded to know.

"The plan to have Aaron sign everything he owns over to Lucia." Joanna considered Lucia's request. It made sense to bring her along. They could use her as bait or a bargaining tool. "We can't take everyone, but we must take Lucia."

"Perhaps I may be of assistance," came a deep, masculine voice from the doorway. Mr Daventry stood like a monument to justice. His black attire gave him a menacing air like he meant to rid the world of sinners. "My carriage is outside. I had a man watching the premises. He sent word to my office when you left. My agents are on hand and are parked at the top of Aldgate Street."

Joanna might have dropped to her knees and kissed his feet if time wasn't precious. "Aaron's stepmother is alive and has transported him to a secret location. She plans to kill him. We think they're heading to the Isle of Dogs."

Mr Daventry gripped her upper arms. "Aaron Chance has nine lives. He won't be beaten, and certainly not by someone as wicked as Natasha. Tell me everything en route." He gestured for everyone to follow him outside. "Aramis. Fill my agents' carriages and tell them to follow mine."

Aramis began ushering everyone outside.

"Wait for me!" Mrs Maloney descended the stairs, Joanna's musket in one hand and her homemade felt bag in the other. "I found this upstairs along with powder and lead. It might be useful."

"A coat might be useful," Aramis said, sighing. "The cold will nip more than your nose. Hurry. Your son needs you."

Mrs Maloney tutted. "This isn't cold. You're too young to remember the winter of 1791. And my boy isn't dying tonight."

"Please hurry," Joanna said, wrapping her arm around Lucia. "While we dally, Aaron is out there, cold, drugged and all alone."

Mr Daventry gave a knowing grin. "He's not alone. The Marquess of Rothley followed you to Lambeth tonight."

# Chapter Twenty

Fortunately, Aaron could take a punch.

The skipper of the crude river barge, a small boat named The Good Hope, thumped Aaron in the gut to ensure he was subdued from the opium. He delivered a jab to Aaron's chin, an uppercut too weak to floor a gnat. Once satisfied his prisoner had downed enough opium to dull the pain, the thug frisked him, a hapless pat of Aaron's body and thighs to search for a weapon.

Aaron swayed and mumbled a few words, pretended his knee had buckled and let the skipper lay him down beneath the canvas canopy. The cove stank of stale sweat and rotten fish. Anyone who caught a whiff of his breath would retch.

"Where are you taking him?" Mrs Lowry asked, pretending to be friendly. "It's too cold to be out on the river tonight."

"I've sailed the North Sea in the dead of winter," the stout Scotsman mocked. "I think I can manage a barge on the Thames."

The fellow snatched a rope from inside a barrel and

secured Aaron's hands behind his back. Then he pulled a knife from a sheath, threatened Mrs Lowry and told her to climb aboard.

"That's not the plan," she said, fear creeping into her voice. "I'm to wait in the house. I'll not leave Lucia there alone."

"Dinnae fret. They'll bring the lass to the meeting place."

Mrs Lowry would be dead once they reached their destination—as would the skipper. Natasha would dispose of the witnesses. It's why Aaron had swallowed half the dose of laudanum, spitting some into his hand when pretending to cough, and wiping the excess on his trousers.

One thing troubled Aaron as he closed his eyes and listened to the skipper wrestle Mrs Lowry onto the boat. Joanna was right. He couldn't kill a woman, not even a witch like Natasha. Which begged the question: how would he free himself from his captor and finish her for good?

"Keep yer mouth shut." The skipper threw Mrs Lowry to the boards and told her to sit still. "Cause trouble, and I'll toss ye overboard."

Another man joined them, a muscled brute named Pike. He'd come to help row the boat but mentioned his friends couldn't find Lucia.

"I left them searching the street," he said, his accent as coarse as a Covent Garden hawker. "She can't have gone far, not on foot."

Mrs Lowry grinned, the news bringing a subtle sigh of relief.

"The girl's nae our problem. We've got our orders and will only get paid if we stick to the plan."

The skipper released the line and cast off, digging his pole into the bank and pushing the barge out onto the murky river.

His friend sat beside him and they took up an oar each, both heaving with the force of each stroke.

Aaron peered through half-closed eyes. They were heading downriver, leaving St Peter's and Westminster Hall behind them, moving towards the Palace of Whitehall and the Privy Gardens.

It would help to know their intended destination.

He recalled the snippet of information Mrs Lowry remembered.

*A woman would destroy him where strong men failed.*

It alluded to Aaron's many fights.

Needing to remain alert as the drug draped his mind in a hazy mist, he trawled through the memory of every battle. The hundreds he'd won, those he'd lost as a boy, too naive to think a grown man wouldn't hit him.

They passed beneath Waterloo Bridge, the men stopping for a brief rest before gripping the oars and propelling them through the water again.

Mrs Lowry tapped his arm and whispered, "Are you awake?"

Aaron met her gaze and nodded. "Hush."

The men were talking as they rowed.

Any information might prove invaluable.

Pike complained about hunger pangs. "Mrs Boyd at The Anchor serves the best rabbit pie for miles around."

"We'll nae stay at The Anchor," replied the Scotsman. "We're to lie low for a while and cannae remain in London. I've a friend in Berkhamsted."

There were five taverns named The Anchor along the Thames. One in Greenwich, a brief ride across the river to a place fighting men called the Dog Pit.

Aaron was fourteen the first time his father dragged him

there. Beating four brutes wasn't the problem. He was fast like lightning, they said, with knuckles of steel. But his last opponent was a woman, a skilled fighter with a face so pretty Aaron's conscience stopped him from hitting her.

Did Natasha know he could not hit her, either?

Is that why she'd chosen his old battleground?

He'd know the answer soon. If the rowers kept their current pace, they would reach the Dog Pit in forty minutes, which explained why Natasha wanted him drugged.

The time passed slowly.

Mrs Lowry whimpered as the murmur of the city dulled and the barge slipped through the black water, gliding around the hulls of moored vessels like a giant eel. They reached the Isle of Dogs. The barge banged against the narrow jetty as the Scotsman dropped his oar and moored the boat.

"Agree with whatever I say," Aaron whispered to Mrs Lowry. "Your life depends on it."

"Wakey-wakey!" Pike loomed over Aaron, dragging him up by his waistcoat. "Reckon you wished you'd worn a coat tonight." The lout chuckled as he cracked Aaron across the cheek, knocking his head sideways.

"Take him to the Pit," the skipper said as Pike hauled Aaron onto the jetty. "I'll deal with the problem here."

Aaron opened his eyes and swayed as he pointed at the trembling Mrs Lowry. "She's hidden Lucia as security," he said, speaking like the drunken lords who frequent the Den. "Your mistress will want to question her before you dump her in the Thames."

The skipper waved his hunting knife at Mrs Lowry and beckoned her ashore. "Tell me where the lass is, or ye'll nae keep yer tongue."

Mrs Lowry drew her shoulders back. "I'll only speak to Natasha."

Aaron let his head flop forward. "Throw her overboard. It will scupper the plans and save me killing her myself once I'm free of these bonds."

Pike laughed. "You ain't leaving the Pit alive."

"Don't laugh," Aaron slurred. "I can beat you with my hands bound and while high on laudanum. Kill the woman." He stumbled for dramatic effect. "I'll enjoy watching Natasha put a lead ball between your brows."

The brutes exchanged wary glances.

While lighting their lamps, they spoke about the risks of not getting paid, before the Scot said, "Aye, best bring the woman to Mrs Chance. Let her decide."

Natasha wasn't waiting at the Ferry House Inn as the men expected. According to the stable hand, she left the tavern when a grey-haired nabob arrived. It was obvious the lad referred to the devious Earl of Berridge.

The two lackeys guarding the path behind the tavern stepped aside for the skipper. Aaron made a mental note of their faces, though few men in London would dare challenge the Chance brothers.

They cut through the fields, the marsh fog obscuring their vision, the ground squelching beneath their boots. Pike shoved Aaron in the back, wanting him to trip, as they followed the track across the boggy terrain to an area of raised ground near a row of alder trees.

The Dog Pit.

Aaron recalled the amber glow of twenty lit braziers, not the measly light from the lamps now hanging from metal crooks. He imagined the crowd gathered around the wooden platform where men fought for a heavy purse, the shouting and shoving, the thud when his opponent hit the boards. The stench of blood and sweat.

The Dog Pit was aptly named. It's where men howled and whined and battled to be named pack leader. Tonight, it was a bleak and barren wilderness, where a corpse might remain undiscovered for months.

He saw Natasha, dressed in a green hooded cloak, her ebony ringlets framing a face of harsh angles and bitter lines. He remembered her cackle, the ugly laugh that followed every cruel jibe.

"You brought him." Natasha rubbed her hands like he was a beef supper. She stopped a foot away, a predatory glint in her eyes, and stroked his bristled cheek. "Goodness, what a handsome devil you are. It almost makes me wish I had kept you as a pet."

"You're too old for me, Natasha," he stuttered, maintaining the facade. Her hair was grey at the temples, the corners of her mouth drooped with the gravity of age. "I prefer a woman with a heart."

"Like Miss Lovelace?" Natasha tapped her finger to her lips. "What will become of your little concubine when she's living all alone at The Burnished Jade? Poor Lord Howard cannot rescue her now he's dead. There's always Mr Parker. He would warm anyone's bed."

It took Hercules' strength not to react. Joanna lived in his heart and mind, but he could not afford to let sentiment make him weak.

"What do you want?" Aaron said though knew full well.

"What any mother wants for her daughter. Stability." Natasha's arrogant gaze shifted to Mrs Lowry, then to the Scot. "Why is she still breathing? I told you. I can't afford mistakes."

The burly fellow squirmed. "She has the girl hidden somewhere. The men cannae find the young lass and are scouring the streets."

Natasha's eyes blazed. "What have you done with Lucia?"

"I'll die before I tell you," came Mrs Lowry's brave reply.

"You'll not be so brazen when Murray puts a blade to your throat." Natasha glared at Pike. "Tie her up. We'll dispose of her when we find my daughter."

Mrs Lowry's eyes widened. "You'd kill me? After years of faithful service?"

"Faithful service?" Natasha's frigid chuckle could freeze hell's flames. "Oh, please. I know about your failed attempts to run away with Lucia. Roberto told me he caught you trying to escape the villa. You can't be trusted and have outlived your purpose."

"So, you throw children to the wolves and murder helpless women." Aaron didn't bother altering his voice. "When you've established yourself at Fortune's Den, I suspect Lucia will suffer a terrible accident and you'll be the sole beneficiary."

Natasha grinned. "Children are useful to a point. What a shame you reminded Ignatius of your mother. He enjoyed watching other men beat you. He couldn't quite rouse the strength to thrash you himself."

Aaron flinched. Hatred for his father lived in the marrow of his bones, but he'd be lying if he said Natasha's comment didn't hurt. It cut deep.

"He must be turning in his grave at your betrayal," he said in this war of words. "Berridge as good as murdered my mother. Now you're working with him to destroy what's left of her memory."

Natasha raised her hands as if exasperated. "All those punches to the head must account for your stupidity. I'm representing your father in his absence. He would have taken your gaming hell, as I mean to do."

Yes, jealous of Aaron's success, Ignatius would have made him suffer. "My brothers will fight you to the death."

Looking bored, Natasha examined her hands. "You know what happens to the hive when the queen dies. The tiny insignificant bees perish."

"My brothers are a damn sight more dangerous than bees." It annoyed him to think his father would be proud.

"Men in love are easy to overthrow. A wife heavy with child is like a chink in their armour."

This vixen knew how to manipulate Aaron's thoughts. She knew where to fire the arrow. "Don't pretend you cared for my father. You let our neighbour bed you while Ignatius was still alive."

Natasha found his retort amusing. "It was your father's idea, a way of protecting me from Berridge when he was gone. Miss Lovelace knows what it's like when wolves come knocking. When you're dead, they'll tear her to shreds."

Aaron didn't dare think about Joanna.

He didn't let his mind invent stories.

He didn't acknowledge the ache in his heart.

"Where is Berridge? The lad at the Ferry House said he accompanied you here. Will you kill him to avenge my father?"

The notion was ludicrous.

What made her believe she could escape punishment?

"Me? Good Lord, no. You'll kill him when you've signed the documents naming Lucia your heir. It will look like you agreed to meet here to fight."

It was Aaron's turn to laugh. "You underestimate me, Natasha. I'll never sign the documents. Besides, there's a flaw in your plan. As Mrs Lowry will attest, I did not come to Lambeth alone tonight. By now, my brothers will know of your treachery."

Natasha didn't believe him. "You'd never risk the lives of those you love. Aaron Chance, the lone hero, fights everyone's battles."

Mrs Lowry begged to differ. "The lady came in the carriage and left Lambeth before I brought Mr Chance to the boat."

With a fleeting look of unease, Natasha scanned her surroundings. Satisfied they were alone, she drew a double-barrelled pistol from the deep pocket of her cloak, cocked one hammer and aimed at Aaron.

"No one knows we're at the Dog Pit," Natasha said, confident his brothers wouldn't think to visit marshland in the dead of night. "They'll be out scouring every back alley, storming the earl's house, hounding that simpleton Miss Stowe. I knew not to trust Lucia or Mrs Lowry with the information." She glanced at the alder trees—ghostly sentinels in the foggy haze—and yelled for her lackey to fetch the Earl of Berridge.

Amid a grumble of voices and gruff shouts, Berridge appeared, shuffling through the boggy grassland, his hands and ankles shackled, the cloth gag sagging beneath his chin.

"Release me at once." Berridge's enraged eyes bored down on Natasha. "You agreed to let me kill him. I've given you the money. Now have these miscreants untie me, and hand me that pistol."

Natasha giggled like she was at the Olympic watching Madame Vestris' farcical play. "Neither of you will leave here alive. How could I honour my dear Ignatius' memory when the two people he hated most are still breathing?"

For a moment, Aaron was back in his childhood home, wondering what he'd done to earn his father's wrath, longing for his parent's love, believing he was undeserving.

"The master didn't hate his son," Mrs Lowry protested. "You poisoned his mind. You made him believe the boy was weak and wouldn't survive if left to fend for himself."

Natasha motioned to Pike. "Gag that woman. If I hear another word from her, I'll shoot you in the foot."

While Pike saw to the task, the earl's temper raged. "You promised me vengeance. You said we'd rid the world of this filthy scourge. You promised me half of Fortune's Den."

"More fool you for trusting a woman," Natasha countered. "Vengeance is mine tonight. Pike, untie the earl's hands but keep his feet bound. Let's watch the men battle it out, just as Ignatius would have wanted."

Joanna hugged herself for the duration of the five-mile journey to the Isle of Dogs. Time was against them. She wished the carriage could sprout wings and cover the distance in seconds, not a painstaking forty minutes.

She looked out of the window as the vehicle charged along the Deptford and Greenwich Road, one of few byways on the Isle. The carriages belonging to Mr Daventry's men stopped near the windmill to allow them to alight. The agents cut across the marshland on foot before disappearing into the foggy blackness.

Everyone else headed to the Ferry House Inn and parked in the deserted yard.

There was no sign of Gabriel's elegant coach, though that didn't worry Mr Daventry, who was quick to reassure Aaron's brothers. "Rothley may have followed by boat. It's easy to find an empty vessel moored at this time of night."

Aramis adopted Aaron's role, insisting everyone remain in the yard while he searched for his brother. "We can't all go charging across the marshland. It's best I go alone. Natasha won't hear me coming."

His wife Naomi disagreed. "We should remain together. We're safer in numbers and your stepmother may have gathered an army."

While Joanna grew tired of waiting, Mr Daventry saw the merit of both plans. "Aramis can have a five-minute advantage and we'll follow behind. There is strength in numbers."

"Let me go," Joanna said, trying to think of a logical reason why Aramis might agree. "I heard Lucia's story and can use it to stall Natasha. She won't see me as a threat. I'll say I never left Lambeth and followed the boat."

"Saving him is my responsibility," Aramis countered.

"We all want to save him." Joanna gestured to Christian and Theo and a determined Mrs Maloney, who clutched the antique musket like she would fire without warning. "But I have a better chance of getting close to Natasha. I'll distract her while you surround the area."

Mr Daventry raised his lamp aloft and looked out over the marshland. "If Natasha runs, it will be impossible to find her in the fog. Miss Lovelace is right. She can approach quietly. We will split into small groups with the aim of surrounding the area. We'll move in on my signal."

Like his elder brother, Aramis vented his frustration. "I'll not follow behind like a hapless sheep."

Joanna touched Aramis' upper arms, arms too muscular to grip. "I love Aaron. If we have any hope of finding the happiness you and Naomi share, let me go. Don't let history repeat itself. Don't shut us all out and tackle this problem alone. Don't treat your brothers like children."

The comment hit a nerve.

After a tussle with his conscience, Aramis exhaled sharply. "You'll need a weapon. Something easily concealed." He beckoned his wife to give Joanna the muff pistol she carried in her reticule. "Leave it uncocked. The slightest bump may cause it to discharge."

"I'll only use it in an emergency," she said, slipping the pistol into her pocket. She still wore Aaron's coat. His scent enveloped her, bringing the calm reassurance needed to complete her mission.

"Go now," Aramis urged her. "We won't be far behind."

Mr Daventry pointed to a path heading into the distance. "It's not far to the Dog Pit. We'll surround the area. Have confidence help is at hand. Aramis will accompany you as far as the gate. Natasha may have posted men there to ensure no one uses the track. You'll need him to dispose of them."

Aramis grinned, relishing the chance to use his fists.

Joanna followed him, circling the stables to the rear of the tavern and heading towards the track. The fog lingered, dense and unmoving, always ten feet ahead. While their next steps were visible, the future remained unclear.

"Aaron is in love with you," Aramis whispered.

"Yes, he told me." She would never forget the warmth in Aaron's eyes when he made the confession, the way his smile stole her breath. It was a moment of bliss. She would walk through fire to see him that happy again.

"He did?" Aramis sounded surprised.

"If we survive tonight, we have difficult decisions to make."

"You mean how he'll commit to you when he made a vow to us?" Aramis didn't wait for an answer. "The role of family patriarch is all Aaron knows. We didn't challenge him because it gave him a purpose, a reason to keep his demons locked in a cage."

"I know life together won't be easy. He lives under the constant threat of attack." From the lofty lords who owed him a fortune. From memories worse than nightmares.

"I have no doubt he will be an exceptional husband and father. It's time he buried the ghosts of the past."

If they survived the night, there was still one obstacle to overcome. "Aaron insists I watch him fight. He thinks I will despise that man. That I couldn't possibly love a beast."

"I'll not lie," Aramis said, his tone grave. "Aaron is savage in the ring. When you watch him, remember how it began and what it means for him to be invincible. Then, he may not appear quite so monstrous."

Aramis spoke like they would win tonight's battle and leave the field undefeated. The possibility grew more likely when they found two unconscious louts near the gate, their hands bound and fastened to the wooden post.

Aramis kicked a lackey but he lay like a lump of stone. "Daventry's agents must have sprinted here."

"I don't think that was the plan." Joanna caught whiff of an exotic cologne, the aromatic smell of myrrh, a deeply complex scent belonging to one man in particular. "Gabriel is here." Relief flooded through her. "He won't let anything happen to Aaron."

Aramis wasn't so sure. "If Rothley kills Aaron, he can marry you."

"Don't be absurd. Gabriel is not a murderer." She gestured to the rogues on the floor. "He bound these blackguards with rope instead of killing them."

Doubt crept into her mind.

She had been wrong about Lord Howard and Lucia.

Was she wrong about Gabriel?

"I can't take the risk. I'm fetching my brothers." Aramis was already making his way along the path. "You'd better hurry if you want to reach Natasha before I do," he called, breaking into a sprint.

Joanna didn't waste a second. She stepped over the men, raised her skirts and hurried along the miry track. Despite hearing a woman's voice heckling men to fight, she crept slowly into the fray.

An older man, who she believed was the Earl of Berridge, stood with his feet in iron shackles, his clothes muddy, a cut to his left cheek. Aaron's hands were bound but his feet were untethered.

The earl threw punches at Aaron, a series of poorly-timed blows.

Aaron dodged them with ease, kicking the earl to the ground.

"Get up you old oaf." A woman in a cloak cackled, then turned to the three thugs watching the bout. "Perhaps we should give Berridge a blade."

Mrs Lowry saw Joanna first. The poor woman sat on soggy moss, a filthy rag fastened around her mouth. Her eyes widened and she shook her head, warning Joanna to retreat.

Joanna cleared her throat. "Stop this!"

Everyone turned in her direction, united in shock.

Aaron met her gaze, cold hard fear flaring in his eyes.

"Miss Lovelace," the woman said, her insidious tone confirming she was Natasha. She was also a member of The Burnished Jade who went by the alias Miss Goswell. "What a delightful surprise." She raised her hand, revealing the double-barrelled pistol.

Joanna did not flinch or exchange pleasantries. "I followed the boat. I have Lucia imprisoned in a secure location. If I fail to return within two hours, she will be taken to the Thames Police Station and charged as an accessory to murder."

Natasha appeared unconcerned. "That is unfortunate. I suppose you want to make a trade. My handsome stepson for my darling daughter. Lucia is quite remarkable isn't she? So innocent yet so conniving. And entirely biddable when she's afraid."

How could a mother be so cruel?

Perhaps Lucia's lesson to learn was courage.

"You will accompany me to fetch Lucia," Joanna said, firming her stance. "Leave with me now and you will both walk free. If you refuse, I cannot be held responsible for what happens next."

In the tense silence, it was like the universe held its breath.

"There appears to be some confusion about who is in charge." Natasha motioned for her lackeys to grab Joanna, but Aaron tripped both men up and a fight ensued.

Even with his hands tied, Aaron fought like a champion.

One thug fell to the ground, blood spurting from his

broken nose. A sharp kick to the knee had a Scottish brute collapsing and howling like a babe.

"Give me the bloody pistol," the irate earl said, lunging at Natasha. "I'll do what you're incapable of doing. I'll rid myself of this vermin for good."

Natasha moved, causing the earl to stumble. He grabbed her cloak to stop himself falling. That's when Natasha lost her temper and shot the earl in the chest.

The loud crack of pistol fire echoed across the barren land. The sharp acrid scent of sulphur mingled with the musty smell of sodden earth.

The wide-eyed earl dropped to his knees, gaping at the spot of blood on his mustard waistcoat as it spread like ink on parchment, darkening with each laboured breath.

With a sinister grin, Natasha watched Lord Berridge die, kicking him to the ground once his chest stopped heaving. "Ignatius will be waiting for you in hell," she cried, then turned to Aaron, her face a mask of pure evil. "Now, you will sign the damned documents or I will shoot you where you stand."

Joanna's heartbeat pounded in her ears. Beads of panic moistened her brow. She had to find a way to stall Natasha. If she drew the muff pistol, the crazed woman might fire.

It was why Aaron's brothers hovered twenty feet away, hidden behind the wall of fog. Help was at hand. She sensed an army moving closer, paused on the brink of attack.

"I would rather die than let you take Fortune's Den," Aaron said with a snarl. "The truth will come to light and you'll hang."

Natasha aimed and cocked the hammer of the second barrel.

"Wait!" Joanna cried, beyond desperate now. "Let me talk

to him privately. Let me convince him to sign the documents." Natasha would untie his hands, and then there'd be hell to pay.

Before Natasha could argue, Joanna flew at Aaron, wrapping her arms around his neck, shielding his body.

"Are you trying to get yourself killed?" he hissed. "If she shoots, you'll die."

"You're the love of my life," Joanna whispered, kissing his lips. "I would rather die than live without you."

Despite their dire circumstances, he kissed her deeply, too. "You should not have come here. You should be safe at home, not risking your life for me."

"Clearly, you've not been paying attention. You're not fighting this battle alone. We're fighting it together. We're colleagues, friends and lovers. And I have no intention of letting you die."

"You've played right into my hands, Miss Lovelace," Natasha said, taunting her. "I did wonder how I might kill two people with one shot. Thank you for providing the solution."

"Wait!" Joanna called. "He has agreed to sign the documents." She looked at Aaron and mouthed. "I have a pistol in my pocket. When I turn and fire you must duck in case she shoots."

But Joanna didn't need to draw the small pistol. They didn't need to pray for a miracle because it came in the form of Lucia.

Joanna turned upon hearing the girl shout.

"Mother!" Lucia appeared from the fog, trying to march like a confident woman towards the virago who'd raised her. "Put down your weapon and surrender. I won't let you hurt my brother. You cannot win. You're outnumbered."

Natasha's face twisted into an ugly sneer. "You ungrateful

wretch. I should have known you'd betray me. Your father would be ashamed."

"No. You're wrong." Lucia stood like David challenging Goliath. "My father needed strong children capable of fighting the Berridge family."

"What do you know, you're just a child? Choose your side, Lucia. Choose wisely because you won't get a second chance."

"I hate you," Lucia cried as a bird call echoed across the wasteland. "I belong here with Mrs Lowry and the family who might come to love me."

"Your brother can't love you if he's dead," Natasha said.

A sudden movement near the trees stole everyone's attention.

Gabriel strode through the fog, his greatcoat billowing, his rifle pointed at Natasha. "Lower your weapon. Don't force me to shoot."

He wouldn't shoot.

From every compass point, people appeared: Aaron's brothers and their wives, Delphine and Dorian Flynn, Mr Daventry and his athletic agents, Sigmund with his fists clenched like mallets, and Mrs Maloney who carried the old musket as well as Wellington's men.

Joanna turned to Aaron. "You see, my love. You've never been alone in your fight against the world. All these people have risked their lives to stand with you tonight."

Aaron raised a stoic chin but water welled in his eyes.

"Spare me the melodrama," Natasha said.

Something in Natasha's tone had Joanna covertly reaching into her pocket and cocking the hammer on the pistol. She slipped her fingers around the handle and firmed her grip.

"Lower the weapon," Mr Daventry reiterated.

But Natasha laughed and aimed at Aaron's chest. "If I'm going to die, I'm taking that devil with me. His father needs some entertainment in hell."

As Natasha fired, a ball from the old musket hit her in the chest, causing her aim to falter and veer off target. A shot from the muff pistol hit her, too, and she dropped to the floor like a sack of sodden grain.

Lucia ran to Mrs Lowry and hugged her tightly.

Joanna turned to Aaron, patting his body, frantically searching for evidence of blood. "Are you hurt? Did she hit you?"

"I'm fine, love," he reassured her. "Natasha missed."

Mrs Maloney approached, tears glistening in her eyes as she hugged Aaron as any distraught mother would. "You gave us all a mighty scare." She brushed his hair from his brow and cupped his cheek. "But no one hurts my boy and lives to tell the tale."

# Chapter Twenty-One

After over a week of peaceful silence, the basement and card rooms of Fortune's Den rang with shouts and boisterous laughter. The contenders had arrived, their complex mix of accents resonating through the corridors like the out-of-tune notes of a symphony. The percussion came in the form of clinking tankards, slamming doors and the thud of clenched fists on the tables.

Arguments erupted. Taunts led to punches out of the ring, with some men taking their grievances into the yard.

For Aaron, the event should have roused the feeling of being home, the deafening racket drowning out thoughts he preferred to keep locked away.

But not tonight.

While he stretched his muscles and waited for Aramis, his mind was consumed with the beautiful woman lounging in his bed. "You need to dress if you want to watch me fight. Perhaps you'd prefer to remain here and pretend I'm still the hero of your dreams."

The muscles in his abdomen twisted into knots.

A fighting pit was no place for a woman.

He'd hurt any man who laid a hand on her.

But that's not what scared him most.

Joanna came up on her elbows, the bedsheets slipping to reveal her bare breasts. "I'll dress when you leave. I don't want you to know what I'm wearing."

She spoke like he couldn't find her in a crowd and wasn't attuned to her scent or the sound of her breathing. Every part of him wanted to climb into bed beside her, talk, sleep, make love, and share a picnic supper like they had for the last three days.

For the first time in his life, he had been selfish, letting Delphine and Dorian take care of Mrs Lowry and Lucia, leaving Daventry to deal with the magistrate. While his family breathed deep sighs of relief, thankful their troubles were over, Aaron still had a major problem to overcome.

"You must focus on the fights, Aaron, not on me."

"I wish I could say I'll be a tamer version of myself." His gaze moved from Joanna's lips to her breasts and the rosy nipples begging for his mouth. "But a part of me will always be broken. I will always need to be the ruler of my domain."

She knew not to get out of bed and distract him. "Is anyone truly whole? Life leaves its imprint on us all. It's a cycle of healing and rebuilding. It should unite us, Aaron, not tear us apart."

Her wisdom and ability to accept people, not judge them, were two of the many reasons he loved her. Still, he couldn't shake this crippling unease, the fear he would lose everything tonight.

"Do you know what they called me in the ring as a boy?"

"No, you've never said."

"I thought Aramis might have told you." His brother had

sat with her for two hours at the Thames Police Station while Aaron gave his statement.

"No, we spoke about the future."

"They called me Satan's Spawn or Lucifer's Lackey." When a man was called something for so long, he was inclined to believe it. "As you'll see tonight. I have something of the devil in me."

She swallowed deeply but seemed determined to drag him out of the mire. "As we all do when we're pushed to the limit. That's why it's important to discuss our thoughts and feelings."

Whatever he said, her balm took the pain out of the sting.

"Shall I tell you what I'm thinking?" He didn't wait for an answer. "If I stare at you for much longer, I'll not make it to the first bout. It's cold. You should dress before you catch a chill."

"Focus on winning your fights, and forget about me."

How could he forget about her? She was his last chance to forge a new life, his last chance to escape his father's legacy. He loved her with every fibre of his being. The love for his family was unaltered. This was a different feeling—a deep intimate connection like they shared the same soul.

A sudden knock on the door startled them both.

"The fights have begun," Aramis called.

"I'll meet you downstairs." Aaron turned to her, not wishing to keep secrets or lie. "I need to tell you something before I leave. It will affect the future and what happens once I've fought tonight."

Joanna yanked back the bedcovers and crossed the room, looking more concerned than intrigued. "You're not sending Lucia away? Mr Daventry assured you no charges will be brought against her. We would never have known about Natasha's plans had Lucia not confessed."

"Joanna," he said, clasping her arms.

But she couldn't quite catch her breath. "Lucia is guilty of asking a man to buy a watch, another to steal a dagger. She doesn't deserve to hang."

"She gave her mother the murder weapon," he reminded her.

"Yes, but she was scared out of her wits. She risked her life to save you. Oh, Aaron, she's just a girl who—"

"Joanna," he said softly. "I'm not sending Lucia away. She will live with Delphine at Mile End. It's all arranged. Rothley spoke to the magistrate on Lucia's behalf."

"He did?"

"Yes, I can't get rid of the man."

"Gabriel wants to help. He despises injustice."

Aaron owed Rothley a debt he could not repay.

The marquess had forced Fitzpatrick to make a statement, confessing he had offered Howard money to ruin his sister. Howard had declined. Rothley found the anonymous letter Natasha wrote—urging Howard to come to The Jade—stuffed down the side of the seat in the lord's carriage.

"That's not all Rothley has done." Aaron inhaled deeply, shocked the words were about to leave his lips. "I have an audience with the King tomorrow." He prayed he wasn't nursing a broken nose and bruised eye. "Rothley will accompany me, as will Daventry and the Home Secretary."

Joanna stared at him, swallowing like she stood at the edge of a forest at night, afraid to take the path. "You intend to ask His Majesty to grant you the earldom?"

"I am the rightful heir. As I have the money and the means to restore the estate, I have every reason to believe he'll accept. I must make a formal submission to the House of Lords, but that's merely procedure."

"But what about Fortune's Den?"

"I shall keep my share of the business but appoint a manager to help run the club." He wanted to say more, to drop to his knees and ask her to be his countess, but she needed to see him fight, and he needed permission from the King before proclaiming himself the earl.

"How will you watch me from the window if you're living in Mayfair?" she said, offering a sad smile.

He slipped his arm around her waist. "I won't need to watch you from the window if we share the same bed." He placed his finger on her lips before she offered reasons why that was impossible. "Wherever I am, I want you with me. Now, you must decide if you feel the same."

Aramis returned and knocked again. "They're waiting for you."

"I'm ready." If he didn't leave now, he never would. "I must go, or my opponent will win by default."

"Don't get hurt," Joanna said, hugging him so tightly her breasts were squashed against his bare chest. "Fight like your life depends on it. I'll be waiting for you, to talk and tend your wounds."

"How am I supposed to hurt men when I'm anticipating the feel of your hands on my body?" A cockstand would hinder him in the ring. Indeed, Joanna would be the death of him, quite literally.

"That's simple. I'll only sleep here tonight if you win."

He smiled, though the primal urge to claim her, to have her living with him, sleeping with him, made him want to put a torch to The Burnished Jade.

"Daventry will be your chaperone during the boxing

event. You'll wait here until he comes for you. I don't expect you to watch more than one fight, but remain with him at all times." He kissed her on the forehead, not the lips. He needed hatred burning in his veins, not this potent blend of lust and love. "I must go before the contenders grow impatient."

"Be careful," she called.

"I will," he said, closing the door behind him.

Aramis pushed away from the wall and uncrossed his arms. "Are you sure you want to fight tonight? I can take your place. It would be an honour."

Aaron gripped his brother's shoulder, reassuring him. "This may be my last fight in the ring. I need Joanna to see what I'm capable of when pushed to my limits. I just pray I don't lose her."

Aramis knew not to argue. "Joanna is an incredible woman, the wife you truly deserve. She would never leave you—why would she? To me, there's no man greater."

A lump formed in Aaron's throat. "And you're everything a man could want in a friend and brother, but unless you want to see me beaten to a pulp, I suggest we dispense with sentiment. Tell me something to get my blood boiling. Spar with me while we're talking."

Aramis laughed and raised his fists. "Two-Teeth O'Toole is here. He's calling you Dandy of the Den. Said he heard you've gone soft over a woman."

Aaron thought love would weaken him, but it was empowering.

One fought harder when there was something to lose.

"You'll tell everyone I'm the Demon of the Den." Aaron swayed and ducked to miss Aramis' skilled jabs. "A fact I'll prove when I win my first bout."

"I'm sure the name will become popular in the salons if

the King grants your request tomorrow. You'll have the lords of the *ton* quaking in their boots."

Aaron smiled to himself. "All I need do is throw a lavish ball that meets their approval, and I'll have them eating from the palm of my hand."

"An earl with a fist of steel will be a tour de force." Aramis jerked from a jab to his chin. "Have you told Sigmund you plan to make him the manager?"

"I thought it best to wait until I've spoken to the King."

"Amongst the corrupt peers, you'd be a refreshing addition to the House of Lords. We'll still hold their vowels. Indeed, interesting times lie ahead."

Christian mounted the stairs, panting like he had raced around the perimeter of Hyde Park. "You're fighting next against that neckless fellow from Manchester. Remember, his left knee is weak, and he'll try to trick you into overreaching. Sigmund has stopped taking bets until the first round is over but says we'll make a fortune tonight."

Aaron straightened, rolling his shoulders and stretching his neck. "Is there bad news? Something that might spark my temper?"

"That beast from Hungary won. Gustav is through to the next round. He's told everyone he's taking the purse home tonight."

The need to prove Gustav wrong lit a fire in Aaron's blood. "Does he still have a habit of leaning forward if he's convinced he'll hit the mark?"

Christian nodded. "Always when he throws a right hook."

"Anything else?" Aaron said, moving towards the stairs.

"Yes, Rothley is here. He said if you lose tonight and are knocked out cold, he will kidnap Miss Lovelace and take her to Gretna Green."

Aaron firmed his jaw against the inner inferno. "Like hell he will!"

The knock on the bedchamber door came as Joanna finished pinning her hair into a bun. Her hands shook as she tightened the belt on her peacock-blue dress. The closed neckline and modest collar would help to avoid unwelcome male attention, though she planned to linger in the background, not take a front-row seat.

Mr Daventry wore black and greeted her with a warm smile. "Are you sure you want to visit the basement? They're particularly wild tonight. A walk through the hallway should convince you the fighters are savage."

Avoiding the basement was not an option. If she didn't witness Aaron acting like the beast he claimed, he would always hide that part of himself.

"Nothing compares to being in the marshes on a foggy night with a lunatic threatening to kill the man I love." Joanna doubted she would ever feel that afraid again.

"It takes a brave woman to fire a pistol knowing the shot will maim," he said, offering his arm.

The memory chilled her to the bone. "It takes a desperate woman. Bravery was never a factor. I'm sure Sybil would fire if your life were in danger."

Mr Daventry gave a proud hum. "Without hesitation."

Since she rarely spent time alone with the gentleman, Joanna asked the questions she found puzzling. "Were you

314

interested in matchmaking before you met Sybil? Is it your mission to rescue all men from bachelorhood?"

He arched a curious brow. "I'm not sure what you mean."

"Please, they say you're the most intelligent man in London."

"One need only attend a scientific lecture to know that's untrue."

"So you have no interest in helping couples fall in love?"

He clutched his chest like the idea was ludicrous. "Have you read the broadsheets of late? Crime is on the rise despite the new police force. I barely have time to sleep, let alone play the matchmaking matron."

"I took you for an honest man," she said, trying to provoke a reaction. "A champion of the truth."

He laughed above the din downstairs. "For argument's sake, suppose there's truth to your claim. Perhaps I'm trying to save men much like myself."

"Men who've clawed their way out of the darkness?"

"Men who've yet to experience the beauty of loving someone."

As they descended the stairs, she considered how Mr Daventry might have manipulated events. An instance sprang to mind, the subtle suggestion that Joanna could depend on Gabriel more than she could Aaron Chance. The gentle nudge to persuade him she should live at Fortune's Den.

Mr Daventry hadn't made them fall in love.

He'd given them space to discover the truth for themselves.

"One wonders who's next on your list," she teased.

"You have a club full of unmarried ladies," he replied before insisting she keep a firm grip on his arm as they entered the basement. "In the game of love, I tend to favour the outsider."

"A wallflower might be considered a misfit."

"And rogues often make excellent husbands."

"I quite agree," she said, thinking of Aaron, though judging by the rowdy men watching the boxing bouts, she might be mistaken.

Spectators lined the stairway, filling every bench, wall space, and inch in between. Men crammed into the large room like cargo in a merchant's hold with nary a hair's breadth between them. Candles flickered in iron chandeliers and wall sconces, yet the room felt like a dungeon—dark and oppressive, where only the lucky escaped alive.

Joanna put her finger to her nose and tried not to breathe. The stench of stale sweat overwhelmed her. "It will be impossible to push through the crowd."

"I suggest you watch from here," Mr Daventry said, ushering men from the stairs, "unless you want to sit with Rothley."

She followed Mr Daventry's gaze to where her brother's school friends occupied front-row seats. Gabriel sat with Lord Rutland, Mr Dalton and Mr Gentry, though the latter didn't look like the professional physician who gave lectures on medicinal remedies. He was in his shirtsleeves, the blood-stained lawn rolled to the elbows to reveal muscular forearms.

The pain of her brother's absence cut deep, a stark reminder Justin would never join them again. While Gabriel was a friend, the other men were acquaintances. Still, they had all been affected by Justin's passing.

"Gentry is the doctor in charge tonight," Mr Daventry said, explaining what she already knew. As a viscount's grandson, Mr Gentry didn't need to work but had personal reasons for tending the sick. "He's already dealt with numerous fractures. One man might lose an eye."

"Don't say such things when Aaron is about to fight."

She watched Aaron enter the ring and pace back and forth like a panther on the prowl. Every honed muscle exuded strength, every movement pulsing with raw power. But who was his opponent? The relentless wait left her restless.

"Aaron mustn't see me."

"We'll hide behind those men." Mr Daventry gestured to the group hogging the lower steps. "You should still have a reasonable view."

Seconds passed as the crowd chanted, "Demon of the Den."

Nausea roiled in her stomach. She wanted to scream and shout, "That's not who he is!" The urge to cry a river of tears had her asking to borrow Mr Daventry's handkerchief.

"This is Aaron's second fight," he said, handing her the silk square. "He floored some fellow from Manchester with one punch."

She closed her eyes, wishing the hands of the clock moved at ten times the speed. The obscene jeers and cruel taunts added to the roar of chaotic disorder.

Aaron remained composed, though she had never seen his eyes look so hard and black. She had never seen every line on his face etched with hatred.

An icy chill ran through her when his opponent entered the ring.

"Gustav! Gustav!" a few men cheered.

Gustav towered almost a foot above Aaron. He looked like he'd spent his life in the stone mines of Gaul and could withstand a hit from a trebuchet.

Tears rolled down her cheeks when Gustav threw a punch.

Aaron ducked and delivered a powerful uppercut to Gustav's abdomen. He was quick, moving with a speed that confused his opponent. Gustav lunged again and took a hit to the face, sending a line of spittle flying into the audience.

Aaron snarled while delivering punishing blows. His sculpted torso glistened with sweat as he circled the giant, landing sharp jabs to Gustav's ribs. He goaded the crowd, raising his bloodied fists and demanding their cheers like a predator basking in his kill.

Who was this arrogant devil who thrived on brutality?

Who was he punishing? His father? Himself?

She recalled Aramis' advice to remember how it started and to think about what it meant to be invincible.

That's when she saw the frightened boy pitted against the beast. The boy who'd taken one knock after another and was still standing. The man who'd sworn never to let anyone hurt him again.

"I've seen enough." She tugged Mr Daventry's coat sleeve. "Can you escort me to The Burnished Jade?"

Mr Daventry jerked in shock like he'd misjudged her character and this was never part of his plan. "You're going home?"

"Yes. There's something I must do."

He tried to defend the savage display. "Men have fought and hunted for centuries. Aggression is in our blood. It's how Aaron saved his family from a life of poverty."

"I'm not judging him. And I'm certainly not abandoning him."

She wouldn't attempt to fix him, either, because Aaron

318

Chance was not damaged or broken. He was a survivor. And survivors were meant to be imperfect.

"Loving someone isn't shaping their character to suit yours," she said, not that Mr Daventry needing reminding what love meant. "Loving someone is granting them the freedom to be themselves."

Mr Daventry looked relieved. "He'll wonder where you are."

"I shan't be long."

Joanna didn't look back as she mounted the stairs and left the basement. Cheers for the Demon of the Den said Aaron had won and would fight in the next round.

The storm outside reflected the current state of affairs. Rain hammered the cobblestones and soaked her in seconds, washing her worries away. The violent rumble of thunder embodied Aaron's battle between the past and the present.

Mr Daventry ushered her into The Burnished Jade, rubbing the cold from his hands, and suggested lighting a fire.

"I'll be ten minutes, no more," she said, hurrying upstairs.

It was dark, but she knew what she wanted. Two tokens she would present to Aaron when she explained what loving him meant to her. She found the first amongst her paste jewellery, the second in her nightstand, tucked inside the paper pocket of her diary.

She was staring at the armoire, wondering whether to pack more clothes, when she heard Aaron call her name. The woeful cry was loud enough to shake the heavens. The shout rang with the pain of a man who was lost.

"Joanna!"

She hurried to the window and looked out onto the street.

Aaron stood outside Fortune's Den, wearing nothing but

319

tight breeches. Rain dripped from his coal-black hair. Rain drenched his bronzed skin, running down his torso in rivulets.

"Joanna!"

Their gazes locked, though his eyes swam with fear.

She raced downstairs and was outside in seconds. She didn't ask what he wanted or question why he was standing in the rain.

"I'm here," she cried, throwing herself into his arms, hugging him so tightly she could barely breathe. "I'll always be here."

They kissed, a wild, passionate kiss, their mouths crashing together, a rampant mating unhindered by the rain.

"You left," he said, panic still marring his voice as he clasped her face in his bruised hands. "I shouldn't have let you watch me fight."

"I'd seen enough. I couldn't stand there waiting for someone to hurt you. I went to The Jade to collect something important."

He kissed her again, a kiss as fierce as it was desperate. "I thought I'd lost you. I thought I'd driven you away." He dashed raindrops from her cheeks. "Ignore what I said earlier. We can leave London tonight. We can live at The Jade if it makes you happy."

She gazed into his eyes, knowing he would move mountains for her. "You waited in the rain for me. You've shown me what it means to love someone. Let me do the same."

She reached for his hand and placed the onyx sovereign ring in his palm. "It's a gift but not for you. You'll merely be the custodian."

He frowned, confused.

"It's Justin's ring." She didn't mention it was found on the body in the woods. "It belonged to our grandfather, and I want our first-born son to have it. That's assuming you'll ask me to marry you and stop alluding to the possibility."

"You know I'd marry you in a heartbeat."

"And this is my solicitor's card." She placed it in his palm, too. "Don't worry if it gets wet. We can acquire another when he draws up our marriage contract. Our first-born daughter will inherit The Burnished Jade when she comes of age. Until then, it's mine. I made a vow to help my ladies, a vow I intend to keep."

Aaron smiled, a slow smile that curled her toes. "I love you. When I'm dry and dressed, I'll ask the question—"

"Ask me now."

Aaron didn't hesitate. He dropped to one knee in the rain. "Marry me, Joanna. Be my colleague, my friend, my lover, my wife. I'll try to be the man you deserve."

"I would be honoured to be your wife, Mr Chance." Tears welled in her eyes. "You're more than I deserve. You're everything to me."

They spent the next minute kissing passionately, a little too passionately, because it sparked a fever in her blood.

"And one more thing," she said, unable to resist stroking his noticeable bulge discreetly. "I like you in tight breeches. Wear them when I come to your room tomorrow night."

His voice was low and husky when he said, "I need you tonight. I have the key to your club. I've often sat in my study, imagining you luring me into your bed at The Burnished Jade."

She touched him again because she couldn't help herself. "Let's pray you want me with the same fervency when we're married."

"I'll want you every damn day of my life."

# Chapter Twenty-Two

*Late December, 1831*

Aaron married Joanna in St George's, Hanover Square, not because marrying in a house of God was part of his penance. The King decreed that the Earl of Berridge must adhere to tradition and marry in the same church as his predecessors.

The King of Compromise was Aaron's new moniker.

His Majesty was happy to overlook Ignatius Chance's misdeeds but quickly reminded Aaron his great-great-grandfather had played a crucial role in brokering the Treaty of Utrecht. His great-grandfather was a patron of science, supporting Gray in his understanding of electrical conduction.

And so, Aaron James Lawrence Delmont-Chance, 9th Earl of Berridge was born, though men knew to address him as Chance when possible—etiquette be damned. Hearing the name Berridge still felt like a knife twisting in his gut, but Aaron was adept at making sacrifices for the greater good.

Hence he stood in the lavish drawing room at Studland

Park, home of The Marquess of Rothley, who had kindly offered to host a wedding banquet while Aaron had builders and architects redesigning his new Mayfair home.

"Do you make a habit of gaping at your wife?" Rothley said, in the smooth aristocratic voice women loved. "Did you hear what I said about Arthur Lovelace?"

No, Aaron was busy watching Joanna from across the room, mentally pinching himself because loving her felt like a dream.

Her pale blue gown accentuated the deep sapphire of her eyes, eyes full of mischief because she was on a match-making mission to find wives for her brother's unmarried friends.

"I'm rarely shocked," he said, dazzled by her smile. His gaze slid over her figure, though he suppressed a sensual hum. They had spent last night apart, every minute feeling like an eternity. "I expected to die a bachelor. When the power of true love grips you, it never lets go."

"Love is like an entity unto its own," Rothley said, his hand shaking slightly as he sipped his port. "Remind Joanna it will take more than an interest in medical procedures to convince Gentry to marry Miss Moorland."

Aaron glanced at the mismatched pair. Miss Moorland hid behind her spectacles and her unflattering green dress. Gentry oozed confidence in his expensive tailoring. He was a man of the world. Miss Moorland was always lost in the pages of her book.

"I believe Joanna is helping Miss Moorland to mingle." It wasn't a lie. The lady lacked confidence in crowds. "And giving her a lecture on how to speak to men and not hide behind potted ferns."

"Most men despise artifice," Rothley said, shifting slightly so the footman could stoke the fire. "A woman is more attractive when she can be herself. Perhaps you should remind Joanna why you fell in love with her. I doubt it was because she excels at mingling at parties."

Aaron recalled the first time he felt a pang in his chest, not his loins. Joanna was waiting in his study late at night, her golden hair tied in a braid, the hem of her nightgown visible beneath her pelisse. She had come to report a crime, her intervention helping to save the life of Christian's wife.

"Joanna shares my passion for justice," he said, his heart thumping that bit harder. "She's not afraid to voice her opinion. I've always admired that about her." She possessed a strength of mind that belied her years.

"Yes, and her capacity to endure hardship sets her apart." Rothley gave a wistful sigh that had nothing to do with Joanna. "If only all women had the same tenacity. Some run at the first sign of trouble."

Aaron wondered if Rothley was speaking from his own experience of lost love and decided to test the waters. "The gossips say you've loved the same woman since you were nineteen."

Rothley stiffened and muttered a curse. "The gossips say I killed my closest friend, that I keep a harem of women at Studland Park and have an opium addiction. None of which is true."

Aaron didn't challenge him and swiftly changed the subject. "What were you saying about Arthur Lovelace? I know you hired a former Bow Street Runner to find him."

Rothley leaned a little closer. "Joanna doesn't know, but I've been paying the fool's debts for years. Arthur left

London when I refused to settle his last lot of bills." Rothley glanced at Joanna, whose smile lit up the room. "I offered to provide Joanna with an income, but she insisted on supporting herself."

Aaron was grateful she'd had the sense to refuse. Rothley cared for Joanna like a sister, but the *ton* would have marked her as his mistress.

"I wish I could say the wastrel is rotting in hell," Aaron said with burning disdain. "But I put my brother-in-law Flynn on the case. He's skilled at finding missing people."

Rothley straightened. "Has he located the devil?"

"By all accounts, Arthur Lovelace boarded a ship belonging to the East India Company, heading for Calcutta." The coward fled London, leaving his daughter to struggle alone. "He has a friend who negotiates with merchants abroad. The gentleman offered Arthur work in exchange for passage."

Rothley snorted. "Good riddance. Does Joanna know?"

"Yes."

With an indifferent shrug, she had seemed relieved.

"Introduce me to Flynn," Rothley said, surveying the guests with interest. "A man of his talents will prove useful in the future."

Rothley meant in his quest to find Joanna's brother. Nothing would persuade him Justin was dead. It's why he refused to attend the memorial service at St Michael's or stand at the graveside when they laid the new headstone.

Perhaps Rothley had another reason to hire Flynn.

Perhaps there was someone else he hoped to find.

Aaron did as Rothley asked. He had no intention of spending his wedding day with the brooding marquess.

Flynn was talking to Sigmund, admiring his new tailoring. "Aaron must be paying you well. I recognise the cut of your coat. It's from Beaumont & Finch."

Sigmund brushed imagined dust off the sleeves. "I could have bought a small cottage in Cornwall for what this cost."

"You run the most notorious gaming hell in London," Aaron said, slapping his friend on the back. "It's important to have a commanding presence. Before long, you'll attract attention from the ladies at The Jade."

Sigmund laughed. "I may look like a gentleman, but I've manners coarser than a sailor's tongue. Though Betsy at The Saracen's Head had no complaints."

A sudden peal of laughter drew Aaron's attention to where his brothers stood near the impressive bow window. The sight tightened his chest. He recalled the terror on their faces that first night in the rookeries—mere children taken from an elegant home in Mayfair and dumped in the street like unwanted dogs.

The road to happiness had been long and gruelling.

At times, he'd thought they wouldn't make it.

But like the rest of England, his family had embraced change. Come the spring, Aaron would be an uncle, and again in early summer. His role as family patriarch was far from over. A fact that brought a broad smile to his face.

"A penny for your thoughts," Joanna said, sliding her arm around his waist and resting her head on his shoulder.

He drew her around to face him and lowered his voice. "I'm counting the hours until we're alone again. I have a deep desire to make love to my wife. I can't wait until tonight."

Her gaze dipped to his mouth with the same fervent hunger. "Anticipation is a potent aphrodisiac. It's said to heighten one's pleasure."

He pulled her close and pressed his mouth to her ear. "I'm on fire. I'll combust before we reach the Adelphi."

"Two nights in the best suite should help to work the excitement out of your system." Her hand slid covertly under his coat, and the minx squeezed his buttock. "Then again, we've been rampant for over a month."

"Perhaps you might surprise me like you did last Sunday."

Aaron had gone to retrieve some papers from his study at Fortune's Den and found the door locked. He entered to see Joanna sitting in his throne with her feet propped on his desk, wearing nothing but her stockings and his silk cravat.

She smiled at the memory. "How many times had you sat at your desk and imagined gripping my hips and sinking deep into my body?"

"More damn times than I'd care to count."

She laughed and patted his chest. "Rothley has a maze somewhere in the grounds. We might imagine ourselves at Mrs Flavell's wild party."

"It's snowing." He was thinking of her comfort, not his own.

"Since when has the weather deterred us?"

"You'll need a cloak," he uttered, arousal pumping through his veins.

"We can't go yet. Lucia is about to sing. She desperately wants to please you, Aaron. Delphine bought her an elegant new dress."

Mrs Lowry was right. Against the odds, Lucia was a kind, caring girl who just wanted to be loved. There was something of himself in her, the part that wasn't hateful and bitter.

He wrapped his arm around Joanna's waist and listened to his youngest sister sing while Delphine played the pianoforte.

Pride filled his chest. The aria stirred a deep sense of grati-tude that he'd found someone he loved so profoundly, and the slight ache that came with knowing it was precious.

Aaron glanced at Rothley. His lips were pressed in a tight line, a furrow cutting deep between his brows. He wore a mask of silent anguish, as if every note pierced his heart.

While they all clapped to cries of an encore, Rothley left the room.

The next song was more uplifting, and Lucia bowed to rapturous applause.

Daventry approached. "Lucia could travel the world with that voice," he said. "Though now you've found her, I don't suppose you're keen to let her go."

"Maybe when she's older," Aaron said. His siblings liked having a younger sister to care for, particularly Delphine. "There's no rush. Lucia needs the stability a large family provides."

Daventry nodded and addressed Joanna. "The Countess of Berridge has a monumental task ahead of her if she hopes to see her ladies fulfil their potential."

Joanna smiled. "I never shy away from a challenge. Ask my husband."

Daventry laughed as he took another glass of champagne from a passing footman. "Your ladies may need to work on their repartee. Miss Moorland asked Gentry if she could examine his implements. The fellow almost choked on his brandy."

Aaron chuckled. "It could have been worse. She might have confessed to having a fascination with men's tools."

Joanna took umbrage at their teasing. "I doubt Mr Gentry will forget her. Sometimes, a lady must do what is needed to stand out from the crowd."

Daventry bent his head. "Gentry will need a lady with a bit more gumption, particularly when he's working as a highwayman out on the Barking Road."

Aaron almost choked at the news and he wasn't drinking brandy. "Whoever told you that must have downed a quart of gin. Why would a professional man risk his neck to steal baubles? I know for a fact he doesn't need the money."

"I'm told he's conducting a private investigation," Daventry whispered.

"Does it have anything to do with Justin's death?" Joanna asked.

Daventry shrugged. "If I were attempting to bring two medical minds together, I might suggest Miss Moorland conduct an investigation of her own. Though she might need both of you to help her in the risky endeavour."

"I'm not playing the matchmaking matron," Aaron said with a snort.

"What if I offered an incentive?"

"You have nothing I want."

The glimmer of mischief in Daventry's eyes said that wasn't entirely true. "What about a written oath? Security for the future?"

Aaron straightened. "Go on. I'm listening."

"A contract between my family and yours, agreeing to come to each other's aid. Would you not want your sons to know they can call upon mine in a crisis?"

With his interest more than piqued, Aaron nodded. "And in exchange, all I need to do is help my wife keep her vow to her ladies?"

Daventry glanced at the door as Rothley returned. "Yes, and assist anyone in this room who's stopped caring if they live or die."

"Draw up the contract, and I'll consider your proposal." At the rate Aaron made love to Joanna, he'd also be a father in nine months. Preparing for the future was vital.

"Excellent," Daventry said. "Though it will also apply to daughters."

"And my siblings and their children."

"Agreed."

While Daventry was in a pleasing mood, Aaron said, "Perhaps you might reassure Lucia that no charges will be brought against her. She still has nightmares and jumps whenever there's a knock on the door."

"Certainly."

As soon as Daventry left them, Aaron gripped Joanna's elbow and propelled her towards the door. "This might be the only opportunity to spend five minutes alone."

"It's pointless sneaking about. People will know we've been outside."

"Yes, admiring the orangery. We're entitled to have time together on our wedding day. Ask the footman for your cloak."

Eager to be alone with him, she retrieved her garment. "My husband loves the snow," she said to the indifferent servant.

"I love you," he muttered. "Come rain, shine or freezing blizzards."

She smiled softly, her eyes shining with emotion. "And I love you, even on the darkest nights."

They hurried outside.

The crunch of snow beneath his booted feet had him glancing at Joanna's dainty shoes. "Let me carry you. We'll keep each other warm."

She let out a squeal when he scooped her into his arms.

"Will it be a quick tupping?" she said in a sensual voice as he carried her through Rothley's ornate garden.

"I don't care what it is as long as I'm buried inside you." He entered the boxwood maze and took ten steps before putting her down. "Now you're in trouble."

"Trouble? But I'm a good girl, sir."

"Like hell you are. Outward appearances suggest you're biddable, but we both know that's a lie. You have me by the ballocks."

She chuckled. "That's wishful thinking on your part."

"We'll save the amorous talk for later. Hike up your skirts."

He unbuttoned his trousers, recalling his desperate scramble to reach her when he saw her leaving the fighting pit. The memory always roused a primal need to claim her, to drive hard and deep and remind her she was his.

"You're lucky I'm not wearing extra petticoats."

Amid a mad fumble, he hoisted her up against the hedge. "I wanted you like this on the night of Mrs Flavell's party. You drove me insane with your sweet little pants and moans."

She blinked snow off her lashes and wrapped her legs around him. "Have me now. Have all of me. I'm yours."

He entered her swiftly, and they both moaned from the pleasure. Hell, she was so warm and wet a man could lose his head.

"Will I get my own moniker now I'm your wife," she said, panting and gripping his hair and urging him to pump harder.

"You're the ruler of my heart. The Queen of Clubs."

"Oh, I quite liked being called Miss Scrumptious."

He met her gaze, shocked to hear the words fall from her lips. Delphine must have told her. Despite refusing to use the moniker himself, he could think of a hundred reasons why the name suited her.

But he smiled, a smile that warmed the once cold chambers of his heart. "Everything about you is delectable. You'll always be scrumptious to me."

I hope you enjoyed reading ***The Last Chance***

That's the last story from the Rogues of Fortune's Den, but fear not, all the characters will appear in the new series featuring the ladies from The Burnished Jade.

Will the new Countess of Berridge help her ladies find matches of their own? Is it true Mr Gentry is moonlighting as a highwayman? Why would such an upstanding gentleman risk the hangman's noose?
Find out in …

***A Lesson in Scandal***
***Tales from The Burnished Jade - Book 1***

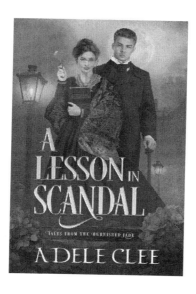

Printed in Great Britain
by Amazon